# PRAISE FOR THE AUTHOR

## BETWEEN ME AND YOU

"A thought-provoking romance that is fresh, insightful, and clever in its execution."

—*Kirkus Reviews*

"Sharply written and well-paced, this will delight . . ."

—*Booklist*

"A smart, thoughtful look at marriage and love."

—POPSUGAR

"Allison Winn Scotch crafts a heart-wrenching tale."

—*Us Weekly*

"Two people, two perspectives, one love story . . . It's heartbreakingly joyful to discover everything that happens in between."

—HelloGiggles

"This reverse timeline is beautifully done . . . Impressively executed and satisfying when the story concludes."

—Bookreporter

## IN TWENTY YEARS

"Scotch hits a grand slam with this novel . . . [A]n absolute must-read that lovers of women's contemporary fi̶ ̶  ̶̶ ̶̶ ̶̶ devour in one sitting."

"Heartfelt . . . Well written and memorable."

—*RT Book Reviews*

"Allison Winn Scotch is the ultimate beach read. If you plan to sink your toes into the sand and need a fab book to kick back with . . . this is the one."

—*Parade*

"The perfect beach read."

—POPSUGAR

"Both heartbreaking and funny, this novel explores how we cope with the disappointments of adulthood and come to terms with our past."

—*Real Simple*

"Both funny and heartbreaking, this relatable story of friendship and how life interferes will leave you nostalgic for your own friends."

—Read It Forward

"A story about youthful dreams and middle-age reality, this is a page-turning book to talk about."

—*The Parkersburg News & Sentinel*

# CLEO
## McDOUGAL
# REGRETS
# NOTHING

# ALSO BY
# ALLISON WINN SCOTCH

# CLEO McDOUGAL REGRETS NOTHING

A Novel

*Allison Winn Scotch*

LAKE UNION
PUBLISHING

Text copyright © 2020 by Allison Winn Scotch
All rights reserved.

No part of this book may be reproduced, or stored in a retrieval system, or transmitted in any form or by any means, electronic, mechanical, photocopying, recording, or otherwise, without express written permission of the publisher.

Published by Lake Union Publishing, Seattle

www.apub.com

Amazon, the Amazon logo, and Lake Union Publishing are trademarks of Amazon.com, Inc., or its affiliates.

ISBN-13: 9781542021227
ISBN-10: 1542021227

Cover design by Kimberly Glyder

Printed in the United States of America

*For my daughter, Amelia.*
*May you live a life without regret.*

*I figure if a girl wants to be a legend, she should go ahead and be one.*

—*Calamity Jane*

# ONE

*Cleo McDougal is not a good person. She* does *good, yes, but doing good and being good aren't the same thing, now, are they?*

Cleo McDougal did not see the op-ed or this opening line in said op-ed on the home page of *Seattle Today!* until approximately seven fif-teen a.m., after she had completed her morning at-home boxing class, after she had showered and meticulously applied the day's makeup (a routine that she admitted was getting lengthier and more discouraging at thirty-seven, but Cleo McDougal had never been one to shy away from a challenge), and after she had roused her fourteen-year-old from his bed, which was likely her day's hardest ordeal.

Of course, she had not yet seen the op-ed. By the time she did, the political blogs had picked it up and run with it, which was why it took off, blazing around the internet and Twittersphere. (*Seattle Today!*, a hipster alternative online "paper," would otherwise really never have landed on Cleo's radar.)

She had made a rule, which was clearly a mistake—she could see that now—to give herself one hour in the mornings before checking her phone. This was not a hard-and-fast rule, and obviously she scrolled through the news and quickly glanced at her emails while still in bed, before the sun rose over Washington. But it had come to her attention that, well, she needed to be a little more . . . Zen. Voters liked Zen.

But they also liked tenacious and prepared and simultaneously calm and confident (and a laundry list of other things—pretty, warm, tough but not too tough, sharp-tongued but not a grandstander . . . you get the idea), and so when Gabrielle, her chief of staff, said that her own therapist advised taking one hour in the morning to unplug so that she absolutely did not completely lose her mind, Cleo thought it might not be a bad idea to test-drive.

It was only day four. She was liking it. She did indeed feel a little calmer, a little more serene, at least until she had to wake Lucas, when the previous hour's tranquility usually spiraled into a bit of a spat, but she defied anyone to enjoy their morning with a teenager who mostly communicated by grunting.

Surprisingly, Lucas was the one who saw the op-ed first. Perhaps not all that surprising, since he and his phone were nearly telepathically connected, but surprising still because Cleo was, need it be said, a senator, and theoretically her staff should have given her the heads-up on a hit piece published in her childhood hometown, which then took off online like a match to gasoline.

"Who's MaryAnne Newman?"

Lucas was hunched over the kitchen island in their three-bedroom condo, picking over an Eggo, one of the few things he'd agreeably eat for breakfast, and Cleo wasn't sure she had heard him correctly. She had never mentioned MaryAnne to Lucas, rarely talked about that time in her life. It wasn't that she didn't think of MaryAnne—she did. But she also spent a lot of time trying *not* to think about her. How can you drive away from your past without even glancing in the rearview mirror? That kind of focus took effort.

"What?" Cleo turned toward Lucas, her coffee perilously close to sloshing over the rim of her mug. (Gabrielle had also recommended that she limit her coffee intake, but that was when Cleo pulled rank and told her she would sooner sleep with William Parsons, the Senate majority leader, who bore a striking resemblance to a walrus, than abandon coffee, and Gaby knew it was not a battle worth pursuing.)

"MaryAnne Newman," Lucas muttered, which was one step above a grunt, and thus Cleo was almost delighted.

"Are you—are you on Facebook?"

Lucas rolled his eyes, which was much more like him. "No. Have you not seen this?"

He held out his phone, and Cleo stepped closer.

"She wrote about you. And . . . I guess me? I got a news alert."

"You have a Google alert on me?"

Lucas's eyes could not have gone farther back into his head. "No. Jesus. It came up on my phone alerts. They do that now, you know, like, send breaking news to your phone." He shrugged. "I guess everyone who has an iPhone probably got it." He swallowed. "Also, I'm assuming what she wrote wasn't true? Or is it? Because then—"

Lucas stared at her, eyelids lowered, an indecipherable mix of teenage disdain and ire and, Cleo detected, something more. Her heart rate accelerated. MaryAnne didn't even *know* Lucas; their lives had diverged well before he came along. What could she possibly be writing about?

Cleo patted her pockets, in a slightly more desperate search for her own phone now, then realized it was still in her home office / boxing studio / guest room (though they never had guests), resting, waiting, recharging, like it wasn't an imminent time bomb.

Lucas pulled his screen closer, read the opening lines.

> *"Cleo McDougal is not a good person. She* does *good, yes, but doing good and being good aren't the same thing, now, are they? In fact, her whole life, Cleo McDougal has been a cheater. She cheated in high school, on the debate team, on the school paper, for a summer internship, and from there it only got worse."*

"That is *not* true," Cleo said to Lucas. Though maybe it was, just a little? Leave it to MaryAnne to thread the needle between rumor and fact. Cleo almost snorted, it was so familiar.

"Keep reading," he said, passing his phone across the counter.

Cleo skimmed the next paragraph, detailing old grudges that felt irrelevant twenty years later, until she saw it. The reason for the hint of whatever it was in Lucas's eyes.

> *"I have recently learned that this pattern of cheating extends all the way to Cleo's personal life. I support women and their myriad choices, but when these choices reflect on their moral and ethical compass—something we must all agree is critical for presidential material—it bears stating publicly. A reliable source recently reached out to me, knowing we grew up together, to disclose that while at law school, Cleo had a torrid affair with a married professor, and, I quote here, 'many people have since suspected that he could be the father of her son.' I share this information not to shame her—"*

Cleo slammed down the phone; she didn't need to read further. *Of course MaryAnne would play the smug card!* she thought. *That. Conniving. Bitch,* she also thought.

"Is that true?" Lucas's voice was softer now, more like the kid he used to be, less like the man he nearly was. Cleo's stomach nearly leaped through her throat.

"No. Sweetie, *no.*" Cleo reached out and mussed his hair, which he did not particularly like and which did not play nearly as naturally as Cleo hoped, a ruse to buy her time. "You know that isn't right—I was already pregnant at law school. MaryAnne is just passing on gossip that she didn't even bother to fact-check. I assume that's why she published

4

it in . . ." Cleo batted her hand around, as if she were shooing a fly. "Whatever this ridiculous excuse for a news website is."

Lucas chewed his lip and digested this. They'd been over this—his father. They'd had long discussions about it, and damn you, MaryAnne Newman, for bringing this back into their lives all over again. Cleo had settled it for Lucas—that his dad wasn't involved and didn't want to be, and that it was just the two of them, it had always been just the two of them, and that was fine. Lucas used to ask more questions about it when he was younger, but lately they'd somehow silently agreed that, like many things, especially in DC, where alliances were often fluid, it was ancient history. His father wasn't around, and that was that, and Cleo and Lucas were peas in a pod. (They weren't really, now that Lucas was an ornery teenager, but Cleo tried to remember that this was all very developmentally normal.)

"So who's MaryAnne Newman? And why would she write this?"

Cleo blew out her breath. She tried to tell herself that she was more perplexed than alarmed, but that wasn't really true. She was alarmed. She was shocked out of her brains and also terrified too. How on earth had MaryAnne Newman heard about Alexander Nobells? Gaby and her whole team of advisors—Cleo had a staff of thirty-five in her DC office alone—had warned her: if you toy with a run for the presidency, everyone will emerge, cockroaches and rats and all sorts of vermin from your past, to share their own stories. But Cleo had led a (mostly) clean life. There was Lucas, of course, the unplanned pregnancy her senior year at Northwestern—*not* at law school, thank you, MaryAnne—but she'd kept him! And she'd loved him! And she'd raised him! So no one on either side of the aisle could point fingers. She'd tried to make the best choices—strategic choices, true—but also at least decently moral choices (there was a sliding scale on most things), always with the eye that one day her record, her history might come to light.

This didn't mean she didn't have regrets. She did. MaryAnne Newman knew that too. She was just wrong about this one.

5

Cleo reached for Lucas's phone and tried not to think of Nobells. She hoped she didn't look as shell-shocked as she felt, with the memories of the affair now reawakened. *Fuck you, MaryAnne Newman.*

"MaryAnne was my best friend until my senior year in high school," she said, and her voice did not shake even though for most people, in light of such a public takedown, it would. But she had years of debate team triumphs and of speaking on the Senate floor (she had been elected at thirty-one, among the youngest senators in history) behind her. Her voice would not quake, even in her kitchen with her son handing her such a grenade. "And she shouldn't have written such lies, much less from an anonymous 'reliable source.' And they should have fact-checked it, and I have no idea why they didn't."

She did know actually—because in today's environment, lurid half-truths garnered eyeballs, and no one really cared to differentiate between fact and fiction when they hit Retweet. Cleo made a mental note to have Gaby call the editors at this "paper" and go absolutely batshit on them. "But you know how it is these days, especially when you're a public figure. People say anything about you, and half the world takes it as truth." She looked Lucas right in the eye. "But, buddy, we know our truth. And this isn't it."

Lucas shoved the Eggo in his mouth, held it in his teeth. Cleo wished that he took better care of himself, but any time she suggested it, it morphed into a fight. He was so handsome, with dark eyes and near-black hair, neither of which he got from Cleo, who burned at the first sign of sun and whose hair wasn't quite blond but wasn't quite brown either. She was tiny, which caused everyone—mostly men—to underestimate her, while Lucas was shooting up like a wild plant that wouldn't stop sprouting. Cleo knew he got all that from his dad. Still, Lucas always looked a little bit unkempt, a little . . . dirty. Maybe that's what fourteen-year-olds liked these days. She wasn't too old to know . . . but really she was.

Lucas brushed back his bangs, which hung about half an inch too low for good vision; bit down on the waffle; chewed; swallowed; gave it some thought. "She really seems to dislike you. For a former best friend."

Maybe this should have bothered Cleo, but she was long past seeking the approval of anyone other than her constituents. And Gaby. And Lucas.

"A lot of people dislike me. That's part of the deal of holding office. It's only going to get worse if I run for president."

"If?" Lucas said. This had been an ever-present discussion between the two of them as of late. Cleo wouldn't do anything without Lucas's green light, but she very much wanted him to give her the green light. As a senator, Cleo's life was mostly undisturbed outside the Capitol. All that would change in the White House. Lucas seemed to think it would be "all right, I guess" if he were the First Son, which Cleo took to be a near go-ahead, and from there she had dropped it.

"When. Well, if. Probably when, though," Cleo said. "When I run."

Cleo grabbed the phone, reread the story, which was less like an op-ed and more like a thinly veiled personal vendetta. Talk of her presidential run had grown louder lately: *The Today Show* had done a walk and talk with her to introduce her to a national audience; she'd done *Meet the Press* last month and fared well. She needed some big endorsements and she needed some bigger checks, but Gaby thought they had momentum, and Cleo had always been one to use momentum in her favor.

"So then, what'd you do to her?" Lucas asked. "Besides, I guess, cheating on the debate team and whatever?"

This was a longer conversation than they'd had over breakfast for at least two years, since puberty had kicked in, and though the subject was dire, Cleo was also delighted. Parents of teenagers took what they could get.

"I didn't do that stuff either," Cleo said. "It wasn't like that—she and I did the same activities. I was just better at them." This was an unkind assessment, but then again, MaryAnne had thrown these punches first. Cleo set down his phone and headed to her office to grab her own. There would be texts; there would be emails. Gaby would already be working with her team on crafting a media response. "Don't worry about this, bud. It's nothing."

"That's what people say when they've done something that they shouldn't have," he called after her.

"Have you brushed your teeth?" she called back. "We're leaving in ten."

"Yes," he said. "Stop asking me that. I'm not eight."

Cleo suspected he was lying about his teeth, but he was right: he wasn't eight anymore; he had to learn about consequences. This was part of her parenting strategy: consequences. Unprotected sex led to unplanned pregnancies; abandoned best friends led to op-eds twenty years later. Choices are made, regrets are managed, consequences arise.

She'd learned all about them too.

# TWO

Gaby was as mad as Cleo expected. Maybe *mad* wasn't the correct description. Gabrielle, like Cleo, practically levitated when faced with an obstacle, particularly one that made her, well, furious, so this was Gaby at her *utmost*. By the time Cleo got to her office—after an emergency speakerphone call while dropping Lucas at school (he wore noise-canceling headphones because that's just what he did in the car anyway)—Gaby, in heels that would cramp Cleo's arches in a second flat, and in a slim navy blazer and even slimmer navy pants, had already written a response to be released to reporters, booked Cleo on CNN, and lined up a nine thirty a.m. conference call with lucrative campaign donors. Her staff of thirty-five was buzzing about like a well-oiled machine, even when faced with calamity, and Gaby barked orders, each staffer scurrying to nail down her own task. (Of her DC staff, only four were men. Cleo's choice.) This efficiency, this competence, was why Cleo had hired Gabrielle for her very first run for office, when she was only a recent law school graduate and the mother of a toddler and brazen in the way that you have to be at twenty-four (elected at twenty-five to meet the constitutional minimum) to presume that you could beat a seven-time incumbent who had previously sleepwalked into reelection. (Incidentally, Martin Bridgewater was indicted on charges of insider trading the next year, so Cleo felt that she had done him a favor beating him so he didn't have to step down to public scorn and scrutiny.)

"This will just be a blip," Gaby said, staring at her phone, reading and talking and strategizing all at once. She looked up, locked eyes with Cleo, who was settling in behind her highly organized, extremely neat desk, unwinding her scarf that warded off the late-spring chill, sinking into her chair that needed some WD-40 again to stop the squeaking. "I'll squelch this like . . ." She snapped her fingers. "Like that."

"I know," Cleo said. "This doesn't worry me." A beat. "All that much."

She reached over and straightened a pile of color-coded folders, then brushed some dust off the silver-plated picture frame with a shot of Lucas when he was a toddler and dressed as a chocolate-chip cookie for Halloween.

"We can have the bitch killed," Gaby said, laughing just a little. She knew, as a black woman, that she had to manage her anger, at least outwardly, though not so much in front of Cleo, who had known her since their second year at Columbia Law. If she said this aloud outside the office, the headlines would go on for days, likely ruining her career and possibly ruining any hope of Cleo's run for president.

"That might be extreme: death," Cleo replied. "She's just nursing a grudge from high school, though the paternity stuff is wildly out-of-bounds. Obviously." She tapped her mouse, zapping the screen saver of the suffragettes and waking her computer. "Still, I suppose I could have been kinder back then."

"We all could have been kinder in high school."

"Weren't you elected, like, homecoming queen?"

"Well, sure." Gaby reached for a protein bar from her bag. She was training for a marathon and had to eat every two hours. "But I didn't get there by being nice. Homecoming queens are elected by playing dirty."

"I wouldn't know. I was not homecoming queen."

"I don't list it on my résumé," Gaby said. "Though it was pretty great training for now. Is Lucas OK?"

"Fine, actually. He knows it isn't true." Cleo sighed. She had real work to do and just wanted this to evaporate. "I can reach out to MaryAnne. I think she still lives in Seattle. I can apologize."

Gaby inhaled sharply. "You only apologize when I tell you to."

"I just meant that I think I could smooth the waters with her." Cleo thought of her old friend, and even with her public betrayal, she recognized that maybe MaryAnne's wounds weren't entirely unjustified. Her tactics? Yes. Her inaccuracies? Well, *sure*. But Cleo had burned the two of them down. That also was true. And maybe it still stung for MaryAnne in ways that Cleo had numbed herself to.

"If there had been a time to make it go away, it would have been before the op-ed on that ridiculous site, which, let's be clear, is not even *journalism*," Gaby said. "Besides, you're a single mother who has a fifty-four-percent approval rating. We can withstand one bump as long as it's managed."

This was true. People did like Cleo. That's why donors were lining up, encouraging her to run. That's why her office was stacked with photos of her with musicians, actors, and plenty of big hitters in DC too. Both sides of the aisle, which was no small feat these days. She was measured and level and generally batted straight down the middle but wasn't afraid to swing at a curveball or a breaking ball, an analogy that she felt she could own, since she was the only girl who'd still played Little League at eleven. By twelve, the boys were outpacing her, and her parents gave her the option of switching to tennis. Initially Cleo had been heartbroken, but then she quickly wised up that it wasn't *baseball* that she loved; rather, it was *winning*, and if she couldn't be the best at second base (her position), well, she'd be the best from the baseline. It didn't really matter all that much to Cleo. She just wanted the trophy. And she knew how much her success delighted her parents—she was precocious enough to recognize it even then. Still, she managed to tamp this ambition down in just the right ways in adulthood: too pushy and you were unlikable, not pushy enough and you'd never run for Congress (or president!) in the first place.

"People do like me," she said. "But maybe apologizing is the right thing to do anyway."

"What did you do?" Gabrielle was now finished with her breakfast bar and was moving on to a green smoothie from the mini fridge that sat under the flat-screen, where news spun around the clock. Cleo eyed the anchor, Bowen Babson—inarguably a man who should have been on Cleo's radar and in her league, but he was five years younger than she and had a reputation for women ten years younger than him, and so she was theoretically over-the-hill while he was just hitting his prime. Cleo didn't think she'd ever gotten more than a collegial smile from Bowen, which was fine, she supposed; she didn't have time or really the inclination for a romance. A quick hit of sex, well, sure. She wasn't going to turn that down. But even that led to complications of publicity, of gossip, and when you are in the public eye, you can't afford a scandal such as occasionally sleeping with the anchor of *Good Afternoon, USA*, even with his green eyes and jaw that looked like Captain America's. Today Bowen must have been sitting in for the regular morning anchor. Cleo didn't mind. She didn't mind one bit, actually.

"What did you do to her?" Gabrielle repeated. "Because you know I don't care, to be clear. High school shit is high school shit."

"Says the prom queen."

"Homecoming queen," Gabrielle corrected.

"Forgive me, is there a difference? We had neither."

"You didn't have homecoming? Or . . . prom?"

Cleo shook her head. "We had both, but I grew up in Seattle, you're forgetting. They didn't believe in anointing women—or men, I guess—into categories. Or winners. Or whatever. We didn't have cheerleaders either."

Gabrielle's eyes grew wide. But she was from Texas, and other than Election Day, the Super Bowl was the most historic day of the year for her.

"So she's not mad at you for going *Carrie* on her at homecoming. OK, I can cross that one off."

"If you seriously thought I was the type to dump blood on someone for wearing a tiara, I feel as if we have other questions to address."

Gabrielle laughed at this, and Cleo did too, deflecting for the moment that Cleo had not always been as likable or as kind. (Was she kind now? She didn't even know.) Gabrielle reached toward the mini fridge and grabbed a second green juice, sliding it across Cleo's desk, which, despite its organization, had too many folders and too many papers for a clear path from A to B. Thus, Cleo did not reach for the bottle when it became moored behind a stack of files.

"Come on, you need your energy. This might be the only healthy thing you eat all day."

Gabrielle, marathon trainee, was practically lit from within. Her skin glowed, her energy was boundless, and her teeth—which had little to do with nutrition and more to do with a wonderful Dallas-based orthodontist—were as white and as straight as those of all the celebrities in the photos in her office.

"Fine," Cleo acquiesced. "I'll try it, but I won't like it."

"Welcome to Washington; that's basically our motto."

Gaby and her comms team had gotten out ahead of the story, true. But like it or not, that hadn't quashed it entirely. The op-ed had over ten thousand retweets on Twitter, and Cleo was also trending, albeit not at number one, so that was a relief. It was nuts, Cleo thought, how this theoretically unimportant—and, more critically, unverified—gossip could take off so quickly. Sometimes politicians used this to their advantage. But today Cleo was playing cleanup. She did one interview: Gabrielle didn't think that Cleo needed to give such a piece wall-to-wall coverage, and besides, she had to be on the Senate floor for votes, and she simply couldn't devote all her time to an old high school dispute with her former best friend.

On CNN, her one interview with Wolf Blitzer, she'd come off as human, flawed (in a good way, which mattered in polling numbers), but not terribly contrite, which Cleo had thought was acceptable.

"Should we all apologize for being self-centered at seventeen?" Cleo had laughed when Wolf asked her if MaryAnne's charges of selfishness had merit. "Because I have a fourteen-year-old, and I'm pretty sure that this comes with the territory of being a teenager."

"Speaking of him—" Wolf didn't have to finish his question.

"Wolf, I can say unequivocally that her lurid insinuation about my son's father—which is our private family matter—is untrue. I don't know who her source was, but her facts are wrong. And I don't want to have to discuss this further." Cleo didn't mention that the accusation of an affair was indeed accurate. Because she didn't want to have to waste any energy thinking about that man, that mistake, and besides, she felt confident that by batting down MaryAnne's gossip with facts, she could bat down the rest of it too. On this, with Wolf, she proved correct.

"Also, Wolf, I should say that I'd rather not discuss my son."

Lucas was going to be pissed that she'd mentioned him publicly, though technically this was MaryAnne's fault—generally, he would have preferred that she ignore his existence in any capacity other than at home and/or when he needed money or food or a ride or whatever else he requested when he emerged from his room, and he certainly did *not* like her to mention him in interviews. But it was true: teenagers *were* assholes, and Cleo didn't want to lose the chance at the presidential nomination because of that.

"Moody teenage years do have the right to be off-limits . . ." Wolf smiled.

"And no one gets out of those unscathed." Cleo smiled.

Wolf chuckled but pressed her. "I have a grown daughter. I understand. But . . . why did your friend raise this at all, if it's all untrue? Just a baseless smear?"

"You'd have to ask her about her intentions," Cleo replied, and immediately she knew this was a mistake. Cleo rarely made mistakes, much less in public, much less with Wolf Blitzer. The last thing she wanted was CNN chasing down MaryAnne Newman and combing through Cleo's childhood—or any of it. She knew some of this was inevitable with a presidential run; with her congressional campaigns—barring her first campaign against Martin Bridgewater, which had been a bit of a nail-biter—she'd easily triumphed, and any opposition research had been limited and squelched quickly, but she didn't need to direct the cameras to MaryAnne's doorstep.

Cleo followed up before Wolf could latch on to her slip. "What I mean, Wolf, is that of course there were petty disagreements. If memory serves, we both chased the coveted editor of the paper position and a junior-year summer internship, and we were both on the debate team. I was captain. Perhaps MaryAnne thought that she should have been instead. It was a long time ago, before . . . well, as you and your viewers know, my senior year was difficult for many reasons—"

"Your parents," Wolf interjected, as if Cleo had forgotten.

"Yes, well, my parents were killed the summer before in a helicopter accident, and I don't think that any seventeen-year-old can be expected to handle that with the grace that's required. Not completely anyway."

Cleo did not want to play the "dead parents card" any more than she wanted to play the "Lucas card." But it was true: her parents had been killed when, as a surprise anniversary present, her dad took her mom up on a new Boeing chopper he was working on, and Cleo then had to move in with her grandmother. And maybe she still would have cut MaryAnne off at the knees to be the editor of the paper—she was the golden child of the household, and she knew, both then and now, that her parents had hung the moon on her achievements—but Cleo couldn't say now. Her dad had taught her to reach for what she wanted, to grab hold and dig her nails in deep, so she didn't think he would mind her mentioning her parents now. With Wolf. On national TV. With the presidential bid calling. Her mother, though . . . her mother may have minded.

"So you do have regrets?" Wolf asked.

"Don't all people have regrets?" She hoped her face didn't twitch when she said this, betraying her. She'd have to rewatch the tape later to be sure.

Wolf nodded at this and let her off the hook. Politicians being human was always a good thing to go to commercial with.

⌒੭

Did Cleo have regrets? Of course she did. But this did not please Gaby.

"I love you, Clee," she said once the CNN crew had left their offices and in between bites of her midday omelet (protein). She passed Cleo a wipe to remove the TV makeup. "But you admitted that you've made mistakes. Men can do that. Women, not so much."

Gaby reminded Cleo of her mother when she said this, which was maybe part of the reason they were such good friends. Cleo had discipline, to be sure. But Gaby had acumen beyond the rigidity and focus needed to become a congresswoman at twenty-five and a senator at thirty-one. Gaby had been the one to nurse the slow but steady drumbeat of support for a presidential run, molding Cleo's messages and tone, which initially were more strident than necessary and probably more off-putting than Cleo realized. MaryAnne wasn't the only one from Seattle who harbored a grudge. And probably Northwestern. And Columbia Law. Cleo was likable enough to get elected but not so likable that she ever would have won a popularity contest of her peers. She didn't care all that much, but Gaby did, which was why Gaby had vision, just like Mona, Cleo's mom, who'd had vision in a different way—she'd been part of the company at the Pacific Northwest Ballet until she first got pregnant, and then she picked up painting, as if that had been a natural course for her all along. She became fairly well-known for her work within the Seattle art scene—not because she was Georgia O'Keeffe or Frida Kahlo (the list of famous female artists was sadly significantly shorter than their male peers) but because she had a unique ability to capture a specific, piercing emotion in each of her works. As if she could see through not just her subjects but her audience too. Gaby was like this: a seer, and it made her extremely excellent at her job and dangerous too.

"I didn't mean to sound weak," Cleo said. Her stomach growled as Gaby tore into her omelet. "And I don't think I did. Isn't part of the human experience admitting your mistakes?"

"Human but not female."

"Disagree." Cleo palmed her stomach, as if this would quell her hunger. "Part of being a good lawmaker is the ability to adapt." Cleo thought of her dad, how he'd tell her to jab left if she couldn't jab right. To dance, to move, to win. And her mom would laugh and laugh when she and her dad did this little jig in their kitchen—his hands up and Cleo punching them, as if her dad were an amateur boxer and not a nerdy Boeing engineer, and as if Cleo were a prizefighter, not a middle schooler who barely made the growth charts. And how happy it made Cleo to see her mom laugh and to please both of them. That laughter and approval and Cleo winning were all knotted together, especially after Georgie, her older sister, had been such a disappointment.

Gaby's phone buzzed before they could get into it further, which Cleo found to be a bit of a relief. She and Gaby so rarely disagreed, and she didn't want to butt heads with her closest advisor, not over MaryAnne Newman.

Gaby's face grew still as her eyes raced over her screen.

17

"Hmm," she said, and it was not a *hmm* of ponderance. More a *hmm* of displeasure.

Cleo's stomach rumbled again, and she pressed her intercom, asking her executive assistant to bring her something, anything that they had on hand in the office. Someone had grabbed a tray of muffins a day or so ago, left over from a meeting. That could do.

"Hmm," Gaby muttered again, and this time Cleo could not wait. "What?"

Arianna, in a blazing fuchsia sweater and wide-legged black pants that reminded Cleo of the shape of the Liberty Bell, entered with the picked-over plate of muffins and a bag of Bugles. This was surely not the job she'd had in mind when she graduated from Columbia Law last May, but everyone needed to start somewhere. (Cleo often worked on legislation with Arianna's father, an environmental lawyer, and when he called her to say his daughter was graduating from Cleo's alma mater and could she find room on her staff, Cleo happily did.)

"This was all I could find. But I can run out?" All of Arianna's sentences ended with a question mark, which Cleo made a mental note to dissuade her from. Women in politics didn't have the luxury of ending their sentences on an upswing, as if they were asking permission, as if they couldn't find the answers themselves, as if they were waiting for someone to guide them. Actually, Cleo thought, women everywhere couldn't afford this.

"Don't worry," Cleo said to Arianna, reaching for a nonspecific flavor that she thought might be carrot but proved to be banana nut. "This is great."

"I'm sorry," Arianna said. She tugged at the hem of her sweater.

"Don't apologize," Cleo replied. "Don't apologize for anything if you're not responsible for the problem."

"OK. I'll try."

"It takes a while," Cleo added. "Eventually you'll refuse to apologize even when you *are* responsible." Cleo thought again of her parents in the kitchen, with her report cards hung on the refrigerator and a giant poster board from the science fair—an exploration of the hierarchy of a beehive—which had won first prize that month. Of how her dad had kept telling her to hit his palms harder and harder, then harder still, and how he was sweating by then, and Cleo was a little worried about him to be honest, but she put some muscle behind it, and then the phone rang, and her dad startled, and Cleo inadvertently hit him square in the jaw. He refused to allow her to apologize. She was just doing what he asked, he said. Cleo felt guilty for the evening but then resolved that he was right. He told her to assert her strength, and she did. She shouldn't be sorry. He was the one who had jolted. (But she did check on him and bring him another ice pack. She loved her dad something fierce.)

"Also, Arianna, can you check my passport and ensure that everything is up-to-date? I am heading out on the delegation trip to the Middle East in a few weeks." Technically all her papers were in order, but Cleo liked to be sure before each trip anyway. There was something methodical about her process that she found reassuring.

Arianna squeaked that she would and shut the door behind her, the hems of her pants swaying as she went.

"So," Gaby said. "This story isn't going away."

"But I did Wolf Blitzer!" Cleo swallowed a bite of the muffin top and wondered if her assessment of banana nut was wrong. What else could it be? It wasn't carrot; it wasn't banana nut. "What kind of muffin is this?" She broke off a piece and offered it to Gaby.

"Technically I'm off gluten, but this is what you pay me for, so . . ." She placed it on her tongue, assessed. "It's vanilla macadamia."

Cleo was impressed not just with her palate but also with her certainty. Indeed, it *was* vanilla macadamia, which she'd never have sussed out on her own.

"It looks like MaryAnne has some clout up in Seattle. Turning this into a bit of a stink." Gaby paused, still scrolling. "She was interviewed on their own local news today . . . and . . ." Scrolling. "She shared the ridiculous op-ed on Facebook, which I guess was seen by some of your old classmates." She tapped her phone. "Hmm. OK, well, some of your classmates are defending you but . . . hmm, OK, wow, well, some of them are not."

"Tell me something I don't already know."

Gaby sighed. Rested her phone in her lap next to her takeout container with the half-eaten omelet.

"So, Cleo, I love you. You know that. I will work with you forever and tirelessly, and I believe that you can and should be president. Even before forty."

"What's the 'but' coming?"

"But we've never really had the conversation about your past."

"I don't have a past," Cleo said. Her muffin was becoming much less appealing.

"Everyone has a past, Clee."

"Well, obviously."

"What I mean is, you didn't have liabilities in your New York race because no one cared all that much. New York wanted you, and they loved you, and it wasn't even close. But this time it will be different."

Cleo nodded. This wasn't her first rodeo. In fact, it would technically be her sixth. Three congressional races, two senatorial.

"I'm not a dummy," she said. "I know what I'm in for."

"Then I need to know what *I'm* in for," Gabrielle said. "I can't protect you if I don't know. Why would MaryAnne mention some married professor? I get that the timing is off with Lucas, but that doesn't seem pulled from thin air."

Cleo laughed but not her normal laugh, and they both knew it. It was her nervous laugh that she'd use whenever she needed to give herself a moment to strategize. It wasn't actually all that often that she needed it. She was almost always prepared (a cable commentator once said *too* prepared) and rarely caught off guard, and besides, she had other ways to distract and deflect. All politicians did. Point fingers elsewhere,

blame the other party, cite oppo research, take a fact and spin it so diz-
zily that no one even really knows what you're talking about by the end
and thus drops it. But none of this would work on Gabrielle. She was
too smart, she was too close, and also, she was one of Cleo's few dear,
true, trusted friends. Probably her only one, actually. Cleo did not have
a wide network of girlfriends, for reasons MaryAnne's only partially
accurate op-ed made clear.

Cleo exhaled, long, slow, measured. "I mean, listen, I have moments
of regret."

"Who doesn't?"

"Right, so? So what? Then there's nothing."

Gaby's phone buzzed, then buzzed again, but she didn't even peek.
"So if I peel back this onion with MaryAnne and the rest of this, there'll
be nothing there? I personally don't care whom you've slept with. The
electorate . . . may."

"MaryAnne is, like, the president of her country club," Cleo said,
as if this had anything to do with anything.

"And those women are exactly who you need," Gaby said, not
incorrectly. "Thus . . . the affair?" She squinted, capturing a thought.
"But I knew you in law school, and I swear, you were never getting laid."

Cleo raised her eyebrows as if to say: *Exactly.* She hoped Gaby
would let it go at that.

"Fine, whatever, but even you mentioning 'regrets' raises the hairs
on my neck." Gaby leveled her gaze, and Cleo knew she was giving her
one chance to tell her version of the truth before this went any further:
into a real campaign launch, into a confrontation with MaryAnne, into
a war with the press. Gaby was not the type of woman who liked to be
caught unaware in the middle of a fistfight.

"Fine. Listen. My dad. He and I started something when I was
younger. My mom thought it was . . ." Cleo hesitated, remembering.
"Well, my mom thought it was 'a tornado of negative energy,' that's
what she would always say. 'Why are you getting caught up in that

negative energy? Go focus on just being a superstar!'" Cleo smiled at this because her parents had been diametrical opposites who also fit together perfectly. They'd had her late—Cleo always assumed that she was an accident, but she was never old enough or bold enough to ask. And they loved her so very much, so what did it matter? She was, they always told her, their shining star.

And then they were gone.

"So what was the negative energy?" Gaby brought her back.

"It's just . . . it's a way of sort of . . . tracking my mistakes."

"We don't make mistakes."

"Fine. A way of tracking my regrets."

Gaby inhaled. "I don't even know what that means, and frankly I'm scared to ask. It's not . . . I mean, please tell me that you don't, like, have some sort of Excel spreadsheet for regrets?"

An Excel spreadsheet sounded exactly like something she would keep. Cleo loved Excel spreadsheets.

"It's nothing. I mean, it's something, a list. But it's mine. And it's private, and no one knows." Cleo said this stridently, like she would in a debate or on the Senate floor while pushing a bill, but she couldn't totally be sure of the list's secrecy. Had she shared it with MaryAnne during one of their hundreds of childhood sleepovers? Had she drunkenly mentioned it during the rare college party she attended when she blew off too much steam to deal with dead parents and a black hole of loneliness and a wandering ambition that she didn't know how to tame now that her parents weren't there to guide her?

Maybe she had mentioned it once or twice unintentionally. She wouldn't hold her hand on the Constitution and swear to it.

"Still waiting for this big reveal."

"My dad, he just . . . he encouraged me to write down all my regrets, so I could look back and see if they truly were mistakes, and if so, learn from them, and if not, learn from that too." Cleo paused. "You never knew them, my parents. They were just encouraging me to be my best. This was one of my dad's tricks."

"Oh!" Gaby looked both mystified and confused. "Most people write down their goals. Or aspirations."

"Right. This was kind of the opposite of that but with the same end result. I think. I mean, I've never done anything with it other than add to it."

"Hmm," Gaby said. Again. Then: "I wonder if we can use this."

"Use this?" Cleo felt something unfamiliar rise in her: panic.

"Yes . . . yes!"

Gaby was on her feet now, towering in her heels, dumping the remains of her omelet in the trash to the side of Cleo's desk.

"Let's tackle some of these regrets publicly!" Gaby was practically shouting now. "Let's build a road trip around this. Your summer recess. Film it, bring a crew, no, wait . . . home video on our phones so no one thinks it's too orchestrated! Could there be anything more humanizing?" She clapped her hands together three times, as if she were applauding herself.

Cleo was on her feet now too (albeit in one-inch wedges). "You literally *just told me* that admitting weakness is a terrible strategy! Why would I air all of my mistakes?"

"Because you are *owning* them. You are showing up at MaryAnne Newman's doorstep and sharing your regrets, *not* apologizing as if she were the victim, rather making amends because you have realized you have grown. People *love* growth in a candidate, people *crave* growth." Gaby went still. "I guess I should ask . . . these aren't egregious? I mean, there aren't any dead bodies anywhere, are there?"

Cleo glared.

"Anything short of murder I can work with."

"I think this is a terrible idea," Cleo said, plunking back in her chair, which squeaked again. *"Arianna, please get me some goddamn WD-40!"* she shouted toward the door, not even bothering with the intercom.

"You're wrong," Gaby shot back.

"I'm very rarely wrong."

"True," Gaby conceded. "But you pay me to tell you the rare times that you are." She paused. "How long is this list? Twenty? Thirty?"

"Two hundred and thirty-three. I think. Give or take a few."

Gaby's eyebrows skyrocketed to the top of her forehead. "Holy shit."

"Some of them are small! Most of them are small. Like, I didn't have enough cash on me, so I couldn't properly tip the Starbucks guy, so I wrote it down so it wouldn't happen again. And in my defense, it hasn't!" Cleo felt a little indignant. Also a little hysterical.

Gaby waved a hand. "We're not filming you returning to tip the Starbucks guy. Although . . ." Her focus wandered to the ceiling as she considered it. "No, not that."

"I just don't see how pointing out all of my flaws makes me electable," Cleo said in as close to a whine as she'd ever emitted.

"Because we're beating everyone to the punch. They're going to pull you apart if you run—for a lot of reasons, but also because of your XX chromosome. You are going to go on a 'no regrets regrets' tour and show everyone how likable, how relatable you are, *even* when you've made mistakes, stepped in the figurative shit."

Cleo probably looked unconvinced. Because she was.

Gaby softened. "Cleo, the easiest, cheapest shot is for them to paint you as *un*likable. If you were the majority leader, who cares; no one would give a shit. That's the luxury of having a dick."

Cleo groaned.

"This will make people fall in love with you. It will be your armor against the inevitable other stuff—the less-than-kind stuff—that will come your way. It's already starting with MaryAnne's op-ed."

Cleo started to protest but then stopped because what Gaby said was the truth.

"We're going to make them love you," Gaby said. "Then we're going to round them up to vote for you."

Cleo audibly sighed, which Gaby correctly took as a concession.

"Narrow it down to ten," Gaby said as her phone blew up again. "I want a list of ten regrets—juicy enough to be appealing but not so juicy that charges will be filed. And then I'll pick five. Maybe more. We'll see how it goes."

"First of all, no charges *can* be filed! I'm not a criminal! I'm a senator."

Gaby laughed. "You know those aren't necessarily mutually exclusive."

"Fine," Cleo huffed. "I'll narrow it down to ten. But we get to agree on the five. Because this is *my* life out there, not yours."

She squeezed her eyes closed. There was no point in arguing this further. Cleo had been brilliant at law school—she'd graduated number two. But Gaby was number one.

Gaby's phone was on fire now, and she was on her feet, pointed toward the door. "Shit, I need to take this. MaryAnne Newman has officially become a pain in my ass."

She headed toward the door just as Arianna in her blinding sweater rushed in, still pale, still nervous, with the WD-40.

"I'm sorry," Arianna said to no one, to all of them.

Cleo did not correct her.

# THREE

The condo was dark by the time Cleo got home. She'd made the decision when Lucas was starting kindergarten to move to DC full-time and commute back to New York, her representative state, on the weekends. With no coparent and no grandparents, there was simply no other way to do it and still provide him stability and also be a (relatively) present mother.

The day the movers came, though, she did jot the move down on her list of regrets. She thought she was doing the right thing—adding her voice to the political landscape—but she was twenty-eight and a single mom and, honestly, though she trusted her decision-making, she didn't totally trust *all* her decision-making.

Thus, she supposed, the list. A way to track her decisions when they went awry.

That's all her dad was trying to say from it, she was sure. She couldn't ask him now. He had a brother who lived in . . . she wasn't quite certain . . . she thought maybe Bozeman, and maybe she could have reached out over the years and asked if he kept a list too and why it started and if it gave him peace of mind, but her father and her uncle hadn't been close, and she hadn't heard from him since just around the funeral. Cleo wasn't the type to chase down estranged relatives in Montana if they didn't want to be involved in the first place.

She flipped on the lights in her kitchen. There was an abandoned half-empty pizza box on the counter, which meant Lucas was home from soccer practice and, she hoped, doing his homework, not rewatching *Stranger Things*, which he had now binged three times this spring and was actually beginning to concern her. She grabbed a slice, shoved the box in the fridge, and tiptoed to his room, devouring half the piece before she even reached his door. (The vanilla macadamia muffin had not been sustaining.) She didn't want to eavesdrop, but she didn't want to burst in there without knowing what she was getting herself into. Teenagers harbored all sorts of secrets.

His room was silent but the light was on, so she knocked, and he grunted, so she entered.

He was sprawled on his bed with his laptop open and his palm curled around his phone, which he immediately shoved under the covers. Cleo hoped he wasn't looking at porn.

"Hey, how was your day? Soccer go OK?"

"Yep."

"Your coach being nicer?"

While Lucas shared relatively little with Cleo (very, very, very little, in fact, but who knew what was normal, since he was her only child and she didn't have very many mom friends), he had confided that his coach this year was being "a total dick." Lucas had been blessed with a bit of a godly foot, something Cleo assumed he must have gotten from his father, who she thought she remembered had indeed been an athlete. Her son's natural athleticism had been seamless until middle school, when his legs grew faster than the rest of his body, and he had to reconsider his gait and his balance, and also the other kids were bigger and shoved and elbowed, and everything about Lucas's game had to be recalibrated. He was up for it, Cleo knew, but he had also had the good fortune of the game always coming easily. And so when he had to exert the effort, he was not pleased.

Which subsequently did not please Cleo. She didn't want to raise someone who got by with half efforts. She would have to add it to her list of regrets in that case, and it would stay there forever. Cleo saw half-efforted people all the time in Congress, and frankly, they disgusted her. Not because you should apologize for being born into a dynasty or for being carried into your position on a wave of charming popularity, but because if you didn't do the work once you held the golden ticket, what use were you to anyone?

This privilege reminded Cleo of MaryAnne Newman, who felt entitled to plenty of things, including evidently publishing disparaging op-eds on *Seattle Today!* about her former best friend. And now Gaby was toying with the idea of Cleo making amends with her? Cleo acknowledged her culpability in the detonation of their friendship, but the salaciousness of the paternity angle was a bridge too far. Really.

"Coach was fine today."

"Mrs. Godwin dropped you off after practice?"

Lucas finally looked up and met her eyes. "I mean, I'm here, aren't I?"

Cleo sighed. She'd learned in debate and law school to avoid stupid questions.

"I just wanted to be sure. My day got hectic, and I forgot to check in with her about carpool."

"She asked me if you were OK after that . . . article."

"Oh!" Cleo didn't quite know what to say to this. Emily Godwin was one of her few mom friends at Lucas's school, but they weren't *friend* friends. She couldn't call her up and say: *My chief of staff wants me to expose all of my regrets; can I come cry into a giant vat of wine with you and watch shitty TV to distract myself?*

In fact, she had no such friends like that, and maybe she should add that to her list of regrets too. It would be nice to have a normal, nonpolitical friend who didn't have an angle and who you did more than text about carpool or covering for you at a PTA meeting. (Cleo had never attended a PTA meeting, my God!)

"I'll text her right now," Cleo said. "And thank her and tell her that I'm fine."

"Are you?" Lucas's face was washed with concern, and Cleo saw him as he used to be, before all the hormones overtook him and hair sprouted from his chin and an occasional crater of a zit planted roots on his forehead. Maybe he'd have been better off with a dad in his life; Cleo didn't know.

"I am. I'm more worried about you." Cleo sat on his bed, just on the edge, because he didn't really like her in his space. "Is there anything else you want to talk about, with . . . that article this morning?" Cleo hoped the answer was no, but she acknowledged that it might be yes, and she'd have to deal with that too. That all this may have reopened questions, wounds about his dad. Obviously Lucas had asked about him from time to time. And she never felt good about her answers: vague, noncommittal, that she hadn't known him well. What else was there to say? She had tried her best, she'd tried to be all things for him, she'd tried to love him from all sides and perspectives. She had tried to be enough.

"I'm OK," he said. "Seemed like typical political bullshit."

Cleo started to chastise him, but what was the point? *Bullshit* was well incorporated into his vocabulary now. She leaned over and kissed the top of his head, and he didn't recoil, which was truly something. She did notice that he needed to wash his hair, but because they were having such an unusual moment of bonding, she let it go.

"Homework?" she asked.

"Already done."

"Superstar," she replied, just like her parents used to say to her.

Lucas gave her the finger, but she could tell he didn't really mean it.

She kept the list, handwritten, in her top desk drawer, which she also locked. She didn't know why. Lucas wasn't the type to snoop (if anything, she should be poking around *his* room), and there wasn't anyone else in the condo. Maybe it was the symbolism—that it needed to be protected, that it was for her eyes only. That, in senatorial terms, it required clearance. And now Gaby wanted to open it to the world. *Ten?* Gaby wanted her to pick *ten?*

Cleo popped the lock and tugged the drawer toward her. She hadn't reread the list in ages. Her last entry simply read: *brownies*, but Cleo couldn't remember if she'd intended to mean that she should eat more brownies (whimsy!) or fewer (gluttony). Cleo remembered her dad encouraging her to use the list as a way to reflect and reset, and she came to think of it more like confession, if she were Catholic (which she was not) and if she went to church (didn't do that either). She'd convinced herself that if she purged her misdeed on paper, recognized it for what it was—anything from an innocent mistake to an intentional obfuscation—she could pick it up and leave it behind her on the side of the metaphorical road, drive away with a clean conscience.

And to a certain extent, this was true. There were small misgivings on there; she flipped through the top page onto the second, then the third—*no high heels* (whoever decided that women had to perilously teeter on three-inch pins to make their calves look slimmer while nearly castrating their pinkie toes?) and *blinker lights, goddammit*, which Cleo remembered she'd jotted down after failing to signal on a turn when she was new to DC and unaccustomed to driving and nearly collided with an oncoming car and instead steered smack into a stop sign.

The notepaper was worn the more she went backward, her handwriting different too. Bouncier when she first started, maybe because she didn't yet realize how exhausting and difficult adulthood would be. Tougher for her than many because of her parents and her loneliness and probably her ambition too, first nurtured out of love by those parents, then left unwieldy and rambling when Cleo was on her own. So

Cleo sank into that drive, gave it space, simply let it take her when it wanted, but it was also true that it made her a little more ruthless, a little less empathetic, a little more likely to sneak onto MaryAnne Newman's laptop in the computer lab to read her notes while she went to the bathroom to touch up her makeup before they debated in front of their peers to decide who should be elected head of the paper. (Everything in her school in Seattle was a democracy. They really believed the children were the future.) Cleo had always told herself that none of this made her a terrible person; it made her a cunning one, and in fact, it armed her for all that came next: her parents, the pregnancy, Congress. So it was a funny thing to have a list of 233 regrets when Cleo also couldn't deny that so many of them led her here, today, to everything that had happened since. How could you define regret if it also put you on top? By your motivation? By your failures? By your successes? Cleo didn't know. Could she see now, from MaryAnne's perspective, how she hadn't been so kind in high school? Well, sure. Did that merit MaryAnne's scorched-earth strategy? Cleo thought not. Firmly *not*.

For a brief hiccup of a moment, she wondered how long her father's own list had been. If it had brought him peace, if it had helped guide him. She'd never read it, never asked to read it, and until now had never been curious to do so. People should be allowed their secrets. People should be allowed their scars. Today there was no room for that—there were glaring headlines at every little misstep (case in point: MaryAnne Newman's now-viral op-ed) or social media frenzies tasting of schaden-freude, but in years past, people like her dad could really step in the figurative horseshit and no one could smell their stink. *That would be nice,* she thought. *Whatever happened to that?*

Cleo located her mouse, which was under a pile of confidential files on New York State white-collar crimes, and woke her desktop. She'd never been on Facebook officially, or not personally anyway. Gaby had their comms team handle the social media accounts, which Cleo glanced at once in a while, but she mostly thought her energy was better served elsewhere. She had Twitter because she had to keep up with the news, but Facebook struck her as a little juvenile and also, she didn't have a huge desire to keep in touch with her high school classmates and see the photos of their grinning family units of four on the beach or their July Fourth parties or, in MaryAnne Newman's case, her posing with a championship trophy from the round-robin at the country club.

She grabbed her phone. Texted Lucas, who was only down the hall but generally responded best to digital requests.

Cleo: Can u come help me for a sec? She added a smiley-face emoji.

Lucas: No emojis, Mom.

Cleo: Fine. Can u come help for a sec, no emoji?

She heard a rumbling from his room, then the padding of his footsteps down the hall. Her office door swung open.

"What?"

"Remember that time you signed me up for Facebook? Do you remember the login?"

Lucas sighed, exasperated. "You're not eighty. You should know how to do this."

"I know," Cleo conceded. "But I'm busy trying to save the world, so please just log me in."

Lucas's eyes rolled so far back that Cleo wondered if they would ever return, but they did, and he leaned over her desk, pounded her keyboard, and voilà!

"Do you want me to add a profile picture? Right now, you look like an anonymous troll. No one can tell it's you. You made me sign up as Cee Mac. It's like a bad rap-star name."

"No!" Cleo pushed his hand off the keyboard. "That's exactly how I want it."

"God, you have issues," Lucas said, but she could tell he was only partially serious, and frankly, to get her teen to rib her was possibly the highlight of her day (though her day admittedly was terrible), so she laughed and replied, "Aren't you lucky that I'm your mom then."

He walked out without answering.

MaryAnne Newman's Facebook page was public, so Cleo had no problem finding not just her profile but her posts and photos and, of course, the op-ed.

> *I JUST WANTED TO SHARE THIS. IT TOOK A LOT FOR ME TO SPEAK MY TRUTH, BUT A LOT OF US REMEMBER CLEO MCDOUGAL, AND I DO. NOT. THINK. SHE. SHOULD. BE. PRESIDENT.*

Cleo nearly giggled because twenty years later, MaryAnne hadn't changed one bit. True, Cleo had been a type-A perfectionist, tap-dancing not just because it made her parents so happy but because Cleo got off on being the best at everything too, but MaryAnne had been her mirror image—all charged up without quite the dexterity or acumen that Cleo possessed, and so while they were perfect best friends (for a while), this was also the reason they were so combustible. Now Cleo could see that it had never been an equal relationship, unlike Cleo and Gabrielle, who were true sparring partners. There were petty jealousies between MaryAnne and her, and an uneasy sense of competition lurked just under the surface (competition that went both ways, Cleo knew, even if she usually triumphed), but as teens, neither one of them was adept enough to recognize this dynamic. They loved each other, they really did, even when they didn't. And maybe Cleo should have just let things take their natural course. She probably would have bested MaryAnne in debate and on the school paper; she didn't have to cheat, to take shortcuts. But part of her—the regretful part—wanted to win more than she wanted to protect her friendship.

Cleo stared at MaryAnne's Facebook profile picture and remembered how, for that internship their junior-year summer, just before her parents died, she gave MaryAnne bad advice on her essay, knowing full well that writing about the day her dog died was trite and clichéd and would never win her a spot in the mayor's office. Just prior, MaryAnne had casually bragged that her parents were golfing partners with the mayor's personal lawyer and that he was going to put in a good word for her. Cleo, feeling undermined and yes, a little less than, could not let that stand. She herself wrote about her relationship with her sister, how she felt like two people—one an only child and one a much younger sibling of a troubled sibling who had dropped out of college—she did not mention her arrest for weed possession—and the expectations this placed on Cleo, the good one, the best daughter they could have asked for. Cleo got the internship. MaryAnne did not.

Cleo inhaled and steeled her nerves as she scrolled down MaryAnne's Facebook page. She was used to criticism. Any politician was. But these were people she knew, who knew *her*, and that made it different because that made it personal. She didn't really want to know what they all thought of her in high school, not because she didn't care but because she suspected that she actually might.

There were twenty-one comments below the op-ed (and MaryAnne's commentary). Cleo didn't recognize all the names at first until she realized that some of her classmates now went by their married names. She leaned forward, squinted at the photos. Their faces, though older, rang bells, loud bells, bells that Cleo didn't really want to hear, to be honest. It wasn't that high school had been traumatic, at least not until her parents' accident, and obviously that wasn't her classmates' fault, but even Gaby had proposed that her campaign motto be "Only Forward" because Cleo wasn't the type who took much delight in looking back or basking in nostalgia. She had repressed nearly all memories of Alexander Nobells; she had moved well past her one-nighter with Lucas's father; hell, she'd made her peace with her strained relationship with Georgie.

The past was the past was the past. Which was at least half the reason that Gaby's suggestion, to revisit her list, to right some of her wrongs, was so irritating. Who really was the better for logging hours on Facebook, posting photos for their former friends from two decades ago? Not Cleo McDougal, that's for sure.

The messages were nearly all words of support for MaryAnne, which immediately raised the hairs on the back of Cleo's competitive neck.

Susan Harris: I didn't know Cleo well, but I remember once in biology, she just HAD to be the first one to dissect the earthworm, and I knew she was nasty then!

Maureen Allen: Word.

Beth Shin: I don't want to dump on her for being smart and doing well in biology, but yeah, wasn't she a bit of a bitch about it? Like, rubbing it in our faces how much better she was? I never liked her. I'd never vote for her either.

Christopher Preston: THANK YOU FOR SPEAKING UP! She always had such a sour look on her face. Never smiled. Amen.

Cleo didn't remember rushing the dissection tray in biology, though it sounded like something she would do, and she didn't even remember Maureen Allen at all! She knew she could drag out her yearbook and reacquaint herself with all those faces, all those names, but really, did it matter? Christopher Preston wasn't wrong about one thing: people see what they want. Her face naturally pointed downward and generally did indeed appear sour, even if she were thinking delightful thoughts. Like, winning the White House or even just envisioning a glass of wine and a massage, which she hadn't had time for in more than a year.

Instinctively, Cleo moved her hand to her shoulder, began digging into the knot that she'd assumed was more or less permanent. She kept reading.

Finally, a word of defense.

Oliver Patel: It seems to me that this is two decades' worth of old history, MaryAnne, and maybe none of us was at our best at seventeen. Did you really need to air this on *Seattle Today!*? I mean, is it even a legitimate news outlet? I remember Cleo as determined and really, really smart and sure, maybe a little better than us, but so what?

Oliver's post had five likes, which made Cleo's heart leap a little more than she'd anticipated.

Below it, he added his own reply:

Oliver Patel: I should offer the caveat of . . . it's not like I knew her well.

MaryAnne Newman: Well, that was my point, Oliver. Maybe none of us did. Even when we were supposed to be best friends.

# FOUR

It was a Saturday, so Cleo had no idea why her buzzer kept ringing at . . . eight fifteen in the morning. As a rule, Cleo didn't sleep late, but she'd forgotten to set her alarm last night, and there was no chance that Lucas would rouse her. He'd sleep until noon if he could. (Which he rarely could because of weekend soccer practice.)

She pulled on a robe that was discarded by the side of the bed. Her building had security, so it wasn't like the media could be literally beating down her door. Besides, despite the now twenty thousand retweets of the op-ed (at least as of last night when she checked), Cleo didn't think the story would stay front of mind for all that long. Political scandals tended to come and go, and granted, this was her first, but she trusted that someone else, likely a man if the odds proved correct, would step in it soon enough. Insider trading. Groping a breast. Affair with a housekeeper. Who knew? That list could be long.

The buzzer blared, this time unrelenting, as if someone's finger had been surgically attached to the button. Such aggressiveness could be only one person.

Gaby was in her running gear, naturally, because Saturday mornings meant long runs for her marathon training.

"Did I wake you?" This was a valid question because it was also so surprising.

"I lost track of time last night. On . . . Facebook." Cleo was embarrassed to even admit it.

Gaby welcomed herself inside. There was no posturing between them; they knew each other too well. Gaby didn't care that she'd just run fifteen miles and reeked of sweat, and frankly, Cleo didn't either. They'd seen each other much worse.

"So I've made a decision." Gabrielle reached for a Keurig pod and a mug in one simultaneous motion, her arms swinging in opposite directions, her brain working on both sides. "And you need to pack."

"What? We already discussed this. I'm not going back to New York this weekend. Lucas has a soccer tournament, and I'm on snack duty. In fact, shit, I'd better wake him."

Gaby couldn't have looked less interested or less convinced. Children were not for her. Not that she couldn't pinch cheeks and buy birthday presents, but priority-wise? She'd made that decision years ago. And she wouldn't apologize for it either. "Don't feel sorry for me," she'd say whenever the subject arose about her marital status (single) or motherhood status (party of one, thank you). "If you don't want to be a mother, you shouldn't be." Cleo would always stand beside her nodding (and often grinning) because who the fuck was anyone to tell anyone else what they should do with their life? Or their uterus? Or their DNA? Gaby's decision wasn't borne from a terrible childhood or mother issues. She simply didn't want children. She didn't feel the tug. She didn't want to vacuum Goldfish crumbs and drive carpools and yell about washing hands after using the bathroom, and Cleo thought that was terrific. Not because Cleo didn't love being Lucas's mom—she did—but because Cleo thought that every woman should do exactly whatever the hell she wanted. (Which, she realized, should make her reconsider how judgy she was about MaryAnne's country club presidency aspirations.)

"Text Emily Godwin. She'll cut up oranges," Gaby said.

"I like Emily; don't shit on her. She's saved me a million times."

Gaby nodded, a small concession that she was being petty. "You're right. Sorry." She plopped a sugar cube into her mug. Cleo's house was Gaby's house. "I've booked us on noon flights to Seattle." She checked the time on the microwave. "So we need to leave here in about an hour. Give or take."

"You've *what*?"

"I checked the weather, and it's beautiful in Seattle this weekend, and we're gonna knock on MaryAnne Newman's door and rattle the shit out of her, and by the time we leave, this turd is going to turn into a diamond." She blew on the top of her coffee, as if what she was announcing were perfectly innocuous, like, *Let's go to the grocery store this afternoon and pick up some Cheerios.*

"I . . . I can't just . . . I'm not going *to Seattle* today!" Cleo tugged her robe around her neck.

"Au contraire. You can and you are. This story spun even bigger overnight. While you were catching up on your beauty rest, CNN led with it last hour."

"So it will go away! Like every other stupid story. I think Malcolm Johannsson is about to leave his wife for their nanny! That will bump it out of the cycle. He's supposed to be a churchgoing, God-fearing devout Christian and is the minority whip! That should stay in the news for at least three days."

Gaby shook her head. "Do you want to have a shot at the nomination?"

Cleo felt her jaw tighten. "Yes."

"Then you do it my way. I ran some numbers last night, read some internal polling. People like you, Clee. But they also see you as . . . robotic."

"What does that mean?"

"It means you are a successful single mom, which they admire—"

"Uh, yeah, this shit is hard," Cleo interrupted.

"Right."

"Also, I'm not robotic," Cleo said flatly, a little too robotically, she realized. "Also *also*, she tried to out Lucas's dad!"

"True," Gaby said. They met each other's eyes. Gaby knew Cleo well enough to know that Cleo wasn't truly offended by this, particularly because MaryAnne had gotten it wrong. If anything, it amused Cleo precisely for that reason: that it was a clumsy, amateur play, and that as long as Lucas wasn't upset by it, Cleo wasn't either. Welcome to Washington. Bring your steel balls.

"Look," Gaby continued. "We just need to have more than one emotional card to play. Voters want to—*need to*—have more of a connection with you. This isn't just New York. This is America."

"Very glad we get to expose all of my regrets to *America*."

"Not all," Gaby said, swinging open the refrigerator and sighing when she found it mostly empty. "Just five."

∽

Cleo hadn't returned to Seattle since her grandmother died her junior year at Northwestern. Her sister had long since fled to California—after dropping out of the University of Washington, she headed south to Los Angeles and had stayed, and what else was left there for Cleo? It wasn't that she lamented her childhood; in fact, she remembered it warmly and was grateful her parents had expected excellence or at least taught her to pursue it, but she'd made the decision—she remembered consciously thinking this at her grandmother's funeral, which she, barely an adult, had organized—that Seattle had offered her all that it could, and, like an orange picked down to the rind, she was ready to emotionally discard it. Over the years, she'd gotten the (very) occasional invitation to weddings and, of course, her ten- and fifteen-year high school reunions, but she had a toddler, then an elementary-age kid by then, and dragging him across the country to reunite with friends she hadn't felt the urge to speak with in a decade didn't exactly sound appealing. Also, none of them were friends by that point. Maybe a therapist would tell her there were other reasons, more complex reasons for turning her back on the place that she came from—that this was where she gained a lot but lost a lot too, and that this was where she learned that playing dirty came with costs (that didn't seem to bother Cleo as much as it should), and that this was where she quite literally mourned the loss of her childhood and learned how much you could get by on your own—but the result was the same: Cleo had left and didn't come back.

That the flight was turbulent was no surprise. As if a sign from the universe, if Cleo were to believe in signs, which she did not. Gaby had booked a ticket for Lucas as well ("it's important that we still see you as maternal," she'd said, to which Cleo replied, "I *am* maternal!" to which Gaby had just said, "Great, then this will be easy,") and Lucas was more pouty than usual because he missed his soccer tournament, but he'd never been to Seattle, and even with all her misgivings, Cleo wanted him to see where she'd grown up. Also, if Lucas had really protested, he could have stayed with Emily Godwin—Cleo's red line was using Lucas for political gain; she wouldn't have brought him if he didn't "kind of" want to come. She wanted to take him to the cemetery where they'd buried her parents. Point out the mayor's office where she'd interned that summer before her final year of high school, maybe even swing by her old school on Monday before their flight out and introduce him to her debate teacher, who had prodded her into another round of revisions on her speeches and also invited her over for dinners once a month after her parents died. Ms. Paul must have been sixty by now, but Cleo bet that she was still as much of a hard-ass as ever, while still knowing when a kid who lost her parents needed a plate of homemade lasagna.

Lucas drank four Cokes on the plane, which both improved his mood and made him too hyper not to be annoying. Cleo had bought him Wi-Fi to keep him occupied, and he'd spent the majority of the six hours texting frantically with . . . Cleo didn't know whom, but she was glad that he appeared to have more friends than his morose demeanor would indicate. His leg bounced as their town car cruised down I-5 toward their hotel, his neck swiveling every which way as he took in the landscape, each turn of the freeway a new memory for Cleo and a new sight for Lucas. The Space Needle, where they'd held their spring dance. The expanse of Lake Washington where she spent summers, before she became so laser focused on moving up, up, up, jumping off the docks of more affluent friends who lived on the water. The looming mountains, where her dad had taken her to learn how to ski.

Gaby had booked them at a downtown Sheraton, and their rooms were not ready upon their late-afternoon arrival.

"I have to share with you?" Lucas whined.

"I won't peek at anything," Cleo said. She made a cross-her-heart sign across her chest and immediately regretted it. Lucas thought emojis were lame; this was not going to endear her to him either. "No, really, Luke, I'll give you as much privacy as you need."

He sighed as Gaby pecked at her phone and said: "Uber's on the way. Lucas, you'll film it from your phone—you probably know your way around the tech better than I do." Lucas shrugged, as if this were totally normal, and Gaby took it as a yes. Then she looked toward Cleo, as if she did not need to be in the know until now. (Cleo always needed to be in the know.) "If you want, because I sprang this on you, we can count this as one of your five."

"My five?"

"Five regrets. After this, we can be down to four. Though, to be honest, I expected to have the ten to choose from by now."

"It's been twelve hours!" Cleo snapped.

Gaby didn't give her the dignity of a reply because they both knew that Cleo could damn well get anything accomplished in twelve hours if she really wanted to.

"Let's go clean up so you're camera-ready," Gaby said instead.

"Wait . . . now? We're doing this now?" Cleo clutched the handle of her roller bag, like this could anchor her to the floor of the lobby of the Sheraton. She wasn't mentally prepared to show up at MaryAnne Newman's doorstep while still reeking of stale plane air and with a stomach filled with only half a turkey wrap that cost eleven dollars on board. "I need . . . I need to shower! I need to think about what I want to say. I need . . ." She caught a glance of her reflection in the front windows of the hotel. Maybe it was the prospect of facing her old ghosts, but honestly, she looked like a ghoul.

Gaby waved her hand. "I want this truthful, and I want it as close to raw as it can get. This is what we need to tap into." She jabbed Cleo in the chest, right where her heart was beating too loudly. "This—heart. We'll get there right as the sun is setting, and it will be picturesque and cinematic and cathartic, and then everyone is going to love you. But yes, let's go swipe some lipstick on."

Cleo exhaled loudly, enough to let Gaby know that none of this pleased her.

"You don't know MaryAnne. It is not going to be that easy."

"How can you be sure?"

"Because if she showed up and did the same to me, I'd never let her off the hook."

MaryAnne Newman lived in the ritzy part of Seattle. Of course. Growing up, Cleo hadn't been lacking, but she wasn't part of the upper echelons of Seattle society. The kids who lived in Broadmoor or Windermere or just off the golf course of the country club were always kind enough—Cleo didn't want to pin her ambition to class differences or bank accounts or that she drove a beat-up Jetta while they got new BMWs and Jeeps. Seattle was a town where, theoretically, everyone was welcome and embraced and peace, love, and understanding were taught and imparted and mostly put into practice too. Cleo never went without—her parents did perfectly well. But as the Uber wound through the wide, manicured streets, punctuated with high hedges and bursting rosebushes and blooming rhododendrons, Cleo so easily reacquainted herself with that steady bleat of "less than," just like she had those first few times her mother dropped her at MaryAnne's in elementary school. It was subtle, niggling—nothing that beat you over the head—just a small whisper of awe she felt walking into MaryAnne's cavernous kitchen, eyeing the lush green backyard with a pool that had a waterfall. In the back of an Uber, she was nine again. Even though she was a senator. Even though she'd made something of her life that few of her high school peers could imagine. That she'd flown six hours across the country to apologize to MaryAnne Newman epitomized this: that despite everything, here she was, all these years later, hat in hand.

Cleo had dragged her feet all the way from the hotel restroom, where she'd polished her makeup and changed out of her merino wool sweater, which stank a little bit of perspiration. She'd snapped at Gaby as she touched up her eyeliner, run a brush through her blond-brown hair that was in need of new highlights that would return it to more blond than brown. She'd tried to pluck out three grays with her fingers but had no luck. She'd have to find time for a hair appointment before the next set of television appearances. Things like this mattered for women senators: shimmering highlights or too-long darkish roots or, God forbid, gray hair, could make or break your Twitter feedback. Cleo had never once seen anything of the sort for her male colleagues. In fact, one of the most reviled members of Congress (on both sides!) recently grew in some stubble, and rather than being met with disdain, this somehow made him more likable. Cleo had read headlines claiming he was now sexy. (!!!) All because of a fucking beard.

"Hold still," Gaby had said in the Sheraton bathroom. "Please keep in mind that I'm not doing this because I want to embarrass you or make you eat crow. God, Cleo. When have I ever advocated for that?"

Cleo pursed her lips, because it was true.

"I'm doing it because I'm trying to protect you. My phone hasn't stopped buzzing; your interview with Wolf didn't tamp this down. MSNBC is talking about it now too; let's not even get into Fox. Don't you want to at least *have* the chance to be considered for the nomination? Because this could be over before it even begins."

Cleo pursed her lips harder and met Gaby's eyes in the mirror. Gaby was right.

"Apologizing is not my strong suit."

Gaby handed her a pink lipstick that would ensure her pallor morphed from half-dead to at least having a steady pulse. "Tell me something I don't know. And you know I don't like you to apologize, not when it comes from a place of weakness. But there are all sorts of ways to say you're sorry, and sometimes it can come from strength too. *That's* what this is about. Besides, what's the point of your list if not to make amends?"

"The list is for *me*! That's what it was for. Who said anything about amends?"

"So your dad would hate that you are using it to become a better person?"

Cleo snapped the lid back on the lipstick and dropped it in Gaby's bag. "I thought we were really doing this to have a shot at the nomination. Not because I needed to become a better person."

"Touché," Gaby said. "But maybe we can do both at the same time."

And now the Uber was nearly at MaryAnne Newman's house. It looked vaguely familiar to Cleo, and she realized MaryAnne must live in—or at least near—her childhood home, like so little had changed twenty years in.

"Wow. This is a *super*-nice area," Lucas said, his head swiveling back and forth as he took in the old mansions from each window. "Did you grow up here?"

"No," Cleo said, a seed of her old class insecurity kicking in, recalling the way that MaryAnne's mom always looked like she had just come from the salon, with blown-out hair and perfectly pink polished nails. Cleo's mom, even with her perfect dancer's posture, was usually covered in paint splatter and wearing clogs. Cleo noticed only when confronted with the differences. "No. Another part of town. We'll go there tomorrow." She hesitated. "Well, I don't know. We'll see what tomorrow brings."

Her old home had been sold shortly after her parents died, the money put away for college, with half of it going to her sister, who had by then gotten her act together, graduated from UCLA, and was working at some New Agey spa that Cleo scorned, even at fifteen when she and her parents last visited. So there was no house to tour in Seattle, really. What, exactly, was she planning—a slow drive-by of the beige ranch home that hadn't been hers in two decades? Maybe that sounded more macabre than it needed to be. Maybe she could just park outside and say, "Hey, I was fourteen once too, and this is where I lived when I was."

Their car rounded a curve and eased to a stop on the right side of the road, and Cleo couldn't help but let out a little gasp of air. MaryAnne actually lived in her childhood home. She and Cleo had spent nearly every weekend here, because MaryAnne had a pool and a ping-pong table, and there was a brief stint in middle school, before they each respectively grew serious and cast all playful things aside, when her older brother convinced their parents to buy him a real-life Pac-Man machine, and that was really something.

MaryAnne had repainted the door bright red, but otherwise, the looming Colonial was just as Cleo remembered. She hesitated before popping the handle to the car door, nausea cresting in her throat. She wanted to grab Lucas and Gaby and yank them back in the Uber and flee. Her misdeeds toward MaryAnne Newman weren't even *on* the list!

(She didn't think.) Now, twenty years later, should she regret them? She swallowed, waited for the unease in her stomach to pass.

She remembered a sliver of a moment their junior year, AP French. She and MaryAnne had both struggled on an exam. It wasn't a big deal in the scheme of their world, but it sure as hell felt like one at sixteen and with college applications looming. Cleo had never come naturally to the language, but she bore down, gutted it out. Neither of them knew what exactly went wrong on this test, other than for the first time in their academic lives, they bombed it. Each sat at her own desk, slack-jawed and stunned, Cleo battling back tears, staring at the C- on her blue book. When she'd told her parents that night, ashamed and disappointed, her mom said, "Well, sometimes you have to fail to know where you can succeed next time," and her dad nodded along, saying nothing. If they shared her disappointment, and knowing them they did, they didn't make it known. Which, in hindsight, Cleo could appreciate. She'd do the same for Lucas. But three days later, MaryAnne asked her to hold her bag when she went into the bathroom to change her tampon, and Cleo—who was not even *snooping*—saw a new blue book with an A- written on the cover in their French teacher's handwriting. It turned out, Cleo found out by sniffing around, MaryAnne's parents had called their teacher and raised a stink, and she had been allowed a retake during lunch two days before. MaryAnne had told her she was having cramps and had gone to the school nurse.

Cleo gazed out at MaryAnne's manicured lawn, so green that it nearly felt like an optical illusion, like a painting where the artist had intentionally used a verdant green rather than a more realistic one. She replayed her own shortcuts, ostensibly, her own regrets—the internship essay, the glancing at MaryAnne's notes before she ran for the paper, the various other small but cutting ways their friendship fractured.

*Yes,* she thought. *I'd do it all over again in a heartbeat.*

So maybe not regrets after all.

# FIVE

Gaby rang the doorbell, then scampered off the front stoop, so Cleo waited by herself, flanked by two towering potted ficus trees. It was an unusually sunny near-dusk afternoon—May in Seattle was hit-or-miss with the weather—and she reached for her sunglasses, an extra armor to shield her from whatever lay behind the door. When no one answered, Cleo allowed herself a small exhale, felt the knot in her stomach untangle.

"Ring it again!" Gaby stage-whispered from the side of the lawn. She was on the right; Lucas was on the left, their camera phones held high so as not to miss either angle of the blessed reunion. (Gaby had decided to film for backup.)

"No one's home," Cleo said. "Let's go. There's always tomorrow."

"She's in town!" Gaby whispered back, though Cleo was honestly not sure why she was whispering. The street was otherwise empty, and they didn't have anything yet to capture on film. It wasn't like this was an FBI raid, which, it occurred to Cleo, she would have been much more enthusiastic about. "Ring. It. Again!"

She pressed the buzzer one more time, praying feverishly that Gaby had gotten her intel wrong, and MaryAnne was currently enjoying the beaches of Maui or the mountains of Whistler or wherever she would whisk her family off to avoid the scrutiny of the press glare from the op-ed. Then Cleo recalibrated: MaryAnne would never shy away from the spotlight. She'd shared the op-ed on her Facebook page! Of course she was in town. Cleo was surprised the front door wasn't flung wide open, with MaryAnne welcoming the inquirers with homemade short-bread and Earl Grey tea. She may have been planning a parade to celebrate. It was easy to envision this, after all, because if Cleo had charted the same course as MaryAnne (country club president rather than senator), it's what she would have done exactly.

Before she could consider this, the *Sliding Doors* possibilities of their lives, she heard footsteps coming too quickly, then the lock unlatching (too quickly!), and then the bright-red door, so cheery and welcoming, flung open too quickly. Cleo squeezed her eyes closed. No! *No, no, no, no, no!* This was not the intention of her regrets list. This was not how junior senators from New York made apologies! She should have stood firm and had Gaby craft a statement of sincere apology and weathered the storm. Then she remembered that they'd tried that (kind of) with Wolf Blitzer, and in the age of social media, one juicy scandal has longer tentacles than an apology, particularly for women. Women couldn't fuck up the way that men could. They were held to a higher standard, as if making mistakes weren't part of the human experience. Cleo understood that she couldn't change society's preconceptions with one Wolf Blitzer interview. She'd have to do that piece by piece, bit by bit, as senator, maybe as president, maybe just by raising her son to be a good human being.

Regardless, here she was on MaryAnne Newman's doorstep, just like she had been so many times in her childhood, and she may as well get it over with.

She opened her eyes, raised her sunglasses to rest on the top of her head.

A girl about Lucas's age stood in front of her.

It was as if Cleo were in eighth grade all over again, and she was shocked to feel the tingle of tears building. She blinked quickly; Cleo

McDougal was not a spontaneous crier, and she didn't even know why she was so emotional in the first place. The girl had MaryAnne's blue eyes, her straight, long brown hair with fraying ends, a nose like a ski jump. Her cropped shirt aired her belly button; her denim shorts put her gangly legs on display.

"Oh my God," the girl said.

"Oh my God," Cleo replied.

"You're, like, you're the senator."

"Oh." Cleo chewed on her lip. "Yes. That's me. But I also know your mom. Obviously."

"I told her not to write it," the girl said, so easily betraying her own mother. "I told her it was petty, but . . ." She shrugged. "I think your generation is different from mine." She twisted her hair into a spiral with her hand.

"Oh," Cleo said again. None of this was what she had been expecting. Cleo was good at confrontation—she'd honed the art after so many years in Congress. But this softer, kinder, younger version of their misspent youth had her off guard, uneasy in a close-to-an-emotional-breakdown sort of way. She could feel it in the sweat building in her armpits, in the staccato of her pulse. Then: "Well, is . . . is she here? Your mom."

The girl shook her head. "They go to the club every Saturday night for dinner."

Cleo turned in both defeat and victory toward Gaby. "She's not home! Can we quit now?"

"It's just, like, a five-minute walk," the girl said. "I can take you. But, I mean, I don't blame you if you don't want to speak with her ever again. It was shady, for sure. Like, the opposite of feminist. The affair stuff? Like, I said to her, *Mom, no one cares who screws who anymore.*"

Cleo tried to laugh. "Well, I'm not sure how true that is, but thank you." A snapshot of Nobells scampering out of her tiny apartment in a rush to get home to his family flew through her mind. She shook her head, as if that could release him from her memory. "Anyway, I guess since I showed up at your front door, I do need to speak with her, but—"

Gaby cut her off, no longer whispering, shouting from the front lawn, "We're in! Just lead the way!"

⁓

Her name was Esme, which Cleo thought was exactly a name that MaryAnne would select—*French*. She was surprised, however, that Esme was nearly Lucas's age. She didn't peg MaryAnne as a young-mom type, but then, no one probably pegged Cleo as the young (single) mom type either. Truth told, Cleo hadn't even been sure if she wanted children, but then her parents died, and when she saw the plus sign on the test the spring of her senior year at Northwestern, she thought it might be nice to go through life with someone. By the time Lucas was born, she knew she'd never have a moment of doubt.

Which wasn't true. She had plenty of moments of doubt. Somewhere on that list of 233 screwups, at least a dozen of them were related to Lucas. Not *Lucas*. She loved him more than she ever antici-pated. Just the whole thing: the struggle; the exhaustion; how like it or not, being a mother at twenty-three and in law school affected her choices; how differently she anticipated it would all go for her. Maybe MaryAnne felt similarly.

"Are you in eighth grade?" Lucas asked her, staring at the cement as they walked.

"Yep. You?"

"Yeah. But I guess I'm old enough to be in ninth."

"No, that's not true," Cleo interjected, and Lucas shot her a look that could quite possibly wither her right there in the fading sunshine on the Broadmoor sidewalk. Cleo popped her eyes back at him. She didn't know the rules of him talking to a girl because frankly, she'd never seen him interact with one. Was she not allowed to speak? Did she have to render herself invisible? She was only thirty-seven! She liked to think that she was at least hip enough to make small talk with her kid.

"Mom—" he said.

"I only meant that when we moved to DC, you started kindergarten as one of the oldest. I didn't hold you back."

"I didn't say that you did."

"Well, it sort of sounded like . . ."

At this, Gaby grabbed her elbow and pulled Cleo back a half pace to let Lucas and Esme find their footing on their own.

Cleo watched Esme stroll down the street, so lanky and at ease. Her gait was exactly like her mother's—MaryAnne had always been good at track, one area where they didn't compete with each other—and Cleo guessed that Esme had it in her to do a mile in less than seven minutes too. It was so strange, she thought, to show up and find a younger rendition of her old friend, as if time had stopped and she were looking at their old selves. Cleo found herself a little slayed at this, at the notion of their fourteen-year-old selves having the chance to do it again, to do it better. So maybe this was what regret felt like: sorry for the fact that they weren't wiser to how they would blow it up.

"I haven't seen him this talkative since. . ." Cleo watched Lucas banter. "I don't know. Birth?"

"I glanced at his texts on the plane today," Gaby replied. Of course she had, because Gaby was such a goddamn smooth operator. "I think he has a girlfriend back home too."

"He *what*?" Cleo actually stopped midstride.

"I could be wrong, but . . . I'm usually not."

"I'm sorry, you mean my fourteen-year-old who usually communicates by grunting and stuffing food into his mouth has . . . what?"

Gaby grinned. "See, look at that, we've only been in Seattle for two hours, and already I'm rocking your world."

"I hate you."

"Tell me something I don't know," Gaby said, and they double-stepped to catch up with the other two who were leading the way.

⌒೨

Esme waved to the security guard at the front gate of the club, and they wound through the walking path to the main building, which was also more or less just how Cleo remembered. Ornate fabrics, overstuffed window seats, bookshelves stacked with leather-bound collections that absolutely no one was going to read in between their tennis matches or golf rounds. Everything about the club was *rich*, and though Cleo was theoretically part of an elite class now, still, it knocked her off guard. Being elite in intellect or even elite with power wasn't the same thing as being elite with wealth, because if it had been, Cleo wouldn't have had to work so hard and fight so hard to land where she did. As a kid, Cleo always shoved her hands into her pockets, curled her shoulders, and kept her eyes down when they strolled through, as if the real members couldn't see her if she couldn't see them and that if she were invisible, no one could call her out (or throw her out) for being an impostor.

Esme checked the time on her phone.

"They're probably getting drinks before dinner. Come on—I'll show you."

Lucas trailed after her like a lovesick puppy, and Gaby giggled a little at the sight.

They strode past the tennis courts, with towering lights just warming up at dusk, and the pool, where a few fortunate toddlers splashed in the shallow end with bored mothers looking on and a few seniors methodically swam laps. Cleo remembered this all so well, the way that MaryAnne would sign her in like they were sisters, the way that in middle school, they would sink into the pool until their fingers pruned, the way that they would linger in the locker room showers, using too much shampoo and conditioner because they smelled like honeysuckle and lemon, and both Cleo and MaryAnne thought such a scent might attract a few suitors. (It did not.) Through all of it, Cleo was grateful for MaryAnne but also always, always aware of that sign-in, that MaryAnne had the entry and Cleo did not. That MaryAnne's parents could call their principal and demand a retake of the French test because her parents' names were on a brick outside the school, and Cleo's parents' names were not.

But Cleo brought other things to their friendship; she was the alpha in nearly everything else, and MaryAnne seemed fine with it all; they each had their power; they each knew their lane. And then they'd gotten to high school, and the stakes became so infinitely higher, and somehow an unspoken pact arose between them: *Do whatever you must at whatever cost.* As Esme opened the door to the bar area, Cleo considered that maybe this had never been their pact; maybe it had simply been an agreement she'd made with herself. *No regrets.* Of which, obviously, she had many: 233.

Cleo's pulse was throbbing at a near-medical-emergency rate by now.

"They're usually in the back," Esme was saying, though Cleo could barely hear her above not just the din of the TVs airing a Mariners game and the clinking of forks and the uncorking of wine bottles and the popping of beer caps but of her own internal voice shrieking, *Get the fuck out of here!* But she too followed Esme, much like Lucas, and then they were there, in the depths of the bar room, and Gaby had her phone out and aimed like a shotgun, and there was nothing to do to turn back time (to an hour ago, a decade ago, two decades ago, Cleo didn't know) because MaryAnne, in a pastel dress and soft pink blush and blood-red lipstick, was right in front of her.

Cleo felt a rush of flop sweat streak down her back. Professional confrontations were her forte. Personal confrontations, she realized only at this moment, were not even in her repertoire. Panic was setting in, and though Cleo McDougal never, ever in her life ran from a fight, her instinct was to turn and flee. She glanced toward her old ex–best friend and for just a tiny flicker of a moment was punctured that this was what it had come to. Then she sewed that lament back up.

"Hi, Mom. Look who I found," Esme said, and Cleo decided immediately that she loved this girl. She was a little bit cunning and also succinct and knew that she was slaying her mom just a bit in her guts.

MaryAnne's eyes moved from her daughter to Cleo, who was doing her best to contain her adrenaline, and her jaw went slack. Just for a moment. Then it firmed up, as did her steely eyes and her rigid posture. ("I have a backbone," MaryAnne once snapped at Cleo, after the mayoral internship debacle. She meant it metaphorically, but MaryAnne was also a debutante, so she meant it literally too. No one had better posture than MaryAnne Newman.)

It was only then that Cleo worked up the nerve to take in a wider view. She'd assumed that the "they" in Esme's remarks had been MaryAnne and her husband, but now she saw that it was a table of eight, all faces she recognized, all faces from her yearbook and probably some of those Facebook comments too.

"Shit," Cleo muttered under her breath. She turned and looked at Gaby, who was recording with the determined furrow of a documentary filmmaker. "Shit!"

Gaby paid her no mind, and Cleo spun forward.

"MaryAnne, um, hello."

The back room had fallen so silent that Cleo could hear a bat crack from the Mariners game out front. Eight sets of eyes on Cleo—well, eleven if you counted Lucas and Esme and Gaby, but Lucas and Esme may have been staring at each other.

MaryAnne rested her hands in her lap and swallowed. It was so odd, Cleo thought, trying to remove the nostalgia and the crest of emotion that had swept through her just moments earlier, to see her after so many years. Her mannerisms were still the same, her face, though older of course, still a mirror of who she had been at seventeen. Twenty years had passed, and yet Cleo could nearly read her mind, just like before when they were inseparable.

"Cleo," MaryAnne said finally. "This is a surprise."

"I think it's Senator McDougal," Esme interjected, and Cleo wondered if she couldn't adopt this child before she left town.

"Cleo's fine. Of course." But she smiled at Esme as she said this, an acknowledgment of their shared feminism, of the power that came with a title that so few women had yet to attain.

"Hey, Cleo!" From behind MaryAnne, Oliver Patel, her sole defender on that ruinous Facebook post, offered a wave. "It's so cool to see you here!"

"Hey, Oliver," she said back, and his eyebrows rose a little bit like he was surprised that she remembered him. But he had always been kind and also extremely handsome—dark hair, dark eyes as big and as entrancing as a full moon, just the right grade of stubble—so of course she remembered him. He was unattainable, a baseball player, someone Cleo passed in the halls and thought that if she were a different type of person—softer, prettier, the girl who laughed at jokes she didn't get when he told them on the quad during a free period, the type of girl who actually spent her time on the quad during a free period—maybe he'd kiss her one night at a party after drinking a beer. Yes, Cleo remembered Oliver Patel. Cleo had been hard-core in high school but she hadn't been impenetrable.

To his right sat Maureen Allen, who had less nice things to say about her, and Susan Harris, then Beth Shin, who, well, ditto. (Cleo didn't remember the names of the three others at the table, though she knew she should have.) They'd all been on the debate team together, but Maureen and Susan dropped out their junior year to . . . Cleo couldn't quite remember why—but she did remember thinking at the time that she was glad they had. Beth had been a decent debater, but those two were barely adequate, and Cleo thought they held the team back. But now, so many years later, well, she hadn't really thought about how they might all still be friends—not just Facebook friends but real-life friends—how their world from back then wasn't so different from their world now. Surely, if MaryAnne had wanted to, she could have made choices that expanded her scope beyond what it had always been. She couldn't hold Cleo accountable for her sitting in the same country club with the same people discussing, likely, the same gossip that she had at fifteen. (Cleo didn't want to judge—anyone should do whatever made them happy—but then MaryAnne dragged her into this whole thing to begin with, so perhaps Cleo had the right to do and think whatever she damn wanted.)

Maureen Allen and Susan Harris and Beth Shin, unlike Oliver, said nothing and just glared.

Then Cleo remembered, as Esme had been trying to remind her, that she was a goddamn United States senator, and MaryAnne Newman shouldn't intimidate her, *Seattle Today!* op-ed or not, lurid (inaccurate) rumors or not, Facebook slander or not. She too righted her posture, and she was sure from the look in MaryAnne's eyes that she remembered Cleo's body language as well.

"I'm here because obviously I saw your op-ed."

MaryAnne's cheeks flushed, which surprised Cleo, because you'd have thought that MaryAnne wanted the fight, the confrontation, what with the public takedown. But maybe she had just wanted to air a bunch of dirty laundry without thinking through the consequences. God, wasn't that at least what half of the internet was these days? Screaming into the void about someone or something or an airline or a coffee shop or a slow pedestrian or a lousy driver and getting it off your chest? Never once did you think any of those people was going to respond.

"Also, I saw your Facebook post, and then, of course, I saw all of your comments."

Oliver Patel grinned, and Maureen and Susan and Beth pulled back from their glares and looked as if they might turn figuratively green. *Consequences. Regret. They're tied together.*

"Well, it was all true." MaryAnne sniffed. "You were not very nice by the end of high school, and I am doubtful that you should be president. If you can't get those who know you well to vote for you . . ." She flipped her hand as if to say, *Well, then you're screwed.*

"It wasn't *all* true," Cleo said. "You didn't fact-check the date of my son's birth." At this, she gestured toward Lucas, who really was not paying too much attention and instead stealing sideways glances at Esme. Gaby had been right: something *was* happening between the two of them, that unknowable alchemy that ignited teen hormones, and Cleo lost herself for a beat, considering the consequences of a romance between the two. These days, with social media and text and FaceTime (did kids use FaceTime?) and who knows what else, a three-thousand-mile lovesick relationship didn't seem far-fetched. Cleo turned back to MaryAnne. "That was low, and I would at least think beneath you."

MaryAnne sniffed. "I went with the information I had been made aware of. And I don't like cheaters. But if that affected you"—she pointed her chin toward Lucas—"I'm sorry. I am. Perhaps that was out of bounds. Children should be off-limits. Not, however, their parents."

"Apology accepted," Lucas said and offered a little shrug. He was used to political sniping, and he was used to his mother defending herself, Cleo supposed. It occurred to her that she didn't want to raise a son who grew up thinking this was all normal. None of this was normal. If she had her list here now, she'd add this one—*have raised son in a toxic bubble of Washington, DC, where he thinks launching metaphorical grenades at your opponents is just your average day.* Cleo considered this notion. Of course Lucas thought this was normal. She was his mother. He'd learned it from her. *Regret.*

Cleo inhaled, exhaled, looked to Gaby, who was all business with her camera phone. She wanted to get this over with now, rip off the Band-Aid and be done with it. Convince Gaby that filming four more of her regrets would only end in disaster.

"Well, I flew all the way here today to apologize." She said it stiffly, not like something emotive she'd rehearsed to argue on the Senate floor. She knew she could do better. She inhaled again, tried to soften. "Teenage girls can be pretty tough, MaryAnne, and I didn't mean to hurt you."

MaryAnne's face pinched for just a moment, and Cleo, aware of her old friend's mannerisms, was sure that this could all be over. That she'd be forgiven, and they could pour themselves a glass of . . . she didn't know what they were drinking but something fancy . . . and move on. Cleo didn't really want to befriend MaryAnne again—she was firmly *not* into looking backward—but a shared drink felt like a peace offering that would be a nice gesture, a neat bow tied around this now-closed chapter.

Instead, MaryAnne composed herself, rose to stand, and said simply, "No."

Maureen and Susan, in the back, gasped and looked a little delighted. Like a real live fight was going to break out right there at the Seattle Country Club among the blue bloods. Well, one blue blood and one just regular blood. (But senatorial blood!) Cleo did think that she could take her, thanks to her early-morning boxing classes, and God knows that with her marathon training, Gaby could deliver one cold knockout punch, but she also knew that physical violence on camera (because Gaby would surely keep filming *while* punching) would not be the ticket to her reputational rehabilitation.

MaryAnne herself, in her sleeveless pink and green floral dress that highlighted her arms, was looking significantly fitter than in high school, even with her stellar track times. Probably spin classes, Cleo supposed. Maybe a personal trainer.

"Mom," Esme interjected. "Please sit down. This is ridiculous. She apologized."

MaryAnne raised her chin an inch, refusing.

"Do you know what you did to my entire life?" she said.

Cleo shook her head. "Your *entire* life? No."

"When you sabotaged that internship at the mayor's office, you changed everything for me."

"Mom," Esme groaned. "Please. Stop." Then, to Cleo (and probably Lucas): "She and my dad separated recently. He became a cliché and literally ran off with a coworker."

"I'm sorry to hear that, MaryAnne," Cleo said, as if she bore responsibility. She did feel sorry for her, and God knew she understood the sting of being disposable.

"And she's spent a lot of time reading blogs about reclaiming her personal power," Esme continued. "Righting what went wrong." She rolled her eyes and looked so very much like Lucas when he did the same, as if a plague infected teenagers with a universal disdain. "And I keep telling her—move forward, but she keeps looking back."

"'Only Forward' would actually be my campaign slogan!" Cleo said, which, she immediately realized, was a stupid thing to say. "I mean, well, when I run for . . ." She flopped her own hand. "Never mind."

"Ugh," MaryAnne replied. "Me, me, me, me, me, me, me." She reached for her (fancy) drink and swallowed the rest of it until the ice rattled in the highball.

"I shouldn't have told you that writing about your dead dog was a great essay topic," Cleo said. "OK? I shouldn't have." She quieted for a moment. "Really, MaryAnne, that was childish."

"But she should have known that too!" Esme said. "Don't apologize for her stupid choice."

"I like you." Cleo looked at Esme. "I like you very much."

Esme grinned, opening up her face into something wide and beautiful, and then Lucas grinned, opening up his face into something Cleo hadn't seen in a while at home, even on the soccer field: joy. For a flicker, Cleo saw a different life, one where she and MaryAnne hadn't detonated their friendship, and their children grew up together side by side, barefoot in their backyards, biking to the 7-Eleven for Cokes, best friends just like their mothers had once been.

"I think you owe me a public apology, and not just for that," MaryAnne said.

From behind her, Oliver interjected: "MaryAnne, at what point do you just let twenty years go?"

"Not at this point," she snapped. "*I* could have been a senator; *I* could have done something with myself! That internship started something for Cleo, and the same thing could have happened for me."

"Like I was saying." Esme sighed.

"MaryAnne, you're only thirty-seven," Cleo started.

"Thirty-eight," Esme corrected. "Last week."

"MaryAnne, you're only thirty-eight, and so many women reinvent themselves these days—"

"No." She cut Cleo off. "I'm not interested in you showing up here and being my therapist or patronizing me. You were my best friend, and you took something from me, and I'm sorry that your parents died and all of that." She paused. "I am. But I don't believe that people change, and you showed me your true colors, and I'm not going to absolve you of that."

That sliver of lament that Cleo had sewn up reopened. Barely, just detectable—not enough for Cleo to really try again with MaryAnne with a renewed openhearted apology—but there all the same. That on a few occasions, she had been small and petty and shitty to MaryAnne, who had sometimes been small and petty and shitty back, but not with the ferocity that Cleo had. Cleo wouldn't really change anything—she loved her life, was proud of her life, and her straight line from Congress at twenty-five to a presidential run at thirty-seven required this linear thinking. But still. In this quiet moment, with her eyes locked with her old best friend, she could allow for the fact that things could have been done differently.

Behind MaryAnne, Maureen and Susan and Beth had gone statue still, and Oliver was shaking his head, like he couldn't believe that he was part of this high school drama. But Cleo still knew MaryAnne well enough to know that she wasn't going to relent.

"OK," she said. "Fine. You can't say I didn't try."

"But you didn't really," MaryAnne snapped. "And I can say whatever I damn want."

So Cleo bounced her shoulders and looked to Gaby, who finally dropped her phone and stopped recording. And then, perhaps for the first time in her life, Cleo McDougal acknowledged her loss and retreated.

∽

At the hotel, Gaby and Cleo lounged on the king mattress in Gaby's room. Well, Gaby lounged, leaning up against the headboard, and Cleo got up and paced. They'd given Lucas his space; he was already half-mortified that he had to share a room with his mother, so Cleo suggested he treat himself to room service, and she'd be back in a bit. She didn't know what he expected—they'd always been a unit, just the two of them, and simply because puberty held him in its grasp didn't mean that she was booking him a separate hotel room. She'd avert her eyes; she'd never enter the bathroom while he was in there. She was doing her very best.

Gaby had ordered two burgers and two fries for them respectively, but Cleo didn't have much of an appetite. She nibbled on a disproportionately long fry (she'd always been drawn to outliers) and considered what came next. She didn't think that MaryAnne was going to stop, and in fact, Cleo was scared to check her Facebook page now. Surely her ex–best friend had teed off about their evening, saying God knows what to God knows who. Gaby stared at her phone while it buzzed and

62

buzzed and buzzed, biting her burger thoughtfully, as if it held the key to their mess.

"Ooh!" Gaby said, a grin appearing on her face, even while she chewed. "Ooooh."

"Good news?" Cleo stopped midstride and hoped for a bit of a miracle. "Did she forgive me?"

"Hmm, no." Gaby looked up from her screen. "But that Oliver guy just texted me asking if I wanted to get a drink." She righted herself off the bed and reached for her suitcase. "And you know what, Oliver Patel? I do."

"Wait, he texted *you*?" Cleo groaned. She wasn't even sure when they had time to exchange numbers.

"You wanted him for yourself?" Gaby was in her bra now, throwing on a bright-yellow silk shirt that complemented her skin tone perfectly and which, Cleo suspected, Oliver would never be able to resist.

"Well, I didn't *not* want him. He was cute in high school—I didn't really know him well, but my Lord, look at him now."

"I know." Gaby raised and lowered her eyebrows, then did it three more times. "I *know.*"

Cleo flopped on the bed, muttered into the pillow, "I'm happy for you."

"It's just drinks," Gaby said, but then she laughed, rich and decadent, and they both knew that it wasn't.

"It's fine," Cleo said, face still in the pillow. "I'll go hang out with my teen son who has more romantic interests than I do."

"Clee." Gaby turned to her, serious now. "If you want . . . I can set up a profile on Tinder." She laughed again, gleeful, and Cleo threw the pillow at her head.

"Don't wait up." She grabbed her purse from the arm of the desk chair and dropped her room key into her back pocket. "Oh, also," she added, like it was an afterthought, "I just uploaded the video to YouTube. So buckle up!"

"You *what?*" Cleo jumped to her feet at a pace that would very much impress her boxing instructor. "It was a fucking disaster; why would . . . Seriously, Gaby, this has to stop!"

"No, it wasn't. I reread all of your internals, and the electorate wants to see growth. They don't expect perfection."

Cleo sat back down on the bed.

"Hey, chin up, Senator McDougal. We're just getting started."

"Honestly." Cleo fell backward and stared at the ceiling. "That's what worries me."

⁓

Cleo had the YouTube app on her phone but had never used it. Why would she? Sometimes Lucas watched . . . she thought they were called "vloggers"? And he for sure caught up with some soccer stars, watching their foot skills, cheering their goals, salivating for whichever products they hocked.

She knew she could head back to their room and ask him to find the video and read the comments, but really, what good was going to come from that? It was disorienting being back here in her hometown, seeing her old friends. Well, maybe not *friends*. Peers. But at some point, she and MaryAnne had truly loved each other like sisters, and there was no way around that fact, even in the wreckage of what came next.

She thought she'd give Lucas a bit more breathing room, and besides, she could use some air herself. She shot Lucas a quick text that she was taking a walk (he wouldn't care, but she was still a responsible parent), then slid on her flats and strode through the Sheraton lobby and out into the Seattle night. The city had changed so much since she'd grown up here—it was a vibrant boom of a town now, expansive and glittering, but still, so much of it felt pregnant with memories—of shopping trips to Nordstrom with MaryAnne's mom's credit card, where they bought electric-blue eyeliner at Clinique or frosty glossy lip shellac at Veronica Kaye, of a field trip to the aquarium in middle school where Cleo had stood so long in front of the shark exhibit that the bus back to school nearly left her, of the scent of Benihana lingering on their clothes after MaryAnne's birthday every year. Cleo could feel the smudge of the kohl eyeliner, smell the scent of the aquarium, taste the fried rice and egg.

She turned right toward the waterfront. She wished that she'd brought her yellow pad of paper with her 233 regrets on the trip because she'd add today to it: 234. She hadn't thought much about how she sabotaged MaryAnne in a long time, probably since . . . college? She didn't know. She'd thought of MaryAnne, sure, from time to time, but not about her role in how, maybe, she had changed MaryAnne's life as much as she changed her own. Though she didn't think it was quite that easy. Cleo had worked her goddamn ass off to be the youngest congress-woman and then the youngest senator, and honestly, mayoral internship or not, school newspaper editor or not, it was entirely possible she'd have landed in the exact same position. But could she be certain?

She crossed the street from Second Avenue to First, the incline dropping perilously as if beckoning pedestrians to Pike Place Market. *No,* she told herself. *I can't be certain.* And maybe that made her shitty or maybe that made her ingenious. She didn't know. She knew only what she did and where it led her, and also that she had been sixteen or seventeen, and sixteen-year-olds and seventeen-year-olds made mistakes. She didn't know what Oliver Patel was doing with his life now (other than being gorgeous), but she hoped that he wasn't paying the price for that time his senior year when he went streaking across the baseball field when he got accepted to Berkeley. (He probably wasn't. Men are forgiven much more easily and much quicker than women, Cleo knew. Hell, *everyone* knew.) Cleo had not been part of that streaking crowd. In fact, now that she thought of it, MaryAnne hadn't really been either. Or maybe MaryAnne had been after she and Cleo broke apart, and MaryAnne had forged on without her.

Cleo reached the Waterfront Park right on Elliott Bay, leaned against the concrete ledge, gazed into the black horizon, which shone with lights from homes across the way. Her mom, who never seemed to begrudge that she hung up her pointe shoes when her children arrived, used to come here and paint at sunrise. By middle school, Cleo was always awake—even set her alarm for six a.m. because she'd read that successful people were early risers, so it seemed like a good habit to get into—and sometimes her mom would make her tag along. "Make" because Cleo had never been creative or interested in her mother's art beyond a simple appreciation for her talent and a bit of reverence for the fact that she had once been a star dancer and had somehow also now honed that spark into a different form of talent. Cleo didn't much see the point of creative fields. She never said as much to her mom, though her mom was often nudging her to tap into something, even when it was obvious that Cleo's skill set lay elsewhere.

"It doesn't have to be painting," her mom would say, and they knew damn well that it wasn't going to be dance. At two, Cleo had evidently run screaming from her first ballet class, and her mother, having endured blisters and broken toenails and pulled hamstrings and fractured ribs, all by eighteen, didn't push it again. Instead, as Cleo grew older, she said: "Anything, anything, sweetheart! Music, art, or pick up a camera! All of this opens you up to new possibilities." But Cleo had already learned that her parents' praise was so intertwined with her success, and even though her mother pushed her to simply dabble, dabbling didn't earn approving murmurs and an extra twenty dollars for spending money and sometimes, a special night out where they all dressed up in fancy clothes and toasted her with wine (her parents) and Shirley Temples (her).

Now, of course, because she was a member of Congress who needed to appear well rounded, she tolerated music and art and theater, and God knows she read too much (usually nonfiction, most often biographies). She supported arts funding and all that, but she was never going to wander through the Guggenheim because she had a free afternoon or attend the ballet because the urge struck her. She just wasn't.

A boat blared its horn in the distance, and something came to her, a surprise. That years ago—maybe ten, maybe five, she'd have to check when she was back in DC—Cleo had indeed added something to her list: *I never learned to paint. Or sing. Or dance. Or anything. Maybe that could have been a nice thing.*

Cleo stared up at the sky, thought of her mother, how strange it was that she had been gone for twenty years and only now Cleo was recognizing pieces of her in herself. She didn't think she'd want Gaby filming her in an art class, but it couldn't have been more embarrassing than what went down at the country club. Her gut twinged, and for the first time in a long time, she acutely missed her mother. When you lose your parents young, there is simply a blight on your psyche that becomes part of your being. Really, it had become background noise to Cleo: she knew the loss was there, but if she paid too much attention to it, it would override everything.

She turned to go, the memories both too poignant and just poignant enough. She'd cleared her head, felt a little more at peace with the mess of the day. Cleo didn't believe in hokey things but maybe it was her mom looking out for her, like she would have back in middle school or high school. When Cleo would wind herself up over a spelling bee or, later, an algebra test, and her mom would stand behind her and rub her shoulders and pour her a glass of orange juice, and it didn't make everything better, but it helped. (Incidentally, she was the spelling bee champion in fifth through seventh grades.) Also, she knew her success was a glue among the three of them, what with Georgie being such a mess, such—though her parents would never have said this aloud—a disappointment. Georgie required so much of her parents' energy, Cleo just wanted to make it easier for them. And she liked how winning felt too.

Now, Cleo angled herself up the hill back to the Sheraton and breathed deeply, wondering if her mom could hear her breath, though she knew she couldn't. But it was nice to pretend that she could. For a moment, Cleo wondered if maybe something was shifting in her, quaking inside.

Or maybe that was her phone notifications. By the time she arrived back at the hotel, with Gaby nowhere to be found, the YouTube video of her confrontation with MaryAnne had 100,000 views, and upon hearing her fumbling with her key card, Lucas swung open the door with a wide-eyed, "Holy shit, Mom, you've gone viral."

# SIX

Cleo had taken an Ambien and slept surprisingly well, though not long. She could get by on nearly no sleep—a by-product of training herself for late nights at work, fine-tuning legislation or reviewing details with her staff. Gaby was still unreachable by midnight (three a.m. Washington, DC, time), so Cleo popped the pill and away she went. Discipline was never one of her problems, so staying off YouTube and Twitter, where the video had of course also taken flight, wasn't difficult. Actually, getting Lucas to put his own phone away was more of the battle, but then it always was.

Their room was dark, the sun barely up itself, when she woke. For a very brief second, she debated rising and going to the hotel gym, giving her that precious hour away from her screen. But then it lit up with a new text, and Cleo couldn't help herself. Truth told, discipline was not her strongest suit until she'd at least had a coffee.

She couldn't bear to read all the notifications, so instead, she focused on the most recent.

Georgie.

Cleo couldn't remember when they'd last spoken. She closed her eyes again, tried to trace back. In the adjacent double bed, Lucas snored just loudly enough for Cleo to hear but not loudly enough to have woken her, and she remembered those early foggy baby days, when he'd get congested and snore and cry and snore and wail, and she'd wonder how on earth either of them would ever make it out of his infancy alive. Georgie had shed all her disaster years by then and had two toddlers at the time (twins), and sometimes Cleo would tentatively reach out for advice. But childhood and sibling impressions are tough to break, and Cleo never quite trusted Georgie's advice and also resented that she had to ask for help in the first place. That part wasn't Georgie's fault—she'd forward her articles on sleep training and why Cleo shouldn't beat herself up when breastfeeding didn't take—but it was hard to bridge the gap between them. Not just the age gap, not just the distance gap, but that elusive sense that though you were blood, sisters even, you really were more or less strangers. Through Cleo's formative years, Georgie had been a disruption around the house, a stressor for her parents, a blight on their family dynamic. Those weren't things that you glided over just because your parents were gone and you really only had each other. Maybe in the movies; maybe in fiction. But the truth was that genetics took you only so far, and Cleo didn't know Georgie any better than she knew anyone else. It's just how it was, with them virtually strangers when they shared the same house and then with Georgie having moved out by the time Cleo was eight. Also, as complicated as their relationship was from Cleo's perspective—that she couldn't help but see her sister as a permanent fuckup, even though Georgie was a heralded success in adulthood—Cleo also knew that Georgie held her own view: that she had been an only child for ten years before the baby came along and upended things. And as Cleo aspired to be the perfect child, Georgie was rebelling against it. Magnetic particles who repelled one another rather than grew closer.

Still, in adulthood, Georgie tried. She really did.

Georgie: R U in Seattle?? Saw the video. I shld come help.

After all the years of teenage and young adult turmoil, after dropping out of the UW and relocating to LA and enrolling in UCLA (and clearing her five-year probation from her weed arrest), Georgie had made a name for herself as a guru / life coach / therapist to the stars. She sold crystals and essential oils and, last Cleo had heard, was in talks to launch a tunic clothing line. (Georgie was always in tunics.) From time to time, she'd text Cleo with advice on how to de-stress with deep breathing or why she couldn't and shouldn't burn the figurative wick at both ends. Cleo always found it at least a little amusing that her sister was famous for doling out wisdom, but maybe Georgie had learned a thing or two on her rockier path to adulthood, and for that, Georgie had earned Cleo's respect, even if the younger sister would never, ever believe in the healing power of crystals.

Cleo typed a reply.

Cleo: It's ok. Leaving tomorrow. Gaby is on top of it.

Georgie wrote back immediately. She'd be awake this early on a Sunday because her twins, like Lucas, played club soccer—were being recruited for college scholarships—and Cleo was certain Georgie had them up juicing or stretching with her personal trainer or in their private home gym. (Cleo wasn't being critical. No one got anywhere in this world without greasing their elbows and leaning in to the work.)

Georgie: Not ok. It's a mess online. Have u not seen? Are u taking care of urself?

Actually, Cleo hadn't seen. Because she really didn't want to look. But she also really didn't want to admit that to Georgie, who would take it for weakness, because, well, it was.

Cleo: Gotta run, Lucas wants to hit the gym. Will circle back. Promise.

Cleo watched as the ominous three dots appeared on her screen, then disappeared.

They both likely knew that Cleo would not circle back, nor did she really promise. Were unkept promises better or worse between sisters? Cleo didn't know. She knew only that her family now was Lucas and, to a certain extent, Gaby. And it probably wasn't what she always wanted for herself, but she was adult enough to know that almost no one got exactly what she wanted for herself. You got what you got, and you could work hard, really, *really* hard, and hopefully shift the tides or change your circumstances, but that usually didn't reframe your foundation. If it did, you were one of the lucky ones—the exception, not the rule.

Plenty of people had it far worse than she did.

∽

Unlike Georgie, Gaby was pleased with the overnight results from the YouTube upload.

"Look." She thrust her phone in Cleo's face while they were in the back seat of an Uber, on the way to Cleo's old neighborhood.

Cleo didn't know what she was looking at and frowned.

"The tide has shifted. At least half of these comments—" Gaby paused and scrolled lower. "At least sixty percent of these comments think MaryAnne was in the wrong."

"Yeah," Lucas said. "But I'm looking at her Facebook page, and no offense, Mom, but the people who actually know you do *not* seem on board." He paused. "Wow, like, I actually had to go on Facebook. Don't tell anyone."

"Fuck those people you know," Gaby said. Then: "Sorry, Lucas. Pretend you didn't hear that."

"I'm fourteen, Gaby; we all say 'fuck.'"

Cleo groaned. "Please, God, is it too much to ask for you not to swear . . . like *that* . . . in front of me?"

They both swiveled their necks toward her, unsure to whom she was speaking.

"You, Lucas, you. Gaby is my chief of staff, so it's OK if she says . . . 'the f word' to me."

"Mom, just say 'fuck.'"

"Oh my God!" Cleo actually slapped her palm against her forehead.

"Oh, by the way, I think I'm gonna get a coffee with Esme later."

This time both Gaby and Cleo swung their faces toward him.

"You're what?" Cleo said. "And since when do you drink coffee?"

"I don't." He shrugged. "But everyone in Seattle does. I think. I mean, I don't know. Would you rather I said I was going to meet her for a beer?"

Cleo groaned again, this time louder, and the Uber driver, perhaps thinking she was ill, said, "You OK? Should I pull over?"

"Sorry, sir, I'm fine. Just having a bit of a midlife crisis."

"You're that senator, right?" His eyes moved to Cleo in his rearview mirror.

Cleo swallowed. She didn't realize that she was recognizable outside the Beltway. Hell, even there, half the time she was mistaken for someone's secretary, someone's mother (she was someone's mother, obviously, but as, like, anyone's mother, since she had breasts and a uterus), or someone else ancillary who hadn't earned her keep or hadn't merited the respect male senators received. (It would be untrue to say the respect that older female senators received, since they still didn't receive as much respect as the men, even when the men were idiots or introduced far less legislation than the women.) Which, even if she were merely someone's mother or secretary or bookkeeper or just restocked the tampon machine in the lower-level bathroom of the Capitol, did it really matter? Was it too much to ask for a little respect regardless?

"It was the YouTube video, wasn't it?" Gaby interrupted, leaning forward to glean the opinion of a man who was not one of Cleo's constituents.

"No, ma'am." He paused, easing the sedan to a stop at a light. "Well, I did see that this morning, but I read that article. By your friend. Saw it on my Facebook three times."

"What did you think?" Gaby pressed. "You can tell us. This is a perfect random poll of an unbiased person."

"You don't know if he's unbiased," Lucas said. "Maybe he thinks all women belong in the kitchen. Maybe he hates his mom. Maybe he chops up women and leaves them in a freezer."

Cleo wasn't sure whether she was raising a feminist or a serial killer.

"What?" Lucas said upon seeing her face. "If you were to, like, actually poll him, you'd find out where he stands before you ran his answers."

Gaby smiled widely. "I think I'd like to hire you."

"Hard pass." Lucas sank back into his seat and resumed looking bored.

From the front, the driver said, "No, I like women, and I think they're a hell of a lot smarter than men, that's for sure. But to answer your question, I thought your friend was pretty petty for writing that article. But then I thought you were pretty petty for being a bad friend in the first place."

Cleo glanced at Lucas. She didn't want him thinking she was a bad friend, even if it were years ago, even if it were true. He met her eyes, offered a little shake of his head. They understood each other, the two of them. He was OK. He knew who she was now, and he was letting her off the hook for MaryAnne Newman. Cleo reached over, squeezed his arm.

It was nice that someone was, even if it were just a small kindness between the two of them, not on display for the world to see.

Cleo's old house had been repainted, and the new owners had added on a floor to only the right side, along with new shingles. So basically it looked nothing like her old house and more like a house that had undergone extensive plastic surgery. This made Cleo think again of her sister, who had not had extensive plastic surgery but many of her clients had. Cleo took a step back from the curb and surveyed the remodel.

They probably should have just knocked it down and started over. Her mother would have found its asymmetry displeasing to her eye, and her father would have called it a structural disaster. It felt strange that both she and Georgie had grown up here, with such wildly different childhoods, with such wildly different experiences. She hadn't been the type of kid who wished she had another sibling—Cleo's parents were company enough for her, though it occurred to her now, standing on the sidewalk with her head cocked, that maybe if she'd had someone closer to her age within her house, she wouldn't have felt so lonely, that she wouldn't have craved her parents' approval and attention and praise. Cleo's loneliness, especially once she moved in with her grandmother, fed her, to be sure—to be better, to stand taller, to pull more attention and eyes toward her. But success could never be a permanent plug for emptiness.

"Do you want to ring the bell?" Gaby asked.

Cleo shook her head. "I just . . ."

She trailed off. She didn't know exactly what she thought. She couldn't impart to Lucas the whole of her childhood by visiting her old home. That it was happy because her mother was warm and wore paint-speckled clothing most days, and her father was pretty brilliant and passed on his love of all things brainy, and yet it was also isolating because she was too smart for a lot of the other kids and also not always friendly, as if her mother's kindness never penetrated and her father's intelligence overcorrected. But MaryAnne got her; they, like she and Lucas, were peas in a pod for a long time—swapping books that were probably too grown-up for them, like *Carrie* and *1984* and *The Handmaid's Tale*, but in those days, parents didn't care about age-appropriateness like they did now, and listening to music that Cleo liked because MaryAnne liked it, not because she had developed any musical tastes of her own. (MaryAnne's older brother was just *obsessed* with Pearl Jam and Nirvana, so basically that.)

It wasn't just the two of them either; that wouldn't be fair. Cleo couldn't go on the campaign trail and say, like, "I had no friends, which drove me to where I am today." She did. She and MaryAnne both had friends beyond each other. They had the debate team and the kids on the school paper and in all the other clubs that they joined (though none of those kids had leaped to her defense in MaryAnne's Facebook post). And Cleo played tennis, and her senior year was elected captain, though this was after her parents had died and she never knew if it was that people liked her or pitied her. She put it on her college applications regardless, so that was good. But all these people, all her friends, well, they weren't much different from Georgie. They occupied a space in her life, but they didn't *take up* space, which were two very different things.

She had a boyfriend her junior year, Matty Adderly. He'd also applied for the internship at the mayor's office, but Cleo hadn't sabotaged him. She knew he wouldn't get it anyway. He was sweet and just the right amount of geeky to be completely devoted to her, but not smart enough to make her want to push it into a forever thing or that she worried he'd beat her out for the job. He also didn't come from connected parents (his dad was an accountant; his mom stayed at home), unlike MaryAnne's blue-blood stock who could call in favors and give her a leg up above the rest of them.

After Cleo's parents' accident, Matty tried to be there for her at every turn. Now Cleo could stand on the curb of her old street and stare at her old house and consider this kindness, how he wanted to bring her tea and help her move to her grandmother's and offered to take notes in her classes when she had to miss school, but back then she felt like he was smothering her. She was used to the unadorned, naked affection of her parents, but she hadn't adjusted—maybe still hadn't really—to that from anyone else. Or perhaps it was that she didn't want it from anyone else. If it couldn't be her parents, maybe it should have been no one.

She dumped him in a study hall about three and a half weeks after the funeral. He was just too much. She didn't want to be rescued. She was wise enough to see this in herself even at seventeen.

From the sidewalk in front of her old home, she stuffed her hands into her pockets and turned to Lucas.

"Do me a favor—look up Matty Adderly on Facebook. See if he's said anything about me." Cleo was surprised to feel something crest inside her, the notion that she might care if he had.

Lucas tapped away on his phone.

"Oh, by the way, I'm logged in as you." He glanced up. "I don't have an account, obviously. I don't think anyone under thirty is on Facebook." He said *thirty* as if it were a dirtier word than *fuck*, and Cleo felt very, very old.

"You shouldn't be on Facebook in the first place," Gaby said to Cleo. "They'll mine everything you ever post, every page you ever search."

"I'm not really on there. It's a dummy account. For things like this."

"Huh," Lucas said. "I found him. Who is he?"

"I . . ." Cleo slid her sunglasses on. The sun had cut through the clouds, and in an instant Seattle was the crystal-clear version of a postcard you'd mail to relatives back east. "He was my boyfriend for a while. Here."

Lucas looked up, surprised, eyebrows raised.

"What? You think your mom wasn't hot enough to have a boyfriend?" Gaby said.

"Gaby . . . ," Cleo interjected.

"I've been told repeatedly by both the media and my teachers that I wasn't allowed to judge girls on their looks," Lucas said. "'Hot' hadn't entered my brain."

"Hmm," Gaby said.

"Fine, 'hot' does enter my brain because I'm fourteen and not blind. What do you want from me?" He paused. "But he wasn't . . . ?" He trailed off, the words forming a question.

Cleo understood his implication. He wasn't his dad. She knew she could give him his name, that with the internet, Lucas could probably track him down before she was done spelling it (though it was not a complicated name that required spelling), but she wasn't up for that kind of trauma, and she didn't want her son to be up for it either. Single parenthood was already so complicated. Dragging her past into it would only make it messier. She supposed that she had MaryAnne Newman to thank for Lucas's curiosity. Curiosity that felt like it would lead only to heartbreak. Couldn't Cleo want to protect him from that? She didn't know if she was doing it right, handling it right, but she just wanted to try to protect him. That didn't seem like it was the wrong thing.

"No, love, not him. I haven't seen Matty since graduation."

Lucas nodded, tapped on something on his phone. "Whatever. I just . . . I can't imagine you with a boyfriend."

"Why not?" Cleo yelped. She didn't want to remain single forever. Or maybe she did. She didn't necessarily want to get married, but a little companionship and a steady date to the movies and perhaps the hot new Italian joint might be nice. If Gaby could make eyes at Oliver Patel and get a text an hour later, why shouldn't Cleo?

Lucas looked at her plainly, with no judgment. "Because for fourteen years, you never have."

"Well, you didn't get here by immaculate conception," Gaby said, just before Cleo could explain the difficulties of dating as a single parent *and* senator.

"You're disgusting," Lucas retorted, then pulled up Matty's profile.

It turned out that Matty Adderly was a mad programmer for Microsoft and had figured out Cleo's thinly disguised alias on Facebook and already sent her a friend request and a message. In fact, he'd done it months ago, long before MaryAnne Newman ever blew this shit up.

Cleo, Lucas, and Gaby began their long ascent up the hill to Pagliacci's, which, in Cleo's memory, served the best slice of pizza she ever had. It was only eleven, but no one had eaten much of a breakfast, so a pizza brunch on a Sunday it was. Lucas read Matty's note aloud.

Cleo-

I hope you don't mind my reaching out. It has been twenty years, but I see you in the news all the time—and this morning I went down the rabbit hole of finding you on socials.

(Cleo interrupted Lucas here and said, "'Socials'? Who says that?" To which Lucas replied, "Everyone, Mom, everyone says that." And Gaby added, "Clee, I think you're already doing it." And Cleo said, "Doing what?" And Gaby replied, "That thing you do where you don't give people a chance before they've had any chances in the first place." So Cleo stopped talking.)

Anyway, I'm still living in Seattle, which can be a little claustrophobic, but I don't really see anyone from school much, so it's less horrible than you'd think. (I don't actually think it's horrible, but I'm sure you do.) ☺

(Cleo couldn't help herself and interjected again. "Did he actually use an emoji?"

"Yes, the smiley face with blushing cheeks," Lucas said.

"Yikes," Cleo replied.

"Give me a break—you sent me that one last week about scoring a goal in my game," Lucas said. And then Cleo really did shut up because maybe she was judging Matty Adderly by standards to which she wouldn't want to be judged either.)

> I don't know if you'll even see this but if you do, I just wanted to say that I'm rooting for you, and it really makes me happy to see you succeed.

> All best,
> MA

Cleo, unprepared for the ascent, was out of breath by the time Lucas had finished. Gaby, because she was training for the marathon, was not, and in fact had taken to running up the hill backward, then sprinting down it to meet them, then repeating it all over again. Also, she had barely slept last night after her evening with Oliver Patel but seemed not at all affected. That women in Washington (and beyond, of course) were judged on their stamina was utterly ridiculous, Cleo thought, as she watched her friend bounce up and back.

"What happened with him?" Lucas asked as she jabbed the crosswalk light. No one in Seattle jaywalked, and Cleo was not about to break the rules of the city and be criticized for anything else.

"It was high school," Cleo said. "What happens with any of that?"

Lucas narrowed his eyes, and because Cleo did not want him to disengage, she elaborated.

"When your grandparents died, I guess my singular focus was moving on. Getting through that grief intact. Living up to their expectations of me, which, I mean, not to be a cliché, I could never now live up to. And part of that meant getting out of Seattle and just . . . getting through things. Forging ahead toward what I told them I would do: rule the world."

"It's so nice here, though," he said. "You couldn't rule the world from here?" They each took a moment to look around, and each concurred that this was true. The air was squeaky-clean, the vibe was hip and electric, the mountains sprang up unexpectedly in the background with peaks dusted in snow. No one was in too much of a rush, but no one meandered either, and everyone seemed placid and accepting and, well, *pleasant*. You could just tell by the way people stood at the corner and waited for the orange hand to turn white and said "excuse me" when they stepped around you to peer at the coffee menu at Starbucks.

Cleo exhaled, and the light changed, and they crossed the street while she considered how to best explain why she dumped an extremely sweet person who had only her best interests at heart.

"It was nice growing up here, which is why I wanted you to see it. And I wish you could have met your grandparents, not just have seen the house that I grew up in. But . . . I don't know. The longer I was here, the smaller it felt. I wanted to be the big fish in the big pond. That's how I think I defined success back then."

"I think it's how you define it now too," Lucas said as he stopped and peered into the window of a tattoo parlor, his hand above his eyes, shielding them from the sun. Cleo yanked his arm.

She didn't press him because it's a rough day for parents when they discover that their child's wisdom has surpassed their own, even if that's the entire point of parenting. So instead, she said, "You have to be eighteen to get a tattoo, and even then, it's stupid."

"As stupid as running away when *you* were eighteen?"

"Eighteen-year-olds make plenty of dumb choices," Cleo said. "And I didn't run away. I got into college. And then your grandmother died. And then what was I going to return to anyway? I wanted to go to law school. And then I wanted to get into Congress. And so on."

Lucas's phone buzzed before he could reply. "Oh. That's cool. He just wrote you back."

"He who?" Cleo asked. She was peering up and down the street, which looked nothing like the street she remembered from twenty years ago. There were espresso bars at every other storefront and impossibly hip clothiers and organic juice pop-ups and one store devoted entirely to essential oils. Georgie would *love* Seattle now, Cleo thought, and reminded herself to text her back. Which she already knew she would not.

"Matty," Lucas said.

"Why would Matty be writing me back?"

"Oh, I wrote back to him writing you in the first place."

Cleo stopped short, and a man with a handlebar mustache, a magenta vest, and rolled jeans, with an adorable yellow Labrador, nearly tripped over her.

"Why would you *do* that?" she nearly screeched. The man did a double take, and so she offered, "Sorry, not you. Him, my son." So the man flashed her a peace sign and went on his way, and Cleo thought this was a very distinctly Seattle interaction. And it slayed her just a little bit in the best of ways. Maybe you couldn't run away from where you came from as easily as she had thought.

"I didn't, like, say that you loved him," Lucas said. "I just said, 'hey, thanks, nice to hear from you.'"

"It wouldn't be such a bad thing for you to have a little romance in your life," Gaby butted in.

"Where *is* this pizza place anyway?" Cleo barked. Nothing about this street looked familiar anymore. Back then, she and MaryAnne could have stomped down the avenue (in their Doc Martens, because in Seattle, even the semi-non-cool kids wore Docs) blindfolded and still found their way to Pagliacci's. She spun around to the west, then the east, and was no better oriented.

"I can ask Oliver about him," Gaby said. They were striding down the next block, simply to move from point A to point B. "Maybe he knows his deal."

"Why would you ask Oliver about Matty? *When* would you ask Oliver about him?"

"Oh, we're having dinner tonight. I figure, we fly out in the morning; why not?"

"Great," Cleo said. "You both have dates tonight."

"Mine is not a date," Gaby protested, but Lucas said nothing, which made Cleo wonder if Lucas really knew what a *date* date was, and if so, how he did and when he'd been on one. Also, should she bring up the fact that Gaby was reading his texts on the phone and maybe he was technically cheating on someone back home? She wanted to raise a man who respected women but she didn't want to be a mom who snooped on her kid. Though she'd read some studies that she *should* be snooping on her kid, so . . . This whole thing was getting out of hand. All she wanted right now was a fucking piece of pizza.

Before everything went south their senior year, she and MaryAnne used to split a Canadian bacon and pineapple pie. They'd trudge up the hill after school, on breaks from their homework and before going to MaryAnne's (with the pool and the ping-pong table and the Pac-Man machine) and were at Pagliacci's so often that the guys knew their order. They'd slurp their Diet Cokes until the ice rattled and pick the bacon off their slices and drop it on their tongues, nearly drinking in the grease. They'd talk about their own versions of ruling the world—it changed by the month. Sometimes it was through politics and sometimes it was through solving the hunger crisis in Africa or ending the Iraq War, and sometimes it was just making some boy who demeaned them feel small in a reciprocal way. Ruling the world could be both literal and metaphorical. This was before every T-shirt in the Gap screamed with quippy slogans like "This Girl Is on Fire" and "I Am My Own Future" and "#SquadGoals." It was just them and their pizza and their aspirations.

Today, in the bright and welcoming Seattle sun, Cleo landed on the block that she was certain was *the* block. But where she expected to find her old pizzeria, she instead found a vegan bar.

"I don't know." She looked to Gaby and Lucas. "This was where it was."

"Maybe it closed." Lucas looked unfazed, like her introducing him to Pagliacci's wasn't about to be one of her seminal parenting moments. "I don't care; let's just eat here. I'm fucking starving." Cleo glared at him, which he ignored.

"You know I'm avoiding gluten anyway," Gaby added. Then she checked her phone. "Hmm. We're back to about fifty-fifty on those YouTube likes." She mulled something over. "Maybe we should rebrand the video with a snappy title, a headline like, 'Cleo McDougal Has Regrets.'"

"That's not really snappy," Cleo said. "That's just a word-for-word interpretation."

"It's a work in progress," she replied, swinging open the door to the restaurant, which smelled strongly of wheatgrass and something so unpleasant that Cleo almost gagged.

All she'd wanted was a piece of pizza, a slice of her old life. She considered that all MaryAnne had wanted was a fair shot, a slice of her envisioned life.

The hostess welcomed them and saw them to a table in the back.

Cleo pored over the menu in search of something that could satisfy her craving. You got what you got. Sometimes you got an egg substitute omelet when you wanted Canadian bacon and pineapple pizza. Other times you were elected to the United States Senate while your former best friend ran for country club president. Cleo wasn't one for tears, really wasn't prone to complaining. Still, she could see where MaryAnne had a point.

She'd much rather be eating a bacon and pineapple pie.

# SEVEN

That night, Cleo was in the bath when the hotel phone rang. She never took baths back home—who really had the time for an indulgent bath as a single mother and senator?—but with Lucas around the corner at his coffee "hang" (his word, not hers) and her emails read and answered, she figured she would pamper herself. She was debating pouring in shampoo to make bubbles when the phone, conveniently placed by the hotel on the wall next to the toilet, buzzed. She sighed, her serenity disrupted, and reached for it, her arm damp and spilling water on the floor. For a moment, she envisioned herself as a heroine in a romantic comedy, taking calls while in a (shampoo) bubble bath and living a delightfully quirky life.

"Hello?"

"Senator McDougal, there's a Matty Adderly here for you."

"A what?" Cleo sat up abruptly, and more water sloshed over the lip of the bath. "I'm sorry, a who?" (Grammar was important to Cleo, naturally.)

"A Mr. . . ." The concierge paused, said something with her hand over the receiver. "Yes, a Mr. Adderly is here."

"I don't . . . What?" Cleo squeezed her eyes shut. Had Facebook developed a technology where you stalked someone on his page and then he was shown your location and just magically appeared? Or

maybe Matty was the one who was stalking her? Had she been photographed entering the hotel, and he just decided to come over? Cleo
knew her recognition was on the rise (thanks, MaryAnne Newman!),
but this seemed a little outlandish.

"Should I tell him . . . ?" The concierge seemed as confused as Cleo,
though not for the same reasons. Obviously. It wasn't *her* high school
boyfriend who had appeared in the lobby out of nowhere after two
decades of distance.

"I guess; I don't . . . Can you please ask him to give me about fifteen
minutes? I'll meet him in the bar."

She heard the concierge convey the message.

"Very good, ma'am. He'll see you there."

Cleo stared at the ceiling, recalibrating, then stood, grabbed a towel,
and pulled the plug on the drain. *Goodbye, shampoo bubble bath,* she
thought. *It would have been nice.* As she shoved her arms into a violet-
hued blouse (she often wore violet, as the color brought out the blue
undertones in her eyes and was always her mother's favorite) and tugged
on a pair of jeans, she resolved to chew out Gaby on the plane for setting off this entire godforsaken misadventure. Cleo was not interested
in revisiting her past, relitigating her mistakes, falling in love with boys
she hadn't really been in love with in the first place. Cleo was *not* the
heroine in a romantic comedy. And frankly, given that, at last glance,
the comments and likes on YouTube and Twitter were trending toward
MaryAnne, Gaby should know this and shut this whole thing down.

She swiped on blush and lipstick and brushed mascara over her
lashes (because she was not a monster) and let out the topknot on her
still-in-need-of-highlights hair. She wondered if she looked too much
like she was indeed prepared to fall in love with Matty and considered
changing. The blouse was a little too romantic, flowy and ethereal, but
when she opened her suitcase, she found she hadn't packed appropri-
ately, so it was this, her workout clothes, or an athleisure hoodie that
she wanted to save for the plane.

As she rode the elevator down to the lobby, she tried to think if she'd ever added Matty to her list of regrets. She wished that she'd reread the 233 items more carefully. He was probably on there somewhere. Nothing sweeping like: *Shouldn't have dumped Matty because he was the love of my life* but something smaller like: *Should have appreciated his generosity. Though,* she pondered as the elevator door dinged open, *that's not such a small thing after all.*

She saw him before he saw her, which was the benefit of arriving second. Sometimes, when she was entering a tough negotiation with her colleagues in one of her Senate committees, she (and they) employed this tactic. Arrive last. It made you appear less eager, less ready to compromise. Of course, sometimes you wanted to arrive first, just to let them know that you were a baller. (Being a senator was sometimes confusing. You'd never hear anyone admit to it, but it was true.)

She held her breath, blew it out, then strode through the restaurant to the bar, which was surprisingly crowded on a Sunday night at eight p.m., but Seattle was cool, so maybe no one worked on Monday. She didn't know.

Cleo tapped him on the shoulder, and he spun around on his stool, startled, like he wasn't sitting there waiting for her, nursing his beer. Even in the dimmed light, Cleo could see that he looked exactly like he used to, only a little craggier, which served him well. His blond hair was still thick; his stubble hadn't grayed. He stood to hug her, and he hadn't shrunk. (Why he would, Cleo didn't know, but still, she thought it.)

"Clee!" he said with nothing but delight. "I'm so happy to see you. Thanks for reaching out."

She pulled back from his hug, because Cleo was always the one leaving hugs first, and plunked onto the stool next to him.

"I didn't know what to order you," Matty said, an apology. "I couldn't remember what you would drink." So still just as nice as ever.

"I didn't really drink in high school, so you wouldn't have known."

"Well, then, that explains it!"

The bartender swooped over, and Cleo ordered a martini.

"I'm glad I didn't get you something," Matty said. "I would have guessed wine."

"In Washington, you need a stiff drink more often than you realize."

Matty laughed at this, and Cleo relaxed just a little bit. She didn't even know quite why she was so on edge. Maybe too many ghosts from the past in one weekend. Gaby had thrown her on a plane, and the next thing she knew, she was standing in front of MaryAnne Newman (and the rest of them), and then she was standing in front of her childhood home, and now she was (figuratively) standing in front of a boy whose heart she had broken (rather callously), and she hadn't really asked for any of this. Cleo swallowed. She did not like to think of herself as a victim, even if it were just a victim of Gaby's plans. She thought of herself as a woman in charge, in control, both hands on the steering wheel.

So of course she went and ruined whatever ease had just passed between them. "Look, I don't mean to be a jerk, but I'm confused about you being here."

He looked confused at her confusion. "Um, you sent me a note on Facebook?"

To which Cleo was even more confused. "I . . . I mean, I don't really use Facebook. My son set up my account." She stopped then and realized exactly what had happened. Lucas, her morose, grouchy teenager, was actually the sidekick in her romantic comedy. "Oh. Oh, OK, no, I see. He must have . . ." She waved her hand and wished very much that she had a martini in it.

Matty took out his phone and offered it to her, the message on display. Indeed, she had invited him for drinks at about eight p.m. So he was less of a stalker than she'd thought.

"My kid," she explained. "He's out on his own date . . . with MaryAnne's daughter. And I think he probably felt sorry for me."

"I don't mind," he said. "I'm just happy to see you." (So, so nice.) "Though that must be weird."

"Having a kid?"

"Out with MaryAnne's daughter," he clarified, and Cleo winced. She was so goddamn off her game.

"Oh yes, well, trying to adhere to the adage that if you tell a teenager not to do something, they'll just want to do it more. If I say he can't speak with her, they'd probably run off and elope. If they could."

Matty contemplated this, sipped his drink. "I don't think I was ever the type of teenager who had to be told not to do something."

"Yes, you were always very sweet." He was the one who winced now, and then the bartender brought Cleo her blessed martini. "I meant it as a compliment," Cleo said, after drinking an oversize swallow quite gratefully.

Matty shared his story quickly, in less time than it took her to drain her glass. He'd been married just out of college but only for two years. "A starter marriage," he said with a casual shrug that belied what Cleo could see was still a bruise that smarted. "In fact, she also said I was too nice." Since then, it had mostly been about his work as he rose through the ranks at Microsoft, and he now had an expansive loft just around the corner from the hotel, with a view of the Puget Sound and flat-screens in too many rooms.

Cleo didn't know why it surprised her to hear that he was so successful—probably because she thought of herself as someone who read people well. You had to be to juggle so many different personalities within your constituency. Matty hadn't been anything special in high school, no gem to be fashioned out of coal, no brilliant mind, no honor roll. But maybe he had layers she hadn't seen, or she had been so wrapped up in her tunnel vision, in her specific definition of *success*, that she'd missed it. Cleo her whole life had been taught by her parents that intelligence and drive were really what you needed to get by. Her dad had been an engineering major, then a helicopter pilot in the army reserves before moving to Boeing. Grit, grit, grit. Even in her artsy mother: you don't become a member of the Pacific

Northwest Ballet at eighteen on luck. Hard work, effort, grit, that's what got her mom there. Cleo glanced at Matty now, content and gracious and certainly accomplished, and wondered what else she placed a high price on that was less valuable than she thought. Whoever said you had to be the smartest person in the room? (Well, in fact, Cleo had said that. But figuratively speaking.)

Cleo sucked the alcohol out of an olive and glanced at Matty again. He really was so very handsome, and she really had dumped him very cruelly their senior year. He reached over, squeezed her shoulder.

"Cleo McDougal." He laughed. "You're a fucking senator."

"It's going great right now, as you have probably heard."

Matty laughed even bigger at this; then his smile fell.

"OK, with the exception of what MaryAnne did. I mean, what she actually wrote about your law professor . . ." He shook his head. "I'm sorry. That really was high school shit, too low of a blow."

"It's OK." Cleo shrugged.

"It's not really."

Cleo bobbed her head. It wasn't really. "Occupational hazard. Public takedowns. You start to get used to it."

"Do you . . . Is there . . . I mean." Matty started to redden. Same kid, two decades later. "Are you seeing someone?"

"Also an occupational hazard, Matty." This wasn't entirely true. Plenty of senators had full personal lives. Just not Cleo McDougal.

"So who takes care of you?"

Cleo's head jutted back, just like it would have at seventeen. "No one takes care of me. I take care of myself!"

Matty's hand found its way to her arm. "No, I'm sorry; I didn't mean it like that. I just meant—when shit gets rough, who do you lean on?"

Cleo started to answer but found she couldn't, because there wasn't a good answer to offer. Matty's eyes met hers, and she thought she saw something that looked more like pity than any form of judgment. She took her right hand, placed it over his, still on her arm. The heft of his grasp was grounding.

"Is it weird that you've stayed here? In Seattle?" she said finally, sliding her hand back around the stem of her martini glass, his curving around the neck of his beer. "With all the same people?"

"Oh, my life is on a different track." He made a face. "That sounded condescending. I just mean that I don't see them a lot. It's not like a constant dinner party with MaryAnne and her crew."

Cleo hadn't been to a dinner party other than a mandated work dinner party in a long time. Emily Godwin, her sole mom friend in DC, was often kind enough to invite her to such things. Every few months she'd try to nudge her out, to come over for dinner. But Cleo was almost always too busy and besides, she knew that these were couple-y things, and her singleness threw off the table setting and dynamic as well.

"I go on a lot of dates," Matty was saying. "Meet a lot of women. I think everyone I know has tried to set me up."

"Ah, the beauty of being a single man at thirty-seven as opposed to a single woman at the same age," Cleo mused, then ordered another drink. She was having more fun than she expected, and Cleo almost never had time for fun.

He laughed, though she wasn't sure why. "Sure. But it also probably has to do with the fact that I am, as you have noted, too nice, an easy fix-up, and you . . . are . . . not?"

Cleo didn't appreciate this intonation because she absolutely hated that female politicians were expected to be placid and nice, as if being demanding and being a bit of a hard-ass weren't compatible with the job, when, in fact, they were much more compatible than being sweet. But before she could chide him, he said, "I think that's why I admire you so much. Your edge. I think I kind of regret being such a pushover. I mean, you were pretty firm with me when we broke up."

"Oh, I am sorry for being so cold back then." Cleo softened. She could be a bit of a hard-ass. "I regret things too, of course." *Two hundred and thirty-three things.*

"But not that, not us," Matty said, laughing again. "No, we never would have worked. You had your sights set on something bigger. I had my nose in a coding book."

"I can't like a nerd?" Cleo found herself very much considering reliking this nerd. And that he was dismissing her made him all the more appealing.

"I find that offensive. We consider ourselves more geeks than nerds," he joked, which kind of astonished her because she didn't remember him ever being even remotely funny, much less sarcastic. "But no."

Something about his *no* felt definitive, and Cleo sank an inch in her barstool. Maybe it was the two martinis; maybe it was the heady whirl of nostalgia these past two days had brought, but she suspected she wasn't thinking very clearly. She very much wanted Matty to kiss her, twenty years later, in the bar at the Sheraton, but perhaps he could see it better than she could, and they really would never have worked. (Something Cleo would have sworn to not ninety minutes earlier.) He had always been good at advice and even better at listening. Back then, she took this as a form of weakness. She had wanted someone stronger than her, but two decades later, Cleo realized that perhaps she hadn't needed, still didn't need, someone *stronger* than her. What she needed was someone to complement her. She resolved right there in the Sheraton bar to make sure that Matty remained in her life, even if he wasn't going to buckle her knees with a kiss right now. (She wouldn't protest.) She wasn't long on friends, and yes, that was a real regret, whether or not she had added it to her list. (She may have, though; she'd have to check.)

"Do you think I was a bitch to MaryAnne in high school?" she asked. Matty would tell her the truth.

"I think MaryAnne is working out some of her own issues, especially with that stuff about the affair. We're rapidly approaching our midlife-crisis age."

Cleo had evaded enough interview questions in her time to know a dodge when she heard one.

"But I was a bitch?"

Matty sighed. "It's a confusing time." He waved to the bartender. Cleo hoped he wasn't signaling for the check.

"High school?"

"Well, I mean, sure, but I was talking about now."

Cleo still wasn't clear on what he meant, but she never liked to betray any unknowingness, so she said nothing. In politics, unknowingness made you a target. Probably in life too. She wasn't sure because she never let on. Instead, she'd research and she'd study and she'd dig deeper, staying all those late nights at the office while the heroic Emily Godwin dropped Lucas off at home, and solve for whatever question mark had been presented. Until no question mark remained. She might have been a bitch, but she was a bitch who did her homework.

Finally Matty said, "I mean, look. I'm just a white dude who lives in a loft with his Microsoft money, so correct me if I'm wrong. And I don't want to speak out of turn. But it seems to me that when women talk about supporting women, neither of you put your best foot forward back then." He hesitated, staring at the grains of wood on the bar, seemingly uneager to meet her eyes. "And now? I'd think that you'd each know better."

Cleo sighed, then rested her head on his shoulder, surprising herself. She had never thought of him as particularly smart, but it turned out that he was actually quite wise. *Regrets,* she thought, *maybe I have one more.*

❧

Lucas wasn't back in the room by the time Cleo headed up, after Matty had paid the tab. (He insisted, then also admitted he was dating a twenty-seven-year-old, and then it was her turn to redden because Cleo had evidently wildly misread his intentions.) Afterward, in front of the elevator bank, they had hugged; he told her not to be a stranger. She promised that she wouldn't, and unlike her promises to Georgie, she thought—she hoped—this was one she could keep.

"It's funny," he said to her after he kissed her cheek, "how people can come in and out of your lives after so many years away and how maybe they matter in different ways than they used to."

"So I have your vote?" Cleo joked because Matty was being sincere again, and though she really, really wanted to appreciate that side of him, she also wasn't used to nearly anyone in her orbit ringing with sincerity. Sure, she was passionate about some of her pet issues—school funding and equal pay and all that—but sincerity also meant vulnerability, and vulnerability in politics meant blood.

"You have my vote," he said. "And now you have my cell. So call anytime."

"I will." She nodded, and she remembered again how wonderful he had been when her parents died, and so she repeated, "I will."

In her room, Cleo pulled off her violet blouse and jeans, folded them in her suitcase, and grabbed her pajamas, which she'd hung in the closet. She preferred them to be unwrinkled; she didn't really know why. Lucas made fun of this, but he balled up all his clothes and dumped them in the corner of his room, so he was in no position to judge.

It was nearly one thirty in the morning East Coast time, so she should have been tired. But everyone knew that Cleo McDougal could run on coffee fumes and ambition, a habit honed early, mostly out of necessity when Lucas was a baby and it was just the two of them. Now this was one of her strong suits within the Senate—not her lack of sleep but her grit, her determination, her ability to work through just about anything.

Like her world upending when the police came to MaryAnne's house that night of the helicopter crash, because they'd already tried her own home, and told her the news. She and MaryAnne had been poring over *U.S. News & World Report* college rankings and assessing where they had the best shot. Then MaryAnne's mother opened the bedroom door, looking like she was about to faint, and then the police guided Cleo to their living room couch, and that was that. Georgie flew up from Los Angeles the next morning and . . . Cleo tried to remember where she had slept that night, at her grandmother's or at MaryAnne's. It came to her—she'd slept at her own house that night, her childhood one. She was hysterical, of course. It was the last time she'd truly ever come undone, and she had refused to go to her grandmother's. MaryAnne's mother wasn't sure what to do, so they drove back to her own house, and MaryAnne lay beside her in Cleo's twin bed, and Cleo shook from the shock of it, her whole body quaking all night. And then they rose at dawn, and Cleo got into her parents' bed, which smelled like her mother's shampoo and her father's aftershave, and she kept crying, unable to stop even if she'd wanted to.

Eventually MaryAnne's mother had arrived and packed Cleo a suitcase and delivered her to her grandmother's, and Cleo wept for three days straight. She stopped eating, and her grandmother fretted, and Georgie, now a responsible adult with a thriving life-coach practice, tried to intervene, but Cleo was also nearly a grown-up by then, and she was strong enough to push them away, to lock herself in her grandmother's guest room and insist that they let her mourn on her own and fend for herself. It wasn't a conscious choice back then to spurn their generosity. Cleo was in shock and adrift; her whole world had been their little insular triangle, Mom and Dad and her, and without this formation, Cleo didn't know who she was. When two sides of a triangle collapse, you're just left with a solitary straight line. Cleo remembered this now—lying on a bed at her grandmother's and literally envisioning herself as a flat black line, and she had stared at the ceiling and considered what her parents would want her to do now. To weep, to mourn, or to get the hell up and light the world on fire. And she knew that it was the latter. So she stopped crying and resolved that her tears were a weakness, and she went to the funeral and sat dry-eyed. It was as if she had channeled her grief into stoicism, and from there Cleo channeled this stoicism and her ability to power through straight into her veins.

You get what you get. You do what you have to do. You stop crying. You stop sleeping. You turn yourself into someone to be reckoned with. You become a straight line, and then you become an arrow.

Tucked into the hotel duvet, Cleo logged on to Facebook on her phone. She clicked out of the app and then checked Lucas's location. (Yes, she tracked his phone. Emily Godwin had suggested it, and it had never seemed smarter than now.) He was still at the coffee place. Surely it would close soon. Surely he couldn't be falling in love with MaryAnne Newman's daughter. Cleo tapped the Facebook app again. She didn't want to tell Lucas whom he could and couldn't fall in love with, but she might have to.

She scrolled through Matty's page and his photos—he liked to fish in the summers in Idaho evidently and also had a dog whose breed was undeterminable. There was a recent picture with a woman, probably the twenty-seven-year-old, at a Coldplay concert, and all this just seemed so Matty. He was right, she thought; she was not the type of girl who went to Coldplay concerts and fished in Idaho, so maybe they never really would have worked. But maybe that kind of life would have been nice, even for a long weekend, even for an occasional long-distance romance. She knew that if she told Gaby about how he showed up and they had a few drinks and she rested her head on his shoulder, that she—Gaby of her firm no-kids policy and her likely no-marriage policy too—would squeal and think that maybe this was the start of something. You can be a staunch independent feminist and still love a Kate Hudson rom-com.

But Cleo knew she would never be the heroine in a romantic comedy. She just wouldn't. She'd made her peace with that years ago. When she left Northwestern on her own with a baby growing inside her.

She typed MaryAnne's name into her search bar, clicked on her profile. She found herself inhaling deeply, as if she were about to get her flu shot or a gut punch or terrible polling numbers (which, incidentally, she never got—her home state loved her) and was steeling herself for it.

The lock on the hotel door beeped, then unlatched, and Cleo threw her phone to the foot of the bed.

"Hey," Lucas said. "How was your night? Anything exciting happen?" He flopped belly-down on his own bed, then angled his face toward her.

"Very funny."

Lucas propped himself up on his elbows. "What? Did something happen?"

Now it was Cleo's rare chance to roll her eyes at him. "I know that you messaged Matty, OK? The jig is up."

Lucas swung his feet out toward the floor and sat up. "Don't be mad. I just . . . I don't know, it's kind of pathetic how you have no life."

"This coming from a kid who is literally locked in his room when he's not at school or soccer."

"But I have a *life*, Mom. Also, that's entirely age-appropriate—teenage boys are supposed to lock themselves in their bedrooms and ignore their mothers. But all you do is work."

His phone blipped, and Cleo lost him to his texts for a moment. A grin spread across his face; then he typed something back quickly.

"Is that Esme?"

"Stop snooping!" Lucas yelped, his smile gone.

"Lucas, you're sitting two feet away from me, typing with a ridiculous look on your face. That is not snooping; that's observing. A mother is allowed to do that."

"Fine." He stood, walked to the bathroom, shut the door. Cleo heard the lock spin.

"We still have a lot to discuss," she called after him.

He didn't answer, of course, because he'd given her as much as he'd wanted to for the night, and then he was gone. He really was her son, she thought. And she didn't know if this filled her heart or emptied it.

# EIGHT

Cleo missed Monday in the office, and despite working for the entire six-hour plane ride home, she was now behind. Cleo McDougal did not like being behind, and anyone, from MaryAnne Newman to Arianna, her junior-most staffer, could have told you that. She was a scheduler, a go-getter, and never once in her history of schooling had she missed a deadline, not even that rocky fall of her senior year when she was still unpacking her boxes from her move into her grandmother's and unpacking her grief from everything else.

She had just made it back to her desk after a committee vote—a bill on the childcare tax cut that she had cosponsored, which indeed made it out of committee, and now the real negotiating began: cajoling, bargaining, duping, and manipulating members of the other party to give her what she wanted in exchange for something they wanted—and had barely plopped into her desk chair when Gaby knocked. This was being gracious, because Gaby never knocked; she just announced herself.

"I just got off a very interesting Skype."

"Uh-huh." Cleo was rooting around in her bottom drawer for a protein bar. She found a box of Girl Scout cookies—Trefoils—and figured that would do. She'd bought a bunch from the custodian's daughter last year. Franklin worked the evening shift, and since Cleo was always there late, they'd struck up a friendship. "Do Girl Scout cookies expire? Do we know?"

"Doubtful," Gaby said. "That's seriously your lunch?"

Cleo tore the box open and placed a cookie smack in the middle of her tongue as an answer. "Oh my God," she managed. "Heaven."

"You were definitely a Girl Scout, weren't you?" Gaby reached for one, despite her admonishment.

"Brownie and Junior. My mom was our troop leader. I probably would have kept going until high school, but MaryAnne convinced me that we'd never get boyfriends if we did." Cleo thought of the two of them, at Pagliacci's, watching Oliver Patel and the other baseball players slide their trays down the line to the cashier and MaryAnne narrowing her eyes and saying, *We can't be Girl Scouts anymore, Clee. It's over. Hot guys don't feel up girls who are Girl Scouts.*

"Was she right?" Gaby reached for another cookie, then reconsidered and placed it back in the plastic.

"Well, we quit. And I did end up dating Matty. Though he was not really the type of boy MaryAnne meant. I mean, you met him."

"I didn't."

"Oh, right. I'm distracted. But she and I weren't beating anyone off with a stick." Cleo stacked two cookies on top of each other and bit down. "I did lead our troop every year in cookie sales, though. One year I had so many that we couldn't use our dining room."

"Of course you did." Gaby laughed. "Let me guess, MaryAnne came in second."

"Indeed." Cleo laughed too, though she felt a bolt of sadness for her old ex-friend. Why had everything between them always had to be a competition? *Regret.*

In fact, Cleo had spent last night poring over her list of 233 regrets to assess if what had occurred to her in Seattle—more friendships, more appreciation for kindnesses, more room for art in any form—had made the list. They hadn't, not really, other than the brief notation from five years back—*I never learned to paint. Or sing. Or dance. Or anything. Maybe that could have been a nice thing.* Nearly everything on there was a concrete wrong or a direct action that Cleo had taken: she was surprised to see *MaryAnne internship essay* buried in the first hundred—she could have sworn she never put pen to paper about MaryAnne. But then there were simpler items too: not taking a probiotic regularly, not ordering Lucas's Christmas presents in the fall during Labor Day sales, the like. Yes, there was a *shouldn't have quit yoga*, but that wasn't really reflective, now was it? That was an action that she would like to undo. But did not. Had not. The yoga itself might lead to a more meditative, thoughtful state, but as it was on the list . . . not particularly insightful. Even, Cleo realized, her regret about her artistic pursuits. She could have tried something, done anything!, but she hadn't. She'd been content to jot it down and carry on. She reread the list of 233 regrets and wondered why she hadn't found them more propulsive, why they hadn't sparked her to change, to make amends, and who she might be, how she might feel if she had.

Indeed, Cleo had instead used the list to purge herself of guilt, of any sort of misdeed—big or small—but she hadn't used it to become *better*. And though her dad wasn't around to ask, she was starting to suspect that was his intention. Her father was a good man. He was faithful and devoted and funny and smart. And maybe his list made him this way or maybe he made his list to avoid becoming anything he didn't want to be—unfaithful, cruel, less informed. Cleo didn't know; she couldn't know now. But she did know that writing things down and using them for good were not the same thing. It occurred to her how much this notion echoed the very beginning of MaryAnne's op-ed.

"Anyway," Gaby said. "Two orders of business. One: Oliver Patel has asked if he can come visit." She grimaced as if this were a terrible thing as Cleo raised her eyebrows. "But I've decided I like him and so I said yes."

"Wow," Cleo said, swallowing the last of her Trefoil sandwich. "That's unexpected."

"I shouldn't have started with that because we'll have to unpack that at a different time." Gaby talked over her. "I should have started with: I just got off Skype, and Veronica Kaye wants a meeting."

"Veronica Kaye? Of *Veronica Kaye*?" Cleo knew it sounded stupid even as she asked it, and she hated sounding stupid. But she, who was pretty hard to stun, was stunned.

Veronica Kaye ran the empire Veronica Kaye Cosmetics, which she had founded when Cleo was in about middle school (Cleo and MaryAnne just loved, loved, loved their frosty pink lip gloss) and which over its first decade became a billion-dollar company. It was female-led from top to bottom, from Veronica herself to the women on the sales floor at Nordstrom and Macy's and now on QVC, which hocked a slightly lesser brand of the goods for a discount price. She was known to write big checks for candidates she supported, but receiving this support was elusive, the white whale of the political world. She'd never jumped into the presidential race, instead choosing to focus on smaller, local campaigns where she thought grassroots work could make a bigger difference. Cleo had always admired her for that. It was easy to write a check for a splashy candidate who got coverage on all the news networks. It was probably more authentic to quietly endorse a state senator or a local mayor who could bring immediate change to a community.

"You led with Oliver Patel when you could have started with Veronica Kaye?" Cleo said. "Oliver was cute in high school and obviously foxy now, but seriously?"

"I know, I know. I'm allowed one swoony mistake at the thought of his cheekbones, and that's it. Oh, also, he FaceTimed me this morning and I was almost late for work . . ."

Cleo held up her hand. "I love you more than anyone in this world other than Lucas, but I really do not need to hear about your phone sex."

"Technically, it was FaceTime sex, but point taken." Gaby checked her phone. "Also, I need that list of your ten regrets by end of day. That's what put you on Veronica's radar in the first place."

"My regrets put me on her radar? Gaby, no one knows about this list other than you."

"Right, but I mean, the video, the buzz. The spunk behind it."

Cleo met her gaze. "I mean it, Gaby. I don't care if you want to tell the world that I'm trying to make some . . . reparations. I do care if you share that I have two hundred and thirty-three of them." She didn't add: *And that this was my thing with my dad. And it was private. And it was ours.* And also, there were items on that list that she did not want exposed, could not have exposed.

"Understood. You have my word. She won't know. And honestly, there's no reason she has to." Gaby nodded, an affirmation. "It's my understanding that she likes the gumption—and that's all she really needs to see. Also, though, she wants to meet on Friday, and I think we should bang out another one by then."

"Gaby, these aren't like . . . items on my grocery list." Cleo debated another Trefoil but felt a stomachache coming on, so she closed the box and opened her bottom drawer, dropping the box back inside. "Besides, the mess of MaryAnne hasn't exactly been cleaned up."

This was true. Lucas had been texting nonstop with Esme (Cleo had yet to ask him about the girl here at home and whether or not he was being unfaithful, though she didn't know what this meant for four-teen-year-olds), and this morning on the drive to school he informed her that her visit had only made MaryAnne more determined. The video of Cleo's escapade was still blazing through YouTube, rocketing all over Twitter, and viewers remained split on who really was in the wrong. Maybe MaryAnne liked her odds of swaying the public opinion tide. Or maybe she was still just furious.

"More determined to do what?" Cleo had asked Lucas.

"She just said *more determined*, then put the rolling-eyeball emoji," he said. He held up his phone to show her, but then the light turned green, and someone behind them honked, and Cleo jolted forward.

"Well, can you ask? Also, I thought emojis were—"

"God, Mom," he interrupted. "I'm just trying to help. I'm not, like, your spy."

Gaby's phone buzzed, and she hopped to her feet, her message to Cleo received. "By the way, speaking of MaryAnne, CNN sent over a request for a comment."

"Comment on *what?*"

"MaryAnne posted something else on Facebook, and you're right, the story isn't going away."

Cleo nodded. One of their male reporters had chased her down the hall this morning before she ducked into a bathroom, just about the only place he couldn't pursue her. She'd waited him out until he finally gave up. Stall tactics. Another thing politicians excelled at.

"I don't think we should give them one," Gaby said. "I don't want to have to answer everything she does with a tit for tat. Let's think on it, put a pin in it. And in the meantime, ten regrets, and I choose four more. ASAP." She paused. "Please." Her phone vibrated again, and she grinned and held it up for Cleo to see. "Oliver."

"Lovebirds already," Cleo said.

"Speaking of good sex, I've been thinking." Gaby sat back down.

"Oh God."

"No, seriously. It wouldn't be such a bad thing if we lined up some dates."

"Whatever happened to being proud of how independent I am? How I don't *need* a man to stand by my side?" Cleo reached back down for the Girl Scout cookies.

"Jesus, you don't."

"So then what?"

Gaby stood again—moving on to her next item, ready to put this one to bed. "For you, Cleo, for you. Not because you *need* one or because you're lesser for it. But because Lucas is getting older now, and maybe I might actually like Oliver Patel." She laughed, corrected herself. "Who fucking knows. But you can't be on your own forever."

"I can be single forever," Cleo snapped. "I am perfectly happy being single."

"Being single and being on your own are two different things," Gaby said, not unlike what Matty had echoed at the bar in the Sheraton. "No one can do anything in this career, much less in this world, on their own. I'd think you'd know that by now."

Gaby's phone blipped, and she said, "Shit," and disappeared out the door.

And Cleo stared at her bottom drawer and wished she had thought to buy a few more boxes of Girl Scout cookies. She'd like to be better prepared.

⌒♋

Emily Godwin had volunteered to drop Lucas after practice again, and this time she came to the door.

"Mom! Mrs. Godwin is here!" Lucas yelled, then stomped up the stairs to his room. Cleo, from her office, heard two pairs of feet and realized that Benjamin, Emily's son, must have trailed Lucas inside. His door slammed, and Cleo rushed out in slippers and sweats to thank Emily personally. She hoped everything was OK; Emily usually just did the flyby drop-off, and though Cleo genuinely really liked her, she was also always a bit relieved not to have to make any chitchat. Chitchat was low on Cleo's list of things to do. With constituents, sure, because that was part of the job, and the job she welcomed. There was *purpose* behind that kind of chitchat.

"Cleo!" Emily said warmly and pulled her into a hug. She and Cleo had been friendly since the boys landed on the same soccer team in second grade, and though they weren't close, Cleo enjoyed her company, as far as she enjoyed anyone's company other than Gaby and Lucas (and now Matty), on the sidelines and those occasional out-of-town tournaments. Most people in town and on the team worked in politics in one form or another, so it wasn't strange to have a sitting senator staying at the Hampton Inn with the team any more than it was to have any other parent. Emily had started her career as a lawyer in the Justice Department but after three kids gave it up for, as she often said, *the sanity of staying at home. Which, actually, is not exactly sanity.* She'd laugh about it, and Cleo always liked her for this. That there was no apology for her choice and there was also a recognition that it wasn't an easy one.

Her husband had also worked for the Justice Department, but around the time Benjamin was born, he jumped to outside counsel for better money. Emily once mentioned that they'd discussed who should quit—with three kids it felt like someone should—and at the end of the day, her husband just wasn't ready to be a stay-at-home dad. Emily had shrugged as if, well, it was what it was, so she became the full-time parent. Not because he was better at his job than she was, not because she was dying to pack lunches and fold laundry and run all the soccer carpools, but because in the default of the gender hierarchy, for some reason, the man's need as usual came first.

Emily didn't begrudge him, and Cleo understood that everyone made choices that kept them sane, which wasn't always the same thing as keeping them happy. But Emily was happy enough, and it wasn't Cleo's life to live. Besides, as a single mother, even an ambitious, ball-busting single mother, of course there were times when Cleo wished that she had the time to pack lunches and fold laundry and run soccer carpools. (Cleo actually had no desire to do any of those things. But in theory, yes, yes, she would have liked that.)

At the very least, it might have been nice to have a partner so every decision didn't have to land on her shoulders alone. When Lucas was a baby, it was exhausting—all those micro decisions that seemed like they might be life-changing. Bottle or breast? Stomach or swaddle? Organic or non?

One morning, early in her second year at law school and in a rush to get to her criminal procedure class, she completely forgot to put pants on him. He showed up at day care with no pants but still smiling and totally unselfconscious and kissed her on both cheeks before she left (which nearly made her crumble right there on the soft padded floor), as if him standing there without pants was entirely normal, and the wonderful caregivers assured her that she was not the first harried young mother to forget her child's essential clothing. (He also lacked both socks and shoes. It was spring; he didn't freeze.) It would have been nice from time to time to have a partner around to remind her to put pants on the baby.

Georgie had tried. Cleo had to give her credit for that. She'd flown out a few days after Lucas was born and slept on the couch of Cleo's small off-campus apartment. Her own boys were three by then, so Georgie surely could have taught Cleo a thing or two. And it was kind, of course, that she showed up. And for the first day or so, Cleo had been grateful. Much like how when she initially started dating Matty, she'd appreciated his own quotient of generosity. But Cleo was so fucking exhausted and so used to making decisions for herself that by that second day, Georgie's help began to feel instead like suffocation. Really like judgment. From someone who, for the bulk of Cleo's life, hadn't been in any position to pass judgment. Actually, up until Cleo's early teen years, and certainly in the time that they'd shared a roof, Georgie had been a goddamn disaster. But there they were, the older sister as an expert, the younger one without a clue: Cleo not knowing what to do about the umbilical cord scab; Cleo having bought the wrong size diapers; Cleo nearly fainting when his poop was bright green and then having to listen to Georgie assure her (in what Cleo thought was a quite patronizing tone) that this was all just *normal.*

Cleo, a rigid straight line, just wanted to *scream.*

She'd read all the books and done her homework, and yet still Georgie tried to grasp her breast and show her how to nurse; Georgie tried to reswaddle him when Cleo's attempts weren't sticking; Georgie knew how to bounce him on her shoulder to get him to both burp and sleep within two minutes. And it was all too much for Cleo—not just her kindness but that her sister was in *her space* telling her *what to do* and *how to do it,* and her feelings weren't even rational—she knew this! She knew that her annoyance should instead be gratitude, but on the fourth night, while Georgie was demonstrating how to give Lucas a proper bath, Cleo could just not take it a second longer—what she perceived as condescension (which she later realized was not, but this took at least a year). She exploded on Georgie to give her some space and that she was his mother. Then continued with plenty of other unkind words about how difficult Georgie made life for her parents, about how Cleo didn't want to be taking advice from someone who had once been brought home with a police escort (a house party where Georgie had been found falling-down drunk)—all words of regret now—shouting so loudly that Lucas cried for an hour straight. And even Georgie's patented bouncing technique would not quiet him.

Georgie left the next morning, and they returned to their monthly phone calls (if that), and Cleo dialed an agency and found a very nice woman, Bernadine, who understood boundaries and didn't try to shove Cleo's nipple into Lucas's mouth and arrived at eight a.m. and left at six p.m., and that was much more civilized than the messiness of family. At least, that's how Cleo saw it at the time. Once she got herself into a routine, she put him in day care, which meant even more boundaries and no one in their home but the two of them. Cleo was happier that way.

Tonight Emily pulled back from their hug and reached down for an (organic reusable) grocery bag at her feet. "I was at Costco today and bought an extra rotisserie chicken. Thought I'd see if you'd eaten."

Cleo reddened. She'd planned to just order a pizza. Again. Lucas could live off pizza if she'd let him. And she didn't want to be Emily's pet project. "I haven't," Cleo said. "But really, it's OK."

"Don't be ridiculous—I have more free time than you. Let me help."

"I just . . ." Cleo couldn't think of an excuse fast enough. She didn't want Emily to think that she regularly needed help for simple things like, well, like dinner. Carpool rides were amazing, but that was because Cleo couldn't be two places at once. Stocking their fridge or making a pot of pasta was simple adult stuff, and Cleo should be more capable. Just like she should have known how to swaddle Lucas or eke out a post-bottle burp.

"You have to eat, and I had an extra, no big deal."

"You're right," Cleo conceded and stepped aside, welcoming her in. "Thank you."

"The boys ran off before I could tell Benjamin that we weren't staying. Someone to FaceTime in Seattle? Does that sound familiar or . . . did I not eavesdrop correctly?"

They landed in her kitchen, and Emily heaved the bag to the counter. She removed the chicken, which smelled, frankly, heavenly and also nutritious, which was a change from Girl Scout cookies and plane food and vanilla macadamia muffins.

"No, you heard correctly. Do kids date these days? If so, I think maybe he's dating someone, my old friend's daughter, there." It occurred to Cleo that Emily might have her ear to the ground on eighth-grade gossip. "But have you heard of any . . . romance here?"

"Oh, Benjamin wouldn't say a word." Emily pulled out a bottle of wine, then a salad. "But I'll ask Penny; she'd know. She's like the town crier." Penny was their youngest, only sixteen months younger than Ben. God bless Emily Godwin—*How on earth does she do it?* Cleo thought. "Oh, I also got you a salad. They were on sale. I figured after . . ."

"You saw the video from Seattle?" Cleo laughed. "This is a pity dinner, isn't it?"

Emily laughed too. "No, just, Jonathan's working late, and the other two kids are accounted for. I hated the idea of you on your own after . . . all of that." She paused. "I hope you don't mind. I know we're not . . . I mean, I'm sure you have other friends to do this kind of thing with."

Cleo reached for a wine opener. "I don't really. Believe it or not, cutthroat young women do not make friends easily."

"I wouldn't call you cutthroat."

"You're not on the Judiciary Committee with me." Cleo grabbed two wineglasses and poured generous fills. "Should we call the boys?"

"Let's drink this first," Emily said. "They'll still be there when we're done."

Cleo clinked her glass to hers. She liked her more and more by the minute.

With a belly full of chicken and salad, Cleo felt better than she had in days. She really should make a better effort with her diet, she told herself. She didn't have to be Gaby and enter a marathon and swear off gluten (and dairy and anything else remotely pleasing to her palate) to be a little healthier. And maybe it was the protein and vitamins or maybe it was the wine (Emily had stopped at one glass because she was driving Benjamin home, but Cleo had poured herself a second), but she finally felt brave enough to cull her list, to whittle it down to ten actionable items that she really did regret and had courage enough to admit to. And possibly face publicly if both Gaby and Veronica Kaye insisted. There probably was not a lot she wouldn't do for a check from Veronica Kaye. In a different line of work, some might call it prostitution. In politics, it was fundraising.

She grabbed a red pen from her desk, unlocked the drawer, pulled out the worn yellow paper. Two hundred and thirty-three regrets over twenty-four years really wasn't all that many, she thought. She made a mental note to raise this with Gaby, who seemed gobsmacked at the number. That was what?—Cleo did the quick math—something like ten or so a year. Imagine going through your life with only one regret a month! That was nothing! That was one bad day's worth.

Cleo clicked the top of her pen up and down, admonishing herself. Frankly, the list should probably be double what it was. She checked the dates next to each regret—she hadn't updated it in some time; the last entry was from January.

She rolled her shoulders forward, then back, trying to assess how best to narrow down two decades' worth of missteps. It was really something to read through them all, to wonder what could have been if she hadn't, say, weaseled out of her required art credit at Northwestern (she had signed up for dance, thinking maybe she had underestimated herself and had a twinge of her mother's talent, but then sprained her ankle on the steps of her dorm one week into school and had happily used the injury and the accompanying doctor's note to get out of the class). Maybe she would have fallen in love, as her mom had, with the movements of Martha Graham or Alvin Ailey, and even if it hadn't changed, say, her trajectory toward law school and politics, maybe it would have made her more comfortable with her body, gotten her on the dance floor at those rare parties she attended, challenged her to take up more space in the world. Maybe she'd have Gaby's posture and her stomach wouldn't sag over her waistband, which it had ever since she gave birth. Or maybe taking that dance class would have given her more confidence in herself—not her intellect, not her drive, just . . . herself, because those were different things—and she would have been someone else entirely. She wouldn't have gotten too drunk at that party her senior year and forgotten to use a condom and gotten pregnant, and Lucas wouldn't be here and everything would have shifted. Maybe she wouldn't have made dumb decisions with Alexander Nobells; maybe she would have stood her ground when she lost her summer position; maybe she would have confronted him and who knows what would have happened from that.

She threw her pen across the room, startled at this realization. It was just a thread she was pulling, an imaginary thread at that, starting with a stupid interpretive dance class. She didn't regret Lucas (of course!) or any of the struggle that came with him. And most of the time, Cleo genuinely loved her life, and she was proud of it. But still. It was easy to see how this list could go sideways. How looking back started to make you question the way forward. And, as her campaign slogan intended to convey, Cleo McDougal preferred to only look forward.

She stood, retrieved the pen from the floor by her office door, then swung the door open and listened for Lucas. It was still early Seattle time. Maybe he was talking with Esme?

"Luc?" she yelled down the hall. "Lucas?"

She heard her phone buzz in her office, so scampered back.

Emily: Town crier knows all. Penny confirms L is "with" Marley Jacobson.

Cleo : What does "with" mean?

Emily: . . .

. . .

Emily: (Checking)

. . .

Emily: She says it means they are "together." I realize this is not more helpful.

Cleo searched for the miserable-face emoji but found it took too long to find and gave up.

Cleo: OK. Ugh. Thanks.

She settled back at her desk, trying to reorient herself and focus. She'd intended to cull the list, and cull it she would. Dealing with Lucas's love triangle could wait. She knew she wasn't the best one to give advice on romance, and she further knew that he would pounce on this weakness immediately. He was her son, after all. He could nearly out-debate her now, if and when he chose to string more than three words together consecutively, which was not often. (So in some ways, also a blessing.)

Cleo flipped the yellow papers. She resolved to cross out any items that were nonsensical to her now—vague, in-the-moment regrets that she couldn't possibly fix or redo because she had no idea what they meant all these years later. She clicked the top of the pen, swiped through a couple dozen this way, easy. What did *steps!!!* or *too many mushrooms* mean after all these years anyway? It didn't matter. She axed through seventy-two of these.

Next she thought she'd categorize the remaining. There were regrets, and then there were *regrets* like Alexander Nobells, among others. He wasn't even the gravest. Those were regrets that were no one's business but her own. She eased back in her chair, squeezed her eyes closed, pinched the bridge of her nose. She'd never intended for some of them to fester as they had. Sometimes an act or a lie or a misdeed started out simply as an in-the-moment impulse. No one ever really thought that they would follow you around, potentially haunt you forever.

Cleo opened her eyes, tore off a sheet of clean paper, and removed a ruler from her top drawer. She drew three parallel lines down the page, then inked a perpendicular line on top. Three columns. The first: *Stupid Things*. The second: *Possible Fixers*. The third: *Off-Limits*.

Cleo figured perhaps she could take a few from the first column, a handful from the second, and keep the third at bay. This should satisfy Gaby and hopefully please Veronica Kaye too, who, according to Gaby, loved the spunk she was seeing from Cleo without—Gaby promised—knowing the impetus (the list!) behind it.

She started scribbling, filling in the lines. She'd gotten only four deep when Lucas stuck his head through the door.

"Hey."

Cleo jolted. She hadn't ever told Lucas about the list and certainly didn't need him reading it. *Couldn't* have him reading it. When do parents grow to be OK with their kids knowing they are fallible? That they tell half-truths to protect their children or sometimes also, yes, themselves? That they do the best they can, which often isn't good at all. She opened her drawer quickly, dropping the papers and pen and ruler inside. She shoved it closed.

"What's up?"

Lucas glanced suspiciously toward the drawer. "What's that?"

"Just a draft of a speech I'm working on."

"You have a speechwriter."

Cleo nodded. She did. "I know. But you know how I micromanage."

Lucas made a face as if this were likely. She did micromanage. It wasn't too far-fetched.

"So listen," he said. "I don't want to alarm you—"

"Oh my God, is this about Marley Jacobson?" Cleo interrupted, though there was no reason to think it was about Marley Jacobson. She realized this as soon as she said it.

"What?" Lucas soured. "Who told you about Marley?"

"No one."

He stared at her, his cheeks basically quivering in what she knew was rage.

"Can't you stay out of my business?"

"Hey, *you* came in here." Cleo stood, walked around her desk, and leaned against the front of it. "Also, since we're on the subject . . ."

"We weren't on the subject." Lucas crossed his arms, just like he used to as a toddler whenever he was gearing up for a fight.

"Fine, well, we are now, and I don't know what's going on, but you can't be 'with,' or whatever, two girls, Lucas. You just can't."

"God, you are so lame."

"I have never pretended otherwise."

"If I had a dad around, I could ask him." Lucas's hands moved to his hips, even more defiant now.

It had been percolating since MaryAnne's op-ed, this rebuke, the sting of how maybe Cleo fucked up and it could have been different with his dad, but still, it smacked her across the face. It was his default way of fighting, going right for her most vulnerable part, and he wasn't wrong: she saw his dad's name there, on the list, a reminder. Cleo tried to spend every moment she had while not working (and, admittedly, much of her time was spent working) with Lucas, putting Band-Aids on scrapes, reading bedtime stories before she returned to her office to review drafts of legislation, attending as many soccer games as she possibly could (so most, though not all), and, until a few years ago, he'd taken her at her word: that it had always been just the two of them, and they didn't need anything, anyone else. He had been curious, sure, about why other kids had present fathers, but he hadn't been pushy and he hadn't been bothered. That changed around twelve, right about when puberty set in, and Cleo had to talk to him about all sorts of things that neither of them particularly wanted to discuss but discussed anyway. Body hair. Erections. She even broached masturbation once, but it was a bridge too far and ended quickly.

But she told him, clearly and with some finality over dinner one night—Cleo knew they were going to get into the heart of it, so she came home early to cook spaghetti and fresh marinara (his favorite and really one of the few things Cleo knew how to make)—that his dad didn't want to play a part. The same line she used when the press had raised it in her first congressional run. And because Cleo took people at their words, she said to Lucas, she had honored what his dad said and reminded him that impregnating someone is not the same thing as being a father. *Besides,* she added, both when he was twelve and anytime he raised it after that, *we are not the type of people who chase down others who spurn us. We never will be.*

Cleo never felt good about it, this discussion and some of the mistruths she represented in it, but Lucas trusted her, and for the most part, that was that.

"Your having a father wouldn't change the fact that it's not fair to Marley Jacobson if you are FaceTiming Esme!" Cleo managed tonight.

She thought of her list, tucked in that top drawer, and remembered why she locked it. Because of this discussion. Because of Doug. Because how that night was such a massive clusterfuck of regret, even when, of course, it couldn't be. Of how Lucas would feel if he saw it or understood it or had any idea the panic that she felt not just when she woke up and realized she'd had unprotected sex with a guy she really barely knew (it was Cleo's only one-night stand both before and since) but also when she realized—ten weeks later—that she was pregnant.

Cleo's period had always, always been reliable. To the afternoon, to the time of day. It was so reliable that she gave it no thought. At that point, she'd had so much else on her plate. Her grandmother was gone, her parents obviously too. She was focused on making dean's list, on her law school acceptances, on completing her honors thesis. It didn't even occur to her that her period was late, because it was one of the few things she could count on. Almost two months later, she woke up in a deep sweat, as if her body were literally waking up to a realization that something was changing, and she ran to the twenty-four-hour CVS down the street from the apartment she shared with two other girls. (Friends she'd made in the Club Against Homelessness!, a.k.a. CAH!, which she enjoyed—they visited shelters twice a month and brought gently used clothes and read to and played with the kids—but she knew looked great on her résumé, to be honest.) By the time she got an appointment at student health and saw the ultrasound, she was almost through her first trimester. Sure, her breasts had been a little sore, but she hadn't been sick, her stomach wasn't pooching, she hadn't been exhausted in the way she figured pregnant women were supposed to be. The doctor (a man) told her the news with a moderated tone, a neutral expression, and Cleo wondered how, for someone so smart, she could have been so dumb.

"Listen, it's ten o'clock," Cleo said now to her son, that blip on the ultrasound fifteen years ago. "I'm not going to litigate why I'm a single parent with you right now. I'm just encouraging you to not be a jerk to these girls."

Lucas flexed his jaw. Cleo tried to envision his father doing the same, if he'd look like him while doing so, if they shared these mannerisms. In truth, she couldn't really remember all that much about him, and that both embarrassed and relieved her. There wasn't much to tell Lucas because, well, there wasn't much to tell.

"Fine," Lucas said. "Duly noted."

"Thank you. That's all I'm saying. I'm out here on the front lines fighting for legislation that makes women true equals, and if I end up raising an asshole . . ."

*"I got it."*

"Right, of course. You'll do the right thing." Cleo relaxed. She thought she might brew some coffee and get back to the list once he went to bed. "Oh, but did you come in here to tell me something?"

"First of all, can I stay home from school tomorrow? I have a headache."

"No." Cleo sighed. She didn't know why this had become a thing lately, Lucas squirming out of school. She'd asked Emily if there were any bullying rumors or drama, but she'd heard of nothing and said, "Benjamin does the same thing. I think it's teenage boys. They want to hibernate." So Cleo, who had let him skip the first two times he'd groused about a nondescript ailment, had started putting her foot down. "Take a Tylenol," she said. "You're fine. But what did you want to tell me?"

"Fine," he huffed, then softened. He chewed his lip. (Did his dad also do this? Cleo had never chewed her lip a day in her life. Or at least certainly not since she held an elected position. Lip chewing implied equivocation, and elected women were not allowed to look equivocal.) "Well, I just hung up with Esme."

Cleo sighed.

"Do you want to hear this or not?" Lucas barked. "I'm, like, trying to be helpful. A good son."

"I'm sorry, yes, continue."

"Well, her mom. She's, like, still pretty pissed."

"Yes, that makes sense." Cleo nodded. MaryAnne could harbor a grudge with the best of them.

"And I guess she's running a full-page ad tomorrow in the *Seattle Post-Intelligencer*."

"A what?" Cleo yelped. "An ad about *what*?"

"About you," Lucas said. "Or against you."

"Jesus Christ!" Cleo screamed.

"I don't know," Lucas said and even seemed a little bit sorry for her. "But it seems to me that this is war."

# NINE

The ad went more viral than even the YouTube video. Frankly, a lot of people thought that it made MaryAnne look a little bit unhinged, which left Cleo conflicted. On the one hand, Cleo appreciated that the tide of public opinion was tilting toward her, but on the other hand, she didn't appreciate the notion of a woman being deemed "psycho," as she was frequently seeing online, because once you called one woman crazy, you opened the door to call all of them crazy. And more often than not, women were not only saner than men but actually less hysterical. Cleo and her colleagues had trained themselves to hold their voices firm, their posture unwavering whenever any of their hearings were televised or whenever a reporter tracked them down in the halls within the Senate building. They couldn't afford to look emotional, couldn't risk even being *called* emotional. As if emotion were something that made them less capable at their jobs. Often it made them better.

One of Cleo's colleagues, Helene Boxer, learned this lesson the hard way. During a particularly contentious Supreme Court justice hearing, Helene had the audacity to rise from her seat and point her finger at the nominee when she caught him in a lie about his voting record, and not only was she raked over the media coals for ten days straight, she lost her upcoming reelection. Her challenger Photoshopped the video of her at the hearing such that she resembled a witch on a broom and ran ads with the image the last two weeks of the campaign. He won by seven percentage points.

So Cleo was understandably torn at the blowback against MaryAnne Newman.

Gaby, however, was not.

"I am going to fuck that bitch up," she said. She'd sent out one of their staffers, Timothy, to the newsstand that stocked the papers from all fifty states, as well as countries across the world, and she was staring down at the open paper on Cleo's desk. "Like, seriously. I could kill her. *Kill her.*"

"You can't kill her," Cleo said.

"True, I'm a black woman in America. I could be arrested just for saying that." Gaby paused, only half joking. "We'll enlist Timothy. He's white, Harvard-educated, and twenty-eight. He'll be out of jail in three months, if he's convicted at all."

Cleo pulled a sheet of paper from her bag. She couldn't sleep last night, not after Lucas announced the declaration of war and certainly not after more obfuscation about his dad. Cleo knew the mess was her own making—perhaps not all the MaryAnne stuff, because MaryAnne was happily digging her own hole deeper, but the father stuff, well, sure. So she had plunked down at her desk, and she had taken another hard look at those 233 regrets, and she had written down ten before she could talk herself out of it.

"Here," she said and shoved the paper at Gaby. "Ten. As demanded."

"As requested," Gaby corrected.

"Same thing coming from you."

"True," Gaby demurred, glancing over her options. "Hmm, OK, OK, no, OK, oh yes, that one for sure." She looked up, met Cleo's eyes. "There are some things we can work with here. You really want to dance?"

"No," Cleo snapped. "I don't *really* want to dance. But you made me write down ten regrets, and I thought that pursuing something creative in the public eye was better than tracking down Lucas's father in the public eye, so does that satisfy you?"

Gaby's eyebrows skyrocketed as Cleo's intercom buzzed.

"Senator McDougal?" Arianna still always sounded like she was apologizing. Cleo grabbed a pen, wrote down, *Speak with Arianna about her tone!*, and underlined it twice to remind herself. Arianna wasn't going to get far in politics, in any career, if she couldn't quell that upward tick, that question mark. Women who were constantly apologizing were at a disadvantage in any negotiation and, of course, taken less seriously, because who wants advice or counsel from someone who is sorry before they've even convinced you of anything?

"Yes, Arianna."

"Veronica Kaye is here? Um. Now. She's outside?"

Gaby's face went slack, and the blood drained from Cleo's.

"Shit!" Gaby said.

"Shit," Cleo said too.

"I wanted to have time to tell her our plan," Gaby was whispering again, a sure sign of her highly unusual and extremely rare panic. "Shit, shit, shit."

"Our plan?"

"The regrets plan! That's what she wanted from us; that's what got her here."

"*Shit.* OK, go with dancing."

Gaby looked even more alarmed.

"I am not a complete rhythmically challenged imbecile, Gaby," Cleo bleated. "My mom was a professional ballerina. It's in me somewhere!"

"OK, OK, we'll go with that." Gaby smoothed out her sweater, grabbed a lipstick (Veronica Kaye Fire Engine Red!), and puckered up. "Here." She thrust it toward Cleo. "You need more help than this, but it won't hurt."

Veronica Kaye swooped in and smelled, frankly, heavenly. It was the first thing Cleo noticed: her scent. Not just that the tones were perfect, some magical blend of vanilla bean and gardenia and perhaps a touch of grapefruit, but she also reeked of power. Cleo sized her up and genuinely thought she was the most intoxicating, most impressive woman she'd ever seen. And Cleo had met heads of state, ambassadors, prime ministers, and, of course, other senators (there were seventeen total, to the eighty-three men). Gaby was nearly salivating. It was hard to quantify who was more stupefied, but together their collective awe spoke to the way that Veronica Kaye commanded a room.

Of course, she was also beautiful, though neither Cleo nor Gaby would have led with that. Praising a woman for her beauty was so retro that it was uncouth. But still, she was. Stunning. As the CEO of the largest cosmetics company in the world, she needed to be, but she sold her products on more than prettiness; she sold them to encourage women to know their worth, to feel comfortable in their skin, to own who they were. Veronica had emigrated from the Dominican Republic as a young girl, and her face was still dotted with freckles from the Caribbean sun. Her caramel skin was flawless without makeup, despite her being somewhere in her fifties. Her eggplant-hued dress was immaculately tailored, her gold watch and jewelry just the right amount of heft on her wrist.

Cleo stood behind her desk and wondered if she weren't a little bit in love.

"Senator McDougal," Veronica said, thrusting out her hand and shaking with the exact measure of firmness that Cleo would expect from such a goddess. A thin blond man in his thirties trailed her, and she turned and said, "I'm fine, Topher; can you please get me a cup of coffee?"

Topher nodded and was dismissed, and Cleo knew that she was more than just a little bit in love.

"Cleo, please call me Cleo, Ms. Kaye."

"And you call me Veronica." She laughed. "Ms. Kaye is my slightly overbearing mother-in-law, who, God bless, I love, but we really don't have much in common." She laughed again. "I guess we both love her son—she maybe even more than I do." She pointed toward the door. "That was Topher. He's one of my VPs—I suppose we have to hire at least one man or risk a lawsuit, no? But he won't be sitting in for this. This is just us women."

Gaby swallowed, her eyes wide with reverence. "We can't thank you enough for coming in," she said. "But I didn't think . . .'."

Veronica sat in the chair opposite Cleo's desk, so Cleo sat too; then Gaby followed.

"I was up on the Hill today. I know this is a surprise. But I find that sometimes surprising people can work in your favor." She assessed Cleo, then Gaby. "Sometimes, it's best to catch people off guard to get a sense of what you're really getting into."

"Well," Gaby said, spreading her arms wide. "What you see with us is what you get."

Veronica narrowed her eyes toward Cleo. "I'm intrigued by what you did in Seattle." She paused. "Obviously, it is not going quite as you expected, but that doesn't worry me."

Cleo glanced down at the open newspaper on her desk and subtly tried to fold it, but you can't subtly try to fold a newspaper. They all waited until she finished, Cleo's cheeks turning a deeper shade of pink as each second croaked by.

"What I liked about it was the gumption," Veronica said. "The end result is often less important than the passion behind it, at least for voters on the national stage. Running a presidential campaign is quite different from running a senatorial campaign, where your voters already know what they want to know."

"That's exactly what I told her!" Gaby said, which Veronica ignored, and Gaby clamped her mouth shut.

"What I mean," Veronica said, "is that I'm intrigued. And you're on my radar. And if I see more gumption, wherever this notion came from . . ."

Cleo started to interrupt, though she wasn't sure with what—she didn't want to tell her about the *list*, which she worried would sound like a weakness, but perhaps if it were framed, as Gaby once said, as a way of growth, of looking more human—but she got no further than a stutter before Veronica cut her off.

"I don't need the details," Veronica said. "I don't even want to know them right now. *Surprise me.* That's what I like out of a candidate."

She stood, her time here already coming to an end. "But keep that up and you'll have my endorsement. And this time out, my endorsement can probably make you president." Then she barked, "Topher? Where's my coffee?" And then she was gone.

❧

After Veronica's visit, Gaby's plan to publicize Cleo's regrets sped into hyperdrive.

"Dancing," she screeched the next morning after their staff meeting. "We are going to make you a dancing queen! And I took a look at the others," she continued, talking too quickly, like she'd had four espressos by ten a.m., which she may have. "While I work on the dancing, I want you to get back on that bill—"

"The free housing bill?"

"Bingo," Gaby said, pointing her finger at Cleo. "That was a smart move—putting it on the list."

"Well, I mean, I should have supported it in the first place. I caved when it became a political stink bomb." Cleo didn't often wilt in the face of political pressure but occasionally, yes. She never liked it, was never proud of it, but polling mattered, plain and simple. The only way you ensured that you got to stand up and fight for your constituents was knowing that from time to time, you had to take a seat to preserve your job.

"But now you can look like a champion, at least in the eyes of Veronica Kaye."

The free housing bill was a controversial proposal that Cleo had been asked to cosponsor the year prior. It recommended sweeping new legislation for lower-income families who, if they could demonstrate five years of steady employment, at least one child elementary-school age or older, and a clean criminal record, could apply for either a free home renovation or a free home, period. It had its detractors, of course: cries that giving away things for free was not the American Way!, and further cries that housing was a temporary Band-Aid for larger, systemic problems in poorer neighborhoods. But Cleo had disagreed. She'd read the research and thought that stability started with a solid roof over someone's head, with a rodent-free kitchen, with water that didn't turn brown from the pipes. Still, her staff had polled her voters, and it was a disaster—positive numbers in the low thirties, and even though Cleo knew it was probably the right thing to do, she demurred when asked to sign on.

"I'll reach out to Senator Jackman and see if we can revive it," Cleo said.

"And I'll be sure to let the press know when you do."

"I'd expect nothing less." Cleo nodded. "Though, I mean, we're not going to film that." She thought of Senator Jackman, a perfectly coiffed, straight-spined sixty-four-year-old ballbuster from the great state of Illinois. As open-minded as she was, she also came from a generation that cared about etiquette, and Cleo was certain she'd nix Gaby's guerrilla-style filmmaking as she and Cleo hashed out the details. Besides, that type of policy work was the opposite of sexy. It would die on the internet vine unless the two of them ended up in some sort of salacious choke hold.

"No, we're not going to film that," Gaby said. "But it can still be a feather in your cap, a reconsideration, a regret addressed all the same."

She clicked her tongue. "That leaves us with two more. Give me the day, and I'll let you know what's next."

"You told me we were doing all this on my recess," Cleo argued. "In case you've forgotten, I'm not yet running for president, and I have to represent the people of New York in other matters right now, *and* who even said I want to do this?"

Gaby froze, literally, her hand in midair, her eyes as wide as globes. "You don't want to run for president?"

"My regrets," Cleo snapped. "After MaryAnne has gone so well, can we at least have a conversation about if I even want to do four more?"

Yesterday's *Seattle Post-Intelligencer* still sat folded on her desk. She'd meant to ask Lucas last night if he'd gotten any further intel from Esme, but he'd had on his noise-canceling headphones and was so focused on his homework (she hoped it was his homework—perhaps she should more accurately say, so focused on his *laptop*) that she didn't want to disturb him. Besides, she hadn't yet figured out how to respond to the ad, much less to whatever was next in MaryAnne's arsenal.

"The regrets list is what got Veronica here in the first place," Gaby said.

"No, not *the list*, because she doesn't know about that," Cleo said. "Confirming?"

"Fine, the act of embracing said regrets. The semantics of it doesn't matter, OK?" She grabbed the newspaper from Cleo's desk and threw it—somewhat dramatically, Cleo thought—into the garbage can.

"Gab, you can't just throw it away and act like there aren't reverberations. That's not how this works. That's the very point of the list. That I did something and maybe there were ramifications. A lot of times, toward me. Some stupid stuff, like not finishing my antibiotics, but some other stuff too, like torpedoing MaryAnne's internship." Cleo sighed. "Just because you do that doesn't make the ad disappear or the mess with MaryAnne disappear either. Besides, people already like me. Why risk that?"

"People like you enough, that's true. But now we're going to make them love you."

"I never needed anyone to love me," Cleo said.

"Well, maybe that's where you're shortsighted," Gaby replied.

# TEN

The truth was that even outside of high school, even well beyond the MaryAnne Newman situation and the "dumping her perfectly nice boyfriend" situation, Cleo McDougal really hadn't ever been such a good person. The opening line to MaryAnne's initial op-ed had been, in fact, quite accurate. Cleo didn't think this was why her dad passed on his habit of noting his regrets—she didn't believe that *he* believed that she was an inherently bad person. But now she couldn't be sure either.

And nothing changed once she entered politics. If anything, politics amplified these characteristics. In politics, this self-involvement made her even more successful. Theoretically, politics was about bridging divides. Realistically, it was mostly every man (and woman) for themselves.

Cleo had removed the crumpled copy of the *Seattle Post-Intelligencer* from her garbage can when she returned from her Budget Committee meeting and before she had to run to a banquet retirement dinner for the Human Rights Campaign. She'd refolded it, carefully, and tucked it in her bag. She didn't really know why. The lawyer in her told her it was evidence—of what, she wasn't yet sure. The regretter in her also told her it was evidence but of her own culpability. Because she knew that she was culpable, even when she'd also been bruised, like with Alexander Nobells, like in her estranged relationship with Georgie.

As it turned out, Emily Godwin's husband did some work for the HRC and was at the dinner too. Cleo had brought Arianna; she wanted to mentor her, to show her how women wielded their power out in the real world, not just on C-SPAN. But Arianna had seen a boy across the room from Senator Frost's office, and Cleo sent her toward him with her blessing. God knew these things could be dull and also agonizing in small ways; why not enjoy a glass of wine with an ally and possibly a man to kiss you at the end of the night? (Maybe, even, as Gaby had suggested, find someone to love you and love in return too. Cleo wasn't so impenetrable that Gaby's comment hadn't resonated just a little bit.)

Senator Jackman, the champion of the free housing initiative, lingered by the bar in an immaculately tailored red pantsuit—she was impossible to miss—and Cleo made a beeline and offered up her full and renewed support of the idea. The senior senator seemed both pleased and amused at Cleo's change of heart, but in DC, everyone's intentions were constantly shifting, and Senator Jackman knew better than to look a gift horse in the mouth. When someone offered to be your ally, you might privately ask yourself *WTAF!*, but you publicly nearly always shook on it. Indeed, Cleo clasped her hand, feeling quite good about herself for following up on her promise to Gaby (and the fact that this was the right policy to pursue for her constituents—New York real estate had boxed out too many deserving families), and then felt her stomach shift. She couldn't remember what she'd eaten for lunch. Or breakfast actually.

So this was how Cleo ended up running into Emily Godwin's husband at the buffet: he went for steak, she for salmon, and they were forced to make small talk (Cleo hated small talk) while waiting for the server to refresh the grilled vegetables. Jonathan was the kind of good-looking you saw throughout Washington—chiseled jaw, hair graying at the temples, wide shoulders—the kind of good-looking that earned him respect before he even opened his mouth, respect earned at literal face value. Cleo was nodding in agreement with him about something having to do with the boys' soccer team but really thinking: *This guy is given the benefit of the doubt in ways that I would never be granted.* He was nice enough; none of this was his fault, but Cleo's gut roiled and she lost her appetite for the salmon, which really wasn't very good in the first place. (The food at these things rarely was.)

Jonathan got ushered out into the sea of other chitchatters, and Cleo found her table, happy to be seated, off her feet in her high heels, which she hated and found sexist but what was she going to do? Show up to a work dinner in flats? Lace up her sneakers, which were really only appropriate (for serious women) at the congressional gym? Across the room, she watched Arianna flirt with the other young aide, and it occurred to her that people all around her were having sex left and right, falling in love left and right, and here she was, elbows on a rented linen tablecloth, staring at her cold salmon, thinking about how much her toes hurt. Lucas's perception of her dating life wasn't *quite* accurate: there had been failed attempts, three dates in a row with a few men, some making out in cars or their bedrooms (if Lucas had a sitter or was at a sleepover), but something sustainable, something real, well, no, there hadn't been that. She thought of Matty at the bar in the Sheraton, how she was surprised that she wouldn't have minded if he'd kissed her. She realized that this was likely because she wouldn't have minded being kissed, not because it had to be Matty. Was that how lonely, how isolated she'd become?

Something had to change.

Before she could determine just what—other than the obvious, that it would be nice to have steady, reliable sex every once in a while, to have a date to see a movie or binge a Netflix show (Cleo had never binged a Netflix show)—and how exactly to solve it, she spotted Jonathan again, just a few people away from Arianna. He was tall, which was probably what caught her attention—she wasn't spying, in any case. She'd remind herself of this later, when she sat at her home office desk, a pen in hand, and went to add this incident to her list, that she *wasn't trying to stir up any trouble.*

But she saw what she saw: Jonathan slipped his hand onto the small of a woman's back who was *clearly* not Emily Godwin. (Who was home watching his three children and probably cooking and cleaning for them too! Cleo felt her pulse accelerate and very much hoped that Emily was not doing Jonathan's laundry as well.) He leaned in close to the woman—a *blonde*, of course—and even from across the room, Cleo could see this woman relax into him, a secret passing between them. Her hand reached back, grazing his shoulder at whatever he said, as they tipped their heads together, laughing.

Cleo felt the betrayal as if it were her own. Emily Godwin had been a bit of a saint to her, for no reason other than she recognized that Cleo needed a saint from time to time. Cleo stood up in her chair, threw down her napkin, and started toward Jonathan to give him a piece of her mind, to tell him just what a goddamn *saint* he had for a wife.

"Senator McDougal!" Before she could get even halfway across the room, a man whose face she recognized before she placed his name—not because she didn't know his name, rather because his face was simply so ubiquitous—stepped into her path.

"Ah, Bowen, hi."

They each respectively tilted toward the other, kissing each other's cheek. Bowen Babson, the anchor of *Good Afternoon, USA,* pulled back from their hellos and grinned. He, like Cleo, had been a young hotshot, on a rocket through the network, landing his own show two years ago, at thirty. Cleo had always admired this drive and naturally admired his confidence (like attracts like), which occasionally allowed for Cleo to daydream about their potential. He also had a reputation for sleeping around Washington (no judgment) and dating women under twenty-five. (Which again reminded Cleo of Matty and how even her relatively geeky high school boyfriend was dating up these days, and no wonder he hadn't kissed her!) But Bowen was TV-anchor handsome, wavy dark hair, penetrating green eyes, whip smart, and even, Cleo begrudgingly admitted, fairly funny. He was easy to talk to between segments, he asked fair questions, and he was always, always prepared. It wasn't difficult to see why he cleaned up on the singles scene. It also wasn't difficult to see why he should have come with a warning label and why he'd never so much as made a single suggestive remark to her. Cleo wouldn't have expected him to.

Cleo peered over Bowen's shoulder, trying to track Jonathan. "I'm kind of in the middle of something."

Bowen's gaze followed hers, his head swiveling toward the back of the room.

"Admiring someone?"

"I'm a senator, Bowen; what makes you think that I'm here in pursuit of romance?"

Jonathan had his back to them now, and Cleo was intent on keeping her focus.

"Sorry," Bowen said. "You're right. That was shitty. Though, just for the record, I'd have said the same thing to a man." He held up his hands. "I'm the furthest thing from a misogynist. I was raised with three sisters. They'd literally pummel me if I had a sexist bone in my body."

Cleo broke her gaze, met his eyes. And she was surprised to see that they were sincere.

"I'm sorry," she replied, then thought of Arianna, who apologized too much, and then she thought of MaryAnne, who refused to accept Cleo's (somewhat sincere) apology. Words were words were words. Intent mattered. "You really weren't being that shitty. I'm just . . . I'm busy."

Jonathan had cupped his hand around the woman's waist now; they were headed toward the exit.

"Oh my God," Cleo muttered. "I'm going to fucking kill him."

"Um, can I help?"

"What? No." Cleo stood on her tiptoes, her calves genuinely cramping in protest, to watch them through the crowd.

"Some investigative reporting, perhaps?"

They were gone, out the exit door, on to God knew where. Probably a room upstairs at the hotel, while Emily waited at home lassoing the children. Cleo hated Jonathan in that moment, hated that he'd forced her friend to become a cliché. She'd given up her job for their family, and he repaid her with this. For Cleo, there was no greater injustice.

"Fuck," Cleo said. "Fuck, fuck, fuck."

"Can I put that on the record?" Bowen leaned in closer. Though his typical fling was indeed at least a decade younger than Cleo, she wondered if she were misreading things: Bowen Babson appeared to be flirting with her, and she found this both intriguing and suspicious.

"You may not." Cleo frowned and returned to her table, grabbing her purse and blazer.

"Hey, can I text you?" Bowen called after her.

"What?" Cleo spun around, genuinely shocked that she was not misreading him at all. Or maybe he wanted to text her about something else; maybe Senator Jackman had run into Bowen and mentioned the renewed free housing bill? She found herself extremely unnerved.

"Can, like, can I get in touch. Maybe a drink?"

"I'm thirty-seven, Bowen." She paused. "And I have a fourteen-year-old."

"Why are you telling me your biography and assuming I don't already know this? Besides, I like kids," he said.

"But do you like teens?"

Bowen looked confused, like he didn't know the difference between a preciously adorable five-year-old and a surly fourteen-year-old who had to be reminded to both wear deodorant and brush his teeth.

Cleo waved her hands. "Look, call me, don't, whatever. I have to go."

"Something's happening here, between us, clearly."

Cleo didn't bother answering. Emily Godwin was her friend. *Her friend*, for God's sake, and she didn't have many of them. She needed to tell her. She needed to tell her immediately. This wasn't going to be another regret.

$\sim$

"You absolutely, unequivocally are *not* telling her," Gaby shouted, so loudly that Cleo turned down the volume on her car speaker.

Cleo hadn't exactly thought through the plan. She'd just peeled out of the valet stand, intent on landing on Emily's doorstep and confessing. She had never been a girl's girl—one only needed to look at the debacle with MaryAnne to intuit this—and for once, she understood both lucidly and emphatically that she could have Emily's back. *Obviously* she was going to drive over there *right now* and tell her.

"You do *not* get into her business," Gaby said, still shouting.

"But she should know!" Cleo clicked her blinker too hard, made a turn out of DC toward Alexandria.

"Maybe she already does. Or maybe she doesn't and doesn't want to. Or maybe she does but doesn't want to. Or maybe they have an agreement. Who fucking knows? This isn't yours to get in the middle of." Gaby had wound down a bit, her voice now hovering just above a low menace. "I'm sorry, Cleo." (Was she really sorry? Cleo wondered. *When are we going to stop using that phrase when we are so rarely truly and genuinely sorry?*) "But you can't just ring her doorbell and blow up her life. Affairs happen. We're adults."

Cleo rolled to a stop at the light. She knew as well as anyone that affairs happened. And yet even after MaryAnne's op-ed, she hadn't told Gaby about Nobells, about that second year in law school. She'd never told anyone, actually. Shame, embarrassment, regret—that's probably what kept her quiet. Culpability too. She'd gotten out of it with little fallout, which should have relieved her. She hadn't destroyed his family; she hadn't destroyed her reputation entirely, which even in law school was as a superstar.

She hiccupped, wondering how much she should share now, with her best friend, who wouldn't judge her. The light changed, and Cleo pressed the gas too quickly, her tires squealing below, as if she could out-race her past, as if it weren't right on her tail, breathing down her neck.

# ELEVEN

If Cleo had just chosen from her list at random as Gaby had suggested, this regret never would have seen the light of day. There was *MaryAnne shameful*, all done in the name of ambition, and then there was this sort of shameful, which, even thirteen years later, still made her sick with disgust. If she hadn't seen Jonathan at the Human Rights Campaign dinner, she would have kept it stuffed down, where she preferred it to be. But there it was, a blight smack in the middle of the pages of her yellow pad, folded in between *NEVER talk back to Owens* (a formidable torts professor who annihilated Cleo in an open argument on product liability) and *lay off bourbon*, which, all these years later, Cleo had little memory of the why behind it but also couldn't ever remember drinking bourbon as of late, so it must have been something. She had a vague recollection of an evening out with Gaby in law school and of . . . *dancing*? She shook her head. It couldn't be dancing. Cleo McDougal did not dance in public, which she realized, now, might soon change.

There it was, one word, on page four of the yellow pad, and she understood its meaning: *NOBELLS*. Thirteen years ago, she had double underlined it, as if not just a regret but a warning too.

Cleo leaned back in her office chair and exhaled, her whole body slumping. She really didn't want to face this reckoning, but the more she thought of poor Emily Godwin, who never failed to cover Cleo's orange-slice duty *and* picked up an extra rotisserie chicken from Costco, the more convinced she became that if she were serious about addressing these regrets—if she didn't just want to use it as a stunt to propel her toward Veronica Kaye's checkbook (a differentiation of which Cleo was not yet sure)—she had to face Alexander Nobells. MaryAnne Newman hadn't been wrong about everything in her op-ed.

As a second-year law student and young mother, Cleo had perfected the art of juggling fine china. Metaphorically, of course. She wouldn't have had time to learn to juggle, even if that had been in the course catalog. (If it had been a requirement in the course catalog, she would have found the time.) Professor Nobells, who ran the Advanced Evidence seminar, had a reputation for being jovial but tough, and Cleo liked him immediately. He wore speckled sweaters with cowl collars and black-framed glasses that were both retro and modern, and sometimes Cleo would watch him, rather than listen to him (an anomaly for her for sure), and think that if life had put him on another track, maybe if he had been less intelligent or less passionate, he could have been an L.L.Bean model. As it was, he was maybe forty or so and looked like a man who had grown into his looks.

He was a partner at the law firm (the best in the city) where she worked the summer between her first and second years and had a reputation for taking an interest in his students' lives, so Cleo thought nothing of it when he stopped her on her way out of his seminar to ask about Lucas. She hadn't publicly shared that she was a single mom, but Columbia was small enough that she assumed people knew, and like it or not, she was asked about it when she interviewed for the summer position. (She had repeatedly assured them that she had excellent childcare lined up, which she did. She also wondered if they'd ever ask a single dad such questions and, furthermore, knew that these questions weren't ethical, but she didn't want to jeopardize her job prospects by pointing this out.) She tried her best to show up to class in non-wrinkled, nonrumpled clothing and with her hair brushed and cheeks blushed, but she knew this wasn't a battle she always won. But what she lacked in style, she made up for in preparedness, which was all that mattered to her in the end. She'd thrived at her summer position at his firm and made Law Review her first year. She didn't give one shit if Lucas's oatmeal ran down the front of her T-shirt if she could out-debate, out-work, and out-gun her peers.

Professor Nobells, whom she had known only by name over the previous summer, seemed to take sympathy on her that day when he stopped her in the doorframe as she left Advanced Evidence. She knew he was married. He often spun his gold band around his finger as he paced on the dais, and sometimes he'd tell adorable anecdotes about his kids, who were a few years older than Lucas (who was just eighteen months or so—Cleo remembered he'd just learned to say two-word sentences when this all started happening).

Still, when he said, "Miss McDougal, do you have a moment," she turned back toward him, not really having a free moment because she was due to get Lucas from day care, and she didn't like to be late because she spent large swaths of her afternoon looking forward to sweeping him up in a bear hug. But she wasn't the type to brush off her professors, so she said, "Of course. Is everything OK?"

His eyes fanned into a smile. "I just wanted to check on you. I know you're pulling double duty. And your work is immaculate, so it's not that."

She waited for more, her breath in her throat. In law school, though she knew she was *good*, she still had a small but niggling perpetual worry that she wasn't as good as she thought. In Seattle, she'd been a superstar because her competition wasn't as stiff. At Northwestern, she'd made dean's list because her academics had been her sole focus. (Barring the very occasional night out and even more occasional drunken night out, which resulted in Lucas.) But at Columbia, she knew her attention wasn't what it should be. Of course it wasn't! She had a toddler, for God's sake, and because it was just the two of them, Lucas had to come first.

"Relax," Professor Nobells said. He reached out and squeezed her shoulder, letting his hand linger, then slide down her arm. "I'm not here to tell you you're doing anything wrong."

Cleo exhaled and wondered if she should find it strange that her professor was touching her, but she also noticed that she didn't mind. It came from a good place, a welcoming place, and Cleo, rather than recoiling, liked it. A decade later, at her desk in her home office, she considered that maybe she liked it just because she hadn't been touched by anything other than tiny hands in so long.

"Oh," she said. "I'm fine. Tired a lot. But fine." She almost told him about how Lucas was teething and she wasn't sleeping because it was easier just to sleep on his floor rather than trudge back and forth from her room, but she didn't want to look unprofessional. She didn't want to look like a harried mother, which she knew would relegate her to the dismissed pile. Motherhood, regardless of how fiercely she loved her son, wasn't going to handicap her. She had resolved this from the moment the plus sign appeared on her pregnancy test.

"Listen, why don't you come by for dinner on Thursday?" His hand was back by his side, and Cleo told herself that she must have misread the squeeze. It was a compassionate touch, nothing more. He was her *professor*, and he wore a *ring*, and he told cute stories about teaching his kids how to *ride bikes*! God, what was wrong with her?

"Oh!" Cleo said again. "Um, OK?"

"Can you get a babysitter? I don't want to put you out."

Cleo nodded enthusiastically. The benefit of going to law school with a child (perhaps the only benefit) was that there were babysitters aplenty all over the college campus. It was odd to be handing Lucas off to a girl only a few years younger, but having unprotected sex your senior year in college did that to you. So. She learned not to explain herself to the sitters whenever they showed up, and frankly most of them didn't give it a second thought. They were there for the money, not to consider all the ways Cleo's life would be different if she'd used a condom.

"I have a list of sitters," she said. "I'd love to."

"I always like to make myself available to standout students," he said. "Guide you through your time here. Send you on your way with counsel and recommendations."

"That would be amazing," Cleo replied. She couldn't believe it. She could, of course; she deserved it, her work merited it, but still, she couldn't believe it.

"Great, it's settled. My address is in the directory. Let's say six-ish?" Cleo nodded.

"I make an excellent chicken." He grinned. "I know, I know. I teach law by day and cook by night. A modern man if you've ever seen one."

"Your wife is very lucky," Cleo said, for no reason other than it sounded like she was.

༄

Cleo clicked her pen, circled *NOBELLS* on her yellow pad, then quickly typed his name into her Google bar. She was not the type to google-stalk her past. She barely knew how to work Facebook, for God's sake. She didn't know that Matty had gone on to become a Microsoft genius; she didn't know that MaryAnne had gone on to leave the majority of her lofty dreams unfulfilled. Gaby's campaign motto, "Only Forward," was an accurate representation of Cleo's general mind-set. She didn't see much use in skulking around her history, which was ironic, she realized, as she scanned the first page of internet hits on Alexander Nobells, given that her father encouraged her to put that history down for more permanent posterity.

Just as she clicked on a recent *Washington Post* article in which Nobells was quoted, Lucas opened her office door. He never bothered knocking, which she didn't really mind, but she also knew that if she repaid him with the same discourtesy, he'd stop speaking to her for at minimum several hours. (Until he needed something from her. Teens were unpredictable but predictable in their demands, at the very least.)

"I need you to sign these," he said, dropping a stack of forms on her desk.

"What are they for?"

He shrugged, like it was a nuisance for her to ask. "I don't know."

"School? Soccer? Can you give me a general sense?" Cleo reached for them, realizing it was probably just going to be more expeditious to figure it out herself.

"School," he said. "Permission slips for our retreat."

"You have a retreat?"

He rolled his eyes. "Yes. They said they sent the parents emails. The end-of-year retreat before graduation? In two weeks, when you go to Syria or . . . wherever?"

"Oh, OK, sure." Cleo had definitely not read those emails, nor had she even seen them. But she must have discussed this with Lucas at some point, since he knew about her Middle East trip with the Senate Intelligence Committee. She wasn't even sure why they were holding a graduation in the first place, since the students just rolled over to the high school within the same school, but she didn't want to sound like a grinch. "Hang on. I'll sign them now."

She grabbed a pen while Lucas scowled at the floor.

"Actually, can I ask you something?" She peered up at him, her handsome prodigy, dark hair, broody eyes. He grimaced in reply. "What do you think of Benjamin's dad?"

Lucas flopped his shoulders. "I don't know. He's a dad."

Something hung in the air between them, or maybe Cleo was imagining it. The emphasis on *dad*, like, did it really matter if he was a great human being, a hero of some sort? He was a male and he had spawned Benjamin and at least Benjamin was lucky enough to have one. She held her breath, wondering if they were going to get into it again.

Then she pressed on. "Is he nice, though? Home a lot?"

"God, how would I know?"

"Because you spend most of your free time there?" Cleo signed his forms distractedly. She realized she had put her signature where she was supposed to print her name and vice versa. She drew two haphazard arrows, indicating that they should be switched, and assumed this was good enough. If any of her staffers had turned in such an error-riddled form, she'd have insisted that it be redone. Cleo exhaled, debating asking Lucas for a new form—she didn't like making mistakes, much less stupid ones. She worried that the administrative staff at school would judge her, find her sloppy. Which she never used to be until MaryAnne Newman showed up in her life again. Now she felt like she was making all sorts of mistakes—maybe *mistakes* was too strong; *missteps* felt better, but she didn't like making those either. She thought of the folded newspaper in her bag with a giant ad about her presidential fitness. *Goddamn you, MaryAnne Newman!*

Lucas was speaking again. "I don't know, Mom, OK? He's . . . fine. I don't, like, talk to him a lot."

"Is he nice to Emily?"

Lucas grabbed the forms, headed back toward his bedroom. "Hey, Mom, not everything has to be turned into some feminist manifesto."

Cleo jumped to her feet. "What does that mean?"

She thought of the two girls he might be juggling—Marley and Esme—and realized she really, really needed to sit him down and make him choose, not just dance around it as she had the other night. She needed to explain why he was being a dick and what a terrible precedent this set. Not just for him but for those girls too. Making them feel as if it were one or the other, making them wonder if they needed to be something more than they were for him, making them morph themselves into something they weren't.

Or maybe teen girls these days would just shove a middle finger in his face and recognize that he was the problem, not them. That actually seemed more like it.

Lucas stopped, turned back. "Sorry, that came out harsher than I meant it to. I just meant that not all men are the enemy. And I doubt Ben's dad is." He swiped his hair from his face and disappeared into his room for what would be the rest of the night. Like it was that simple. Men and women. How people make you believe that what you see is who they are.

Cleo slunk back into her chair. *Of course all men aren't the enemy!* She noticed her search results still in her tab. Alexander Nobells. *But sometimes, it's just a fact that they are.*

Cleo had arrived at Professor Nobells's apartment on the Upper West Side with a bottle of wine that she hoped was good. No one had really taught her how to buy wine—her parents were dead by the time she realized that she should know about it, and her sister was across the country now, working and therapizing and doing a good job being an adult (surprising), and Cleo wasn't going to bother her to ask about vintages and grapes, especially after she'd screamed at her when she came to help just after Lucas's birth. Besides, Cleo was busy raising a baby on her own, and thus the long and the short of it was that she hadn't been drinking much wine anyway.

But the nice man at the wine store recommended this Italian merlot, and though she wasn't a fan of trusting people without doing her own research, she had to acknowledge that this time, she simply was not an expert. Nor could she become one between the time Nobells invited her and now. So she swiped her credit card and hoped for the best. She didn't love wine or any alcohol to begin with. It made her lightheaded too quickly and sometimes it flared up her rosacea, though that was unpredictable at best. If Cleo liked anything in life, it was to be in control, so whether it be wine or a skin condition, she did whatever she could to mitigate unpredictability. (The irony of her unplanned pregnancy was not lost on her. Maybe a therapist would tell her that part of her skipped the condom intentionally, so she had something, someone to call her own. Cleo wasn't sure. Georgie probably had some thoughts too, but Cleo wasn't interested in asking.)

His building was fancier than she expected, though she didn't know why. Maybe it was his low-key professor vibe, which quelled his smarmier, flashier law-partner vibe. The doorman called up and announced her; then she was shown the elevator, and then Professor Nobells was opening the door to his rambling three-bedroom. He had books stacked upon books and a bunch of oil paintings that looked expensive. Cleo hadn't taken Art History at Northwestern, but these paintings, in gilded frames and highlighted with overhead lights, reeked of wealth, and Cleo felt a little bit over her head. After retiring from the ballet, Cleo's mom had painted for the love of it, to keep that part of her alive; though she had a following in Seattle, it wasn't as if her works were commissioned by MoMA, and Cleo had never paid close enough attention to differentiate what set good art apart from great art. Georgie had taken most of her mom's paintings when she, Cleo, and their grandmother packed up the house; Cleo had a few in a closet wrapped in Bubble Wrap.

"I brought wine," she said, and she was already embarrassed. This wasn't a date, for God's sake! He was her teacher, and he was married with two children a little bit older than Lucas! "I didn't know if you and your wife drink red, but here you are."

The apartment smelled like butter and chicken and rosemary, and though Cleo didn't wish for a man to cook for her in perpetuity, she was glad that for tonight, one had. She wondered what his wife was like, if she was as beautiful as he was, if she was as intelligent. She thought, despite her mildly palpable crush on Professor Nobells, that she could learn from both of them. How to negotiate a mortgage on a three-bedroom on the Upper West Side, how to cook a perfect chicken, how to raise kids in a world where it seemed like, soon enough, big tech would be able to implant chips in their brains.

Nobells ushered her into the kitchen, his hand on the small of her back.

"Oh, my wife, Amy, she's away with the kids. Florida." He pulled an apron over his head in one swift motion. "I'm sorry. Maybe I should have told you when I proposed this?"

Cleo felt blood rise to her cheeks, and she worried that he could see straight through her naivete. That she had quickly debated that this might be romantic, dismissed the idea as preposterous, only to discover that maybe it was. She wasn't sure how she felt about that: it was one thing to stare at your professor from the third row while he lectured. It was another to be invited into his home under the guise of wise counsel and realize that he actually wanted to woo you.

Cleo reminded herself that he was married. And she wasn't reckless. But he had gripped her shoulder outside of class and run his hand down her arm and palmed the small of her back just a minute ago, which sent an electric pulse up her spine.

Nobells uncorked the wine and reached for two crystal wineglasses he had at the ready. He poured them generous fills and then raised his glass, so Cleo followed, her head still spinning, her brain trying to keep up, her heart racing so quickly that it felt like it might explode inside her chest cavity. She wondered if he would say something suggestive, something even mildly romantic. She hoped not, not because she didn't every once in a while fantasize about him kissing her from her seat in the third row, but because she knew this wasn't how she wanted to be seen. Cleo McDougal was a serious person, a serious student, and she wanted to be treated as such. (She thought. Mostly.)

"To hoping my chicken is as good as I promised." He grinned.

And she grinned too. "I can drink to that."

They clinked their glasses, and then they did.

∽

It wasn't until years later, when Cleo had extricated herself from the messiness of the affair, that she had seen it for what it was. She had written it on her list, yes, but that was just the regret. The pain, the secrets, the shame, all of it. They had been careful. Meticulous. Because it was in both of their natures. Amy hadn't ever caught them, and if she suspected anything, Cleo never heard.

Back then, she had blamed herself as much as she had blamed him. She could have left that night. She could have turned him down. She hadn't gone there seeking anything physical, but she hadn't gotten up and left when his motives became clear.

Even now, she understood that there was still plenty of blame to go around. She wasn't one to shirk that. Never had been. But years later, her perspective had shifted. That it was never an equal decision, that he was her professor, that he was the one with the power and the advice and the recommendations, and though, yes, she was a consenting adult, what they both did was wrong. But what he did was more wrong. He knew she wanted a full-time position at his firm; he knew her grades were in his hands; he knew that by initiating the affair, he left Cleo with few good options. To spurn him in that moment in his kitchen meant she risked all of the above; to spurn him down the line meant the same. Cleo knew, in hindsight, that she probably should never have gone there in the first place, to that dinner, eaten his chicken, toasted with her wine. But like so many regrets, once you'd set those actions in motion, they felt impossible to undo.

Certainly back then, Nobells, once it started, seemed impossible to undo. And even now too.

Cleo stood and clasped her hands together, stretching her shoulders and rolling her neck. She had lost track of time, and her whole body, not just her head, ached with a dull throb. She reached into her bag, pulled out the *Seattle Post-Intelligencer*, and splayed it on her desk.

MaryAnne's ad had been an echo of her op-ed. A large-font headline about Cleo's marred character, some lines about her ethics and her judgment and how she was a *cheater*. How *cheaters* shouldn't run our government, how *cheaters* shouldn't be our collective moral voice. (Cleo knew that MaryAnne walked it right up to the slander line, probably consulted with lawyers, probably could back it up with facts. MaryAnne was smart enough not to risk a lawsuit, and so was the *Seattle Post-Intelligencer*.) Cleo ran her fingers over all the *cheaters*, then pressed her palms against the paper, its grit chalky on her fingertips.

The plan came together in her mind quickly, and she moved ahead, without consulting Gaby, without second-guessing herself. These were usually her best decisions—the ones that came from her gut. She knew this next step, hell, this next regret—undoing what she thought to be impossible—had to be big, to be a real reckoning, and she knew exactly the person who could help her.

She sat in her chair and cracked her knuckles. Grabbed her phone.

Cleo: Going to New York this weekend for something kind of top secret. Want to tag along? No questions until I say so.

He wrote her back within seconds.

Bowen: Mysterious. I'm in.

# TWELVE

Cleo had been set to return to New York for the weekend for a few events with her constituents; thus it wasn't even all that hard to slip away from Gaby, who was distracted by Oliver Patel's arrival. He was landing Thursday night, so though she and Cleo and Cleo's five legislative assistants were ostensibly set to prep for a meeting with Senator Jackman on the free housing deal, Gaby left the office early to "beautify," and Cleo could make her New York plan in peace.

"This whole thing," Gaby had said earlier that morning, swooping her hand from the top of her head to as far as it could drop. "I'm cleaning up this whole thing."

Arianna happened to be in Cleo's office at the time and piped in unprompted.

"Natural is back, by the way," she said, and Cleo and Gaby both tilted their heads and stared. Arianna's cheeks flushed. "I'm sorry? Should I not have said that? Oh God, oh God, I'm sorry! You're a senator. I mentioned pubic hair in front of a senator."

"Well, for one," Gaby replied, "you didn't mention pubic hair until now. But for two, OK, thank you. Noted."

"We're tired of putting our bodies through pain for men," Arianna said, and for the first time, Cleo thought she had potential. Not because she wasn't interested in having hot wax near her vagina (because when you thought about it, Arianna was much saner than Gaby), but rather because it was a strident notion that shouldn't have been strident at all: *that these things we do for beauty cause us pain, and who ever said that pain should be a requirement?*

"I like that." Cleo nodded. "I like the point your generation is making." She herself had recently been considering Botox, not for a man but because youthfulness mattered to public perception. She gazed at Arianna for a beat. Actually, maybe that was for men too. Men had for so long dictated what was and wasn't beautiful, what was and wasn't youthful, and let it not be forgotten that youthfulness was more coveted than age. She resolved right then, with Arianna sorting through her files and Gaby rethinking her bikini wax, to skip the Botox. Unless, of course, it was for *her*. How she could even determine that, though, was unclear. The notions of beauty and power were all very messy. She thought of Veronica Kaye. Maybe she should ask her. She seemed like she might have the answers.

"I will think about all of this during my appointments," Gaby said. "Extremely illuminating."

Arianna seemed a little embarrassed but for once not apologetic.

"These are our bodies." Arianna shrugged. "Men should be grateful to be seeing them at all."

She finished with the files and left, and both Cleo and Gaby made "well that was a surprise" faces at each other, their eyebrows reaching toward the top of their foreheads, their chins pressing toward their necks.

"Kids these days," Gaby said, shaking her head.

"Did *not* see that coming," Cleo replied.

Cleo didn't know whether they were referring to Arianna's bravado or the newest trends in bikini waxing, but it didn't really matter either way.

Bowen met Cleo at Union Station after lunch on Friday. Cleo usually tried to bring Lucas back for her trips to New York, but he didn't have friends there anymore, and he was old enough to launch genuine gripes about why he didn't want to spend his weekend holed up at their apartment while she held town halls or did ribbon cuttings or 5ks for various cancers. When he was littler, though he required more from her, he was also easier in some respects. He did what she said; he was simply an extension of her, and questions weren't asked or argued in the same way that they were now. He would whine, sure, but he could be easily bribed, and besides, he didn't really know any other way. It was them, the two of them, in it together, and he did what she did, peas in a pod.

Now, at fourteen, he would still come along from time to time, but he preferred to stay with friends in DC, or when she was really, really hard up, Gaby would babysit. ("Don't call it babysitting," she snapped once. "I do not babysit. This is me pitching in to get you back to your constituents.") But this weekend, Emily Godwin (anointed saint) had been happy to have him. The boys had soccer practice for half the time anyway—"It's easier this way," she'd said. "Then Benjamin doesn't have to talk to us at all. He's much more delightful when that's the case."

Cleo had laughed and wished that Lucas had someone else to talk to besides her. Well, and Benjamin. But the two of them, mother and son, their little unit, she could see how it might be getting claustrophobic for him. Maybe that's why he had two girlfriends, she reasoned: more options. More outlets. Then she chastised herself for such a cavalier thought. *Gross,* she told herself. *You're part of the problem. Women aren't options.*

These weekend arrangements had been made before Cleo had caught Jonathan Godwin in his act of betrayal, which was a bit of a relief—Cleo didn't know if she could call Emily and ask for a favor while keeping such a secret from her. Though Cleo was indeed excellent with secrets—she sat on the Senate Intelligence Committee, after all—this one was different; this one was personal, and Cleo didn't have it in her to lie to one of her few friends.

So it was just the two of them—Bowen and Cleo—for the train ride up to Manhattan. Cleo had emailed the staffer set to travel with her—she nearly always went with at least one minder—and gave her the weekend off. This was a semipersonal trip, and the last thing she wanted was a lackey. Bowen was dressed down, and Cleo found she liked it. Jeans, a crisp light-green button-down, trendy navy sneakers. She was suddenly aware of how much she would like to sleep with him. This was not a feeling she welcomed or found particularly useful. He was here because she needed his help. She willed this notion out of her mind. It proved harder than she thought.

Bowen bought them both Starbucks and himself a giant scone; then they headed to the tracks and waited for the train to blow by. He asked no questions—she didn't even know where he was staying in New York—though she imagined he had a penthouse in Tribeca that was wall-to-ceiling glass windows. He seemed, she thought, genuinely amused that she had texted him but not condescending or patronizing about it at all. Amused in a kindhearted way.

They settled into their seats and finally, as the train's engines masked the sounds of their conversation, he said: "OK, Cleo, you have my attention. I'm headed all the way to New York for you. I assume this is not a whirlwind date." He paused. "To be clear, if it is, that's entirely fine with me too." He read the look on her face, which she imagined was a bit like a schoolmarm's. "All righty," he continued. "Definitely not a date. So, then . . . what?" He furrowed his brow. "Are you OK?"

"I want you to cover a story. About me," she said quietly, and she didn't know if he could hear her over the rattle of the train. "Not just about me. About something I did." She inhaled, stopped. Tried to start over. This wasn't coming out correctly. "A long time ago, at law school, I made a bad decision—I mean, you probably read about it, sort of the half-truth about it, in that op-ed. And until recently, I blamed myself.

But I think what I'm realizing is that I was young and he . . . wasn't. And . . . maybe something should be done about that now."

Bowen's eyes were wide but compassionate. He nodded.

"I'm not very good at . . . ," Cleo started, then stopped again. "Well, I'm really terribly shitty at asking for help. But I thought I could trust you. You're smart. And you'd tell me if this were a bad idea—"

He cut her off. "It's probably a bad idea."

Cleo glared at him.

"Why are you asking me this instead of Gaby? Isn't she your other half?" he asked.

"Because she'd talk me out of it."

"And you don't want me to?" Bowen asked. It was a fair question, and Cleo liked him precisely because his questions always were.

"I think it's the right thing to do," she said finally. She thought of Arianna, of all the other girls who might have endured the same, from Nobells, from men like Nobells. She was in a position of power now, and she'd tried—really—to spur change with that position. But if she couldn't confront the abuses of power in her own past, how could she expect other women to do the same?

"The right thing to do is often not the most prudent thing to do," Bowen cautioned.

The train was picking up speed now, flying out of the DC corridor and headed toward Columbia, headed toward her past.

"I know." She met his eyes. "That's why I asked you along. To get it down for the record. So once I realize how stupid this is—because Senator McDougal does not do stupid things—you can remind me that it was the right thing to do regardless."

⚬

Cleo kept a small apartment on the higher streets of the Upper West Side. When she bought it in law school, the neighborhood had been dicey at best, but over the past decade it had gentrified, and now her little two-bedroom was worth four times what she paid. Maybe five. She knew she was privileged: to have the money to purchase a small apartment in a so-so building in Manhattan at twenty-four. But after her parents died and her grandmother sold her childhood home and the life insurance came in, the money had been split with Georgie, then placed in a trust and released to her upon graduation from Northwestern, where she accepted her diploma with only her sister in the audience.

(Georgie had insisted on flying in, though Cleo also insisted that she needn't.

"It's just a ceremony," Cleo had said.

"I'm coming," Georgie had replied.

She had young twins at the time, and had Cleo chosen to confide her terror over being newly pregnant, surely Georgie would have understood. But Cleo didn't breathe a word about it to her. She already felt out of sorts that Georgie, who had never been particularly reliable, was now steadfastly reliable and showing up to offer her support in lieu of their parents. Looking back on it, Cleo wondered if she might have made different choices with Nobells if she'd had anyone else she trusted or felt that she could rely on. So maybe she should have told Georgie about the pregnancy back then, not when she was eight months along. Maybe depending on one person leads to depending on other people, and then you don't wind up making self-defeating decisions because you are lonely. *Regret.*)

Now, in the hallway of her apartment, she reached for the keys in her bag, digging past a half-eaten chocolate bar, a few Veronica Kaye lipsticks, a bunch of pens that worked only on occasion, and dental floss, and remembered how Nobells, a few months into the affair, had been the one to push her toward it—home ownership, that she wouldn't regret it. He hadn't been wrong. She didn't begrudge him that. It gave her roots and made her feel a little more grounded once she moved in with Lucas, whose room she painted a bright royal blue. He was almost two by then, and so she read magazine articles that said it was time for a big-boy bed, and she took him to Pottery Barn Kids and bought him the one that looked like a race car. He couldn't believe it. That he got to sleep in a race car! And though Cleo so rarely gave herself over to pure joy, she remembered thinking that she'd found it, right there in Pottery Barn Kids, and she had Alexander Nobells to thank for it.

It wasn't difficult to see why she had been so ingratiated to him. He taught her things, he believed in her, he made her think that she was more special with him than without him. So many years later, Cleo hated this last thing the most: that she could allow a man to convince her that somehow she was more valuable, more coveted, more exceptional because he had chosen her. Also intertwined with this approval was, of course, the fact that he held her future at his firm in his hands. Cleo forgot that a lot of the time when she was with him. She didn't know how often he forgot it, or if he forgot it at all.

The apartment smelled of lemony 409 cleaning solution, which pleased Cleo. She paid an older woman, Dora, to clean it every Thursday, even when she wasn't coming into town. But she knew Dora needed the paycheck, and she'd been with her (legally, on the books) since Cleo was in her third year of law school. Back then, Dora had pitched in with an extra set of hands when Lucas was wild or filthy or cranky or hungry—even with the reliable day care, Cleo sometimes felt like she was drowning, and now, when Cleo could repay her, literally and with gratitude, she did. They weren't friends, rather something akin to friendly business associates, and this level of relationship suited Cleo perfectly.

Cleo hadn't expected Bowen to accompany her back to her apartment, but he insisted.

"So . . . this is my place," she said, dropping her keys in a little yellow glass bowl that sat on her foyer console table, just as it had once sat in her childhood home. Her grandmother had given some of her parents' furnishings to Georgie, who was twenty-seven and in a real home after their accident, and sold most of the rest. But a few trinkets, like vases and their china and picture frames and, of course, most of her mother's own paintings, she stored away for when Cleo would want them. When her grandmother died, Cleo kept paying for the storage space until she was finally a grown-up of her own. Then, when she put the down payment on this apartment, she paid the storage facility a fee, and they shipped her the boxes via freight.

Cleo glanced at Bowen, a little insecure, a little off her game with him in her space. She didn't entertain often, well, ever, and she rarely brought men to the apartment. Having him here felt invasive, even though she'd invited him. She hadn't completely thought it through— that he'd trail her back here, that she'd feel as if she were jumping out of her skin.

"Um, I guess I have a guest room if you're staying?" she asked, praying quietly that *please please please*, he wasn't staying. "It's my son's. So the sheets have soccer balls on them."

"Cleo, I'm not sleeping over." Bowen laughed easily. "Relax."

Cleo allowed herself a tiny exhale and padded to the small kitchen, which she'd redone a few years ago. "Good. I just want to be sure that this is professional." She opened up the fridge, found a Diet Coke, offered him one.

"With due respect, Senator, if I wanted something personal, I'd be back in DC right now. Getting personal."

Cleo raised her eyebrows. "Your reputation precedes you."

He bounced his shoulders, put a playful lilt in his voice. "Only good things, I hope . . ."

Cleo held up her free hand, stopping him from taking it any further. He was attractive, *yes*. More than attractive, *fine*. But she'd told him on the train why she'd asked him along. She'd explained the mission and the pain behind it, and though Cleo McDougal never really found much use for flirting, she certainly did not find a use for it now. *Now* was a time to stay focused.

"Please, can we just get through tomorrow and keep this . . ." Cleo drifted off, trying to find the right words. "Can we just . . . I'm a senator. You're a reporter. That's it."

"But I did ask you to drinks last week," he said, and she glared at him. "Fine," he continued, "but I'm still not sure I get what we're doing here. Listen, I *do* get Me Too. Time's Up. I support it. I'm here for it. My sisters are constantly texting me articles they want me to cover on the show. Knit me a pink hat, and I'll wear it and march with you."

"Knit your own damn hat," Cleo said. "Also, how on earth would I know how to knit? Do I look like someone who has time to take up knitting?"

"Point taken," Bowen acknowledged. "But . . . this isn't just about that. It's about something else too. And the reporter in me wants to know why."

Cleo was tired and didn't want to rehash what she'd shared on the train, which had been about as honest as she could reasonably expect herself to be while also not being completely honest. So she'd told him the stuff about Nobells—about the shame she had repressed over the affair (MaryAnne did get that right) and about the power he held over her when it ended. He had listened as thoughtfully as he'd listen to one of the guests on his show, interrupting only to ask imperative questions, and in this way he reminded her of Matty: a deeper thinker than the surface would suggest. And just as she had reevaluated Matty back in the bar in Seattle, she had found herself reconsidering Bowen as the train whipped through the northeast landscape to New York.

Still, though, now was not the time to consider even a hint of that attraction. Over the years, Cleo had become an expert in talking herself out of romantic connections—thus, her dating life almost never went past three dinners and/or occasionally fooling around. Romance was messy and unnecessary, and she wasn't looking for a husband or another child and certainly not gossip headlines, so she compartmental-ized romance the way she would, say, buy fresh flowers. They'd be nice to have, but no one ever couldn't get by without them. She relegated making out with Bowen to buying flowers. That was that.

"Seriously, Cleo, why are you doing this?" Bowen asked again.

She sipped her Diet Coke and thought of all those nights at Pagliacci's with MaryAnne, draining their cups and going for refills. Bowen wanted to know *why*, and she wasn't even sure herself. Why had she done a million things in her life? She just pointed herself north and went, especially after her parents died—following the ambition in her gut. But this time it wasn't about that. This time it felt like she was running counter to that ambition. This time it felt personal. *Why?* Because she had caught Jonathan Godwin leaving the HRC dinner with a young replacement for Emily? That was too easy. Maybe it was because once MaryAnne aired the truth, Cleo couldn't repress her shame any longer. She couldn't tout herself as a role model for Arianna and her generation while also having wronged Nobells's wife *and* having been a pawn in his game. Maybe it was time to address the power imbalance that ran top to bottom through not just the legal profession but educational systems too, and a million other systems beyond that. Or maybe it was simpler than all that: maybe it was just that Gaby, though she would be angry to know Cleo was running this show without her right now, was pushing her to face her regrets in order to launch a presidential bid, and Nobells simply couldn't be ignored.

She could have chosen about a hundred other regrets from her list, though, and she hadn't. And she'd come this far—literally about two hundred miles—to do it. But why now? Why this? Cleo wasn't emotionally intelligent enough to clarify the heart of the *why* for Bowen. It wasn't that she didn't want to; it was that she couldn't.

She shook her head as he watched her. She wasn't about to tell him about her list. That was too far, too much, like stripping herself naked in front of him and pointing out all her flaws, asking him to circle them with a Sharpie.

Instead, she said, because this was also true, "Maybe it's just time."

She raised her shoulders, then lowered them, and though she understood he wanted more from her, he was also keen enough to accept that, for now, this was the most she had to offer.

∽

Though Cleo expected Bowen to have fancy plans—a nightclub or, at the very least, dinner at the Soho House—he was happy, eager, almost, to stick around the apartment, loitering as if there were nowhere else he'd rather be. He hunched over, peered at pictures that lined her bookshelves—mostly of Lucas over the years, a few of her parents too. Cleo tried to relax and be, well, normal, that he was here, in her space, but she was not so easily adaptable. She found herself skulking into opposite corners and making excuses to straighten up Lucas's room or refill the bottomless glass of Diet Coke in the kitchen.

She hadn't heard from Gaby all afternoon, so Cleo assumed that she was knee-deep with Oliver Patel, and though Cleo liked Gaby's input and feedback on her working weekends, she was relieved to have fallen off her radar. Arianna had uploaded her schedule to her phone, and her staff who worked out of Manhattan had touched base, ready for the few events and the meet and greets that she had with her voters. Cleo didn't always head to New York City on her working weekends. Sometimes it was Buffalo or Schenectady or Albany or even the North Fork. Her constituents were varied and diverse, and ironically, though Cleo was a loner who despised small talk, she truly loved making the time to meet with them. Part of it was that they had chosen *her*, which, anyone with any sort of power can tell you, is a little bit intoxicating, but part of it was that they had chosen *her* to make a difference in their lives. She might be the type of woman who would sabotage her best friend's hopes for an internship, but she was also the type of woman who could still carry around hope for change. *Only Forward!* Those two things weren't incompatible, even if they seemed like they should be.

Cleo's stomach growled, and she palmed her abdomen with embarrassment when Bowen jolted upright from a photograph he was admiring of her in London with Lucas. He'd heard it from across the living room.

"Sorry," she said. (Why did she just apologize for being hungry? For her intestines shifting? Like she had any control over that!) "I haven't eaten anything since DC."

"I offered you my scone."

"Ever the gentleman." Cleo looped her right hand in two circles in front of her like she was a queen taking a bow, then realized she had no idea why she was doing this and stopped.

"Where can we go to get something to eat around here?"

"You don't have plans tonight?" Cleo asked in a tone that probably betrayed her discomfort.

"Why would I have plans tonight? I came to the city at your request."

"Right, but, um, I mean, we don't have to spend twenty-four hours t-together." Cleo found herself stuttering, and she did not like finding herself stuttering one bit. She also was aware that she would like to shower, that the grit from the train and the taxi and the few blocks they'd walked here when the taxi was at a standstill left her hair matted, her underarms a little damp. It wasn't that she wanted to look her best for Bowen, but it wasn't that she didn't either.

"God, Cleo, *relax*." Bowen grinned. "I'm staying at my sister's tonight. I did make those arrangements."

"I figured you had a penthouse in Tribeca made of glass." Her gut rumbled again, and she sat on the couch, as if repositioning herself would quiet her insides.

"Why would I have a penthouse made of glass?"

"Everything about you makes me think that you'd have a penthouse made of glass." She hunched over an inch, trying to squelch any chance of her intestinal tract shifting. She gestured toward him. "Like, everything about you. Top to bottom."

"I thought you were smarter than judging a book by its cover," he said. He picked up the photograph from London, examined it, rested it back down.

"Are you the book or are you the cover?" Cleo said.

Bowen laughed riotously, as if he didn't give two shits if he were the butt of her joke.

He didn't, Cleo knew, and she hated that she found this appealing.

# THIRTEEN

It was eighty-five degrees the next morning, and Cleo had a fun run in Central Park with her local staff and about five hundred people who each raised money for GreenUpNow!, a nonprofit dedicated to refurbishing downtrodden urban areas in the state that sorely lacked both funding and grass. She shook a lot of hands, took a lot of pictures, and tried not to make too many promises unless she was sure she could follow through. This was one way that Cleo stayed in the good graces of voters—she never lied to them, never told them things they wanted to hear just to gain their votes. Almost inevitably when you glossed over difficult truths, it meant that you got their votes but eventually lost their trust, and that was not a viable long-term plan. It was part of the reason she had initially spurned Senator Jackman's free housing proposal: she'd told her constituents she wouldn't give away something for free, even while knowing that many of them didn't understand that by lifting up some members of their community, they lifted up the community as a whole. But still. She had promised, and she kept her word. Until last week, when she realized that part of her job was convincing her constituents that an unpopular proposal was still the right proposal. That's why they'd elected her. Not just to be a mirror to their own reflections.

She was enjoying a free Clif bar (breakfast) and an orange at the finish line when two young women approached. She figured that they would press her on her broader GreenUpNow! plans—what could she promise them about a hope for a better tomorrow? She was running through her standard lines, but they caught her off guard.

"Hi," one girl said. Cleo didn't know if they were even old enough to vote. She thought they looked older than Lucas but maybe not by much. *My God,* she thought. *Is this what Marley Jacobson looks like now? With actual breasts and legs like a gazelle's and eyes wide enough for Lucas to convince himself that he's in love?* No wonder he was smitten with more than one girl. She had realized, obviously, that her son was smack in the middle of puberty, but seeing young women so close in age to him and seeing them as, well, adults—those were two separate realizations.

"Hi," the other girl said.

"We're best friends," they said together.

"Hi!" Cleo said, pushing her smile as wide as it could go.

"Do you have any advice for us if, like, we want to be successful together, as a team?" the first one said.

"Oh." Cleo furrowed her brow. "In politics?"

Girl One shook her head, her ponytail swaying behind her. "No." She looked at the other one. "Well, maybe?"

Her friend said: "We saw your old friend's article, and, um, we didn't want to end up like you guys. We're, like, best friends forever."

In just a flip of a second, Cleo's smile fell, and she worried that she might throw up. It had been only a 5k, so she knew it wasn't from that. The New York air was too humid for May, and her tank top was sticking to her stomach, but it wasn't that either. She looked from Friend One to Friend Two, their eyes wide, their words said with only openhearted generosity.

"You're still in high school?" Cleo asked finally. Both girls nodded.

"Sophomores," they said together. Cleo told herself that Lucas wasn't even yet a freshman. He couldn't yet be in this deep with breasts and long legs and beguiling eyes.

Then one added, "We think women can run the world. And you're doing it. But . . ." She waved a hand, as if that ended her sentence.

"But we don't want to do it being mean girls," said the other one.

Cleo swallowed, found she couldn't find her tongue. Why was it so hot out in May? Was this global warming? Why was she sweating more after the run than while she was actually running? She glanced around for members of her staff, but she'd already told them that once the photo ops were over, they should head home. They were reconvening tomorrow for bagels and lox at a Westchester synagogue, then moving on to muffins and coffee at a nearby church. *Mean girl? Really?* She'd never once, ever, ever considered herself a *mean* girl. Yes, obviously, what she had done to MaryAnne was *unkind*, but that didn't rise to the level of those horror stories she sometimes heard from other moms on the sidelines of Lucas's games. Those mean girls did all sorts of untoward things: texting ugly photos of their friends, spreading rumors about their rivals, acting sweet but ultimately pushing the knife into someone's back just a little deeper. She was ambitious, but she wasn't ruthless. She was cutthroat, but she'd never stab you in the back.

She found her breath, steadying herself. One of the girls offered her a water.

"Here," she said. "Are you, um, OK?"

Maybe she had been all those things, though. In the pursuit of more, more, more, maybe she *had* been exactly the type to slice MaryAnne right through the trapezius, even if she had done it simply to get a leg up, to propel herself out of Seattle and away from her grief and on to something better. Cleo felt a little dizzy and closed her eyes, pointed her face toward the sky until it passed. *Jesus.* She'd justified her behaviors toward MaryAnne for so many years that she hadn't considered them objectively: that after her parents died and maybe before that too—with MaryAnne's leg up from her own parents' connections and with Cleo's just a bit more promising work ethic and acumen, she had believed she deserved the success, that she was the worthier one, so she stripped those opportunities from her best friend.

That wasn't deserving at all.

"What I would tell you," Cleo said finally, once she righted herself and looked from one set of wide eyes to the other, "is that . . . well, the truth is that I'm not great at friends. Obviously. I wish I had better advice, but being an adult sometimes means that you make choices. And I made mine. And then you live with the consequences, which sometimes work in your favor and sometimes, well, they do not." She tried to smile, but she worried she just looked nauseated.

"That's not very reassuring," the first girl said.

"We've been told we can have it all," the second one echoed. "You're telling us that we can't?"

"I'm telling you that sometimes you find yourself at a crossroads, and maybe you guys will be best friends forever, and I hope that you will." She smiled then, genuinely. She wished that so very much for these girls who had not yet faced what the world would throw at them, how it would ask them to work harder, fight better, climb faster than it would ask of any man. "But what I'm also telling you is that sometimes you have to make choices, and sometimes this means that you'll choose . . . you." Cleo thought of *Beverly Hills, 90210*, which she and MaryAnne had considered appointment television, and that episode where Kelly Taylor chooses herself. She hadn't meant to quote Kelly Taylor, but maybe she should rewatch (when would she have time to rewatch?) and see if Kelly Taylor wasn't a bit of a feminist.

"You?" one of the friends asked.

"You," Cleo answered, pointing a finger at her. Would it have been so hard if Cleo had chosen *them*? She and MaryAnne together?

"OK," one girl said. "Well, thanks."

Cleo didn't want to leave it on a down note. She hadn't meant to discourage them. "Would you like to take a photo?"

They each shook their head, turned their back, walked away.

Bowen met her on the corner outside her apartment, just in front of the Korean deli, which had been there since she bought the place and had saved her more than a few times when her pantry and refrigerator were empty and she had a toddler to feed.

She had showered since the fun run and stood in front of her mirror for too long, trying to figure out what to wear. She knew that, especially for women, clothes told your story before you even opened your mouth, and she had a story to tell today. Also, she wanted to look nice for Bowen, even if she pretended that she didn't, but she wanted to look *amazing* for Nobells. She might be a buttoned-up senator, but drop-dead gorgeous still felt like its own sort of revenge.

She settled on the same violet blouse she'd worn to meet Matty in Seattle, which reminded her of MaryAnne, which reminded her of those sophomore girls from the park. She tugged on a pair of skinny jeans that she already knew she'd regret with today's humidity, then reached for her phone and pulled up Facebook. Clicked on MaryAnne's page. The comment thread to her op-ed had grown even longer, what with her ad having run a few days past. Cleo had told Gaby to stop giving her updates on the YouTube ratio because she didn't need the approval of strangers. (Theoretically she did, if she were to run for president, but for now, no, no, she did not.) But the people she knew . . . well, she was learning that after thirty-seven years, maybe she did actually care about their opinions.

With Oliver jetting back east to his rendezvous with Gaby, she had one fewer defender in the comments. Instead, what she read was a frenzy, a pile-on, an online mob scene that she was familiar with because anytime she was featured in a big news piece, Gaby reminded her not to read the comments. *Never read the comments.* And here she was, reading them all. Cleo chastised herself: before MaryAnne blew this up, she'd never, ever have read the comments!

Susan Harris, Maureen Allen, and Beth Shin were still particularly worked up. They were using words like *angry* and *bitchy* and *too tough for her own good*. It was amazing, Cleo thought, her thumb scrolling downward through the comments, how society had done this—conditioned women to eat their own likenesses so they didn't realize that if they banded together, they'd be unstoppable. Cleo's thumb hovered as it struck her: she had done exactly the same thing to MaryAnne.

"Shit," she said aloud. "Just fucking shit." As an adult, and especially in Congress, Cleo had been careful never to alienate another female congresswoman (there still weren't that many of them) and truly didn't see women as competition. But maybe that lesson was learned only after she'd stepped on a few shoulders (and a few aspirations) to ascend the ladder to her current position. "Shit," she said again.

She exited out of MaryAnne's page and clicked over to Matty's. He'd taken his twenty-seven-year-old girlfriend to Snoqualmie Falls for the weekend. There were lots of pictures of them hiking and eating hearty meals with jams and bacons and honeys. This made her a little sad—for him because it seemed like maybe he could use someone more complicated, and also for her, Cleo, because maybe she could have used someone simpler. *Regret.* She made a mental note to send him a gift basket from an amazing fishery that her colleague from Alaska was always heralding. It seemed like the type of thing Matty would get a kick out of—a delivery of salmon from Alaska on dry ice! She grinned, just thinking about the look of pure joy on his face. Then she recalculated: maybe she didn't know anything about his girlfriend and whether or not she were simple or easy or right for Matty, and who was she to make snap judgments when she had just wished that everyone else would stop making them about her? Still, though, she'd send the salmon.

She checked the time and realized she was late, so she did her makeup in a hurry and scrambled out the door to meet Bowen, who was punctual and greeted her with a hug, which she did not recoil from.

"We can just walk from here, if that's OK," Cleo said as they started up Amsterdam Avenue.

"You're the boss," he said. "Though I'm still not *quite* getting this."

"I told you," she said, because she had told him on the train. "It's about accountability."

"Whose?" Bowen grabbed her elbow as she started to cross without a light, but then the traffic slowed and he let go and they crossed together, side by side. "And why?"

Cleo sighed. On the surface, without explaining the regrets list, maybe it did sound crazy: digging up the worst of yourself from your past, facing it publicly. But Bowen didn't push it—he wanted the story, she knew: prominent senator confronts the man who may or may not have taken advantage of her a decade earlier—these stories were *en vogue* and generated eyeballs and frenzied Twitter threads and buoyant comments sections too. But he also wanted to protect her. She could sense that even without him saying so. *I don't need protection,* she wanted to tell him. Single moms who have clawed their way up and through and beyond have long learned how to protect themselves.

Cleo didn't want Bowen, or even Gaby, to tell her how to stay safe in a storm. She didn't want Matty to ask who looked out for her. *She* did. That was just how it had been since she was seventeen.

Besides, sometimes you choose you. Bowen had every right to choose himself over her, to go for the story. If Cleo had been in the same position, she'd have done the same.

"I'm just trying to make it right," she said.

"Make it right for whom?" They both did a little dance to the side of the sidewalk when a child blasted by them too fast on a scooter. Her mom yelled out from half a block away, sprinting to keep up.

Cleo thought of her list. She thought of MaryAnne. She thought of those two girls this morning. She thought of Emily Godwin and of Jonathan with his hand on the curve of another woman's back. She thought of how angry Gaby would be that she was doing this without her. She thought of Veronica Kaye, who told her to lean in to difficult choices because that's what turned you into a leader.

"I don't know," she said, pulling on her sunglasses, arming herself for what came next. "But sometimes making it right is just what you do, even if you don't know what happens after."

Bowen watched the child disappear around the corner of the block, the mom still flying after her. Something passed between Cleo and Bowen then, an understanding that he wasn't her savior, and she wasn't asking him to be either.

"I'll follow your lead," he said.

"Only forward!" she replied but found that the intended humor belly flopped, neither of them in the mood for jokes.

Tracking Nobells down was the easiest part. Cleo still had an alumni log-in, so she quickly accessed his lecture schedule and office hours, which remained the same as they had been more than a decade ago. Maybe it shouldn't have been such a surprise. He, like her, was methodical and by the book (until he wasn't). Of course, she couldn't be certain that he'd be there. She reminded herself of this as she felt her pulse palpably accelerate as they drew closer. People change, habits deviate. But she remembered that he used to love spending Saturdays on campus, usually tucked in his office reading, away from the chaos of his family. Though technically these weren't his official office hours, he made it known—or he had certainly made it known to Cleo anyway—that students were welcome to disturb him. She didn't want to show up at his apartment; that wasn't the sort of score she wanted to settle. Besides, this felt like neutral territory, in his old office, on their old campus, now that she was a senator. The balance of power having been leveled.

Cleo and Bowen reached the campus on 116th Street. Undergrad was still in session, wrapping up in the weeks as spring ebbed into summer, and younger versions of who she used to be scurried around them everywhere, backpacks weighing down their shoulders, messy buns atop their heads, iced coffees on hand to push them through their weekend cram sessions.

Cleo looked for the single mothers, the ones pushing infants or toddlers, with purple circles under their eyes and stains on their T-shirts. She saw none. She reminded herself that at Northwestern, in fact, she'd been unencumbered. No Lucas just yet. Not even a notion of him. If you'd asked her who in her life would have gotten pregnant her senior year of college, she would have said *anyone but me*. And yet, her fourteen-year-old was currently two hundred miles away at a pool party for his soccer team, so Cleo was starting to understand that she was not the best narrator of her own story.

"This way," Cleo said to Bowen and pointed toward Greene Hall, which was a rectangular slab of concrete with more slabs of concrete running vertically through it. There had been a long-standing on-campus argument as to whether it was a hideous eyesore or a beloved near–work of art. Though at the time Cleo had sided with eyesore, she now viewed it from afar with affection, even with her growing nerves and her hard-to-ignore flop sweat. (To be fair, this morning's humidity had given way to a sincere heat wave, and with not a cloud in the Manhattan sky, Cleo felt as if she were walking on the surface of the sun.) Beside her, Bowen swept his hand through his hair, which stayed aloft, right in the same position where his hand had exited, held there by his own perspiration.

Cleo swung the door open to Greene Hall and was met with the blessed blast of air-conditioning. "Oh sweet Jesus," she said.

"And you tell me you're not religious," Bowen replied, then let out a little moan of his own.

Nobells's office was on the sixth floor, so they wound their way through the lobby, garnering a few glances, but Bowen more than her. Senators might be celebrities in DC because they wielded power, but here, in New York City, his star-power star outshone hers. He waved to three girls giggling by the elevator bank before the two of them ducked inside.

"Press six," she said. She was too nervous to do so. She wondered if she even had feeling in her arms. She lifted them to test it, and yes, demonstrably, her brain still connected to her limbs, so at least that was set. Bowen watched her raise her arms like a zombie, then lower them to her sides. She did it again.

"Are you sure you're OK?" He squinted, really looked at her, took a step closer. "I'm just following your lead here, but . . . I mean . . . Cleo, is it rude to say that you are looking a little . . . peaked?"

She *was* looking peaked, she knew. She could *feel* herself growing more peaked with each floor they ascended. But she thought of that yellow pad of paper, and she thought of her 233 regrets, and she thought that some of them were silly but some of them were profound, and if she, Cleo McDougal, junior senator to New York State, couldn't right this wrong, address this grievance, then maybe she was not the woman she assumed herself to be. She stared at the ceiling and realized she truly wasn't here to merely address her own regret. *She wanted Nobells to confess to his too.* MaryAnne had tugged at this thread, and now that Cleo was pulling it, she couldn't stop until the whole thing unwound.

She wiped her palms on her jeans. This didn't really help.

"I'm fine," she said. Bowen did not appear convinced.

The elevator dinged, and Cleo pushed her breath out, then stepped over the gilded divide between the elevator and her past and onto the cold tile floors that she'd walked down so many times, so many years ago.

༄

Nobells's office door was propped open. *People don't change,* Cleo thought as she rounded the corner and saw it ajar, then came to such an abrupt halt that Bowen tripped over her.

"Shit, sorry," he whispered, retreating again behind her.

Cleo was too anxiety-ridden to answer.

"Last chance," he said. "Let's just go. Get a drink. This doesn't matter."

That rattled her, brought her to. She turned and met his eyes.

"It *does* matter, Bowen. That's the point." She started to say: *acknowledging my wrongdoing matters*, but she wasn't quite there. If she'd been ready to take that leap, she would have circled back to MaryAnne and apologized with sincerity. Instead she said: "He nearly ruined my career. What if he's done this to other women who weren't as lucky?"

Bowen bounced his head and unlocked his phone.

"OK, let's go," Cleo said.

She straightened her posture, brushed her hair back, and strode down the hall, pausing only momentarily outside Nobells's door. Cleo raised her fist, knocked, though it was just a courtesy, since the door was open and welcoming.

His face fell for just a second; then it washed with confusion and then, finally, recognition. Nobells leaped to his feet, his chair squeaking just as it used to, the air smelling of books and an illicit cigar and that musky aftershave, just as it used to.

"Cleo!" he exclaimed and moved toward her. He pulled her into an embrace. As her muscle memory kicked in, Cleo thought that she might throw up.

She pressed her hands against his chest, putting space between them, then untangling completely.

"Should I call you Senator McDougal now?" he asked. "I always knew. I always knew." He wagged a finger at her like he had been part of her success, like he hadn't been anything other than a blight in her history. He eased back into his chair, then peered at her with sudden surprise, as if it were just occurring to him—this brilliant legal mind who had taught the best and the brightest at Columbia and had been a Big

Law partner for twenty years—why his former student and ex-mistress might be showing up unannounced on an otherwise unremarkable day.

"Please, come sit." He gestured to the leather love seat. "To what do I owe this pleasure?"

Cleo did not sit. To begin with, she didn't want to. They used to have sex on that same couch or at least one markedly similar. She glanced at it, as if she could replay their movie reel, and then she wondered how many other young women had fucked him there too. But beyond that, she worried, despite her steely exterior, that if she moved even a step, her legs would betray her and she might collapse from nerves right there. And that, quite obviously, would be a mess. She could already see the headlines now. **Senator McDougal Collapses from Heat Exhaustion in an Air-Conditioned Building!** Or: **Senator McDougal Suffers Emotional Breakdown in Front of Former Professor!** The opposing party could fundraise off that for years. Market her fragility. Claim that she was basically half-dead or completely out of her mind with hysteria, when she was confronting a man who was twenty years her senior and probably relied on Viagra to get an erection. But, she knew, the headline would be about her.

"I'm not really here for pleasure," she said.

Nobells's brow furrowed. The decade-plus had treated him well. The lines on his face had grown deeper, but they added to his charm. His hair was still thick and espresso with no grays; his stubble was still intoxicating. Cleo remembered how he used to kiss her with that stubble until her cheeks felt raw, how she'd slather on coconut oil the next morning to try to disguise how he had left his mark.

"Do you need legal advice?" he asked.

"No." Cleo let the silence rest between them. She wanted him to squirm, to feel as off-kilter as she did, or as she had, especially that night with the roast chicken and the Italian merlot and with his wife and children out of town.

Cleo had still been uncertain about his intentions, even when they clinked their wineglasses and he pulled the chicken out of the oven and insisted on serving her. He led her to the dining table, pulled out her chair, then placed a linen napkin on her lap. It was so intimate that Cleo couldn't meet his eyes when he asked her if she'd like a refill on her wine.

Dinner was exceptional, as promised: the chicken and warm rolls with butter and a salad with pears and pine nuts and a champagne dressing that he also made from scratch. For Cleo, who was used to eating microwavable macaroni and cheese or the remnants of whatever Lucas left on his high-chair tray, it was, honestly, a bit of a miracle. Like manna from the heavens.

They went through Cleo's bottle of wine quickly. Even the next morning, back at home with Lucas, Cleo realized that they'd gone through it too quickly, and maybe if they hadn't, she wouldn't have been so reckless. But they had, and she couldn't turn back time.

She stared at him now, all these years later, and remembered how his bedroom had smelled of cologne and of sex and also of waffles, which he whipped up for her at ten p.m., once she begged off staying the night (she had never spent a night apart from Lucas and had no intention of doing so even then), and in lieu of the breakfast he said he would have made. She could hear him singing along to Toto's "Africa" while she was still tucked under his duvet, naked. And maybe that was the moment to get up and walk away—while he was cracking eggs and adding vanilla extract, only one mistake made rather than a hundred of them, but she was twenty-three and exhausted and had no way of knowing how far in over her head she was.

After dinner, Cleo was certainly drunk. She didn't know if he were or not: she hadn't been around many middle-aged men and really didn't have any idea how many glasses of wine it took them to wobble their way to the couch. She certainly wobbled her own self over, plunked down, and wondered what on earth would happen next. She remembered feeling like a bystander in her own story, telling herself that if he kissed her, she'd allow it, and if he didn't, she could leave without embarrassing herself. Of the list of many concerns that Cleo had in her life, embarrassing herself was certainly up there. Top three, perhaps.

But he joined her on the couch, his leg pressing against hers and then his arm slipping around her shoulders. He told her a story about how, in his days just out of law school, as a newbie clerk for a federal judge, he slept in his office some nights because he was so terrified of missing filing deadlines or otherwise disappointing his boss, and Cleo closed her eyes and imagined this superstar professor, who was shining all his attention now on her, as a young man not much older than she was. She hoped that he was sharing these words because he saw the same potential in her. Even in her wine-soaked haze, she could tap in to her ambition, how closely it was tied to her self-perception. She liked to think that's what Nobells saw in her too: that she was on a rocket ship to the top, and honestly, though she thought he was sexy as hell, if he hadn't invited her here, if he hadn't stopped her after class and run his hand down her arm, if he hadn't kept refilling her wineglass, she never, ever would have considered him anything more than a brilliant professor who was extremely easy on the eyes. Maybe she'd have hoped to be his summer associate that next summer. That would have been enough.

She planned to say all this, to make her intentions known. She wanted to be *sure* that he understood this about her: Cleo McDougal was a serious law student. She was a serious young woman. She demanded to be seen as such. And what she really wanted was his mentorship, his counsel. But then, just before he finished his story and she could press him on his intentions, she felt his hand on her chin, and he tilted her face just so, and then his lips were on hers, and she sank into the couch, and oh God, it had been so long since anyone had touched her other than Lucas that she let all the rest of it go.

*Regret.*

She filled up on his waffles and made it home to relieve the sitter by midnight.

Now, with hindsight, she could see how much easier it would have been to get up after that first glass of wine or after his roast chicken and walk out before it even started. But once it had, once he had kissed her and all that came after, extricating herself proved much more complicated. That was how regrets worked, she supposed, there in his office, with the heavy cloud of hindsight. It wasn't the murky middle parts or even the earth-shattering consequences that you so often wished you could go back and redo. It was the inception, of stopping something even before it began, that you lingered on. That moment, that was the one to change—the one at the start before it all got messy.

She couldn't, of course. So today, standing in front of him, she was left only with what she could do about it now.

She felt her voice catch in her throat, then regained it, as strong as she needed it to be.

"I came here to tell you that what you did with me was wrong."

Nobells's features pointed downward, as if she had posed a question. Which she had not.

"I don't understand."

Cleo knew that he did understand. Surely he had caught at least a little bit of the coverage of MaryAnne's stupid but viral op-ed. Surely he knew that this would awaken old ghosts. Or maybe he just thought she'd never do anything about those ghosts because she'd let them go for so long. But he underestimated Cleo McDougal.

"What you did with me. Sleeping with me. Seducing me. That whole year. It was wrong. For a long time, I thought that it was a mutual . . ." Cleo shook her head. "And what you did to me afterward—"

He cut her off, now on his feet. "You were a consenting adult."

"I was twenty-three. You were forty-three. You were my professor." Cleo stood up taller, refusing to be cowed. "And that makes it wrong. It doesn't have to be illegal to be wrong, Alex. And I want to know how many others." She gestured to the couch. "How many other second-years did you invite to your office hours or bring into your home under the guise of offering a homemade meal and some counsel?"

"Cleo," he started.

"Senator," she corrected.

He pursed his lips together, refusing her request. "Ms. McDougal. I am sorry that you seem to have misinterpreted our situation from so many years ago. I cared very much for you, and I thought it was reciprocated. In fact, I am certain that it was."

"I was your student." Cleo kept her voice steady. She wouldn't be called shrill or hysterical or emotional.

"And you were an adult. And I helped you."

"It was an abuse of your position," she said. "And I want to make sure that you haven't done it since." She paused. "And we both know that not only did you not help me, in fact, you later tried to do the opposite."

His eyes flared wider at these two notions, the bold accusations that she came to level. But Cleo thought of Emily Godwin and also of herself when, just before the end of her second year, she saw Nobells on the street with his wife and two kids, and how he saw her too, and crossed to the other side as if she were an inconvenience or, worse, as if she were a distraught stalker who intended to blow up his life. She wasn't and she hadn't, and she found that more insulting than anything else. She had known the whole time that she didn't love him. She didn't expect him to leave Amy and the children; she didn't envision moving into his three-bedroom. She did, however, expect respect, and when he scurried down the street, fleeing past her as if they weren't neighbors and this sort of thing might happen, and then he emailed her and said it would be for the best if their arrangement ended, well, that's when Cleo McDougal realized what an insouciant piece of misogynistic garbage Alexander Nobells was. That after eight months, he'd peg her as a crazy stalker. That after eight months, she wasn't worth more than an email. He added at the end of it that he was proud to be part of her story, to have contributed to her next chapters. And Cleo started to reply back: FUCK YOU, YOU DO NOT GET TO CLAIM OWNERSHIP OVER MY SUCCESS, but she decided that flaunting how wildly she would succeed without him was perhaps the best revenge. And she had.

It was only the next day that she got a second email—revoking her summer position at his firm. And then the third email, from the dean of the law school, who had offered to put her in touch with the New York attorney general, in case Cleo wanted to pursue that path, rescinding the offer, ostensibly under the guise that the AG was "underwater right now" and "perhaps we can revisit this down the road." But Cleo knew they weren't going to revisit it. And Cleo knew that Nobells had torched her.

And that's when he went from being a philandering asshole to a vindictive one. So she had scrambled. All the summer positions were locked up by then, obviously. None of the big firms was hiring, and besides, they'd want to know why she'd been let go at the other one. She made phone call after phone call in her two-bedroom apartment, while Lucas slept or was at day care or toddled around in a Pull-Up singing "Itsy Bitsy Spider" and spilling Cheerios, until finally, because they sounded as desperate as she was, she landed an interview at a women's health nonprofit. It paid next to nothing and was not the shining star she wanted for her résumé. But ironically, it pushed her into public service—it was gratifying in ways that reviewing briefs for law partners could never be, and it helped Cleo see that her privileged voice could perhaps help less-privileged ones. Her next step out of law school was running for Congress.

So maybe she had Alexander Nobells to thank for everything after all.

But she wouldn't. Because he'd tried to cut her off at the knees, and she had risen to her feet anyway. So fuck him.

"How many others, Alexander?" Cleo felt bolder now, more like herself, not the version of her she had been in his shadow. More like the girl had been at twenty-four, rising.

"None, Cleo, none."

"I am a fucking senator, so you can address me as such," she said, though she wished she hadn't sworn, because she knew Bowen was behind her, doing what she'd asked.

"Calm down, please." He moved to put his hands on her shoulders, just as he had so many years ago in the precipice of his classroom. Cleo was faster, though, and stepped aside. "Look, I can see that you are quite upset," he offered.

"Don't tell me that I am upset," she said. "Don't tell me to stay calm."

"Well"—he opened his palms toward her—"it appears to me that you are very much upset."

Cleo wasn't surprised that he went for the overly emotional patronizing bullshit. He wasn't the first man to be on the losing end of an argument to do so. He wasn't even the hundredth, the thousandth.

"You tried to alienate me; you tried to wreck me."

His voice dropped to a lower register, a menacing one. "You enjoyed yourself in my bedroom, Senator."

"I was a twenty-three-year-old who was stunned that her professor took an interest."

Nobells recalculated, softening. "What do you want from me? Amy left me three years ago. Are you here to seek revenge? To tell me that I was an unfaithful husband?"

Cleo thought of Jonathan Godwin. No, this wasn't just about that. It was about protecting another second-year student who might not be as game when he ran his hand down her arm outside the classroom but felt obligated to accept his dinner invitation nonetheless; it was about stomping out the perversions of lecherous men preying on less-powerful women, making them appear as if they were equals, then rattling off an email eight months later letting them know that not only were they never equal, they were, in fact, disposable. And to add insult to figurative injury, maybe also believing he was responsible for these young women's triumphs. But not too responsible, because now they were no longer employable. No. Fuck that.

"You were a piece-of-shit husband," Cleo retorted. "But that was between the two of you. I'm here for your job. I'm here for your reputation."

Nobells, on instinct, jumped closer to her, as if he were gearing up for a physical fight. Cleo didn't flinch.

"You say one fucking word about any of this, and I will sue you for defamation faster than you can run a reelection poll," he said.

"I thought I was the only one you ever did this with," she replied, her voice even, her tone serene. "So what's your concern?"

"Fuck you, Cleo."

"Senator McDougal, Alex."

He looked less handsome then, Cleo thought. His cheeks flushed, a little spittle in the corner of his mouth. Cleo wished that all the young women in his law classes could see him as he was, a panicked shell of himself. She cocked her head and thought he looked like a cornered, defanged reptile, hissing and quaking but without its teeth, unable to puncture her skin.

"Fuck you, Senator McDougal. It didn't have to be this way."

"You're right, Alexander. It probably didn't." Cleo shrugged.

"If I read a word about this, you can expect a lawsuit."

Just then, Bowen stepped out from his angle by the door, his phone aloft, his hand steady.

"Sorry, Professor," he said. "Too late for that. We've already gone live."

# FOURTEEN

It had been Cleo's idea—to livestream it on her Instagram account, with Bowen mentioning it in his own to direct more eyeballs (he had 300k to her 48k)—because she knew if she'd done it any other way, asked him to report it like a standard story, edit it, interview her, all the usual paces—she'd have lost her nerve, and addressing her regrets list couldn't be done without complete commitment. (Bowen had insisted on fact-checking the whole thing on the train, and Cleo had come prepared—forwarded him the aftermath emails, had shown him her GPA and her Law Review accolades, and, of course, some of Nobells's texts when he was still heady in lust. Those were, for better or worse, stored in the Cloud forever.) Still, though, she was shaking by the time they hit Amsterdam Avenue, and she actually had to stop and lean over, her palm flattened against the window of a Taco Bell just next to Greene Hall, to ward off the nerves that had presented in the form of an extremely angry bowel.

Bowen was rubbing her back, telling her to take deep breaths, and trying to be as comforting as possible without violating any of her personal space. They were friendly, the two of them, but they weren't exactly friends, and he, unlike Nobells, had been raised in a generation where you didn't touch a woman unless she really, really wanted you to. (Or unless you were an asshole. Plenty of those too.)

Cleo heard the notifications on his phone, dinging one after the other. She felt the vibrations of her own phone, a steady buzz in her back pocket.

"Don't tell me what people are saying," she muttered to him, still bent over, still palming Taco Bell. "It was the right thing to do. So . . . just don't tell me, OK?"

"It's not all bad . . . at all," he said. He scrolled down with his thumb, one hand resting on her back, as if he were checking to ensure that she was still breathing. "Actually, a lot of it is quite good."

"OK." She righted herself. Felt a little less green. She hated that her body betrayed her like this. She didn't want her stomach to collapse into a mosh pit of gaseous nerves every time her past resurfaced. Or every time she resurfaced her past. She'd worked her whole life to be tougher than anyone expected, to be less penetrable than anyone demanded. She hated that these regrets made her more vulnerable, made her more porous. And yet now that she'd started down this path, she wanted to see it through. Even when it backfired, like making MaryAnne even angrier (though she was also beginning to see how she could have handled that one differently—this was not yet a perfectly oiled machine), like hearing Nobells threaten to sue. Maybe it was just that Cleo McDougal had never started anything that she hadn't finished, or maybe it was because she really did believe that, at least for now, Nobells wasn't going to touch another unsuspecting twenty-three-year-old, if he were so inclined, or box her out of a deserved position at his law firm, and what she lacked in power back then, she made up for now. And that had to be something.

"I could use a drink," she said to Bowen, who was typing fairly frantically into his phone.

"What?"

"I could go for a drink."

He stopped typing for a moment, looked toward her. "It's two o'clock in the afternoon." His phone buzzed again. "Oh shit. Here, this one's for you."

He held his screen in front of her, and Cleo squinted against the midday sun to read it. It was from Gaby in all caps.

Gabrielle: WHAT THE ACTUAL FUCK, BOWEN?

. . .

. . .

Gabrielle: TELL CLEO TO CALL ME NOW.

$\sim$

Cleo did not call Gaby. She did not call her sister, who did not call herself because they did not have that type of relationship but indeed texted to express concerns for her mental health and please, could Cleo reply? She did not call Lucas, who had been sent the livestream from his friends and texted to say: WTAFuuuukkkkk? and so she banged out a reply that said: I'll explain, I promise. She would. Once she got ahold of herself.

Gaby left six more voice messages, but Cleo was in the liquor store by then, and all this seemed to matter less and less as she grew more and more eager to pour herself a bourbon. She knew she had sworn it off years ago on her list, but now it seemed too appealing to resist, calling out to her like the temptation of Alexander Nobells's scruff used to, and for once, Cleo McDougal was going to be irresponsible. Or better phrased—for once, since she had become a mother and since she had become a senator, Cleo McDougal was going to get absolutely plastered.

"Do you really think you should?" Bowen kept asking, which she found extremely annoying.

"Yes," she barked at him each time he asked. "I really think I should. And I have asked you to join me repeatedly, so you're either in or you're out, Bowen." She grabbed a bottle off the shelf and spun around to meet his eyes. "In. Or. Out?"

"I'm . . . in? Only because I think you shouldn't be alone."

Cleo almost screamed right there in the liquor store on 105th street. She didn't need a hero, and if Bowen Babson thought he could be hers, she'd rather drink alone. What she needed was a release.

Though she hadn't betrayed it in front of Nobells, his very presence had triggered so much, too much, of who she had been thirteen years ago. Arrogant, sure. She couldn't have undermined MaryAnne in the way that she had without arrogance. Brilliant, yes. She couldn't have made Law Review as a single mother without brilliance. But also gullible—that she showed up to his apartment alone with a bottle of wine. Also complicit—that she'd sunk into his couch and didn't pull away when he kissed her. Also guilty—that she let it go on for eight months, knowing he had a wife and kids—and it ended on his terms and through a fucking email and with him taking credit for who she was yet to be and on top of it all, firing her from the law firm—a position she had earned long before Alexander Nobells swooped in, saying whatever he said to the dean to ruin a chance to learn from the AG too.

So yes, she thought that she deserved a fucking drink.

"My producer is already making calls," Bowen said as the cashier rang up Cleo's three bottles. "He's digging in, seeing if there are others. If there are, you'll be a hero."

"If there aren't?" Cleo wondered if she could open the bourbon in the store and take a swig. No, probably not. She was still a senator, after all. "Then I guess I'll just be a crazy ex-lover who slept her way to the top."

"I didn't say that!"

"No, you don't have to." Cleo grabbed the paper bag, thanked the cashier. "Everyone else will instead."

◦———

Cleo finally succumbed to her phone just as they arrived back at her apartment. She was actively ignoring Gaby, but her son, well, she needed him to know that she was hanging in.

"I'm OK, Lucas," she said when her phone buzzed again and she saw his caller ID.

"You're OK?" he screamed. "You think I'm calling to see if *you're* OK?"

Cleo quickly ascertained that she had miscalculated. Maybe she should have taken Gaby's call instead. It probably would have been less confrontational. She hadn't told Lucas about her plan because she didn't want to worry him, and honestly, she thought he'd be proud of her once he understood.

"Luc—"

He cut her off. *"Do you have any idea how mortifying it is to learn at, like, my soccer pool party that my mother is chewing out some guy she used to sleep with?"* (He really did screech this in all italics.)

"Lukey, please stop; give me a chance—"

He cut her off again. "I don't get you. You're all Miss Follow Every Rule, and now you're, like . . . you're blowing everything up! You're making a mess, and I want to die!"

"You don't want to die, sweetie."

"If. I. Could. Die. Of. Embarrassment. I. Would."

Cleo glanced at Bowen now, who looked more than a little concerned, but she waved a hand, as if her son dying of embarrassment were standard Saturday stuff. Actually, with a teenager, sometimes it was.

"Buddy, I did this because it was important to me. I'm supposed to be the voice of my generation. And I did something really, well, it was wrong. But what he did was more wrong. And I couldn't see that for a long time, and now, when I could, I wanted to rectify it."

The line was silent for a long time. She thought he may have hung up on her. She wouldn't have been surprised. He was a fourteen-year-old who had just learned that his mom had been sleeping with a forty-something-year-old married man—her professor—while he toddled around in diapers. She could see it from his perspective. It was a little disgusting.

"I don't get why you're doing all of this," he said finally.

"Because I want to make the world as level for young women as it is for young men, Lucas. It's important. And it matters. And if I can't do that now, what is the point of my power, of my position?" She paused, remembering something. "Speaking of which, please tell me that you broke up with one of the girls you're dating?"

"Mom! Oh my God!" he screamed. "Jesus Christ! When will you ever stop turning me into one of your causes? I'm not!"

And then he really did hang up on her. Which shouldn't have startled her but did anyway.

Cleo sighed deeply, fell backward into her couch, stared at the ceiling for a beat. Things were probably easier with Lucas when she didn't meddle. She didn't want to be a meddler! She didn't even have time to really meddle. But if she didn't, what if her son ended up just like goddamn Jonathan Godwin or Alexander Nobells, and then she would have failed at the one thing that truly mattered?

*I raised an asshole. I'm sorry.* Add that one to her list of regrets.

Bowen eased himself next to her.

"Should I go? It feels like I should go. I have . . ." He checked his phone. "Seventy-eight emails and a hundred and twenty-four texts to return."

Cleo groaned. "About me?"

"Well," he said, trying to soften the blow. "About this whole thing."

"Kindly pour me a drink," she said. She glanced at the time on the cable box. It was three fifteen p.m. Nearly five o'clock. That seemed fine.

Bowen rose and rattled around her kitchen, returned with a tumbler half-full of bourbon.

"No, you need one too." Cleo shook her head. "If I drink alone, I'm basically on my way to becoming a cautionary tale."

Bowen nodded a small nod, retreated to the kitchen, and returned with a tumbler in each hand.

She gulped down her entire pour. "More please."

He dutifully retrieved the bottle from the kitchen rather than continue to make the back-and-forth trip, and this time he filled her glass nearly to the brim.

"You don't seem like the type to get intoxicated in the middle of the day," he offered, sipping his own drink quite slowly.

"Oh yeah, for sure, I'm not." Cleo swallowed a good third of her round. "You see, Bowen Babson, I'm a very buttoned-up, important senator who has to maintain her composure at all times. If I make even the smallest mistake, the interwebs and the men on those interwebs and also sometimes extremely self-hating women come for me."

Bowen started to interrupt, but she talked over him.

"You don't know Maureen and Beth and Susan. From Seattle. And the things they say about me. Also, I am a *mother*, even though I'm just thirty-seven and never had much of a life, and mothers don't do things like get drunk at three fifteen in the afternoon."

"Well," Bowen said in an attempt to slow her down, "some do. But they probably aren't very good mothers."

Cleo polished off the remainder of her second round. The bourbon felt warm in her belly; her blood felt warm throughout her body, actually. The room was feeling a little bouncier, the situation with Nobells feeling a little less pulse-pounding. She glanced at Bowen and suddenly found him extremely, extremely attractive. It was probably the bourbon talking, but then she reminded herself that she always found him extremely, extremely attractive. She had just never had the opportunity to indulge that.

She reached for the bottle on her coffee table, pouring her own refill this time. She held up the bottle to refresh Bowen's glass, but he was still nursing his first round.

"I'm going to regret this tomorrow," she said. "I have bourbon on my list, but I can't for the life of me remember why."

"You have bourbon on what list? Your grocery list?" He looked at her peculiarly. Cleo found this even more attractive, even at the same moment realizing her mistake. Only Gaby knew about her list, and probably her sister, but Cleo didn't want to text her back and ask her and end up in a therapy session with Los Angeles's life coach to the stars. Telling Bowen Babson, who seemed like the type of guy who wouldn't have even one regret in his life, about her 233 regrets felt like an admission of failure. Cleo was well on her way to drunk, but even now, she knew that she could not present herself as a failure.

"Nothing, no list," she said. "I just, I probably shouldn't drink this." Then she finished her glass anyway. The confrontation with Nobells and all that it stirred up was washing away, which was the point. She didn't want to acknowledge that seeing him again, even all these years later, made her feel not just vulnerable but weak, even when this time she met him with strength.

"It's funny." She rolled her head toward Bowen. "I mean, it's not *funny*, but it's funny how even a decade later, seeing a shithead of a person can make me feel like I'm less than."

"Less than what?"

Cleo rolled her head back to center, then dropped it on the back edge of the couch. "Just . . . less than him. Powerless. Alone." Cleo thought of those first few days, when she couldn't stop crying after her parents died and how that was how she felt exactly. Powerless. Alone. And how you didn't have to lose your parents in an accident to tap into those feelings all over again. That's what Nobells had done to her at twenty-three, reduced her to that naked fragility where she held none of the cards and he was running the table.

Bowen was silent.

"I guess I just regret it," she said, quieter now.

"Regret confronting him or regret the affair?"

Cleo shrugged, squeezed her eyes shut. "What you don't know about me, Bowen Babson, is that I have a lot of regrets. They are piled high, like, boom, boom, boom." Cleo used her hand, karate chopping the air, to demonstrate. "Boom!" she said one more time, and this time inadvertently added an extra flourish and hit him in the eye.

"Ow, shit!"

"Oh God," she said. "See! There's another."

Bowen winced and blinked a few times but did not appear blinded by her martial arts.

"It's OK," he said and managed a smile, which she thought was absolutely, unequivocally magnetic. She raised her hand to reach out, to touch his lips—she wanted to run her fingertips right over them—then realized what she was doing and plopped it back in her lap.

She aimed her face toward his again. She was feeling looser now, and she knew it was the bourbon, but the tricky thing about alcohol is that even when you know that you're drunk, you very rarely say to yourself: *self, you are drunk*, and thus it doesn't stop you from acting in ways that you wouldn't if you weren't drunk. It's as if you are both in control and out of control, though inevitably the next morning, you conclude that it was the latter, not the former.

"I think you should kiss me." She was staring at his lips, convinced that there was nothing she would rather do.

Bowen nearly spit out his drink. *"What?"*

"I think you should kiss me now."

"I . . ."

"Bowen, I think it's very obvious that there is something between us—you *did* ask me out, need I remind you, so let's consider this our little date, and I think, therefore, that you should kiss me." She paused, then added, "I'm a modern woman. I can ask for what I want."

Bowen did not kiss her. He sat instead frozen beside her, looking more than a little alarmed, but because Cleo was well past tipsy, she ignored this particular emotion.

"Oh God," she lamented. "Is it that I'm too old for you? Jesus Christ. That's how it is now, isn't it? Men only go younger, and women, I mean, let's face it, I'm basically being told that I should settle for a man in his midfifties and will essentially be doomed to providing sponge baths and feeding him soft foods in the later years of our relationship." She set her drink on the coffee table. Looked pointedly back toward Bowen. "This is bullshit, Bowen Babson. Complete bullshit. I don't want to be giving sponge baths. Why can't I date younger too?"

Bowen reached out, rested his hand on hers. "It's not because I date only younger. It has nothing to do with that."

"Is it because your generation—"

"We're the same generation, Cleo."

"Is it because your generation needs, like, written consent? You have my consent, Bowen." She grabbed his chin, forced his eyes toward hers. "You have my consent."

Bowen gently removed her fingers, nearly clamped on, from his face. He stood, tucked the hem of his shirt back into his jeans. Cleo could hear his phone buzzing in his back pocket. She could hear her own phone buzzing from the kitchen. She wasn't yet ready to face the outside world again.

"Please don't go," she said.

He cleared his throat.

"It has nothing to do with age or consent," he said. She felt him taking her in, really, really breathing her in, in her wretched condition on the couch, full of self-pity and a little false bravado and a lot, a lot of bourbon. Cleo suddenly realized that she hadn't eaten lunch. "It's that, well, Cleo, it's obvious to me that you have some regrets. And, to be honest, I'd rather not be another one."

"You wouldn't be, I promise," Cleo said.

"Then we'll reconvene without the bourbon," he said before he backed toward the door. "That's really the only way to find out."

# FIFTEEN

Nothing, not one thing, was better by the time Cleo returned to Washington on Sunday night. Lucas was still barely speaking to her, back to his usual grunting and holed up in his room. (Emily Godwin had dropped him off late Sunday afternoon before Cleo arrived back. For the return trip, Cleo rented a car rather than run the risk of making chatter on the train or, worse, running into Bowen on his trip back as well.) Her son had mumbled a hello when she poked her head through his doorway, and when she asked if perhaps they could sit and talk, he glared, and she acquiesced that they could discuss it at another time. She was also still avoiding Gaby, who had left her twenty-two messages and did not seem to be enjoying her weekend with Oliver Patel, mostly because of Cleo going rogue and having little to do with Oliver Patel himself.

Though Cleo had tried her best to ignore the breaking news about her confrontation—one thing she had learned over the years was that headlines rarely changed the nature of her decision-making, though polling from her constituents would, of course—this time the news was impossible to avoid. Alerts were sent to her phone, and commentators debated her tactics (and motives) on talk radio the entire drive back, until she settled in on an easy-listening station, which didn't do much to soothe her.

Even at thirty-seven, Cleo had never developed a specific musical taste. She clutched the steering wheel, her nerves frayed from listening to strangers argue the gritty details of her choices in her early twenties, and wished she had. She hadn't found time for art; she hadn't found time for music. Maybe, she considered as she cruised down the interstate, if she'd leaned in even just a fraction to that part of herself that must lie dormant—she was her mother's daughter after all!—she would have found comforts in something other than career success. She wasn't apologizing for her ambition, and she wasn't even sorry for where it had led her. But she could see how having a singular focus might have narrowed her perspective. She flipped to an alternative station but didn't for the life of her see how the song playing was considered *music*, and then she tried the pop channel Lucas preferred, but my God, Cleo thought, the girl singing about losing her man was really selling herself short. And thus, she ended right back on the easy-listening channel, a milquetoast choice for aging millennials and Gen Xers who had no musical taste at all, which was worse, perhaps, than having terrible music taste.

At least then, Cleo thought, you had an opinion.

Bowen called her Sunday night, when she was tucked in her home office, reviewing her schedule for the week, and she quickly hit Decline, jabbing at her phone like it was radioactive. She wasn't exactly sure what her strategy was here—with Bowen, with Gaby, even with her sister, who had sent another slightly alarmist text about her emotional well-being—but, much like her musical tastes, Cleo decided, maybe for the first time in her life, not having a hard line or a strategized plan was the best way to move forward.

This was not the best way to move forward, quite obviously. Cleo McDougal's whole life, barring her pregnancy, was fine-tuned down to the minute. And she attributed much of her success to this stream-lined, organized vision. But without any instinct on how to proceed,

Cleo decided to chuck it all, to abandon everything. She gazed at the lights in her home office and wondered what would happen next if, say, she just stopped giving so many shits about being the best, about being anointed. Would MaryAnne Newman like her then? Would she still write op-eds? Would she still claim she was a bad person? Would Cleo still aspire to be president and crave Veronica Kaye's approval and the massive check that came with it? Would Cleo have shown up at Nobells's apartment for a dinner in the first place all those years ago if she'd just been content to be another law school student who passed the bar just fine, went on to a perfectly good firm, and pulled in six figures until she was forty-nine and decided to retire to open a used-book store?

After declining Bowen's call, Cleo stilled herself and heard the throb of the bass coming from Lucas's room. Normally he wore his headphones to shut her out, but this time, with this specific rage, he blasted his speakers instead, as if to say: *even if you could come in, even if you were welcomed into this part of my world, I still wouldn't hear you, and you still wouldn't have access.*

Her phone buzzed on her desk, another news notification.

**Has Cleo McDougal Pushed the Women's Movement Too Far?**

She swiped up, clearing it from her screen.

∽

On Monday, Cleo got to her office early—she had been so thrown off her routine that both her boxing class and hour-free phone time had gone out the window—but she still rose with the sun, a habit ingrained from the time Lucas was tiny and needed a feeding, and now a habit reinforced because it was quiet time to work. She usually dropped Lucas at school, then made her way in at a reasonable hour, but today he mumbled that he had a ride with Benjamin's older sister, so Cleo commuted early, and Arianna was the only one in the office when she arrived. She was filling the coffee maker and nearly spilled the grounds when Cleo swung the wood door open.

"Oh! Oh my God, Senator McDougal! I'm sorry!" Arianna steadied the carafe, a look of genuine alarm on her face.

"Why are you sorry?" Cleo sighed. She was exhausted, not just in her usual exhausted way, which really didn't faze her, but deep in her bones—emotionally drained too. It wasn't even because of the news coverage—it was simply, Cleo was learning, the unending fatigue that came from stirring up the wreckage from your past. "Only Forward!" Wasn't everything so much easier that way? When you didn't have to unearth why you had sabotaged your best friend, when you didn't have to consider how you turned over part of your future to an ill-intentioned professor? "What could you have to be sorry about, Arianna?"

"Oh, well, like, I didn't mean to disturb you."

"I disturbed *you*," Cleo pointed out. "You were here before I was."

"No, I know, you're right. Sorry." Arianna poured the water into the machine, clicked it on, waited for it to hum to life.

"You did it again." Cleo wanted to curl up on the floor and take a nap. Could she do that today? Under her desk? On her rug?

"Shoot, dammit." Arianna caught herself. "It's a terrible habit, I know. S—" She stopped just in time.

Cleo swept by her on her way to her office. She did want to solve Arianna's problems, but she couldn't solve them today.

"Oh, Senator McDougal?" Arianna trailed her, watched Cleo flop into her chair.

"Yes?"

"I, well, I just wanted to tell you that I admired what you did this weekend. When I was at Columbia, we had a list of men . . ."

"A what?" Cleo was sitting up straighter now, not sure she had heard correctly. "A list of men?"

"Yeah, a list. Of, like, predatory professors."

Cleo was suddenly awake, her eyes open wider, her heart pulsing faster. Maybe she really had underestimated Arianna. She raised her eyebrows as if to tell Arianna to continue.

"Right, and, I mean, he was on it. I don't know why; I don't have any direct knowledge of his behavior, but . . . I didn't realize you were his student too." She hesitated. "Maybe it doesn't make it better to know that other women had concerns about him too. But, I don't know, maybe it does."

Cleo felt the sting of tears behind her eyes. She didn't want to cry in front of Arianna, and she bit the inside of her lip to distract herself with a different sort of pain.

"I appreciate that, Arianna; I really do."

"It sucks that he did that to you."

"I was consenting." Cleo didn't know why she kept excusing the situation with that. Consenting and unethical were two different things. Also, he could have cost Cleo her entire career. It was only true luck that she had called the nonprofit on the day that they were hiring and that the advocacy the job required stuck. Nobells couldn't have anticipated that.

"Right, but, I mean, yeah, so what? That's why we made the list. Well, not me, *I* didn't make it. I carried around mace, so . . ." She trailed off, like mace could have prevented Cleo from showing up at Nobells's apartment with a bottle of wine. But maybe what she meant, Cleo realized, was that she was already well prepared, aware of the fact that unexpected threats lurked in innocuous corners, even at an Ivy League law school. "But what I mean is that people don't have to be, like, *evil* to be bad." Arianna thought about this for a second. "Like, what he did was disgusting, and maybe what made it worse is that he *wasn't* evil. It's those guys, you know? Those are the ones you have to be more worried about, I think."

Cleo thought of Jonathan Godwin. She did know. But she also thought of Matty and of Bowen, and she didn't want Arianna to think that all men were the enemy.

"There are some good ones out there; don't convince yourself that there aren't."

"Oh my God, I know!" Arianna squealed. "I mean, I *love* men." Cleo remembered her flirtation with the aide from Senator Frost's office. "But still . . . that doesn't mean that they can't be complete douchebags."

Cleo laughed then because Arianna was indeed wiser than she had given her credit for. Certainly wiser than Cleo had been at twenty-four, and she was a new mother at that age and had graduated at the top of her class from Northwestern. She thought of Bowen and how you shouldn't judge a book by its cover. Maybe she was guilty of that with a lot of people: Arianna, Bowen, even herself.

"Listen," Cleo said, ready to start her day. "If you hear of any specifics, will you let me know? I worry that out here by myself, the story will turn into exactly what it wasn't."

"Oh yeah, for sure. Like the desperate twentysomething sex-starved woman who seduced her professor." Arianna practically snorted, and Cleo didn't know if she loved this young woman for her clear-eyed bravado or resented her for pinpointing exactly what half the country would say and repeating it back to her. "All I know, Senator McDougal, is that I got about a million Snaps from my friends last night—"

"Snaps?"

"Snapchat."

"Oh, right." Cleo should have known that. Lucas's phone was constantly pinging.

"I got a million Snaps last night from my friends saying how lucky I was to work for you."

"I really appreciate that, Arianna." For the second time in their conversation, Cleo worried she might cry.

And never, in the history of her political career, had Cleo McDougal cried.

⁓

Cleo, awash in memories of a good man, remembered to order Matty that gift basket from the Alaskan fishery. She even wrote a silly note to accompany it: *Matty—they say there are other fish in the sea, so I thought you might want to try this one, since I guess it's clear that it's not me.* ☺ *Your friend, Cleo.* Was it too much? She was about to ask Arianna if it was too much when Gaby blew in. Cleo hit Order and exited out of the page quickly before she could give it further thought. Across from her, Gaby plunked down in a chair and scowled.

"How was your weekend?" Cleo asked, as if there were nothing else to discuss. "How's Oliver?"

Gaby steeled her jaw, threw her hair over her shoulder.

"He was, is, extremely sexy." She glared at Cleo. That discussion was now over. "I'd ask you how *your* weekend went, but I saw the livestream."

"Uh-huh," Cleo said, because that was obvious.

"Why would you do that without me? Why would you not ask me first?"

"I didn't want to be talked out of it."

Gaby smacked her hand flat against Cleo's desk. "Why would I have talked you out of it?" She pulled her hand back. "No, you're right. I may have. This was reckless, Cleo, and you hired me to ensure that you don't do reckless."

"Have you met me, Gaby? *I* don't do reckless! You were the one who told me to embrace my regrets."

Gaby held up a finger, stopping her right there. "No, I told you to get me a list of ten—"

"And I did!"

"And then I was going to pick five—well, four after Seattle." Gaby finished her sentence.

"Well, cross one more off your list. Now we're down to three." Cleo considered it. "No, two—I forgot the Jackman housing bill. You said we could count that."

Gaby, fuming, just stared.

"What?" Cleo shot back. "This was what Veronica Kaye wanted. This was what *you* wanted."

"Have you seen the news?" Gaby said. "It's all they're talking about!" She reached for her phone. Has Cleo McDougal Pushed the Women's Movement Too Far?

"I thought the motto was 'no press is bad press.'"

Gaby jumped to her feet. "If that's your motto, then you haven't been paying attention. Of course there is bad press! And this press . . . it's not just bad for you; I mean, you literally handed the other side a loaded gun—"

Cleo was on her feet too. She was exhausted, yes, and a little battle-weary, but she wasn't about to roll over and play dead just because Gaby wanted her to.

"Not *literally*—"

"You *figuratively* just handed all these men, well, and some women, a loaded gun! Spurned ex-lover shows up at the doorstep of her revered professor! Or worse—"

"There's not a worse to that," Cleo snapped.

"There is," Gaby pressed. "Because half the talking heads are now wondering if you didn't sleep your way to the top, if he didn't call in favors for you."

"Well, that is *ridiculous*," Cleo screeched. "I barely sleep my way anywhere!"

Gaby nodded. "I could, of course, leak the sad details of your sex life, but I don't think that would sway anyone."

Cleo, still amped, yelled on top of her, "Arianna *just seconds ago* told me that her friends are cheering for me!"

"People can be cheering for you, Cleo, and also thinking you're starting to lose your mind. Two things can be true at once."

This was one of Gaby's favorite sayings, as if Cleo weren't aware that sometimes the universe presented dichotomies, both of which were justified. The responsible twenty-three-year-old who also slept with her married professor. She damn well understood that two things could be true at once. Tell her something she *didn't* know, Gabrielle!

Cleo started to reply, but Gaby talked over her. "After MaryAnne, we needed to be cautious. This . . . this was the opposite of cautious."

"You one hundred percent told me last week that we were all signals go on regrets."

"Yeah, but I was talking about adopting a dog or . . . I don't know, getting bangs!"

Cleo sank back in her chair, so Gaby did the same.

"A) I am not getting bangs—"

"It was a spur-of-the-moment suggestion," Gaby conceded. "It was not a good one. Bangs wouldn't suit you."

Gaby sighed. Cleo sighed. Both of them knew that neither of them really came out on top when they argued. They were too evenly matched and also each too stubborn to really give up much ground. Also, this wasn't the part of the romantic comedy where Kate Hudson started fighting with her best friend. It wasn't even a romantic comedy, actually. Bowen Babson hadn't even fucking kissed her.

"Also, there's something else to consider, which really, honestly, Clee, I wish you'd come to me first."

"What is it?" Cleo didn't have any fight left in her either.

"This whole film-before-you-think culture, well, people are wondering if you made Nobells look guilty without giving him a chance to defend himself."

Cleo felt the blood drain from her face. "He *is* guilty; he *was* guilty. I have emails! Bowen vetted it before we did anything!"

"We'll see how that plays out, I guess. And I should say it's not all terrible. A lot of it isn't, actually. I'm running some internals, trying to see where your voters would come down. It seems like you've locked up women. The men, well . . ." Gaby flipped her hand at the implication. "Of course."

"I'm not interested in internals, Gaby. This is my life, not a policy issue. I thought that was the point? I thought you wanted to make me look . . . less robotic; isn't that what you said? *Exploit my gumption*, if I were to quote Veronica Kaye?"

"I just don't want anyone calling you crazy."

Cleo folded her hands underneath her chin. "Aren't they going to call me crazy anyway? Isn't that just what people do? To a young woman—"

"Youngish."

"To a youngish woman who is considering running for president? Isn't that just what people are going to do?"

Cleo thought of Lucas then, and for the first time really did understand why this was excruciating for him. Her past, her sex life, the gossip, the way she went about it without giving him any warning. She had thought she was protecting him by slipping to New York and leaving him to his idyllic soccer pool party, but he wasn't a child now. She could see why it felt more like a betrayal. She needed to pay better attention to him, she realized, her heart splitting open just a little. She needed to recalibrate her life to ensure that it was in sync with his. If it wasn't, what was the purpose of this whole thing?

Gaby lost herself for a beat too. "I have to ask: we were friends in law school. Good friends, I thought. Why wouldn't you tell me? Why did I have to first hear the hints of this from MaryAnne Newman's op-ed, and I mean, how the hell did she even know?" Gaby looked pained at Cleo's exclusion, at her silence. Cleo saw it in the wince of her eyes, the hunch of her shoulders.

"I don't know," Cleo said. And she really didn't. In law school it was probably out of shame, first for the affair, then out of the notion that perhaps someone could think she was benefitting from the affair, and then, finally, because of how humiliating it had been when he ended it. In the years since, likely because it was easier to stuff it down and move on. That was how Cleo got through just about everything. "I didn't tell anyone. Hadn't told anyone until this weekend. I have no idea about MaryAnne other than she was always an excellent gossip. She would have made a kick-ass reporter, to be honest."

"You could have told me. I wouldn't have judged you," Gaby said.

"It wasn't about judgment," Cleo replied, though maybe it was. Women judged other women all the time. Just ask Susan and Maureen and Beth, who had made up their minds about Cleo two decades ago and also how she probably made up her mind about them too. "I was just protecting myself, I guess."

"I think you were protecting *him*," Gaby suggested, rising, ready to get on with their day.

Cleo thought about that for a long time after Gaby left, after she'd drunk the coffee Arianna had brewed, after Gaby returned and said that internals for women were looking even stronger than she anticipated but that the blowback was poised to be formidable too. Cleo thought about how tangled up it can all get, love and ambition and life and sex and doubt and acceptance and loneliness and, yes, regret. And how sometimes, in the mix of all that, you no longer see yourself clearly and instead you start to view yourself through someone else's lens, for better and also for worse. Cleo was lucky enough to have disentangled herself from Nobells before he convinced her he could mold her into whomever he wished, before he enticed her to believe that he was the reason behind her success, that they were the Pygmalion myth brought to life, with him carving her out of stone, then giving her breath.

But she didn't regret confronting him. She didn't regret asking Bowen to livestream it. She didn't regret burning it all down. If she had to do it all again, she would. Tomorrow.

That was the opposite of regret, she decided. That was living.

# SIXTEEN

Arianna was the one who first saw the hashtag, which made sense, since neither Gaby nor Cleo spent anywhere near the same amount of time on social media as she did.

"Oh yeah," she said the next morning. "I have a search set up for you. You don't?"

Timothy, one of the four men who worked on her staff and who was theoretically charged with being her deputy communications manager, wandered in and said, "Wait, you don't have a search on yourself?" Then he wandered out, like he had contributed all that he needed to.

Cleo had looked at Gaby, who was unpeeling an orange and licking the juice off her fingertips. "Do you have a search set up on me?"

Gaby shook her head. "I thought we brought Arianna and Timothy in specifically to *do* this so I didn't have to?" She broke off an orange wedge. "If I tracked every mention, I wouldn't have time for anything else. Not after your little rendezvous to Columbia, that's for sure."

Things were still not totally settled between the two of them. They weren't going to fight about it, Cleo knew, but that didn't mean that Gaby had altogether let it go—not just that Cleo had ostensibly ruined her weekend with Oliver but that she hadn't consulted Gaby about the whole thing in the first place. Cleo didn't blame her. She probably would have nursed the bruise too. She did trust, however, that Gaby would never pen an op-ed about her no matter what, and because of this trust, she gave Gaby the space to be a little pissy and then move on.

"You guys should definitely have a search," Arianna said, the student becoming the master. "Like, that's where I see so much good stuff."

From another office, Timothy echoed: "Yeah, for sure! Searches turn up all the good stuff."

Cleo didn't know if "good stuff" meant juicy gossip, and thus not really good stuff, or genuinely good stuff, as in Cleo was a saint. It didn't matter. Arianna was still talking.

"So, like, I saw this hashtag last night, and I thought it was a one-off, but look, this morning . . . there are hundreds of them." Arianna jabbed at her phone with the dexterity that only a child who has been raised on an iPhone can. She thrust the screen toward them. "See?"

There, on Twitter, were hundreds of tweets, more coming in by the second.

#pullingaCleo

"What the hell is 'pulling a Cleo'?" Gaby asked before she sucked on the rind of the orange. Cleo made a face. "What? All of the nutrients are in the rind. I'm training for a marathon."

"I haven't forgotten."

Gaby blew out her breath like Cleo was testing her patience.

"It's . . . Wait, here." Arianna swiped and clicked a few more buttons, and then there was a video playing. "See, look? Senator McDougal, you've inspired all these women to confront the men who took advantage of them. And they're filming it, so it's all captured in real time. Like, there aren't any take backs."

"Oh!" Cleo said.

"Oooh," Gaby said, then reached for her own phone in her back pocket and pulled up the app.

"It's all over," Arianna said. "I think this could go seriously viral."

"It *is* going seriously viral," Timothy yelled from a door away.

"Oh!" Cleo said again.

"We do need to be cautious—the backlash, Cleo; we can't ignore that," Gaby replied, looking at neither of them, her singular focus on her screen. "I'm making a call." She placed her phone to her ear and left.

Cleo herself was late for a meeting with Senator Jackman about the free housing bill. Also, she wasn't sure if she wanted her personal story with Nobells to be trending or not. It was one thing to stride into his office and say her piece; it was another for it to become a nationwide phenomenon, which, if she had thought it through, she should have anticipated. Of course she wanted young women to reclaim their power or not abandon it in the first place, but reclaiming that wasn't as easy as simply speaking your mind and putting it on camera. Putting it on camera meant exposing your trauma, and that potentially unearthed all sorts of secondary complications. Cleo didn't want young women to think they had to air their emotional bruises just because she had. And then there was the other fallout, the equally as unsavory blowback: the steady stream of disgusting, misogynistic emails and phone calls that had come into the office all morning. Not to mention the angry missives about the "film first, think later" tactic that Cleo had employed and that her copycats were employing too. Cleo didn't regret that because it was the only way she could have seen it through. But still, she didn't want other women to step in shit just because she had.

Cleo checked the time again and, with the phones a nonstop bleat in the background, she grabbed her notes and briefcase. The internet and the hashtag and the furious calls would march on without her, whether or not she stewed over it. She resolved that stewing would give Alexander Nobells the win, and he'd already come out on top far too often. She was a senator, goddammit. She was about to craft the Jackman-McDougal Free Housing Bill that might genuinely change lives for the better. No one, not even her lecherous law school professor, who almost took credit for her worth and simultaneously cost her a job in Big Law, could stop that.

She slid her feet into her dreaded heels and went. Her toes pinched and her calves hated her, but she had to admit that she was standing taller.

⁓

By the afternoon, a counter-hashtag had been started. Because of course it had been. A particular set of men was *angry* that they were being held to account, and a particular set of women was *angry* on their behalf.

"Yeah," Arianna said. "But it still has two thousand fewer posts than ours does."

#notallmen had taken flight thanks to Suzanne Sonnenfeld, who had a considerable Twitter following and a cable show in prime time, where she frequently conjured up trouble from nothing. Lucas had once said she probably hid a broom behind her desk so she could fly home, and though Cleo was firmly against the sexist nature of his joke—*she's not a witch, Lucas,* she'd snapped, *and even if she were, we aren't against witches, per se!*—she really only chastised him out of principle. Not because Suzanne wasn't possibly a witch—to be clear, she was a horrible, miserable woman. But Cleo would not bring herself to call her a bitch either, because that was even worse. *Language matters,* she'd yapped at Lucas, whose eyes could not physically have rolled farther back into their sockets. *If you want to insult someone, make it smart. Insult her for spreading lies when she knows that they're not true. That's where you go for the jugular.*

"She's an irresponsible piece of shit," Gaby said when they were once again gathered in her office. Cleo didn't argue because she was figuratively correct about that. Suzanne had been known to incite online mobs and stoke partisan and gender and class and race divides, just for ratings. They'd once been seated at a table together at a fundraiser for ovarian cancer, and in person, Suzanne wasn't even particularly putrid—she was also a single mom with a son around Lucas's age, and in that moment Cleo found her perfectly—well, relatively—normal, which made her on-screen persona all the more repugnant. She didn't even believe in the flames she was stoking, but they'd made her famous and they'd made her rich, so she poured on gasoline and watched the blaze.

"She's like your friend MaryAnne if MaryAnne had been given a cable show," Gaby added.

This wasn't fair, and Cleo said so. "I actually did something bad to MaryAnne—" she started, but Gaby cut her off.

"Don't admit your full culpability; that's where they get you. Since when have you gone so soft?"

Cleo started to argue—she wasn't going soft! But a twinge in her gut *did* feel guilty over MaryAnne, and she *had* sent Matty an Alaskan gift basket with a semiflirty note, and she also tried to maul Bowen Babson. So maybe she was suddenly gooier than she realized. Normally she and Gaby were aligned in their steely spines, in their "do not pass go" attitudes.

This new vulnerability could not stand.

"Fine," Cleo said. "Tell me what to do. I'm listening."

"Bowen has issued an open invitation to go on his show," Gaby said over a lunch of pizza delivery for the whole staff. Cleo preferred to order in (or have Arianna do it) when she remembered that it was lunchtime (which was less often than you'd think), because it meant everyone stayed at their desks, maximizing productivity. She knew it was spring and the weather was seductive and some people liked to run to a yoga class, and she didn't mean to be a sly little hard-ass (she did, though), but if she were going to run for president or even be the most effective senator (last year she'd placed second on the number of sponsored bills signed into law), she had to insist that they stay in.

Admittedly, a few of them were paler than they should be and looking not as healthy as their vibrant twenties and thirties would suggest, but welcome to Washington, friends. Also, since the livestream, their phones, both at the DC and her local New York state offices, had not stopped ringing. It was all hands on deck, even if that meant her staffers didn't reach their Fitbit step count for the day. Gaby had the team tallying the positive versus negative calls, and right now there was a 73 percent posted on the whiteboard in their common room. That meant that 73 percent of constituents had her back.

"I'm not doing Bowen's show." Cleo ripped the crust off her slice and ate that first.

Gaby looked at her with a particular peculiarity. "Did you also sleep with him in New York? On top of everything, God, please tell me you didn't sleep with him?"

"I thought you were actively encouraging me to get laid." This was more of a statement than a question, since they both well knew that Gaby was and they both also well knew that if they counted backward to the last time Cleo had headily made out with someone in that rip-your-clothes-off, heat-of-the-moment, can't-stop-an-oncoming-train type of way, that Kate-Hudson-romantic-comedy-climax kiss, they might never find that moment. *Regret.*

"I am encouraging that," Gaby said. "But not with him. Conflict of interest all around. You can see that, right?"

Cleo nodded. She hadn't seen that, actually, but now, when presented with the notion, she could. Opponents would accuse her of manipulating the press with her diamond vagina, and there'd be an entire movement against her that mostly revolved around slut shaming and, once again, how she slept with a man for the sole purpose of bettering her position. It was the easy blow, the salacious one.

"When will it ever be OK for women to have sex just for sex's sake?" Cleo asked.

"You can. I did this weekend. A lot."

Cleo scowled.

"I just mean that it can't be with someone who has something to offer you," Gaby said. "It's not fair. It's the opposite of fair. But, Clee, we don't want to give anyone anything to use."

Cleo sighed. "Well, I'm still not going on his show later. I made plans with Lucas."

Arianna poked her head through the door. "Senator McDougal? I'm sorry to interrupt—"

"No, you're not *sorry*, Arianna; that's your job. To interrupt me."

"Right, I'm sorry. But the majority leader's office just called? He wanted you to stop by."

Gaby's chin dropped simultaneously with her eyebrows rising. "Well, that sounds important."

Arianna continued. "They said he has about ten minutes in about ten minutes."

Cleo stood, looked around for a napkin. Her desk was just papers and files and more papers and files. She grabbed a spare copy of the *Seattle Post-Intelligencer* with MaryAnne's ad from the week before and wiped her hands. Then she slipped her heels back on, reached for her Veronica Kaye lipstick and blush, and pulled her hair into a bun.

"I haven't forgotten about Bowen," Gaby called after her. "So I'm putting it in your schedule for tomorrow. Did you hear me? I'm confirming you for tomorrow."

Cleo had heard her. But tomorrow was another day. She'd triage that situation when the time came. That was one of her specialties.

# SEVENTEEN

William Parsons, the majority leader from the great state of Arizona, was sixty-eight years old and had been in the Senate for four consecutive terms. Cleo rushed down the halls of the Russell Building, her heels clacking and echoing. A few reporters lurked around corners, looking bored and scanning their phones, until they eyed Cleo flying through, and then they raised those phones-turned-mics to inquire about Nobells, inquire about the hashtag, inquire whether this whole thing didn't make her look a little bit unhinged. She stopped only for that one.

"No," she snapped. "I will not allow you to portray me as crazy for confronting a man who had something to apologize for." And then she kept on running and arrived outside the heavy wooden doors of his office with one minute to spare. Senator Parsons was known to run an even tighter ship than Cleo: he did not tolerate tardiness, he notoriously hated both grammatical mistakes and even the tiniest of factual errors, and he did not suffer fools. For all these reasons, Cleo generally liked him. He was usually dispassionate, and he was tough, and he held his staff to exceptionally high standards, which meant that stories had circulated for years about his occasional temper tantrums and his frequent use of extremely creative profanity, but Cleo figured that no one came to the Senate for a playdate, so you either put on your big-girl pants or you got a job in lobbying.

Senator Parsons's office was nearly empty when Cleo arrived. An assistant with a phone pressed to his ear waved her in, then held up a finger. Cleo found it both amusing and terribly rude and presumptuous—that a twenty-three-year-old was beckoning her into the senator's hallowed space but also indicating that she wasn't yet allowed to speak.

The aide, Albie, whom she had seen scurrying after Senator Parsons on occasion, finally clunked down the phone, and Cleo was ready for him to apologize in the way Arianna would have. Instead, he said: "The senator is ready for you." Then he returned to his keyboard and started typing.

Cleo knocked on Senator Parsons's door and entered when he said, "Come in."

His office, actually a fairly posh suite, was much more impressive than hers, a perk of being not just the leader of the majority party but being one of the senior-most members of the Senate. Washington was a hierarchy, after all, even with office space. There were photos with all the living past presidents, more photos with global leaders at various world conferences. There were opulent vases and decorative gilded candlesticks and, naturally, a United States flag in the corner. Light bounced off the overhead chandelier; a velvet couch enticed a nap. On one wall, a flat-screen was set to mute and played CNBC. Cleo knew that before his rise in politics, the senator had made a fortune as an investment banker, and he liked to keep an eye on his portfolio.

Senator Parsons rose from behind his desk and embraced her.

Cleo for the life of her had no idea why she was here, but perhaps the senator had heard the whispers about reviving the free housing bill (she loved the sound of the Jackman-McDougal Bill—not least because it was the first policy she'd worked on all year that felt pure and honest and impactful, not laden down with compromise and favors—and kept saying it over and over to herself in her mind) and wanted on board.

It would be surprising, what with his banking background and what Cleo assumed was his general distaste at the notion of giving something out for free, but every once in a while, politicians made morally correct choices, rather than politically expedient ones.

He sat, and so she sat. He cleared his throat, and she smiled. (Polling showed that men of his generation liked women much more when they smiled.)

He held the silence for a moment, so Cleo thought perhaps she was supposed to know why she was here and made an opening statement.

"You let your staff take lunch?" Cleo said. "I made mine order in."

Parsons laughed. "No, no. They're in a meeting down the hall. Getting their asses chewed out by my chief of staff. I like to do that every once in a while for no reason—just to put them on notice." His smile dropped. "So, Cleo, let me be frank."

"I would expect nothing less from you, William." Cleo sat up straighter, ready to welcome his support for the free housing bill and get down to the nitty-gritty of how it could benefit his own constituents, how the road to its passage was going to be tough but not impossible, and how Cleo always rose up for a fight.

"There has been . . . quite a commotion about your . . . situation this weekend."

"Oh." Cleo felt a quiet clang of alarm in the quickening of her pulse.

Senator Parsons waved an age-spotted hand. "Before we go any further, let me say that I support women! I am here for you! I have a daughter about your age, you know."

"I do know," Cleo said, wondering why on earth she should give a shit that he had a daughter in her late thirties, much less what it had to do with her situation with Nobells.

"You know we are supposed to be taking a delegation to the Middle East next week," he said.

"Of course, the CODEL. One of my favorite parts of the job. Getting on the ground and speaking with the troops."

"Yes, well." Parsons let his voice drift. "I worry that this situation . . . with the . . . 'hashtag'"—he mimed air quotes—"I worry it has become a distraction. My office has been getting calls."

"I'm sorry?" Cleo said. She wanted to retract that immediately, because she was not fucking sorry at all. She was confused how one thing was related to the other in the least.

"Right. My suggestion is that you sit this trip out," he said.

Cleo's already straight spine shot up even taller. "Sir, with respect, why would I sit this trip out?"

He leveled his eyes at her. "Senator," he said. "I *admire* what you . . . what your generation is doing; I'm an *ally*, but—" He paused, perhaps due to the look on her face.

Cleo could feel the heat of her rage rising to her cheeks. She sensed that she was barely going to contain herself from screaming: *You are on your third fucking wife! You think that you're an ally, but your staff is 95 percent male! You are sitting here demoting me because I caused an outrage! That isn't an ally; that's a wolf in sheep's clothing.*

When Cleo said nothing, he continued. "As I said, I'm an ally, but I've conferred with the committee chair, and we both agree that you on this trip will be a distraction."

"A distraction? William, I can walk and chew gum at the same time. I can speak with the troops and tell young women that they shouldn't have to deal with lecherous older men at the same time."

At this, Senator Parsons's forehead rose, and he clicked his tongue loudly. A reprimand. As if Cleo were attacking him by attacking his peer group.

"I didn't ask you here to debate me, Senator McDougal. I asked you here to inform you of . . . the discussion we've been having with the senior members of your committee."

"So now you're conferring with the committee without me?" Cleo was nearly on her feet, but then what? What was she actually going to do? Clock him? She settled back down.

"No, but there has been some talk that you violated this man's right to a defense—that your actions framed him as guilty before he had a right to prove otherwise."

"He *was* guilty. He *is* guilty." Cleo steamed.

"Be that as it may, I fear this is going to escalate, take away your focus, distract the men and women we are there to support. Distract the embeds we're flying over with us. I don't want the journalists to be asking you questions about . . . this . . . when it has nothing to do with our mission." He folded his hands in front of him on his desk. "I believe this is the best decision for everyone."

Cleo wanted to point out that technically this wasn't his decision to make. The entire Intelligence Committee and a few stragglers were going on the trip, and by benching her, he was placing her at a deficit. Which reduced her effectiveness as a senator and therefore impeded her duty to her constituents and her oath to the Constitution. But Cleo had scaled these mountains before, fighting the fight against men who weren't going to be swayed, even when they were in the wrong. There was something remarkable about this arrogance, really. How easily they could plant their flags on the erroneous side of the facts and stare you straight in the eye and almost convince you that the world was flat. Cleo could surely still go on the trip if she insisted on escalating what Parsons wanted her to quell, if she released Nobells's emails and texts, if she demonstrated a pattern of his retaliatory behavior. Or if she simply showed up with a packed bag on the tarmac. She knew he wouldn't boot her in front of her peers. But politics was a bit like chess: you had to move with an eye on the whole board, with a 360-degree view of what would come next and the move after that. Both she and Senator Parsons knew that if she checked him now, he'd find a way to checkmate her later.

She stood, exhaled, tried to compose herself. He wasn't the first asshole who would shove her down the steps while pretending to out-stretch his hand. In fact, that was Alexander Nobells.

"Message received, Senator."

"I hope you understand, Cleo," he said to her back, because she was already headed out. "I'm only suggesting what I think is best."

She almost turned and asked him: *Best for whom?* But why bother? She wasn't going to change a privileged sixty-eight-year-old man. She'd rather save her breath for when she really needed to scream.

She closed the door behind her, then spun and flipped him the middle finger with both hands. When she saw Albie's eyes widen in shock, she said, "Oh, fuck him."

And he said, "Wow, that time of the month?"

And then she got right up close to his acne-riddled chin and said: "Fuck you too."

And she didn't regret that at all.

Cleo was in an exceptionally bad mood by day's end, even with the promise of dinner with her son, who had been avoiding her since her return and since the rise of the #pullingaCleo hashtag. As of that morning, more than a hundred videos of women confronting their superiors had been filmed and uploaded, and Arianna was squealing that Cleo had started a revolution. Lawsuits were being threatened all over, naturally, by many of the accused—and Cleo wondered if Nobells would dare to try. She supposed that Senator Parsons wasn't entirely wrong—that by filming first, thinking later, she had gotten out ahead of Nobells's right to defend himself but, she thought as she stewed at her desk, *boo-fucking-hoo*. It wasn't the most prudent political thought, but she had it all the same. Cleo had learned that when dishonest men were faced with the unavoidable truths of their past, they tended to posture and point fingers (often while screaming in quite hysterical tones), but she also still knew that with Nobells, at the very least, she was right. She also recognized that women risked so much by speaking up that false accusations were rarely a reality, and she hoped that if the women were strong enough to face the men who had made them feel powerless in whatever form that took, they were strong enough to endure the threats.

She hated, of course, that women were threatened in the first place. That it was simply understood that if you took your story public, you would endure not just scrutiny but public shaming and terror too. This was the price women paid to speak their truths. Cleo couldn't change that. She could only speak hers.

And then there were other prices to pay too: getting stripped of the delegation trip, being whispered about in the hallways when you walked by a huddle of men from the other side of the aisle, listening to Suzanne Sonnenfeld suggest that she had your home address and why don't people show up and protest. Maybe Cleo should have seen all this coming because she was usually quite prescient, but this time she simply hadn't.

She had hoped Lucas would be proud of her defiance. She didn't pretend to understand the teenage boy mind—she hadn't even understood it back as a teenager; just look at how she dumped the very kind, tenderhearted Matty—but still, that was her aspiration. For her son to beam with pride in the way that Arianna had. Even Timothy, her deputy comms director, seemed impressed.

Lucas, however, quite obviously was not. Thus, this morning on their way to school, before Senator Parsons sent her into a rage spiral, she gently asked him if he would skip dinner at Benjamin and Emily's tonight and if instead she could pick him up after soccer and they could go to their favorite burger joint, PATTIES. It had been their regular thing since they'd moved to DC—mother-son midweek dinners, when Cleo would turn off her phone for the hour and before Lucas had a whole life of his own, and he wasn't angry with her, and she wasn't confronting ghosts of her past that made her angry with herself as well. They'd order three different types of fries (curly, sweet potato, and shoe-string) and laugh about how Lucas liked mustard on his, which Cleo couldn't believe and didn't know where he'd gotten that from. She did, probably she did know—it must have been from his dad, but then, she didn't know Doug well enough to be sure about that either.

Lucas had begrudgingly agreed to dinner tonight, only after putting up a fight because Emily was making homemade meatballs and he loved them, but Cleo charged her voice with just enough authority to let him know that the invitation wasn't really a request. Not unlike what Senator Parsons had done today. Lucas huffed "fine" and then put on his noise-canceling headphones that Cleo probably never should have bought him to begin with. Besides, Cleo worried that Emily might start to think she had nearly abandoned him. Also, she really hoped Emily didn't hold this whole hashtag situation and general public outcry against her, not least because part of the impetus of the whole caper had been her rotten unfaithful husband in the first place.

Lucas was waiting for her outside the soccer field. Cleo had aimed to get there early and watch the last few minutes of practice, but naturally, she was running late. Gaby had exploded into her office as she was packing up to leave and announced with breathless abandon that Veronica Kaye was starting a Pulling A Cleo Legal Defense Fund to help any and all women who wanted to come forward about their own experience.

"*A legal defense fund!*" she'd screamed. "This is basically an endorsement!"

Then Arianna rushed in behind her, without any apology, and shouted, "Senator McDougal, another woman came forward about Nobells! You did it!"

And Cleo lost her breath a little at that, at the solidarity that comes from establishing a sisterhood, and that maybe Nobells would get what was coming to him, even so many years later. But then she noticed the time, and she threw some files into her briefcase and didn't even have a chance to celebrate all the news, much less tell Gaby about the Middle East delegation boot, which was maybe for the best, because Gaby might have considered literal murder of the majority leader once she heard. Instead, Cleo raced around them both and out the door, offering general remarks of enthusiasm, certain that if she were late for Lucas, any sort of progress she hoped to make with his overall demeanor and communication through grunting would be lost.

But she was late anyway, and he was the last one to be picked up, so already she was behind in her quest for redemption.

"I'm not feeling well," Lucas said when he slid into the car. He groaned and curled over. "Can we just go home?"

Cleo noted, unfortunately, that he likely had not used deodorant this morning as he promised but bit back her temptation to comment. She made a note to ask Emily Godwin how she got Benjamin to wear deodorant daily. It didn't seem like such a herculean ask, and yet here they were.

Lucas had always been an obstinate kid, and Cleo generally had never minded. She herself was obviously headstrong, and she thought it had served her well. You don't become the youngest congresswoman in government without the ability to brace against a storm. During his toddler days, back when she was rendezvousing with Nobells about twice a week—in his office, at his place when Amy was away, the occasional hotel, but always during the day so she could be back with Lucas each night—well, that was the worst of it. The two of them, mother and son, trapped in an unending cycle of who could be more stubborn. Usually, because Lucas didn't have the vocabulary that Cleo did, which meant that he screamed and screamed until she worried that someone in their new apartment building would call CPS, he won. He went through one particularly brutal phase when he refused—just refused!—to wear anything but shorts, even in the dead of winter. Cleo didn't have any mom friends. It wasn't like there was a gang of student mothers at Columbia Law, and how else was she expected to meet women who were raising young children? She didn't have time for those weekday music classes where the kids sat around with dirty fingers and smacked bongos; she certainly didn't have time to work with him on his flexibility or forward roll at gymnastics. They did take a mother-son swim class at the Columbia pool together, but Lucas hated the smell of the chlorinated air, and Cleo hated the very judgmental instructor who couldn't believe that Lucas, at two, did not want to learn to float, so they stopped going after the second lesson and instead got croissants and cocoa every Saturday morning. That was their moment of peace before he jutted his chin in revolt of whatever else Cleo wanted, and she sighed and sat on her couch and felt in over her head, even when she adored this willful creature more than anything else in the world.

She could have called her sister, but she didn't. Not because Georgie wouldn't have helped. Cleo knew that she would have done more than help. She, then well on her way to becoming an A-list therapist, would have sent parenting books and recommended websites and probably shipped some bath oils and organic towels too.

But Cleo didn't want that sort of help.

She'd been on her own, emotionally if not practically, since her senior year in high school, and frankly, she'd learned to navigate it. It didn't mean that she didn't need help. She knew, empirically, that she did. But she'd figured out enough shortcuts to get along by herself that she simply couldn't bring herself to tolerate Georgie's kindnesses. Even when she had to take Lucas out in the snow wearing shorts and endure the withering glares from other self-righteous mothers, she knew she would have found these kindnesses oppressive. Not because kindness wasn't wonderful, but rather because Cleo would have, like so many other times, taken them as a signal that she was less than. That she was a less good mother than Georgie. All these years later, Cleo considered this excuse and how stupid it sounded. No one knew how to be a great mother in all ways on instinct. Why had she assumed otherwise?

In the car, Lucas's stink had muted a bit. Maybe Cleo just adjusted to the smell. She wasn't sure.

"I really don't feel well," he said again. "Can we please just go home?"

Cleo had pinned her night on their dinner. She wanted to talk to him about juggling two girls: Marley and Esme. She wanted to talk to him about his life. And, she supposed, she needed to talk to him about hers. About Nobells, about the shitty decisions she made in law school, about everything that was blowing up.

She reached over from the driver's side, felt his forehead. She had never been good at assessing temperatures. Once, when he was in second grade and she was a freshman senator, he was whining at breakfast; she couldn't find the ear thermometer, and she was late for a meeting with, ironically, Senator Parsons (*prick!*), so she palmed his forehead and scoffed and stuffed him into the car and sent him to school. Ninety minutes later, the nurse called and said he had a 102 fever and couldn't she come *right now* to pick him up? Cleo remembered, even now, the criticism in the nurse's voice. *Of course no one knew how to be a perfect mother on instinct!*

"You do feel a little warm," Cleo said. She had no idea if he was warm or not, but his cheeks were drained of color, and she supposed that they could go to PATTIES another time. Lucas groaned and sank lower in the car seat. Cleo didn't want to give him an out, another missed day of school just because—and she wondered if this weren't part of a longer con that would stretch into the morning—but she didn't want to be negligent either.

She made a U-turn and headed toward home.

❧

Lucas immediately got into bed, mumbling that he was going to sleep for the night, and then slammed his door. Cleo poured him some orange juice and brought him two Tylenol and hoped that he could shake this or admit he was being melodramatic, because she was supposed to go on Bowen's show tomorrow, and Gaby was going to hit the roof if she bailed. He pulled his duvet up to his neck and moaned, and then he told her to get out, so she did.

She wound her way back into the kitchen and made herself a PB and J, then padded to her office. The free evening meant that theoretically she had time to review all the files she'd brought home, and yet after she eased into her chair and sat in silence without her phone or computer and devoured half the sandwich, she unlocked her top drawer and reached for her list.

She flipped the pages and found herself suddenly and unexpectedly missing her mom, who had always been excellent at assessing a fever just by the touch of her hand. Cleo guessed that Georgie was the same: even in her chaotic teen years, she was always more of their mom while Cleo was always more of their dad. And though their parents were a perfect pairing, she and Georgie just so rarely found common ground, as if a romantic partnership worked when it came to opposites but the same was not true of siblings or even friendship. Cleo ran her fingers down her list, searching for the entry. She'd told Gaby she'd consider some sort of public dancing (eek) and she would, but she needed to see it there again, concretely, on the page, as if not just to commit to the follow-through but also as a reminder of her lament in the first place. How much more of her mother she could have been. How much she regretted that she wasn't. Cleo thought back to her trip to Seattle not even two weeks prior, down by the waterfront, of those times her mom dragged her out to watch her paint and how antsy Cleo had been. How she considered it time wasted, how she thought it was wholly unproductive, just staring at the land and the lights across the water and committing it to canvas.

She returned to the second page, which had been penned during college. Nearly the entirety of the entries were devoted more to achievement—an American history exam she appeared to have gotten an 84 percent on—or pursuit of a future achievement—not making enough friends on the student government to be nominated for class president—than anything personal. Obviously, her senior year at Northwestern, there was an extremely personal, terribly intimate entry—two, actually.

She flipped forward and back and then forward again, and there it was: *I never learned to paint. Or sing. Or dance. Or anything. Maybe that could have been a nice thing.*

She stood suddenly. At seventeen, Cleo had happily given the bulk of her mother's paintings to Georgie; she didn't have the wall space nor the decorator's vision for them. They weren't what she anticipated hanging on her dorm room walls (she didn't end up hanging much), and now Cleo could see that they were reminders of her loss and, even back then, she preferred to look only forward. But when her grandmother died, Cleo took three paintings from her home, and over the years they'd traveled from house to house with her, never once leaving their Bubble Wrap. That was enough for Cleo until tonight—knowing they were in a closet somewhere, a hidden reminder of her mother and her gifts and that maybe somewhere, deep inside Cleo, she had a tiny, microscopic bit of an artist in her too.

Not an *artist* artist, Cleo thought as she rounded the corner in her hall, on the way to the storage space in her foyer. Just . . . that there was room inside her for something beyond the rigid and the logical and the straight and narrow. Her mom's paintings were always a little off, a small bit askew. Her dad used to rib her about it, the slightly awry perspectives. But her mom would just laugh because of course this was intentional; she was seeing things differently than everyone else, and she wasn't about to apologize for that.

She had to move all of Lucas's soccer gear and a bunch of snow stuff that he'd outgrown, but she found the paintings in the back of the darkened space. She tore the tape away, then the padding, and she lost her breath a little bit once she had. Her mother's artworks weren't glorious masterpieces. Cleo didn't need to study art history to know that. But they were masterpieces to her mom—and to her father too—and Cleo sank to the dirty floor of her storage space and considered that this had been enough for both of them. To make a little art, to paint a landscape that only your brain and imagination could, and to share it with someone you loved.

# EIGHTEEN

Lucas was still sick the next morning.

Cleo had hammered a hook into the wall to hang her favorite of her mother's paintings, and he hadn't even woken. Finally, ten minutes before they needed to leave for school (and work), she shook him awake and felt his forehead, which seemed clammy but she didn't think feverish. (But who really knew?) Overnight, forty-six more #pullingaCleo videos emerged, which meant thousands upon thousands of retweets and comments, which also meant that Gaby had texted her six times before she even showered, to ensure that she unequivocally absolutely *would not* back out of Bowen's show.

Cleo very much wished her home were better organized so she could find the thermometer and gauge whether or not she should force Lucas to school or if this was food poisoning or if this was just him wanting to skip. He'd been known to be an extremely excellent faker too.

"Lucas, please, buddy. You already missed school for our Seattle trip."

Lucas grunted again, then rolled away from her and pulled the pillow over his head.

"OK," Cleo conceded. "It will be a mental health day. Your last one. I'll call you around lunch to check in."

She retrieved the bottle of Tylenol and left another glass of orange juice on his nightstand.

Lucas was back asleep before she was out the door.

༄ༀ

Cleo was due on Bowen's set in the early afternoon, which gave her the morning to get her ordinary business out of the way.

"First of all," she said to Gaby as they waited for their coffee order near her office, "Parsons booted me from the trip this weekend."

"He *what?*" Gaby barked loudly enough that the barista stopped foaming the milk and stared. Gaby met his eyes and barked, "Does it look like this concerns you?" The barista took heed and kept foaming.

"It's fine," Cleo said. "Not *fine* but . . . I have some other things to deal with anyway. I'll have a quiet weekend. Lucas has a school retreat."

Cleo had second-guessed her decision to leave Lucas home alone sick the entire drive into the office, but what else was she supposed to do? In addition to the Tylenol and orange juice, she'd left him a note (which she realized too late he'd never read, so she texted him the same note verbatim) that said there was more orange juice in the fridge and bagels in the bread bin, and he should feel free to order in chicken soup. She couldn't help herself and added a tip that doctors had found real research on the fact that chicken soup was a natural remedy. Lucas hated soup and would probably find her suggestion incredibly annoying, but oh well, she had to try.

"There's another thing," Cleo said after they had armed themselves with caffeine and headed toward the office. "Where are we on the dancing?"

"It's harder than you would think to find just the right forum for a senator to dance." Gaby slowed her stride as a pack of men walked past and turned to stare at her (maybe at Cleo too, but more likely her) as they went. "On the one hand, I want Veronica to see your sass—"

"Would we say that I have sass?"

"We would say that you *will* have sass." Gaby laughed. "But on the other hand, I'm not so confident in your dancing skills that I really want to make this a public spectacle."

"We could cut the dancing. I could take a pottery class. Or glassblowing."

"You're not taking a pottery class."

"It's just about the art, about me trying the art," Cleo said, and Gaby made a face as if it should never just be about one thing when you can make it about so much more.

Cleo swung open the door to the Russell Building and held it for Gaby to enter, then for three more people—two men and an older woman—to pass through as well. She wasn't at all put off that the men hadn't offered. She wasn't looking for special treatment or gentlemanly gestures.

Still, though, she didn't much mind when the door swung closed behind her right as she saw the majority leader lumbering up the steps and asking her to hold it. She kind of hoped it smacked him in the face, bruised the crown of his nose, split open one of those dry, crusty lips.

It wouldn't make up for anything, but at least she'd enjoy watching him taste blood.

⁓

Gaby tasked Arianna with sifting through the mail to find an invitation to something . . . arty.

"Let's start there," Gaby said. "Anything that might have a live band with a few boldface names. Even if I film Cleo out there on the dance floor myself. I'll make it work."

Arianna raised her eyebrows and surely had something to say but did not. Over the years, her staff had made it known around town that Cleo would show up for a fundraiser for a cause she believed in (or for her own campaign's funding, naturally), but given her disdain for both small talk and art appreciation, she was not likely to waste her time on, say, pop-up art gallery shows to raise money for the homeless. She wanted to help the homeless, *of course*. Whichever staffer had to RSVP would emphasize this, and it wasn't even untrue. But she wasn't going to show up and eat cheese cubes and sip dry wine and nod at art that she didn't understand or think was all that good to do so. She'd rather spend the night writing legislation that made a difference. Like the Jackman-McDougal Bill.

"Well, this is something," Arianna said. "You . . . were invited to a prom?"

Gaby was midgulp in her latte and laughed so hard that she had to lean over the trash can and spit out her drink.

"I feel like that would garner bad press, like, something illegal?" Cleo replied. Then to Gaby: "What? I can't be hot enough to go to a prom?"

"Did you even go to your own prom?" Gaby retorted once she got control of herself.

As a matter of fact, Cleo had not. She had long since dumped Matty, and no one else was interested. Besides, by then she had been accepted to Northwestern, and she was well on her way to plotting her exit out of Seattle, so she spent prom night studying the course catalog and drinking Diet Cokes and listening to her grandmother answer the questions on *Jeopardy!*.

"Fine," Cleo said. "I'm obviously not going as someone's date to prom."

The phone kept ringing as Arianna sifted through the mail.

"Don't get that," she said to Cleo and Gaby, as if either of them had taken to answering their own phone lines. "It's just more stuff about the hashtag. Pros and cons." She looked toward Gaby. "Don't worry—I'm still tallying them."

They all paused and looked toward the whiteboard. The pros were creeping up toward 77 percent, but underneath, Arianna had also written in all caps and underlined: *FIRST LAWSUIT*.

"There's actually a lawsuit?" Cleo asked, a little alarmed.

"Not against you," Arianna replied. "A high schooler in Omaha who outed some big-deal friend of her dad's. She filmed it, and it's gotten, like, fifty thousand YouTube likes, and now he's suing her for defamation."

"Jesus Christ," Gaby said. "What is wrong with people?"

"A lot." Arianna shrugged.

Gaby turned to Cleo. "This is what I warned you about. This 'film first' tactic gives these dickheads an opening."

"I know." Cleo nodded. "But still, with Nobells, it worked." In fact, Columbia had just issued a press release announcing the illustrious professor was taking a "sabbatical" while they investigated.

"Clee." Gaby sighed. "We both know that just because something works doesn't mean that it's not reckless. Veronica Kaye knows that too. We have to be smarter, OK?"

Of course they had to be smarter. They were women.

Arianna returned to the mail pile, then looked up, remembered something, stuttered, then stopped.

"Well, I mean, something came in a few weeks ago?" She shook her head. "I'm sorry; it's stupid."

"You did it again," Cleo said. "You apologized."

"Shoot, I'm sorry!" Arianna's face went slack. "Goddammit!"

"What was that one?" Gaby asked.

"Oh God, I shouldn't have even mentioned it. It's just that, well, no offense, Senator McDougal, but no one is really after you for your arts patronage."

"Maybe I can just take a class," Cleo said. "It doesn't need to be a grand gesture."

Gaby bugged her eyes like it very much needed to be a grand gesture. "What was the one from a few weeks ago, Arianna?" she pressed.

"I replied no, but maybe I can switch it. You're here this weekend, right?" Arianna flipped through some papers in the bottom drawer of her desk.

Cleo nodded a curt *yes*. No delegation. Lucas on his retreat. She was begrudgingly available.

"Whatever it is, as long as it's legal and not a prom, she'll do it," Gaby said, then dragged Cleo into her office. They had Bowen Babson to prepare for.

༄

On the way to the studio for Bowen's show, Gaby was talking a mile a minute, even faster than her usual rate. She had informed Veronica that Cleo was not only pushing through the free housing bill (Gaby had not yet figured out how to make that one sexy for the public, but all parties agreed that writing good and valuable legislation could be used to Cleo's advantage regardless of sex appeal) but that Cleo may very well *dance in public* this weekend. Veronica Kaye had loved it.

"She *loooooved* it!" Gaby shrieked and pumped her fist in the air.

Cleo wanted to share in her joy, she really did. She knew it was no small thing that Veronica Kaye was boarding her train, going Only Forward!, but she was anxious about facing Bowen and she was worried because she'd called Lucas twice around noon and texted him three times and even figured out how to Snap him (Arianna had to help her, obviously), and she hadn't heard back. She'd missed a call from him about an hour ago when she was on a conference call with Senator Jackman going over the budgeting of just how they were going to ask Congress to subsidize their free housing, and now she couldn't get him to pick up.

"He's probably just sleeping," Gaby had said as they got into the town car, when Cleo wondered aloud if she should cancel. "Don't teen boys do that all day? Besides, I know you're avoiding Bowen, and honestly, Cleo, your hashtag has been trending for twenty-four hours, and you need to put your face out there as the woman behind the movement."

Neither of them mentioned that the hallway outside of her office was now teeming with protesters, angry men and also some angry (Cleo thought confused) women, carrying signs that screamed NOT ALL MEN and MEN HAVE RIGHTS TOO! and MEN DON'T RAPE—WOMEN DO! Cleo had to read that one twice to be sure she had seen it correctly, but Gaby yanked her by the arm before she could point out the (mostly) failed logic in this poor woman's argument. Cleo even had statistics to raise on-air, though she knew it would be a lost cause. In her experience, once people were so entrenched that they picketed outside your office building and took the time to write insane signs, they weren't open to being swayed.

"I'm putting my face out there," Cleo said. "Stop telling me that. I get it. I know that I need to address this. I just . . ." She stared out the window as they rolled to a stop at a red light by an Au Bon Pain. This made Cleo wish she were eating a croissant and reminded her that, in fact, she hadn't eaten since the PB and J last night, unless you counted this morning's latte. "Look, Bowen rejected me, and granted, I had had too much bourbon—"

"Oh my God, you can't drink bourbon."

Cleo nodded. "It was on my list. I couldn't remember why."

Gaby's eyes grew three sizes at least. "You didn't start dancing in front of him, did you?"

"What? No, why?"

"You really don't remember? The night at the end of our second year? The bourbon and . . . the bar . . . on which you danced? And subsequently fell off?" Gaby had an air of such astonishment that you'd think Cleo had told her she decided to retire and teach yoga.

Cleo squinted and tried to recall it. She could not for the life of her piece together the evening, but the timing checked out. Of course, back then, Gaby didn't know about Nobells, but Cleo remembered giving herself one night—*one night*—to be furious and to drown her sorrows and to wash away her shock at his disloyalty and her contempt at that disloyalty and then to put it behind her, inasmuch as a young woman can do that. Perhaps she did end up dancing on a bar. That certainly would be something for her list; she could see that now.

"And you're still pushing me to dance in public?" Cleo asked. "You can't get why that might be a terrible idea?"

"I think the bourbon more than the dancing was the problem," Gaby said, and Cleo took her point.

The town car started moving again, but her eyes lingered on the Au Bon Pain. Why was it so difficult for her to take care of herself? Was this why people had partners? Was this why they made room in their lives for someone else? Cleo knew, because she was not an idiot, that she could feed herself. But there was something in the underlying notion of it all: that she was constantly fraying at one end. By God, Emily Godwin had to show up with a chicken from Costco. She thought of Emily just then and how she really still very much wanted to cross jab Jonathan square on the nose.

Her phone buzzed alive in her lap. She didn't recognize the local number, and she'd normally never accept an unknown caller, but Lucas was ghosting her, and maybe he was stuck at a pay phone, in a store, a friend's, and trying her? Cleo didn't even know if they had pay phones anymore, but regardless, she picked up her cell. Beside her, Gaby folded a piece of gum on her tongue and offered her one too. Cleo shook her head, then reconsidered. This would have to be breakfast and lunch combined.

"Hello?"

"Cleo McDougal?"

"Yes, speaking."

"Hi, ma'am. Are you Lucas's mother?"

Cleo's heart jumped, and she reached to her side and clutched Gaby's arm so tightly that Gaby said, "Shit, ow!"

"Yes," Cleo managed.

"He's OK, ma'am," the woman said. "But we had to bring him in to Inova Alexandria—"

"The hospital?" Cleo dug harder into Gaby's arm.

"Yes, ma'am. He called 911 himself." She paused. "Don't worry, ma'am. I'm a single mom myself. I know how it goes."

"Oh shit, oh shit, oh shit, oh shit." Cleo released her grip on Gaby and felt tears behind her eyes, then down her cheeks. Why was she so fucking bad at feeling his forehead? Why wasn't she better organized and knew where the thermometer was? She was a goddamn United States senator and a future candidate for president. How hard was it to see that her son was sick? "Is he OK? Jesus, what is going on? I didn't think he was that—"

"It's his appendix." The woman cut her off. "It came on suddenly, so don't feel too bad. I think most moms would have mistaken it for a tummy ache. He's a responsible boy, ma'am. That's why he knew what to do. They're taking him into surgery now—it was quite emergent—but of course, Mom, he was asking for you."

"I'm on my way." Cleo hiccupped, barely managing the words, weighed down by the recognition that she couldn't even do right by the one person she was responsible for.

She had thought he might even be faking it! That's how awful her instincts were.

No wonder she was always alone. Maybe this was just how it was meant to be. Maybe when you compiled a list of 233 regrets (and she hadn't even updated it recently), this was the life you deserved.

# NINETEEN

Gaby had the driver drop them at the entrance of the hospital, then let Cleo rush in while she lingered behind to deal with her own type of triage: explaining to Bowen's producers why Cleo wouldn't be available for the taping that was set for less than an hour from now. As the car slowed, Gaby had offered herself up instead, which Cleo considered a kindness. Gaby hated doing live TV. She saw other strong, insightful black women too often portrayed instead as hysterical angry black women, and she found the tap dance around this stereotype so irksome that she often didn't even want to bother. But Cleo trusted her so implicitly, believed in her so empirically, and Gaby, equally hell-bent on putting a positive spin on the entire hashtag situation, agreed (somewhat begrudgingly) to be her messenger on Bowen's show.

Cleo ran through the halls toward Emergency as Gaby negotiated the situation on the sidewalk, much like she had rushed through the Senate halls toward Senator Parsons, only now with the recognition of the importance of one and not the other. She threw herself at the nurses' desk and reconsidered this notion. She wasn't going to be one of those women who suddenly deemed her life's work unimportant. She literally shook her head while ringing the desk bell—she slammed her hand down three times and spun around looking for someone on duty—and reminded herself that other than Lucas, her work was the only thing that mattered in her life, and she didn't have to disparage one to embrace the other. This wasn't going to be that type of story.

A young nurse appeared from the filing room, and her eyes widened in recognition.

"You must be Lucas's mom." She smiled a little shyly. She had long, sparkly purple nails and luminescent dark skin and a tiny diamond in her nostril and whiter, straighter teeth than Cleo had ever seen. In fact, Cleo thought she looked a bit like an angel. "I'm a huge fan, ma'am. I mean, I'm considering 'pulling a Cleo' tomorrow with a girlfriend." She shook her head. "Man, fuck that asshole. Screw the patriarchy." She held her fist out, and Cleo, feeling a bit like she was having an out-of-body experience, held her own fist out, and they bumped them together.

"Is he . . . ?" Cleo said.

"Oh my God!" The nurse thumped her hand to her chest, her purple nails shining under the bright lights. "I'm so sorry!" The nurse looked genuinely mortified, so Cleo did not tell her to recant her apology. "Your boy, I should have told you about your boy! He's going to be OK. He's in surgery now."

Cleo leaned against the nurses' station and thought it might be the only thing keeping her from complete collapse.

"You're not looking so great yourself, and I don't mean that disrespectfully, ma'am," the nurse said. She reached out and pressed the back of her hand against Cleo's forehead.

"No, I'm fine. I'm just . . . I haven't had time to eat all day. And obviously, I mean, this news, while I was at work." Cleo started quietly crying. She didn't even have to ask what was wrong with her—crying in public! She would normally be eviscerated for such a thing, but she found that she couldn't care. She knew what was wrong with her: her son was in emergency surgery and her blood sugar was dropping by the second and whoever the fuck said anything was weak about tears? "Do you . . . I mean . . . do you need my insurance or whatever?"

"Oh, ma'am." The nurse's name was Mariann. Cleo stared at her ID and wondered if maybe there actually were signals from the universe. Mariann opened the little swinging door to the back of the nurses' station and ushered her inside. "Come on, let me feed you. We have cookies. A lot of them."

"You don't have to—I mean, thank you, but I know you have work to do."

"Girl, we all have work to do. You do yours for me, just like you did when you filmed that teacher of yours, and I do mine for you, just like I am now by giving you some coffee and Oreos, and maybe I can rustle up some Jell-O. In fact, I know I can. The nurse on the shift before me hoards it. No one really knows why."

"Thank you." Cleo bowed her head and found that she couldn't stop crying.

"No woman is an island," Mariann said as she rubbed Cleo's back. "Even VIPs like you."

⌒

The surgery had gone well, the doctor told Cleo. They'd gotten to the appendix in time, well before it burst, and now it was just the standard recovery—rest and TLC for a few weeks.

The doctor kept addressing Cleo as "Mom," as in, "Mom, can you give him some TLC for a few weeks?" and Cleo very much wanted to direct him to use her name—she was more than just Lucas's mom!—but after neglecting her son and his (now) obvious fever and his (now) obvious distress, she didn't have the heart to push it. She'd thought it might have been a bit of spoiled food! She'd thought maybe he just wanted a mental health day! "Mom," the doctor was implying, was a compliment, and she didn't need to fight every ingrained battle when she knew the surgeon didn't mean anything by it other than that she was Lucas's caretaker, even when she hadn't been a very good one.

Lucas was still groggy, so Cleo sat with him, enveloped by the quiet tranquility of his room. She held his hand, which was bigger than hers now and warm and occasionally trembled when, she supposed, he dreamed, and which he'd never allow her to do if he were awake. It was just the two of them, as it nearly always was. Cleo squeezed her eyes shut and rested her head on his bed. She was so weary from everything. Maybe that's just how it was, with their little compact duo bracing against the world, but maybe it was also that it was so often just their little compact duo period.

Fifteen years ago, Cleo didn't tell a soul about her pregnancy. At some point it became obvious in the late summer when she was entering law school, but Columbia was a fresh start—she literally didn't know anyone—so she didn't have to explain herself other than the occasional, "No, no partner, no husband. I'm doing this alone." She called Georgie around the holidays when she was about eight months in and said, "Um, so I'm having a baby," and it was clear from her reaction that Georgie didn't know if she should be hurt that Cleo hadn't told her earlier or overjoyed that her twins would have a new cousin.

Her labor came two weeks early. Because Cleo was Cleo, she had a birth plan lined up and a bag at the ready. She hadn't taken a birthing class because she figured women had been doing this for centuries without learning how to breathe and push properly, and beyond that, she didn't want to be the only one to go through a fake labor on the floor of a school gym without a partner. When her water broke while she was frying an egg for dinner, she efficiently flipped the cooktop off, called her doctor, grabbed her bag, and hailed a taxi. All on her own. It wasn't that hard.

The contractions came quickly, so quickly that by the time she made it to the delivery ward, she was doubled over in true, visceral agony every two minutes. For a brief moment, she very much wished she *had* taken that Lamaze class, and if she were thinking about it later, she would add this to her list of regrets. Cleo McDougal was always prepared, and she didn't know why she had forsaken that aspect of god-damn birth preparation because she would have had to acknowledge that she was single and lonely and a little bit terrified. She tried to get through a contraction and admonished herself for being so shortsighted, for giving in to the weakness of choosing emotion over preparedness. Yes, she had a bag packed and yes, she had read a birthing book, but would it have been the worst thing to have learned how to breathe?

It was too late for an epidural, and from there her envisioned serene birthing plan flew out the window. She grunted and she pushed and she listened to strangers—the doctor who was not her usual OB-GYN because her usual OB-GYN was skiing in Vail, the nurses who held back her legs—and twenty minutes later, Lucas, red-faced and mushy and looking a little startled to have arrived on the planet, emerged. Cleo had counted on a relaxed, measured birth, but you got what you got, something she'd remind her son over and over again as he grew older.

Lucas stirred from his anesthesia-induced sleep but didn't yet open his eyes.

Cleo stared at him now, her handsome young man, and wondered how the time had gone so fast. She reached out, cupped his chin. She dropped her head back on his bed, waiting for him to finally rouse, realizing that just like when he'd emerged from her, tiny and perfect, it was the two of them, all alone in a hospital room.

For a long time, Cleo had figured this was the only way to do it. Now she wondered why she was so often alone in the first place.

*Regret.*

∾

Lucas awoke and was feeling a little better, texting his friends, Snapchatting away. He complained that his wound was uncomfort-able, and the nurses re-dressed it, and Cleo sat in the corner wishing there were more she could do to heal him.

A girl appeared in the doorway clutching a bouquet of GET WELL! balloons. Cleo recognized her as Marley Jacobson, one of Lucas's paramours. She thought of Esme, all the way in Seattle, and wondered if she knew that she had only half his heart. Then she wondered if maybe Lucas wasn't overcompensating by filling his life with loved ones to make up for the dearth of companionship that he saw in her own. She needed to talk to him about this, she knew, but for now she was touched that Marley was here, showing up for him, even if he'd probably also texted Esme for sympathy.

Cleo excused herself and wandered into the waiting area, hoping maybe someone she knew—Gaby, Emily—would have shown up, even though she hadn't asked them. She knew Gaby was likely still at the office, fielding the calls and comments from her stint on Bowen's show, which Cleo had watched on her phone while Lucas slept. Bowen had been both understanding and firm in his questioning, whether or not blindsiding these men was fair, whether or not filming them without giving them the opportunity of telling their side was just, even when he'd taken part in the very video that got it all started. Bowen had gotten his own blowback about that, of course, the journalistic integrity of it, but he opened the show detailing his fact-checking and why he thought it was a story worth exposing. The network stood behind him, though if the story had gone bust, maybe they wouldn't have. Also, he was an extremely gorgeous white man. He was a moneymaker. His face was on billboards and buses. Of course he was easy to defend.

"I know why I got involved with this," Bowen said as they were wrapping up. "But what about Senator McDougal? What sparked her to this now? And why?"

"I think the reason she did it," Gaby said, taking a beat, "is because we all live with regrets. And Senator McDougal is addressing those regrets she can change now. Wouldn't it be nice if we all had that luxury?"

"So there are others?" Bowen asked. Then clarified: "Other regrets, not men. That's Senator McDougal's business."

Cleo worried for a beat that Gaby would betray her, share the revelation on national television that not only did she have further regrets but that she had a lengthy list of 233 of them that she kept in her top desk drawer where most people stored pens and paper clips.

"Bowen Babson, you know as well as I do, as well as any of your viewers do, that you don't get through thirty-seven years of your life without making some mistakes. He who has, let him cast the first stone."

"Or she," Bowen pointed out before they cut to commercial. "She can cast that stone too."

In the waiting room, Cleo stared at the ceiling, and then she stared at the floor. Gaby wasn't coming. Emily wasn't coming. Bowen, obviously, wasn't coming. Matty wasn't coming. MaryAnne wasn't coming.

She understood that she hadn't asked. Maybe, she thought, it was as simple as that: asking.

She picked up her phone and dialed Georgie.

# TWENTY

Georgie flew in within hours. Literal hours. Cleo couldn't believe how quickly she showed up.

"Oh." She waved a hand and at least a dozen gold bangles clinked together. "A client was flying back and offered me a ride. We worked through some of her issues and we did some meditation, so it was a fair trade."

She pulled Cleo back into a second embrace, and Cleo inhaled deeply—much like Veronica Kaye, Georgie smelled magical. They hadn't seen each other in at least a year, likely longer. Cleo had done a fundraising stop in Los Angeles about sixteen months back—big donors at a mansion in Pacific Palisades—and she'd spent the night at Georgie's and said hello to the twins and Peter, Georgie's husband, who worked in real estate development. She wished she could say, there tangled up against her sister, that it was as if no time had passed, but it wasn't like that. Time had passed. Their lifetimes—thirty-seven years for Cleo, forty-seven for Georgie—had passed, and she didn't know her sister much better than she knew Mariann, the saintly nurse who had provided Oreos and a clipboard to fill out Lucas's insurance forms.

"Hi, Aunt Georgie," Lucas said when he woke, and honestly, Cleo was a little relieved that he remembered her. He barely knew his cousins, and he'd met Georgie on occasion but no more than half a dozen times. He offered her a shy smile, and Georgie rushed to him and clutched his cheeks and said, "My God, you are so goddamn handsome. How many girlfriends do you have?"

And Cleo said, from behind them, "Two, actually. It's a bit of a chauvinistic problem."

And Lucas groaned and said, "Mom, it's under control. Please stop. I was raised by a woman half the country considers their feminist true north right now, so Jesus, I'm not going to become an asshole."

Georgie laughed so hard that her bangles all clanged together again, and so Cleo managed a smile too, and already, just by adding one person to their small tribe, Cleo felt a little more optimistic.

"Besides," Lucas said, "Marley is committed to, like, her camp boyfriend too." He winced a little, and Cleo wasn't sure if it were at his incision or at the camp boyfriend. "It's all fine, Mom; no one has to be *together* together. Your generation is the one hung up on labels. We're just cool with, like, whatever."

Cleo didn't know what to say to that, since she thought half her life's work was dedicated to redefining labels, so rather than reply, she gazed at her son with wide, teary eyes and thought that she'd never been prouder of him in her life than now.

Lucas stared back at her, a little horrified that she was weeping openly, and said succinctly: "I've never seen you cry, Mom, like, ever."

"I'm sorry," Cleo said, though she still couldn't stop.

"It's OK," he said back. "Crying is fine. It doesn't bother me at all. Coach Beckett is always saying leave everything on the field, even your tears."

Cleo thought that she should spend more time around men like Coach Beckett and less around men like Senator William Parsons.

Georgie took her house keys and promised to stock the kitchen.

"You're too thin," she said and then paused. "My God, when did I become Mom? I promised myself it would never happen."

Cleo started crying again, batting her hands in front of her face as if that ever in the history of meltdowns slowed the crest of tears. She hadn't spent a lot of time missing her mother until recently and now, having unearthed her paintings from the storage space and having also evidently unearthed a swarm of unresolved feelings about at least five to a dozen regrets, she found that she was an open wound. She wished very much that Lucas's nurse could come in and re-dress hers as well.

"Oh, Cleo," Georgie said. "I didn't mean anything by that. You look fine. Really."

"Thank you for c-coming," Cleo sputtered and spotted Lucas staring at her with astonishment.

"Oh, baby sister, all you had to do was ask."

∽

On Thursday, the next day, Cleo was working from home, which she never, ever did during the week, but the condo was closer to the hospital than the office, so she allowed herself this convenience. Senator Jackman, who had raised two children of her own, told her that she and her legislative staff could put the finishing touches on the housing bill before they sent it off to Leg Council for the legal jargon, but Cleo didn't want to sit it out.

"It's nice to actually be putting forth some policy that really will spur positive change," Cleo had said in their last sit-down.

"Spoken like a presidential candidate," Senator Jackman had replied and winked, then grew serious. "If you run, I'll do everything I can to help you. God knows that women of my generation didn't have a shot."

Cleo promised her that she would be among her first calls.

"Not really *if* I run," she had said. "Rather when."

Senator Jackman thumped her manicured hands against her heart and beamed. Cleo wasn't even sure when she had made the concrete decision that she would, that she was wholeheartedly going to chase the presidency. She hadn't had much time to really weigh it, what with one recent calamity after another, but maybe it was one of those ideas that lurked around your subconscious, hidden but quietly calling out, until one day you woke up and you just knew. Maybe deciding to run for president for Cleo McDougal was a little bit like falling in love. One day she realized that she was done for.

Emily Godwin stopped by with two casseroles just after Cleo wrapped up doubleheader conference calls. Lucas had a steady stream of friends stopping by the hospital who were, she guessed, ditching school to say hi, in and out, so he practically begged her to give him some privacy and/or not embarrass him in front of them. Georgie had gone to a yoga class that she'd researched online. ("Why don't you come?" she'd implored, as if Cleo couldn't think of many things more embarrassing than attempting to morph herself into a pretzel in public, and then Cleo remembered that she'd agreed to *dance* in public this weekend.) So it was just Cleo, home alone, when Emily rang her doorbell.

Emily stood in her kitchen, and Cleo fumbled with her words. She hadn't seen her since that night when Jonathan had tucked his arm around that (extremely) young woman and exited the ballroom. It felt like two years ago, but Cleo met Emily's eyes and realized, good Lord, that was *last week*.

"Listen," Emily started. "I saw what you did with your old professor. I was really proud. I hope you aren't second-guessing it."

After Gaby's stint on Bowen's show, the protests outside her office had grown even rowdier. Arianna had emailed this morning to say that she was calling the Capitol police in to help. I did make sure to give them all the finger tho, she typed, then added the middle finger emoji.

Cleo shook her head. "No, not second-guessing it, though I probably didn't think it through as well as I should have. A lawsuit has been filed against one of the young women. I didn't mean it to spiral that way."

"Well, he deserved it," Emily said emphatically. "Fuck that guy."

Cleo emitted something like a hiccup, which she meant to sound like a laugh. Then she said: "I wasn't the only one he did it to, I guess. He's taking a 'leave of absence.'" She bounced her shoulders. Nobells facing his comeuppance felt good, but maybe not as good as she expected. But then, she didn't know what she expected.

"Also," Emily started, then stopped, wrung her hands and dropped them.

Cleo felt a swell of panic rise in her exhausted guts. She didn't want to be the one to tell Emily that her husband was just as much a piece of shit as Nobells. She didn't want to change everything in this simple, wonderful friendship that for Cleo was both rare and precious. She didn't want Emily Godwin to be yet another one of her regrets. She thought of MaryAnne then and for one short, piercing moment missed their complementary friendship, their Canadian bacon and pineapple pizza slices, their quest to be the highest scorer on her brother's Pac-Man game. God, why had she been so shortsighted back then to think the mayoral internship trumped their sisterhood? That the editor of the paper mattered more than MaryAnne's loyalty?

"I know—" Emily started.

"I ran into Jonathan the other night—" Cleo said.

"I know." Emily exhaled and focused on Cleo's countertop, which Georgie had cleaned that morning with a nonchemical expensive-smelling cleaner and looked better than it had in quite some time.

"We talked by the buffet. But I left early," Cleo said, hoping they could leave it at that, knowing that they probably couldn't. She didn't want anything to change between them; she didn't want to sacrifice this one woman she hadn't yet done anything to hurt.

Emily inhaled, then exhaled sharply. "I assume you saw him; I mean, I know what he does at these dinners."

"Oh," Cleo said. She very much wished she could disappear. "It's not . . . it's not what it looks like."

"You don't have to explain." Cleo flapped her hand. "You don't owe me an explanation."

"No, you're my friend, and it's OK."

Cleo silenced herself at this. She couldn't remember the last time, other than Gaby, that anyone had called her a friend. MaryAnne, but look how well that ended up.

"About three years ago," Emily continued, looking a little ashen but more sure of herself too, "I found . . . I found myself having feelings for someone else."

"Oh!" Cleo exclaimed and hoped it didn't sound judgmental.

"I didn't *do* anything, or at least then I didn't." Emily paused, and Cleo gave her the time she needed. As a *friend* would. "It, well, *she* was a woman."

"Oh!" Cleo said again.

"It's been . . . complicated. I love Jonathan, and he loves me, and we are a great team, but relationships grow and expand and don't always conform to what you expect them to be at the start." She shook her head and smiled. "We were so young when we got married, you know? How was I supposed to know that I might want to sleep with a woman from time to time?"

"Oh!" Cleo repeated and wished she had something more articulate to offer. *Labels.* More peeling them off, shredding them up, leaving them in the garbage.

"Anyway." Emily shrugged. "I didn't want you to think I was the victim here. We decided, mutually, that we were still partners but that . . . we could also find other 'partners'—oh my God, I hate that word, but it's the one we use, the one our therapist suggested—and still . . . be OK."

Cleo took her time, wanted to be sure that she said the right thing to her friend whom she admired for many reasons, including speaking her truth.

"I think that's pretty wonderful," she said finally. "I never had that type of . . . flexibility. It was always black or white with me. And . . . maybe that hasn't always worked out so well."

Emily laughed. "Cleo, you're a fucking United States senator. With an amazing kid. And if rumors are true, you're about to get Veronica Kaye's endorsement for president. Black and white works for you. Don't sell yourself short."

"Maybe." Cleo shrugged and thought about how she had been alone with Lucas in the delivery room and alone again with him in the emergency room and how, in the span of fourteen years, not much had changed.

Cleo met Emily's eyes and loved her friend a little more for seizing the moment to redefine herself. She thought of her father and of her regrets list and also of MaryAnne Newman calling her a bad person, and she wondered if you couldn't redefine yourself so many years later while still staying true to who you were. Emily and Jonathan had navigated all this, and that gave Cleo hope that she could too. Maybe that was at the heart of the list; maybe that was the purpose. To look back, to acknowledge who you were, to see where else you might be going. Cleo didn't want to not be a senator, to not be president, but she wondered if there weren't another route too, one that opened up her world a little wider, one that relabeled her beyond how she'd always seen herself: "Only Forward!"

She was so glad that Georgie had flown in and even gladder that Emily had shown up with two casseroles.

"Anyway," Emily said before she had to run and drop off her eldest daughter's basketball jersey because she'd forgotten it that morning. "I just wanted to tell you: you know"—she laughed and held up a fist—"Not All Men."

Cleo laughed too. Not all men. Not Jonathan. Not Lucas. Not Benjamin. Not Matty. Not Bowen either.

"But some of them are still pricks," she said.

"Oh," Emily said as she walked out the door, "some of them are still pricks for sure."

# TWENTY-ONE

Georgie and Cleo brought Lucas home from the hospital on Friday. Marley and Benjamin had insisted on decorating his room with over-the-top get-well decor—streamers and banners and balloons found at the grocery store—and Cleo watched from the hallway as her ornery son became someone else around his peers.

That afternoon, Georgie was stirring a homemade chicken soup, and the entire condo smelled of sautéed onions and garlic when Arianna called to confirm that she and Gaby had locked in a last-minute dancing event for tomorrow night and to say that she was forwarding the details. Cleo grabbed her phone, read the fine print, and went into red alert. With everything else, there was no way, *no way* she could dance in public tomorrow. (If ever! she had decided.)

"Cancel it—you just booked it; how hard can it be to get me out of it?" Cleo screamed at Arianna on speakerphone.

"I don't—I can try?" There she was again, Cleo thought, ending her sentences in question marks. This wasn't a request from Cleo. This was a demand. She heard Gaby in the background of the office. "Hang on, Senator; Gabrielle wants to speak with you."

Cleo paced the kitchen while Georgie made some hand gestures that Cleo thought indicated that she wanted her to take deep breaths, but she was past deep breaths now. She was well on her way to rage or panic or a mix of the two, and she didn't see how breathing would help her with that.

"Clee, I know you have a lot on your plate, but you can't cancel. I actually called in a favor and squeezed you in—Arianna remembered that we had initially said no weeks ago, before, I mean, all of this," Gaby said, officious as ever, like Cleo hadn't just brought her son home from the hospital after his insides turned putrid and could use some quality time with him, and as if she hadn't gotten enough publicity in the past two weeks, between MaryAnne and Nobells—like she needed to humiliate herself on the dance floor!

"It was just some stupid idea!" Cleo shrieked. "I don't need to face it tomorrow, to address this regret right now! Look through the ten I gave you, find something else. Do you want me to adopt a dog? I'll adopt a dog. Do you want me to go backpacking through Europe? I have August off!" Cleo, in fact, did not regret not backpacking through Europe after college, as she was pregnant by then, but she could see how it would make a nice video diary for Gaby to exploit. She also didn't really think they had time for a dog, but she wouldn't rule it out. Voters loved dogs.

By now Georgie had stopped with the gestures and threw her hands on her hips. Cleo heard her say, "Oh no," and then she became as still as a statue, which Cleo had never seen in her sister and terrified her nearly as much as public dancing.

"Veronica Kaye is on the board of the foundation," Gaby said. "She called me personally when she saw that you recommitted. She asked what changed your mind, and I told her you were newly impassioned about the arts, and she practically howled with glee, Cleo!"

Cleo reread the email Arianna had forwarded.

"And she believed that? She really thought that I'd start *with a public dance performance* if I were trying to turn arts education around?"

Gaby hesitated. "I explained that it was all about your new commitment to your gumption—which was Veronica's word, not mine.

You're not going to argue with me. Instead, I will see you bright and early tomorrow at eight a.m.—"

"That's not bright and early; that's practically lunch."

Gaby did not laugh at her attempt at humor and instead quieted. "Cleo, impress Veronica tomorrow and I'm pretty sure you'll be a lock as her pick. Which means you'll be a lock for the nomination."

Cleo let out an audible sigh. How could she say no to that?

Which was how she wound up saying yes to *Dancing with the Stars: Washington, DC (Charity Version!)*.

~⑨

Georgie waited until Cleo had cooled off from the phone call to bring it up. And that took some time, to be honest. Cleo looked in on Lucas, who had fallen asleep with his headphones and computer on—she checked, because she couldn't help herself, to make sure it wasn't porn, but it was actually *The Simpsons*, and she started crying again because it really did appear that he was not going to turn out to be a world-class asshole. This alone was a triumph of modern parenting. Then she laced up her sneakers and ran around the neighborhood for what felt like seven hours but turned out to be twenty minutes and two miles, and then, with a cramp in her side and her anxiety over public dancing only slightly in check, she slunk home.

Georgie had ladled up a bowl of soup and also made some chai tea (Cleo had no idea where she'd gotten chai tea).

"Sit," she said and pointed toward the kitchen table, and because Cleo had not yet adjusted to having a big sister push her around and having the instinct to push back, she sat.

"Let me start by saying I like that you hung Mom's painting in the hall. It makes me really happy to see it."

"Me too," Cleo said.

"Now, the other thing. Regrets?" Georgie asked, scooting out a chair and blowing on her own mug of tea. "You . . . you haven't been doing that all these years? Dad's thing?"

Cleo blinked quickly. Why was she always crying now?

"I mean, well, yeah. Of course I did, or . . . I am."

"Cleo . . ." Georgie exhaled, and Cleo wondered if she was going to treat her as a patient or as a sister. "That was Dad's way of keeping score or of micromanaging. He spent a lot of time worrying about mistakes he made or different paths he could have taken."

"Well, I hope you're not about to tell me that he made mistakes with Mom!" Cleo was indignant. So much of what she was learning about people in the past few weeks had upended her. She didn't know if she could bear to unearth her parents' secrets too.

"No, not with Mom." Georgie's hand found Cleo's, and she squeezed. She started to speak, then stopped, then found the words. "But maybe with me—I mean, obviously things weren't great with us, between them and me." She paused, lost somewhere in a memory. "I've spent a lot of time trying to figure out why—why I was so mad at them, and why we never really clicked, and why I let that affect our relationship—yours and mine."

"Did you?" Cleo asked.

"Not really. It would be easier to point to something, you know? Something concrete to say, 'I had a terrible childhood,' but I didn't. You know that I . . . we didn't. I just was how I was, and they were how they were . . ." She drifted again. "I guess I had more time with them, so I was able to see them more fully formed, as adults. You never got that space between childhood and the growth that comes with recognizing that your parents aren't perfect."

"I never felt that they were perfect!" Cleo didn't like being put on the defensive. She didn't like, frankly, not being the one in the room with the most knowledge about any subject, any one thing, even if that thing were her parents, and her sister knew them for a decade longer than she did.

Georgie sighed and reached her right hand around to massage her left shoulder. "I wish you and I had been closer. It was hard, with the age gap and with me always rebelling and then them gone, and we didn't have a house to come home to. And, look, you can catalog your regrets; you can do whatever you want. You're an adult, and you have succeeded beyond anyone's wildest dreams."

"Not beyond mine." Maybe calling Georgie had been a mistake.

"No, that's not what I meant. I meant you're . . . a whirlwind, a shining star. The twins print up news stories about you; they revere what you did to that professor; they are in awe that you live in this rarified air of elected officials who determine the course of our nation." She paused. "And I feel the same, Cleo. I feel the same. Pride. Please don't misunderstand that."

"Thank you." Cleo nodded.

"What I mean is that Dad spent a lot of time cataloging these regrets, which was fine. It made him happy, I guess. But it really *didn't* make him happy, actually. He used it, well, Dad was very anxious, which was probably part of our problem—he was a micromanager, and I couldn't handle it. Now, today, he'd be diagnosed and given Lexapro or Ativan or something. But back then there was a stigma, and he'd never have even thought he was . . . off."

"Dad wasn't off," Cleo protested.

"No, he wasn't. He was wonderful," Georgie said. "But he also had an unhealthy need to be in control, and over time, with my job, I came to believe that's where this started. He started writing things down so *he* could control his regrets rather than have *them* control him. Because you don't remember that—but that's what his anxiety did. He compensated by being meticulous and extra, extra sure of everything—like with his work and, of course, with me. And that probably also explains why he thought he could fly a helicopter without any other approval."

Georgie sighed. "But anyway, you can't beat back anxiety by working hard, and you can't manage your teen by breathing down her neck." Georgie fell silent. "That's just my theory, obviously. He knew I wasn't really like him, so he never pressed me to do it, to keep a list. But, Cleo, Dad wasn't like you in the ways that you think."

"I don't even know what that means," Cleo said flatly.

"I just . . . You've accomplished so much, and you are fearless and you are a force, and Dad was amazing, he was, but . . . you don't have to be him, just because he thought his way of controlling his fears and stressors could also be yours." She sighed. "Look, I have a lot of people in my practice who use the past as a crutch."

Cleo felt her chest spin. She loved her father; she revered her father. She didn't want to learn that he was fallible, that his example shouldn't be the one she strove for.

"That's not what I'm doing, using it as a crutch," Cleo protested. "I'm doing the opposite. I'm finally looking at my past to clear the path for the future."

Georgie, having worked out her knot, took a sip of her tea and considered this. "Fine, but then promise me that once you have, once you're done, you'll let go of this list and these regrets and stop living by Dad's rules and start living by yours."

Georgie clasped Cleo's arm and then stood to refill her tea. "Look, I just worry that this is weighing you down. And if you let it go, I really believe that you'll fly."

# TWENTY-TWO

The ballroom at the Grand Hyatt, just across the way from the Smithsonian, had been transformed into a *Dancing with the Stars* set—spotlights, wooden floor, side area for the band. That was Cleo's first sign that she was in over her head. She'd never watched the show—did Cleo McDougal seem like the type who had time for reality TV?—and she hadn't really understood the scope of the situation until she stepped onto the dance floor in her black workout capris and a cotton tank top, with a disco ball hanging overhead and extremely limber professional dancers stretching into positions Cleo hadn't realized the human body could achieve—that she grasped this wasn't just going to be a regret, but it was going to be an all-caps REGRET. She supposed that no one ever claimed that one regret couldn't beget another one.

The event was being heralded as a competition among Washington's best and brightest, all in the name of fundraising for Arts East!, a nonprofit that brought arts education to at-risk children. And with all that Cleo was juggling, Cleo had forgotten to ask Arianna who else had said yes. Which was how she discovered that one Bowen Babson and one Suzanne Sonnenfeld were participating. She nearly dropped her coffee when she saw them chatting across the ballroom.

An extremely perky twentysomething with a clipboard and a headset approached.

"Senator McDougal! You're right on time." She checked something off on her clipboard. "We're going to be going over the schedule and rules in a few, and then we'll pair you up with the pros."

"Do I get to pick my partner?" Cleo looked around and noticed a highly muscular, highly flexible man about her age who she thought could likely compensate for her lack of skills with his own. This may have been the first time in the history of Cleo McDougal's life that she wanted to fade into the background.

"No, ma'am. We made the selections to ensure fairness."

"Based on what?" Cleo saw Bowen take notice of her, and she glanced away. "I mean, how can you know how well any of us can dance?"

The assistant laughed like this was a preposterous question. "Oh, ma'am, dancing isn't just about raw talent. It's also about chemistry. We let the professionals choose."

Cleo couldn't imagine that any of the professionals rushed to write their names next to hers, but she realized she couldn't upend the system. Besides, now Bowen was waving at her, and embarrassing herself on the dance floor became secondary to embarrassing herself in the moment.

He ambled over in stretchy workout clothes, and she tried to look nonchalant. She had mastered this body language when going head-to-head with her peers in committee or while delivering a speech on the Senate floor, and yet she doubted very seriously that her face was looking at all serene, at all like she had no cares in the world. She had too many cares in the world, frankly, and even the very best politician (of which she considered herself) displayed her tell from time to time.

"Hey," he said, like the last time they'd seen each other, she hadn't been both drunk and handsy. "I've been trying to reach you. How's the kid?"

Cleo was grateful that he was pretending the bourbon-filled afternoon in Manhattan never happened. A decent portion of politics was pretending that certain events never happened: that you hadn't said something monumentally stupid a few years back (you had) or that you hadn't supported a bill that your constituents now rallied against (you had). So much of it was theater—not all of it but plenty, and Cleo relaxed just a bit knowing that Bowen was willing to act his way around that afternoon too.

"On the mend," she said. "My sister's with him today. It's nice to have the help, honestly."

The lights flickered, and a man in dance tights and a tank top walked to the center of the ballroom. He clapped his hands and shouted: "Can I have all the talent form a circle around me?"

"Are we the talent?" Bowen whispered.

"Joke's on them," Cleo replied.

Once they had all formed said circle, which took some time because Suzanne Sonnenfeld kept insisting it should go boy-girl-boy-girl, the choreographer explained the rules. They would each be matched with a professional; they'd spend the day working on the professional's dance of his or her choosing; they'd perform it that night, where the crowd would vote on the winner.

"What do we win?" Suzanne asked.

The choreographer scowled. "It's a fundraiser, Ms. Sonnenfeld."

"So pride?" she replied. The rest of the circle tittered, because for this group, pride was enough.

The pairings were handed out one by one, and Cleo regressed back to PE class in middle school, standing shoulder to shoulder with MaryAnne, waiting to be picked for teams. Neither was ever in the top half of the selection, for obvious reasons. After each classmate was selected, the two of them would mutter one of the terrible nicknames they'd given said classmate under their breath. *Craterface.* Or *Spaghetti brain numbskull.* It was their way to feel superior in the face of being inferior, Cleo could see now. At the time, it was self-preservation.

To her dismay, Cleo was not paired with the highly muscular, highly limber hero type she was hoping for. He, naturally, went to Suzanne, who squealed and ran her hands up and down his washboard abs in a completely inappropriate and objectifying way, but Suzanne was usually inappropriate and objectifying, so no one so much as raised an eyebrow.

"It's amazing," Cleo said to Bowen. "How we all lower our standards to what we come to expect from her rather than raising our standards to demand that she's not an asshole."

"So what you're saying is: Not All Men?" Bowen replied with a grin on his face.

Cleo rolled her eyes.

Bowen was paired with a lithe ballerina who didn't look much older than Marley or Esme, and as he walked off to the practice rooms, Cleo was gutted with a pang of jealousy. Which was pathetic, she knew. She'd given Bowen his chance, he'd firmly passed, and what was the point of pining? Cleo wasn't the pining type. She literally could not think of a time in her life or a man in her life she'd pined for. Not for Matty, though there had been a twinge, perhaps, at the bar in the Sheraton. She thought of him now and how kind he was and how cute he had looked. She reminded herself to check and be sure he got the care package from Alaska. Not even for Nobells, who was obviously off-limits even while they were sleeping together.

Cleo's partner was a skinny jazz dancer who had been part of the national touring company of *Chicago* and *A Chorus Line*, among others, and now ran the Dance DC studio, which catered to bigwigs who thought they had missed out on their chance in their youth and thus burned calories and stress in leotards and headbands and tights after their work on the Hill. Francis was slight and had a frenetic energy about him, and though it wasn't gracious, Cleo thought he looked a bit like a mouse. She thought of MaryAnne again and how they would have nicknamed him something like *Mousecheeks*, and she was surprised that this made her sad—not the nickname but that she and MaryAnne had so deftly obliterated their friendship, that just thinking about middle school PE now depressed her. (To be clear, there was a lot about middle school PE to find depressing, but the secret monikers about their classmates were not one of them.)

Francis, who couldn't have been more than five foot six, informed her that they were going to be doing a mambo and asked if she knew anything about the mambo. Cleo immediately felt defensive and wanted to turn it around and demand if he knew anything about eliminating the trade deficit but caught herself just in time.

"No," she said. "I don't know the first thing."

If this displeased Francis, he didn't let on, and Cleo resolved that he must be a very good teacher if he could convince Washington, DC, types to spend their evenings living out their misplaced dreams and not become jaded or judgmental, so she decided right then to let him take charge.

"That's OK," he said. "I chose it because its history is born from strength and passion."

"Oh!" Cleo said.

"I watched your video," he said, and Cleo wondered if there would ever be a place that she could now go in the entirety of her life and not be defined by that video. "And you have both."

Cleo was not the type to blush, and yet she found herself blushing quite unexpectedly.

"Strength, yes . . . passion . . . I'm not sure."

"Have you seen *Dirty Dancing*?" he asked. "That's the mambo there too. I call this dance *Dirty Dancing* Lite or Mambo for Beginners."

Cleo had seen *Dirty Dancing* because who hadn't? But not for years. She wasn't the type to flip listlessly through the channels late at night and stumble upon a movie that rendered her nostalgic. If she were, she'd remember that MaryAnne had been *obsessed* with Patrick Swayze in seventh grade, while she, naturally, had gravitated toward Baby's independent streak.

"Wait," Cleo said. "Please tell me we're not doing that lift? There is no way I can do that lift."

"Dance isn't about what you can't do," he said. "It's about retraining your brain and your body to prove that you can."

Cleo started to point out that they had only six hours, and no miracles, in the history of life, had been pulled off in such time, but she was trying to be more trusting, so she decided to stay mum and leave it, literally, in Francis's hands.

∽

Cleo had always been competitive, too competitive really. Just look at what she did to MaryAnne. So she was determined not to lose the competition, even if they were only playing for pride. Pride! What else *could* you be playing for? Wasn't that ultimately the point of anything? Cleo was surprised that Suzanne Sonnenfeld even had to ask.

By the time they broke for lunch, Cleo had a decent sense of the choreography, though Francis kept barking things like "Cleaner!" and "Hit that beat!" and "Come on, show me your paaaaassssion!" and she really didn't know what that meant, much less how to show it.

"All I want to do is not humiliate myself out there," she said to him as sweat poured from her brow and her armpits and also her belly button and lower back. "I'm giving it my best."

"That's not all you want," he snapped. "You want to win!"

"Well, sure."

"So then stop apologizing for yourself with words like *humiliate*! The body senses what the brain is thinking!"

Cleo didn't mean to apologize, so she reached for her water bottle, and they trudged back to the ballroom for a catered lunch of finger sandwiches and kale salad. Cleo checked in with Georgie, who reported that Lucas had perked up significantly at the notion of watching her perform on YouTube this evening, and then she checked in with Gaby, who had promised to stop by for moral support.

"What's your dance?" Bowen said, pulling up a seat at her empty round table, which later this evening would be adorned in gold and silver linens and crystal wineglasses and butter knives and rolls and a fairly average lobster salad followed by prime rib.

"Mambo." Cleo shrugged. "Like from *Dirty Dancing*."

"Ooh." Bowen's eyes went wide. "I had such a thing for Jennifer Grey."

Cleo wondered if there was a woman in the world Bowen wouldn't sleep with other than her.

"We're doing a jive," Bowen said.

"Yikes."

"Yeah, it's not gonna be great," he replied. "I think they overestimated my abilities."

"Tends to happen with men," Cleo said.

"What does that mean?" Bowen stopped chewing his sandwich.

"Just, you know, the producers probably took a look at you and thought: What isn't he capable of?" Cleo knew she was being petty, but she didn't feel like being kind.

Suzanne Sonnenfeld slid up right at that moment, so Cleo dropped it.

"You guys ready to taste blood?" she said.

"Oh, eat shit, Suzanne," Cleo snapped.

Bowen, who had been sipping a Perrier right at that moment, nearly choked.

"Well, well, well," Suzanne said. "Look who suddenly isn't hashtag Team Woman."

"I'm not hashtag Team Woman for women who suck. 'Not All Men'? Give me a break." Cleo narrowed her eyes.

"Oh, Cleo, lighten up. It's all for show. It's all for *my* show. I think your professor got what was coming to him," Suzanne said.

Cleo stood, dabbed her mouth with her napkin, and threw it on the table. "I'm a senator, Suzanne. You can address me accordingly."

⁓

The truth was that six hours was just not long enough to master the *Dirty Dancing* lift. Maybe for someone else who was not Cleo McDougal, it would have been. But there were a couple of issues in play, most of which revolved around trust—that Cleo didn't trust that they wouldn't topple over; that Cleo didn't trust Francis (though she was trying), who was maybe four inches taller than her, to carry her weight; that Cleo didn't trust herself to take the leap in the first place.

The rest of the steps were mostly memorization. Once that was down, Francis kept screaming at her to "put some passion in your hips" and "feel the sway, Cleo, feel the sway," but Cleo did not feel the sway, and she sadly worried that she had no passion left in her hips because, honestly, it had been so long since there'd been a reason for it to be there.

With one hour to go before hair and makeup, Cleo was exhausted. She hadn't worked her muscles this hard for this long in, well—she never had. Gaby, with her marathon training, would have been much better suited to this task, but it was too late for that. And besides, Veronica Kaye wasn't showing up to see Cleo's chief of staff leap into Francis's arms.

"One more time," Francis said and pointed to the far corner. Cleo skulked back and turned around to face him, chastising herself for ever agreeing to this stupid thing in the first place. Georgie was right: revisiting your regrets was ridiculous! Whatever made her think that one stupid day of dance could make up for thirty-seven years of not paying attention to the arts? This wasn't connecting with her mom or her past or anything of the sort. She'd been a fool to think that it would, and now she'd have to be a fool in front of five hundred of Washington's elites, not to mention YouTube subscribers. (She hadn't realized there'd be video until this morning—Arianna hadn't put that in the email.)

But Cleo McDougal did not like to lose. So she eyed Francis across the room and saw his outstretched arms and heard him shriek, "Now, Cleo, now!" and so she ran, and then she leaped, and she was as surprised as anyone that she nailed it.

# TWENTY-THREE

Gaby ran into the greenroom, breathless, with just minutes to go before the show.

"Shit, I'm sorry!" she said. "There were so many follow-up calls after Bowen's show, and a second lawsuit has been filed because of this hashtag—don't worry, it has nothing to do with you—and then Oliver FaceTimed . . ."

She tilted her head and finally took Cleo in. Hair and makeup had tried their best to morph her into Jennifer Grey, but it hadn't gone as well as anyone had hoped. Cleo had never in her wildest dreams envisioned wearing a shirt tied in a knot to expose her belly button, nor had she ever wished for wavy hair tied back in a bandanna or, frankly, false eyelashes and extremely pink lip liner, which the makeup artists said was necessary under the lights to make her features pop.

"Yes." Cleo sighed. "This is really happening."

Bowen joined them and double-kissed Gaby on the cheeks.

"We've gotten so many hits from your clip. You're welcome back anytime."

Cleo didn't love the sound of that, not because she didn't think that Nobells deserved to be dragged forever, and she was elated that #pullingaCleo was still a life force of its own, but because part of her worried that the longer this story stayed in the spotlight, the more the real rationale behind it—her long list of regrets—would be exposed. She knew this seemed paranoid. But still. She was sitting in the greenroom of the Grand Hyatt, set to do the mambo, dressed as a character out of a movie she'd loved in middle school, while her sister, with whom she had previously been more or less estranged, tended her son whose appendix had nearly exploded, so Cleo wasn't about to be shocked at anything anymore.

"You look extremely adorable," Bowen said to her. "If that's OK to say."

Bowen was in a vest with no shirt underneath, old-timey striped trousers, and a top hat, and somehow, though Cleo knew she and MaryAnne would have nicknamed him *Mr. Peanut*, she thought the getup made him even more attractive. She hated this.

"It's OK to say," Cleo said. "But don't worry—I won't take it the wrong way. I won't try to kiss you or anything."

"I wouldn't . . . ," Bowen started, then stopped. "Look, can we talk about this later?"

"We don't have to talk about it ever," Cleo said and then saw Francis gesturing to her because he wanted her to stretch out before they went live.

"Cleo, that's not—"

But Cleo was already halfway across the room, having mentally added Bowen Babson to her list of regrets. Two hundred and thirty-four now.

∽

Cleo's nerves kicked in just as the lights went down and the emcee welcomed the crowd. Her intestines contracted and her hands started to shake, and honestly, she wished Georgie were here to talk her through some breathing.

Gaby was seated at the table with Veronica Kaye, who was trailed by her staffer Topher. Gaby and Veronica said a quick hello once Cleo and the rest of the contestants emerged from the greenroom. Ostensibly, being graced by Veronica Kaye should have calmed her nerves, but it did not.

"I just love that you are out here taking a risk," Veronica said. Then she leaned in closer to Cleo's ear and whispered, "No regrets," which sent Cleo off into an entirely different anxiety spiral. Surely it was just a coincidence that Veronica had used such a common phrase, but Cleo—rational and pragmatic, her father's daughter still—did not fully believe in coincidences, and she was unable to shake the sense that Veronica knew more about her than she wished.

Suzanne was up first. She and her partner were doing the Sandy and Danny "You're the One That I Want" scene from *Grease*, and while Cleo was not keen on her own belly shirt and clamdiggers, she was greatly relieved not to be wearing vacuumed-on black latex. Suzanne was in her early forties but rose each morning to hit the six a.m. SoulCycle class, and though Cleo didn't want to appreciate one thing about Suzanne Sonnenfeld, much less objectify her because that felt wholly un-feminist, she had to admit that she pulled off that latex quite well. Suzanne loved the spotlight and played to the crowd, and even though she was a horrible bottom-feeder who catered to the lowest common denominator of politics, she received rousing applause. Washington was apolitical when it came to dominance, Cleo supposed. And as she bounced off the dance floor and past Cleo, she leaned over and said, "I'd never eat shit for you."

And then Cleo forgot about her nerves and her exposed belly button and Veronica's odd encouragement, and she furrowed her brow and refocused and told herself that she was going to murder it out there. Cleo was quite good at *willing*. She was going to *try* to enjoy it too, she told herself, like her mother would have, but she was also going to murder it out there. Just to shut up Suzanne fucking Sonnenfeld.

A handful of congressmen and women and a few prominent lobbyists did their routines, no one embarrassing him- or herself, yet no one coming close to Suzanne's. Bowen was second to last, and Cleo saw him shaking out his hands and legs with his gorgeous young thing of a partner and then, as the emcee called his name, shedding any sign of nervousness and throwing his arms in the air, encouraging the crowd to cheer louder, then louder still. He took off his top hat and bowed as if he had already won, which was pretty rich, Cleo thought—like a subliminal message to the audience that he had it in the bag.

His routine was not terrible. Quite a bit of flying elbows and snapping fingers, and there was one point when his kicks were totally out of sync with his partner, but he sashayed and shimmied and jived with everything he had, and Cleo couldn't help but smile. It wasn't that he was good; it was that he *believed* that he was good, much like Cleo had to *believe* she could nail the lift, and that went a long way in entertaining a crowd. Hell, Cleo realized, it went a long way in politics too.

The crowd gave Bowen a standing ovation, and he bowed three times, soaking it up. He was clearly the one to beat, unless Suzanne Sonnenfeld found a way to rig the ballot, and honestly Cleo wouldn't put that beneath her. Still, though, Cleo thought that hers could be a sweet, sweet victory, triumphing over Bowen and putting a nail in the proverbial coffin of the bourbon situation once and for all.

Francis massaged her shoulders.

"You ready?" he whispered.

"Yes." She wasn't, but this wasn't the first time she'd faked it.

"You trust me? Because there can't be any doubt out there. When you run toward me, the only way it works is if you're all in. I'll catch you. I promise."

"I'm all in," Cleo said. She *believed*.

And then the emcee called her name.

Her routine went viral almost immediately. Cleo wouldn't know this until the next day because she had other things to deal with, but she and Francis were trending within twenty minutes of the YouTube clip airing.

She was doing well from the very beginning. Very well, in fact. Cleo thought that her hips were shaking with quite a bit of passion, as requested by Francis, and her sway was swaying as instructed as well. They were three minutes in, and Cleo couldn't believe how much fun she was having. This must have been why her mother danced! This must be why people sang and acted and lost themselves to a rock concert! She felt at one with the music and at one with Francis, and she saw Bowen watching her and grinning like he was rooting for her as much as he was rooting for himself, and she felt, honestly, like she could soar. She thought that maybe she'd even take a class or two at Dance DC with Francis once she had more time, after she officially launched the presidential bid, after all the hubbub that came with it. Surely she could find a night or two per week to dance.

There were only thirty seconds left to the song, and it came up so fast, Cleo hadn't realized that they were nearing the end. She couldn't remember the last time she'd lost herself like she had mamboing it out with Francis in front of five hundred of Washington, DC's finest. Francis pulled her into a twirl and then spun her out toward the corner of the dance floor and yelled, "You got this, Senator!"

As the music quieted, then grew into a crescendo, Cleo quieted as well, then wound herself up, willing herself to run, willing herself to leap. To believe. She thought of her regrets list, and how she was so often alone, and how she now had Georgie and Gaby and Emily Godwin too, and how, if she didn't just let go of her need to be in control and her need to win and have faith that Francis would catch her, when was she ever going to?

She started running, just as they practiced, and Francis stood on the other side of the ballroom with his arms aloft, his eyes trained on her, and he screamed again, "Come on, baby—I got you!"

And she remembered Georgie's advice from just the day before, and so she ran, and then she leaped, and for a brief moment in time, she truly believed that she could fly.

# TWENTY-FOUR

Unfortunately for Cleo, that moment was short-lived. Halfway through her leap, caught up in the moment and the energy, she shocked herself and showboated and did not heed Francis's immaculately timed instructions from rehearsal. And thus, she threw up her arms too early and made a face toward the crowd, and her momentum therefore was slightly askew and she somehow angled her torso toward him rather than straight to the ceiling and ended up flattening her poor instructor against the band's drummer and drum set, which then knocked over the cellist and, subsequently, the violinist too.

Bowen was the one who ran over first and helped Cleo to her feet. She thought that if it were possible to die of embarrassment (again), surely this would be the moment. Instead he leaned in close to her neck and said, "Go bow."

Cleo was dizzy from the fall and surely hadn't heard him correctly. "What?"

"Go bow. They won't know the difference."

Cleo knew that of course they would know the difference, but one thing she'd learned in Washington was that you could frankly fart in an elevator and, if you were savvy enough, convince the person next to you that they'd been responsible. Politics was half policy, half illusion. So she patted her hair down and reached for Francis, who was not yet moving or ready to bounce to his feet, and then she marched solo to the middle of the ballroom and she took her goddamn bow.

Cleo McDougal was not going down without a fight.

The applause was admittedly tepid at first, but then one table in the back started cheering, and so the one next to them started cheering and so on. No one in Washington liked to be outdone. Soon, just as they had with Bowen, they were on their feet, and goddammit, Cleo started laughing because she knew that she had just convinced them all that they'd farted in the elevator, and even if she didn't win the competition, that was really something. Almost presidential.

Bowen won, and Cleo, grateful that he had rescued her just moments before, hugged him and said, "At least it wasn't Suzanne Sonnenfeld."

"That would have been the shame of my lifetime." He laughed. "I think I was a bit of a ringer, though. My sisters used to make me go to ballet with them."

Cleo made a face like she wasn't sure how much that had helped, because he really wasn't all that good, and Bowen laughed and said, "Well, I guess I have bragging rights now."

"That's no small thing in this town."

Bowen nodded. "Listen—"

"Oh God, I've already humiliated myself enough tonight," Cleo interrupted.

"I was only going to say that I had a nice time in New York—I mean, right up until the bourbon." His eyes met hers, and they were honest, and they were warm, and Cleo, having survived a true humiliation for the evening, realized that he wasn't trying to spurn her or embarrass her as she'd assumed. Why she'd assumed this in the first place probably said more about her knee-jerk judgment of Bowen (and everyone!) than what had transpired between them in New York anyway.

"Oh," Cleo said. "Well, I should know better. Bourbon is my kryptonite, evidently."

"It renders you weak?"

"Something like that," Cleo said. "Last time I ended up dancing on a bar. So the rumor goes."

"So, worse than tonight?" Bowen laughed.

"Possibly even worse than tonight." Cleo managed a grin.

"Well," he said, leaning in close, resting his hand on her waist, then around it. "I don't regret any of it. Not one bit."

⁊

The headline didn't get much attention at first, which was why Cleo circulated around the ballroom with ease and allowed herself a (very) brief amount of small talk before she made an excuse to retreat to Veronica Kaye's table, where Gaby sat beaming. In fact, no one at the fundraiser was any the wiser because their phones had been checked at the door, the better for privacy of the bigwigs. Inevitably a few people found their way around the rules because half the people in this room were paid to find their way around the rules, and one of those people was Cleo, who had tucked her phone into her gym bag, which was in the greenroom.

Veronica had hugged Cleo and congratulated her on the triumph.

"It wasn't a triumph, but I appreciate that." Cleo had laughed.

"It was, my dear. You took absolute shit and turned it into filet mignon. That is a triumph."

So Cleo accepted her accolade, and when Veronica turned back to her table, Gaby gave her a double thumbs-up, which Cleo took to mean that a very big check and endorsement were on their way, and Cleo wanted to call Georgie and Lucas and share the news: that she was officially going to announce her candidacy as president of the United States. And she was going to do it without regret. If she could take a bow after a literal face-plant, she thought, she could do anything.

Though she'd been away from her phone for only an hour or so, she had thirty-one missed texts and five missed calls, which was surprising, since Gaby was the primary one to blow up her phone, and for a moment she worried that something had gone wrong with Lucas, that he was back in the hospital. Her pulse throbbed and her heart raced as she punched in her passcode.

The texts were from Lucas. The calls were from Georgie.

She didn't need to speak with her sister, though, to understand what had gone wrong. She read his very first message.

Lucas: U have a list of regrets?

Then:

Lucas: Mom???

Lucas: What the fuck?

Lucas: What the actual fuck??

She grabbed her bag, and she raced toward home.

She knew, even without reading the rest, that it was already too late.

# TWENTY-FIVE

Cleo had gotten careless. The other night, when Lucas was sick and just after she'd been taken off the Middle East trip, she'd forgotten to lock her top desk drawer. And as she raced down the darkened streets toward Alexandria, she remembered exactly why she had started locking it in the first place. Because of the calamity that was unspooling in front of her.

Georgie was pacing the kitchen when Cleo threw open the door and raced in.

"Where is he?"

"His room," Georgie said. "But, Cleo, I think he's very upset. Maybe take a minute and compose yourself. Generally, when you match hysteria with hysteria, it doesn't calm the waters."

"Please stop treating me like a patient and treat me like your sister!" Cleo screamed, though she hadn't meant to raise her voice.

Georgie wasn't fazed. She'd probably seen this all a million times. Not this specific thing but parents betraying children. Theirs wasn't a new story.

"I *am* treating you like a sister," Georgie said. "Two things can be true at once."

This phrase reminded Cleo of Gaby, and it occurred to her that Gaby must be responsible for this mess. She couldn't believe that she'd do such a thing—share Cleo's most vulnerable admissions with the world. But perhaps she loved Gaby so much because they were so alike—she'd do anything for the win. Maybe Gaby just thought the list was another tool to use to her (and their) advantage. None of this rationale made Gaby's betrayal sting any less. Cleo thought of MaryAnne and wondered if this wasn't how she felt when her parents had called their connection at the mayor's office and learned that she'd have been in contention for the internship if not for her terribly trite, unimaginative essay.

Cleo blew out her breath. She was used to problem-solving, and she knew that the best way was to tackle one issue at a time. First Lucas. Then Gaby. Maybe, eventually, MaryAnne too.

"Can you walk me through what happened?" she asked. "And look, I'm sorry; I didn't mean to yell."

Georgie accepted the apology by pouring her a glass of merlot from an open bottle that was sitting on the counter.

The long and the short of it was that while Georgie was watching the YouTube feed (and presumed that Lucas was doing the same in his room), a story broke and spread on Twitter that Cleo McDougal kept a list of regrets, which was not a particularly lurid story in and of itself. But one fringe website grabbed the piece and posited that it was actually a hit list on her political enemies, and that was all the internet needed—the scent of the potential gossip was too much for the Twittersphere to resist. Never mind that this was incorrect; never mind that very little of Cleo's list had anything to do with politics, at least not in recent years once she'd hit her stride as a senator.

Of course, from there, Twitter blew the story into theoreticals, what-ifs, and I bets—it didn't take long for people to leap from her confrontation to Nobells to postulating on Lucas's paternity, that perhaps the father was a powerful political figure, that perhaps Cleo had been protecting him all these years, that perhaps the personal and the political were all tied together and they resulted in her son.

Georgie explained to Cleo that she hadn't initially seen the story and grew concerned only when she heard loud thuds coming from Cleo's office, where she discovered Lucas upending her files and bookshelf, which he shouldn't have been doing for a variety of reasons, not least because of the delicate state of his surgical incision.

"He was understandably quite upset," Georgie said. "But the twins have their moments too. It was all very . . ." She took a long swallow of the wine. "Well, I thought it was a fairly reasonable reaction."

"To learning that his mom has made mistakes?"

Georgie leveled her with a look. "You know that's not what he was upset about, Cleo. You do him a disservice by pretending that he is naive enough to believe everything you've told him." She paused. "I just think it didn't take him long to connect the dots, you know. To hear about your list and then hear the speculation on the paternity stuff, to, well . . . here we are." She sighed. "I am always supportive of my clients writing down their mistakes or composing letters to those who have wronged them. But, Cleo, then they burn them or toss them in the trash. They never send them! I told you: there's a danger in carrying your past around with you."

"I *don't* carry my past around with me. That's half my problem! That's why I am always on my own."

"But you do, Cleo." Georgie nodded as if this were fact. "You do, in not telling Lucas about his father or not acknowledging your role in whatever stupid teenage stuff happened with the girl who used to be your best friend. You can act like it doesn't exist by shutting it out, but then it just takes up more space, not less."

Cleo didn't feel like being psychoanalyzed. She set her wine down too hard on the counter, where it sloshed over the lip of the glass and spilled. It would leave a stain if she didn't attend to it, but oh well. Regret. Maybe that would just be the permanent reminder of this entire terrible night. The red blot on her marble counter—*just look at that metaphor!* she wanted to scream at Georgie, but instead she turned and plodded up the stairs toward her son.

Lucas was back in bed with his navy duvet pulled up to his neck and his noise-canceling headphones on his ears. Her yellow sheets of paper, torn from the pad, were scattered on the comforter. Cleo paused in the doorway at the sight of the list, out in the world, and she didn't think she'd ever felt more exposed.

His eyes were closed, and she wasn't sure if he were sleeping, so she sat delicately on his bed and gathered up the papers and tidied them in her lap. She knew she was buying herself time. She stared at her son, so handsome and nearly an adult, for an inhale of a beat. His long eyelashes, his lanky body that extended almost the length of his bed, his bone structure that wasn't hers, she knew, his near-black hair that wasn't hers either.

Cleo touched his arm, then let her hand rest there, and he stirred, opening his eyes but unwilling to look her way. She could feel her heart beating and wished, so very much, that it hadn't come to this. That of the millions of ways they could have discussed the truth of his father, it didn't come down to him seeing the entry from the spring of fifteen years ago that read:

*So stupid!!! Why would I not insist on a condom!! Thought getting drunk would help but when does it ever help??*

And then, eight weeks later:

*Pregnant. I can't believe it. Now what.*

And then, a decade later:

*Hate lying to Lucas. Hate it hate it hate it. But remember it is for the best.*

And then a year after that:

*Dad questions again. Maybe I should have told him the truth about Doug from the beginning.*

"Lucas." Cleo shook his arm. "Please talk to me. I want to talk."

Lucas stared at the opposite wall. Cleo could see he'd been crying, which shattered her already fragile heart. Lucas, like Cleo, had never been a crier, though it was clearly a habit that she had taken up lately. But looking at his ruddy cheeks and pinkish eyes, she knew how wrecked he must have been, and she also knew that she alone was responsible.

"Is your music on?" she asked.

He firmed his jaw, and she knew he could hear her.

"OK, I just . . . You don't have to say anything," Cleo started, then couldn't imagine what to say next. She didn't know what she thought—that they could go their whole lives, just the two of them, their peas in a pod, and she'd never be honest with him? Maybe, selfishly, yes, that's what she had thought. When she made the decision fifteen years ago, she hadn't been clear-eyed on what it would mean, the ramifications of the choice she made as her zygote became an embryo, which became a child who became an inquisitive teen. It was easier to just say: *he hadn't wanted to be involved,* which Lucas accepted, often begrudgingly, but accepted all the same, until now. Cleo considered that it was easier *for her,* not for Lucas, and the shame of her selfishness spread through every cell.

"I didn't really know your father," she said, then corrected herself. If she were going to tell Lucas the truth, it needed to be whole. "No, I should say, I didn't know him at all."

Lucas registered something like disgust at the notion of his mother's one-night stand. *Fair,* Cleo thought.

"It, well, I . . . I did not have an active social life in college or really an active romantic one," she continued, and Lucas rolled his eyes and returned his stare to the wall. "I was very singularly focused on my next steps and my future, and I just didn't see the point of fun." Cleo knew he was still listening because his eyebrows rose and lowered as if to say: *what a surprise.*

"Well, my suitemates were going out one night, and they invited me. And I'd already gotten accepted to law school, but I had had a terrible day—my thesis professor had told me he thought my work was subpar and that I was going to have to redo four chapters . . ." Cleo drifted at the memory of how personally she had taken the criticism. How much she spiraled, how in hindsight, her professor was just trying to prepare her for law school by demanding excellence. "Anyway, I guess I needed to blow off some steam, to just . . . not be Cleo McDougal for a night, and so when my roommate, Anna, begged me to go out with her—I mean, she didn't have that many friends either—I let her convince me."

Cleo lost herself for a moment, as she used to in the immediate months following the positive pregnancy test, considering all the ways her life would be different if she hadn't said yes to the invitation, if she hadn't gotten sloppy for the first time in her life that March evening and had turned in a better first draft of her thesis, if she hadn't been so reactive to what was really just constructive criticism.

"Anyway, Anna knew of this party on campus. She said it was the computer geeks, so I wasn't expecting much—but then, I wasn't in a position to adhere to any social hierarchy." She thought of Anna and how they immediately lost touch after graduation. Who knew what happened to her; who knew if she had any idea how that night changed Cleo's life? "And we got to this house, and the boys weren't nerdy at all. They were playing beer pong, which I didn't know how to play, but, well, I'm competitive—"

Lucas sniffed at this, and Cleo stopped to see if he had something to say, but he didn't, so she continued.

"Right, well, I mean, obviously I started taking the beer pong too seriously, because, I mean, I'm me. And a cute boy I'd never met paired up with me, and . . . Look, four hours later, I was very drunk, and so was he, and, well, one thing led to another . . . I don't want to spell it out for you—"

Lucas finally interrupted and said, "Please don't."

"Sure. Sure." Cleo exhaled. She didn't know what she was getting right about this story and what she was getting wrong. "Anyway, I was so embarrassed the next morning. It was so out of character for me, and honestly, I just wanted to put it behind me and go home and rework my thesis."

Lucas, God bless him, turned to her and said (with enough disdain that Cleo understood this wasn't a peace offering): "Wait, you've told me my whole life that girls can do whatever they want with their bodies."

"Sweetie, I didn't know what I was doing. Women then, well, I mean, we were strong, I guess, in our ways, but we weren't like your generation—or I wasn't, at least. Like Marley having two boyfriends or Esme speaking up to her mother." Cleo hesitated. This wasn't what she wanted to say. "This isn't about that, though. This was about the fact that I was so ashamed of myself for doing something reckless, for not being in control, that . . . I think I wanted to pretend that it never happened."

"So you wanted to pretend that I never happened?" Lucas said, his face a mix of heartbreak and rage.

"No, no!" Cleo wanted to get through the rest of the story now. "This had nothing to do with you and only to do with me. Lucas, I had spent so long making sure that everything was in alignment and propelling me to the next step that I couldn't forgive myself when I believed that I'd screwed up. And that screwup ended up being the best part of my life." Cleo thought of her dad, how similar they were—but different too; Georgie was right about that, and she reached for Lucas's hand. "I promise. There was never any doubt about what I was going to do—keep you, I mean. If anything, you made me realize that I couldn't be on my own forever."

Lucas didn't reply, and Cleo quickly realized that framing the pregnancy as a screwup was exactly what she didn't intend. This was why she was always prepared. Accidents happened, mistakes were made when she was not.

She swallowed. She knew what she had to say next, and she knew that however he reacted, she deserved it. All she wanted to do was stand and leave and close Lucas's door and slink back to the kitchen and not ruin the past fourteen years she very well realized she was about to ruin. But she owed him more than that; she owed her son his truth, even when it meant he would finally see her as she really was: flawed, deceitful, human, but also, his mother who tried her best. She really thought she had. She could see now why she hadn't.

She said it quickly, before she lost her nerve. "Anyway, this isn't your father's fault. I left Northwestern without telling him. He never knew. He doesn't know."

Lucas started crying then, his chin quivering and giving way to real tears, and Cleo wished she could go back and redo the entirety of his life.

"I'm sorry," she whispered. "I just didn't know how else to do it."

"There were a million other ways to do it," he managed.

"Yes," Cleo said. Because she knew now that there were.

They sat that way, in silence, mother and son, until Lucas stopped crying and closed his eyes and turned toward his wall, and after a while, Cleo thought he'd fallen asleep. Which was just as well. She didn't expect to get much further than they'd gotten. Not now anyway. She watched his back rise and fall, and she missed both her parents so acutely, she was certain she felt an actual hole in her heart. Maybe that's why she kept the list after all these years: it was what she had left of them, especially her father, to carry around, to plug that hole.

She rose from his bed. She wanted to share this with Georgie, to see if maybe she thought this made sense.

"You shouldn't have done it that way," Lucas said, not asleep in fact and still facing the wall.

"I know," Cleo said, because all that he was accusing her of with those few words was fair. And she thought of her evening, of Francis, of their fall. "I didn't want to admit that I was wrong, that I'd made an absolute mess of the most important thing in my life."

"So fix it," he snapped, turning to look at her, to meet her dead in the eye.

Cleo stepped forward and kissed his forehead and then made her way out of his room, closing the door behind her. But not before she promised that she would.

~⊘~

Georgie was waiting in the kitchen with a new glass of wine and the merlot stain wiped clean.

"Are you OK?"

Cleo nodded.

"Is he OK?"

Cleo shrugged. "Not really."

"He will be," Georgie said. "Teens are resilient. Just look at you."

And then Cleo started crying again, and Georgie opened her arms to her. Cleo leaned in to her sister and dropped her heavy head onto her sister's shoulder, leaving a damp circle of tears in just seconds. And when she had finally sputtered to a stop, she untangled from Georgie and was amazed at how much stronger she felt, just by making herself vulnerable, just by allowing herself to be held up.

# TWENTY-SIX

Cleo couldn't sleep. She checked on Lucas twice and composed an email to Gaby—who had called three times, which Cleo had ignored while tending to her son—demanding an explanation, but thought of Georgie's advice and opted not to send it yet. Gaby had been her best and really only friend for more than a decade, and rather than deploy her usual slash-and-burn tactics, Cleo opted to lean in to her growth and consider that she should give Gaby the benefit of the doubt. So for tonight, she let it go.

She logged in to Facebook.

MaryAnne had cooled it a bit with her scathing posts, though she had already posted the YouTube video on her page. The comments below, however, were unexpected.

Oliver Patel: Hey, MaryAnne, can we maybe ease off this vendetta? Aren't we all adults now?

Beth Shin: Far be it from me to defend Cleo, but I'd never have the guts to attempt the Dirty Dancing lift in public.

Maureen Allen: OMG, remember how obsessed we were with that movie???? Wine and rewatch soon?

Cleo giggled in the darkness of her office. News cycles came and went, she supposed. But Patrick Swayze was forever. She missed MaryAnne and the simplicity of their middle school friendship, before the complications that came next, so acutely.

She rolled her neck and shoulders, which were stiff from the evening's fall, or maybe stiff from the stress of the enormity of everything.

On a whim, she typed in his name:

*Doug Smith.*

Facebook offered the promise of connecting with anyone at any time from your past. She held her breath and waited.

There were thousands of Doug Smiths. She tried to narrow it down to Northwestern, but that didn't help. She tried Chicago. But that didn't help. She scanned the first few pages of profile photos, squinting and leaning close toward the screen, but that didn't help, and honestly, she wasn't even sure how well she'd recognize his face, fifteen years later and sober, all those beer pong chugs long forgotten.

She tried Google, but the generic universality of his name was a nonstarter. Google Cleo McDougal, and you knew exactly who you were getting. Google Doug Smith, and it could be a mechanic in Denver or a PE coach in Phoenix or an accountant in Buffalo. (Her home state! Would it be ironic if he'd voted for her? she thought briefly, then dismissed it.) All these men were Doug Smith and yet none of them was her Doug Smith. Not *hers. Lucas's.* She didn't need to find Doug Smith for herself. She'd never wanted the white knight: not with Matty, not with Nobells, not even tonight, when Bowen had graciously lifted her to her feet.

She reconsidered that last one, then pulled up her email quickly.

> Bowen—I have found myself behaving like an asshole too many times in your company. I'd like to say that it's because you intoxicate me, but it's also probably that I can be an asshole. I'd like to get that drink with you. But I insist on paying.
>
> -Cleo

She read it over once and, unlike her note to Gaby, she hit Send immediately. It went off into the email-sphere and now out of her control, but she had no regrets.

⌐

Lucas was still grouchy on Sunday, and Cleo gave him his space. She went for a run and put her phone on Do Not Disturb so she wasn't inundated with the updates from the overnight news slog, which saw the YouTube video crowding out the regrets list headline, which was still slightly overshadowed by the #pullingaCleo hashtag. She was happy to read, however, that both lawsuits from the hashtag confrontations had already been dismissed when the men were faced with evidence their victims made public. Women weren't willing to take this shit lying down anymore, and Cleo sprinted up a hill in her neighborhood and pumped a fist just because. She typed out a quick text to Gaby—she had longer thoughts that needed to be unpacked between them—but at the very least, they should celebrate this. That two young women had spoken up. That they had been heard. That two older men were being held to account.

Then she turned off her phone entirely, because she knew that thrusting herself into the presidential conversation meant a thorough examination of her life, but she also knew that like most things, this would all pass. Maybe not all of it. She could already see how the conversation about her regrets was being framed in some outlets: "Can We Trust a Woman with So Much Baggage?" and "How Many People Does Cleo McDougal Owe Apologies To?" and so on and so on.

She ran through her local streets with her hat pulled low and resolved that she did owe apologies to a few people—like Lucas, like MaryAnne, and like Doug Smith, whom she should have tracked down on campus because he deserved to be part of Lucas's story, but at the time Cleo, fairly or not, had been so let down by everyone she'd come to count on—her parents were dead, her sister was absent, her high school boyfriend too smothering, her best friend, well, that was Cleo's own doing—but as Cleo saw it at the time, she was her own best shot. It wasn't how she would do it now, and she didn't want to excuse it, but then, that's what regrets were, after all. How you looked back and realized how different it should have been.

She felt a cramp building and slowed her pace. And then the idea came to her all at once, though it had probably been twenty years in the making. That's how easy and how hard it was to ask for help.

She scrolled to his number in her contacts, where she'd located his address not too long ago to send that salmon from Alaska. She shook her head and smiled, looking at how he typed it in back in the Sheraton bar: MATTY!

It was early in Seattle. Not yet eight. But she remembered that, like her, he'd always been a morning person, and so she took a chance.

He answered it on the second ring and sounded like he was inside a wind tunnel.

"Am I catching you at a bad time?" Cleo shouted.

"One second, hang on!" he shouted back. He adjusted something on his end, and then the line was quiet. "Sorry," he said. "I'm on my bike. Training for a triathlon."

Cleo grinned at the notion of her geeky high school boyfriend morphing into a triathlete but then realized that anyone could be anything if they worked to redefine themselves, and maybe with this call, Cleo was aiming to redefine herself too.

"I've been meaning to call you," he said. "That salmon! Best I've had in my life. Think I'm going to book a cruise up there, just to see if I can catch some for myself."

Cleo grinned wider now, at the ease between them, at how happy she was to be able to pick up the phone and connect with her past.

"Listen, I was hoping I could ask a favor," she said. "I mean, if you wouldn't mind, I could use a little help."

Matty laughed for what felt like a minute. Cleo imagined him pulling over on the side of the deserted road to get a hold of himself. "Are you kidding me, Cleo? I think this is probably the first time in the history of Senator McDougal's life that she has asked someone for help. I'm fucking honored. Tell me what I can do. I'm ready."

⁓

Matty said it would take a couple of days. He thought they had some data searches that he could run internally to track down the generically named Doug Smith.

"I'd think you'd have better access through the government," he said. "Don't you have big intimidating databases that can do things like this? Like, not only find Doug Smith but tell you his last eighteen purchases and what he's craving for dinner and what side of the bed he sleeps on?"

"We do," Cleo said. "But this one is personal. And for once in my life, my job has nothing to do with it. And I'd prefer to keep it that way."

Matty whistled his approval. "I guess people can change."

"I'm not changing, Matty. I'm improving. There's a difference."

He laughed again and said, "Goddamn it, you are such a fucking politician. I can't believe I ever thought we could make it."

And Cleo laughed too, because, to paraphrase her chief of staff, both of those things were true at once.

⁓

Cleo knew she needed to deal with Gaby, who had texted her back asking if they could talk about how the list got out, but she didn't know how or what to say yet. Georgie, who was heading home on the latest flight out Sunday night, suggested honesty.

"It seems to me," she said, "that other than Lucas, she is the foundational relationship in your life. She's been your family, and you should treat her accordingly."

"But I've been terrible with family!" Cleo pointed out.

"But not anymore," Georgie said, her bangles jangling and her tunic flowing, as she folded her clothes into her suitcase. "Not anymore."

Gaby was waiting for her in her office on Monday morning with a latte and a breakfast burrito.

"I wanted to offer sustenance," she said, her hands thrust forward like a peace offering, her tone suggesting the same.

But Cleo had already eaten. Lucas was out of school for the week to recover from the surgery—and she'd lured him out of bed and sat with him at the breakfast table, and they shared a plate of scrambled eggs with cheese. Cleo couldn't remember the last time they'd done that, and she ruffled his hair on her way out, and he mildly grunted his annoyance, and then she told him not to watch Netflix all day, but he said he made no promises in an extremely irritated voice.

"Did you find him?" he asked.

And Cleo told him the truth, unlike too often in the past: "I'm trying."

He nodded and returned to his screen. So things were like they were before, but different too.

Cleo slid back her chair and shook her head at Gaby's breakfast offering. Her stomach was flaring with nerves as it was. She didn't want to believe that Gaby had released her list, and she'd promised Georgie honesty—and she knew it was the only way through, but still, even with Cleo's newfound emotional growth, none of it came easily. "I ate already."

"Oh, OK." Gaby's face fell. She delicately set the latte and burrito on Cleo's desk, as if they were fragile, as if, in fact, they were their friendship.

Cleo folded her arms and stared at her best friend and her chief of staff and a woman whom she had admired for as long as she'd known her.

"I want to believe the best, I do, but I think you owe me an explanation," she said.

"I promise, I didn't say a word to the press," Gaby said. "I swear on anything that matters to us. It wasn't me. I called . . . Didn't you listen to my voicemails?"

They both knew that Cleo never listened to voicemails. If you wanted to reach her, you put it in writing or you went through her staff. Cleo supposed now that this was one more thing about herself that she would have to revisit. *Listen to your goddamn voicemails!* She thought that this was something she could do. But perhaps she hadn't wanted to listen to Gaby's. That was the more truthful answer here. She hadn't been ready to hear that Gaby had betrayed her. Because then what?

"Gaby, you were the only person who knew. Do you know how vulnerable I felt? To see my private life all over the news? Do you know what it did to Lucas?"

Gaby's brow furrowed. "What does your list have to do with Lucas?"

Cleo stared, and something passed between them, as it can between best friends, and Gaby understood.

"Shit. Oh shit. Cleo . . ."

Cleo exhaled. She didn't want to detonate everything like she had with MaryAnne. She thought of their confrontation in Seattle at the country club, and for the first time, Cleo truly understood what MaryAnne felt—the sting of the betrayal—and what she needed—the acknowledgment that circumstance had trumped friendship and an honest, gut-sucking apology. Why had that been so difficult for Cleo to provide?

"Explain it to me," Cleo said to Gaby. "Other than Lucas, you're just about the only person I trust, and with this . . ." She shook her head and shrugged. She didn't think she needed to elaborate. "I believe you, Gabs, but the math here doesn't add up. So please, before I say something I'll regret . . ." *Regret.*

Gaby sighed. "Veronica called me. She was happy with the press you were getting with, you know, the hashtag. And she knew you were doing the benefit, the . . . dancing thing. But she was worried. Not about that—"

"You specifically told me to do it because she wanted me to," Cleo interrupted.

"No, she did. She does." Gaby regrouped. "Her people were starting to get concerned that with all of your recent press—MaryAnne, the two lawsuits . . . that one more misstep would make you a liability."

"You told me she loved all the recent press!"

"No, Cleo, she—yes, *she* does. But you know that Veronica Kaye is bigger than just . . . Veronica Kaye. She has a board and a team, double the size of yours, and the whole thing . . . Look, I step in a ton of shit to keep your feet clean."

Cleo narrowed her eyes. "What does that mean?"

"It means that I make bargains all the time with people to get you checks or endorsements or . . . whatever. It's my job, and I am happy to do it. But this time, when Veronica called and expressed that a few people on her team were starting to worry, I only wanted to reassure her. They had watched my interview on Bowen's show, when we discussed regrets—I mean, I didn't even want to do the show in the first place, but I was trying to take one for the team!"

Gaby stopped and waited as if she expected Cleo to thank her, but Cleo did not, so she continued. "Anyway, she kept circling back to how he and I had touched on 'regrets,' which I didn't think was a big deal at the time on the show—at the end of the day, it's just a word! And really . . . I don't know. I got nervous that she was going to second-guess her support—which we have pinned your whole presidential launch on—so I told her. As a way to explain why you were doing some of the things you were doing and that you were coming to grips with some laments from your past, and how that actually made you a *stronger* candidate, not a weaker one."

"Well, don't do me any favors," Cleo said, which was petty and she regretted as soon as it was out of her mouth because she wanted to do this honestly.

"It wasn't a favor; come on. Cleo, I've been on your side since the beginning. I told her it was confidential, and she promised that it was. I don't know, maybe someone in her office overheard. And I'm sorry that Lucas got hurt, and I'm sorry that you feel exposed and betrayed. I did what I thought was right because I thought playing the long game mattered more than the immediate consequences."

Cleo knew all about playing the long game. She also knew how it could backfire.

Her phone buzzed in her briefcase, and she ignored it.

"Look," Gaby said, her eyes pleading now. "She kept asking me, and I didn't know what to do."

"What, specifically, was she asking you?"

"She said that you seemed different—not just because of the 'gumption' but also a little more open, I guess a little wilder, but . . . that's not the right word. *Unpredictable*, that's what it was, which, by the way, is a *good* thing for you. Not just in your polling but for *you*, Cleo McDougal." Gaby sighed, looked genuinely pained, which Cleo knew was rare for her. "Anyway, she wanted to know what had changed, what caused you to go from a little sassy to a little volatile. She wanted to be sure that she was backing the right horse."

Cleo's phone buzzed again, and she reached for it. It could be Lucas, and she wasn't willing to risk missing any more of his calls.

"Before you take that," Gaby said, as close to tears as Cleo had ever seen her. "Cleo, just know I really am sorry. I should have protected you, and I thought that I was, but I can see now why I wasn't."

Cleo stared at her best friend, who had had her back for so many battles, who had never asked her to change, who had never demanded an apology from her, even when she was in the wrong. And Cleo knew that she had been in the wrong plenty of times.

It was so rare to offer a truthful naked expression of apology, Cleo thought. Not with any motivation, not with any edge or angle or motive. Gaby had hurt her, and she had acknowledged it and made amends. Cleo didn't want to be like MaryAnne, who held a grudge like a lifeline, or like the person who had wronged MaryAnne—her teenage self and maybe her adult self too—who deserved that grudge in the first place.

It was the least she could do, Cleo realized, to accept her friend's grace with the same amount of generosity. And so she did.

It was easier to do than she ever would have thought.

∽

Matty had found Doug Smith.

He was pretty surprised himself, he told Cleo once Gaby had left her office and Cleo had shut her door. She had meant it—that this was personal, that Lucas deserved to know his story before anyone else, even before her best friend, and she intended to honor that.

Matty sounded like he was on his bike again.

"Have you turned into a cycling enthusiast?" Cleo asked. She never envisioned Matty, who had managed to be both skinny and doughy in high school, ending up as a jock.

"What? No, I just commute to work this way," he said. "I've really gone full-blown Seattle, I guess." He took a breath. "Anyway, so there's a reason you couldn't track him down on Google."

"Because there are fourteen thousand Doug Smiths in the United States?"

"Well, that," Matty said. "But also, he's a computer privacy expert. He's the one Doug Smith who would never show up on Google even if you wanted him to."

"Well, fuck," Cleo said.

"Nah." Matty laughed. "Not *fuck*. You have me, and it turns out not only did I find him, I have his place of business."

"You do?" Cleo had never really loved Matty enough in high school, but she was finding that she was a little bit in love with him now.

"It's a pretty small world," he said. "He's here. In Seattle. He works on our campus—Microsoft, I mean. A different division, I mean, of course, because I'm not cool enough to be black ops. I just do the programming, but—"

"Hey, Matty, stop being so self-deprecating. You're a hero."

He laughed into his headpiece. "No one ever calls my department 'heroes,' so thank you. Anyway, it all checks out. That's him. Doug Smith. In Seattle." He paused, and it sounded like he was slowing down, and Cleo pictured him pulling in to work. She didn't want to take up more of his time. "So now what?" he asked.

Cleo stared out her window of the Russell Senate Office Building at the dogwoods in full bloom. She thought about her regrets and how they shadowed not just her life but Lucas's now as well. She thought about what parents pass on to their children: their burdens, their traumas, their complications. She knew her dad wouldn't want her to be weighed down with his own stuff forever. She knew also that the gift she could pass along to Lucas was lightening her own load too.

"Now, I guess," she said to Matty, "I'm coming home."

# TWENTY-SEVEN

Cleo and Georgie texted all week about how best to approach Doug. Cleo wanted to call him before their trip, but Georgie felt that Lucas should have the chance to introduce himself without her baggage. That this was her mess, but it was his future, and she shouldn't fuck it up any more than she already had.

Finally, they asked Lucas. Georgie was on FaceTime, and the twins waved on their way to soccer practice, and Georgie ran out of frame for a second to hand them organic protein bars before they left. It was funny, Cleo thought, how food really was a symbol for a nourished soul. She herself had eaten eggs every morning that week for breakfast, and it was a start.

"OK, I'm back, sorry," Georgie said. She was out on her deck in the Los Angeles sunshine, and Cleo had a flash of a whole different life she could have had. If she and Georgie had found a way to be closer through her childhood, been in better touch once they were grown. Maybe she would have been an entertainment lawyer and lived around the corner and dated broody celebrities and Lucas would be best friends with his cousins. Cleo loved her life, was proud of her choices, but now that she had opened new doors, she did from time to time catch herself envisioning what would have happened if she walked through them.

"So, Lucas, you break the standoff," Cleo said. "Do you want me to call Doug, um, your dad, and ask if we should come? Or . . . do you want to go out there and meet him and just see what happens?"

"Wait, we could go to Seattle?" Lucas asked. He hadn't been paying attention, evidently, when Cleo had proposed it.

"Yes, if that's what you want."

"So, like, I could see Esme?"

This aspect of the trip had not crossed Cleo's mind, but the brain of a lusty teenager never ceased to surprise her.

"If . . . that's what you want, I'm sure we could make that happen. This whole experience is your call," Cleo said, and she smiled at Georgie, whose joy was practically bursting through the camera. They had discussed, leading up to the conversation, that this one time in Lucas's life needed to be about him. Not about her needs, not about her job, not about her issues or regrets. Just . . . him. Lucas hadn't quite forgiven her for her years of mistruths, and Cleo knew it would be a long time before she earned back his complete trust. That was fair. They had a lifetime together, and she also believed they could get there. Peas in a pod. They had to.

"Yes," Lucas said. "That's the one I choose."

Cleo disconnected with Georgie and called Arianna at the office and asked her to book two tickets for the next day.

"Should I let Gaby know?" Arianna asked.

Cleo and Gaby had settled their differences, though it would take a while for the feelings to subside entirely. But that's not why Cleo said what she said next.

"It's OK," Cleo said. "This isn't a work trip. This one is for family."

❧

Gaby, of course, wanted to come. Likely to see Oliver Patel but also, Cleo surmised, to make sure that nothing more could go awry. The hashtag protesters had cooled off; their office hallways were no longer clogged with angry, often pimply men and the confused women who ran behind them; the phone lines were starting to quiet too. The *Dancing with the Stars* video was still hot as ever, but Cleo never expected to get through life in politics as a woman without being laughed at once or twice. It would pass. And the regrets list? Well, Cleo had personally written a press release about it. And she knew that it had landed and made its mark when she watched Bowen read it on-air.

(Incidentally, he still hadn't replied to her email in which Cleo proposed a drink [her treat].)

The gist of it was that of course she had regrets. That made her human. She didn't think that it made her less of a senator or less presidential, she'd said. If anything, she'd written, *it made her a better one.* She had thought that the list was her form of confession—to jot down the error of her ways and be absolved simply by acknowledging her mistakes. But that wasn't restitution; that wasn't taking a wrong and making it right. And over these past few weeks, she said, she'd learned the difference between recognizing that she could be fallible and accepting ownership of it. And wasn't that, after all, what the point of this whole thing was? Not governing, she noted. But *living*. The point of all this was to try to be as good as you can while you can. And she had regrets, but who didn't? All she could do now was apologize, sincerely, to those she had aggrieved and try to hold herself accountable for the future.

Bowen held his breath for a moment when he finished reading it, and then he smiled and looked into the camera and said, "That, my friends, is the most we can ask of anyone."

Cleo told Gaby that she wanted her to stay in DC, that this trip was just for the two of them, mother and son. Gaby looked a little disappointed and asked Cleo again, as she had done all week, if she really wasn't still angry over the list leak.

Cleo wasn't. And she told her as much. She called Veronica Kaye instead and told her that she welcomed her endorsement, but not if it meant that she or someone on her staff was willing to sell her out. Gaby had relayed Cleo's distress, so Veronica was not put off by Cleo's bluntness.

Veronica quieted on the other end of the line, then pressed a button, and Cleo heard her call Topher, the man who always lingered one step away from her, into her office.

"Topher," Veronica said into the speakerphone. "Did you leak the confidential information about Senator McDougal's list to the media?"

"No," Topher said.

"Topher," Veronica repeated with seemingly significantly less patience. "I spoke with the editors at two sites, and they forwarded your email that you sent to them, explicitly leaking said information."

Cleo did not hear Topher reply because Topher had not, in fact, thought of something to say.

"You're fired," Veronica said, and Cleo slapped her hand to her mouth in disbelief.

"Ms. Kaye," Topher started to protest. "Her regrets and behavior made her a liability. You couldn't see that! The intentions behind my actions were to protect you."

"Oh, Topher," Veronica said with even less patience than before. "Only a man would think that regrets were a liability."

"Ms. Kaye—"

Veronica cut him off. "I don't like telling anyone something twice."

Cleo, a little bit reverent, didn't dare to speak until Veronica took the phone off speaker.

"Veronica," she said. "I . . . I didn't ask for that."

"No," Veronica agreed. "But you and I both know that an office with one less duplicitous prick is already a better place of work."

Cleo laughed. Then Veronica said: "Oh, fuck him." And Cleo laughed harder.

Gaby did drive them to the airport on Saturday morning, just to be there for support.

"I know I didn't get to all five regrets," Cleo said on the sidewalk outside departures. "I think this is a first—you and me not crossing a finish line." She pulled her into an embrace. "But thank you for pushing me into the others. And thanks for understanding why I'm doing this one without you."

They disentangled, and Gaby actually looked a little moved.

"And if I see Oliver, I'll tell him hello," Cleo added.

"Oh God," Gaby groaned. "I like him too much."

"Fine, can I also tell him that I know you have FaceTime sex nightly or is that overstepping?"

"Jesus Christ, Mom!" Lucas shrieked from the sidewalk at Dulles. "I mean, seriously!"

The doctors had cleared Lucas for flying, but Cleo was nervous and doting anyway. She insisted on checking both bags because she didn't want him carrying his duffel, and she indulged him and bought him two scones and a vanilla Frappuccino at Starbucks, which reminded her of Bowen. She checked her email again, but there was no reply, and she assumed that maybe that was just how it was going to be. Bowen had twenty-four-year-olds throwing themselves at him, for God's sake. He certainly didn't need to sign up for the mess that Cleo dragged along with her. And she wasn't going to chase him. Cleo was a thirty-seven-year-old single mom, likely candidate for the president of the United States. Her story wasn't going to begin and end and hang the moon on a man.

Still, though, they were boarding the plane in search of a different boy, and Cleo didn't know how to feel about that. Doug Smith was as much of a stranger as the person sitting in the aisle seat next to her, and she had no way of knowing how he'd react, if he was married, if he had children, if he'd want another one. If he'd be angry, if he'd be resentful, if he'd be happy. She and Lucas had discussed all this, and he was still OK flying, literally, into the unknown. Her boy was braver than she was, but then she reconsidered and thought of how far she'd come from the seventeen-year-old girl who had been orphaned, and she gave herself credit because she was pretty brave too. Not perfect. But brave and perfect didn't have to be synonymous.

Matty picked them up at the airport, which was sweet of him, because, well, Matty was still Matty, and too good in some ways for her. Cleo could see how wrong she'd gotten that. Lucas FaceTimed Esme the whole ride to the hotel, and they made plans to meet later at the same coffee shop of their first date later that night.

"So you chose Esme?" Cleo asked, because she couldn't help herself. "I mean, not Marley?"

Lucas rolled his eyes. "God, Mom, I told you. We don't have labels."

"I know, but—"

"Why can't it just be that we are happy in the moment, and as long as no one is being dishonest, that's what it is?"

Matty reached over and squeezed her leg, a grin on both their faces, as if the notion were both completely preposterous and ridiculously endearing.

"OK," Cleo said. "I won't ask again."

"Thank you." Lucas sighed, but Cleo suspected that it was better to ask too many questions of your child than not ask enough.

Matty helped them with their bags and lingered after they checked in to the Sheraton (again).

"Want to grab a bite?" he proposed.

"How don't you have plans for the night? I saw those photos at Snoqualmie Falls and the Coldplay concert. Doesn't your girlfriend want you to herself?"

Matty turned a shade that looked familiar because he was often turning such a shade—deep scarlet—in high school.

"Oh!" he said. "You go on Facebook now?"

Cleo smiled. "Not really. But I had to see what else MaryAnne was saying about me. And I had to verify that this so-called girlfriend was real. I mean . . . twenty-seven? You?"

Matty laughed. "I know. Who'd have thought?"

Cleo hugged him. "I bet a lot of people did, Matty. I wish I had too."

☙

Cleo begged off dinner because she had other plans. She made sure that Lucas was settled and knew how to get to the coffee shop ("oh my God, Moooooooom," he'd whined before he slipped under his sheets for a nap), then hailed an Uber outside the hotel.

She pressed her forehead against the car window as they wound through the wide, beautiful streets of Broadmoor, the spaces of her memory plugged with nostalgia. She thanked the driver and stood outside MaryAnne's house and stared up at the cloud-streaked sky and remembered how braided they'd been, the two of them, their own peas in a pod, until Cleo detonated it. And for that, she owed MaryAnne an apology. Cleo couldn't know if she'd ruined MaryAnne's life, if her decision to sabotage her essay or undermine her for the school paper position or any of that stuff had thrown her off her anointed course, if instead of being president of her country club she'd be mayor or serving in Congress alongside Cleo. *Life happens,* Cleo thought. You make a million decisions in the moment that may change your trajectory. And sometimes you get lucky, like when Cleo got Lucas, and sometimes you don't, like when MaryAnne chose to listen to Cleo's truly terrible advice to write her internship essay about her dead dog or when Cleo gave in to her petty jealousy of MaryAnne's blue-blood connections and offered her that advice to begin with and wrecked their friendship. The point of life wasn't to go back and litigate all those mistakes. The point, Cleo supposed, was to do better.

So here she was. At MaryAnne Newman's literal doorstep. Trying to do better.

∽

She rapped the brass knocker against the red door three times, then stepped back and waited. A Range Rover was in the driveway, so she figured MaryAnne was home, and if not, Cleo knew she'd be at the club. But before she had to reassess, however, she heard footsteps, and then the door swung open, and then her old ex-friend stood in front of her, speechless.

"Hi, MaryAnne," Cleo said. "I'm back."

"What are you . . . ?" MaryAnne was dressed down in yoga pants and a tank top, with a messy bun atop her head. She looked more like Cleo remembered her than when she was made-up and tailored at the club. MaryAnne peered over Cleo's shoulder. "Are you filming me again? Is that what this is?"

"No, could I, can I . . . would it be OK if I came in?"

MaryAnne took a second long look around the front yard, as if she couldn't take Cleo at her word, which, frankly, was fair. "Fine," she huffed. "But I was working out, so you have, like, a minute."

MaryAnne had redone the house since her parents lived there. Their walls used to be bright yellow and the wood a rich mahogany. Now it was all crisp white, even the couches, even the rugs. But the bones were the same, the high beams and the arched doorways, and Cleo felt as if she were stepping back in time. She realized how it must feel to MaryAnne—to never, literally, have left home. Not that staying home was a wrong decision for plenty of people—Cleo wasn't judging. But for MaryAnne, with her ambitions, maybe it had been, and Cleo could see why MaryAnne blamed her, though we all make our choices, and even with Cleo's misdeed, MaryAnne chose to stay. She couldn't hold Cleo accountable for that. The world was pretty vast, and even if it had been the harder path, MaryAnne could have gone anywhere, done anything.

MaryAnne sat at her kitchen table and stared; then, because she was a debutante even all these years later, she exhaled and said, "I suppose I should offer you some lemonade."

"I'll get it," Cleo said, and MaryAnne didn't protest, so Cleo found the glasses exactly where she knew they would be, and she found the pitcher in the refrigerator, and then she grabbed two coasters because she knew that MaryAnne wouldn't want rings left behind, and then, finally, she sat across from her old friend to drink some lemonade.

"I owe you an apology," Cleo said. "A real one. I was a true asshole, and I justified that to myself for a long time, but it really doesn't make me any less of an asshole."

MaryAnne bristled, and Cleo didn't know what she had said that was untrue. She was determined to be honest, and she felt that she was.

"I don't . . . I don't really like that language in the house," MaryAnne said.

"Oh, well then, I apologize for that too."

MaryAnne wrinkled her nose like she thought Cleo was being snide, which she wasn't.

"MaryAnne, I am here without agenda. I think . . . You know, for a long time it was only me. Then it was Lucas and me. And that's just how it's always been." Cleo thought of those two girls who had approached her at the Central Park fun run, best friends who never wanted to be apart, and how she told them that at some point they might have to choose themselves. And then she thought of Mariann, the kind nurse who admitted Lucas into the ER, who told her that no woman was an island. "For a long time, I just thought that I had to . . . pick me. I thought that was strength. And all I wanted to be was seen as formidable. But what I didn't know is that out there on my own, I was actually making myself less formidable. No one can do anything in this life alone. Asking for help when you need it—that's the real strength.

So is apologizing when you've really stepped in shit." Cleo stopped and worried that she'd screwed it up again. "Sorry, crap, not shit."

MaryAnne took a deep breath, then a long sip of lemonade.

"I don't know why I'm OK with *shit* but not *asshole*," she said finally. "Do people even consider *shit* a swear word these days? Esme says it on the phone to her friends, like, every other sentence, even when I make her put her allowance in the swear jar." She paused. "Maybe I need to lighten up a little."

"I guess we kind of are who we are, even all these years later." Cleo grinned, and then they both fell silent.

"I'm sorry I took out that ad," MaryAnne said.

"You don't have to—"

"I'm not sorry for writing the op-ed, but the ad was a little too far. Well, actually, I'm sorry for the op-ed too—bringing Lucas into it was wrong. I hate that I did it," she said. "This wasn't just about you. My husband leaving me for a woman in his office, Esme needing me less and less." She shook her head. "It's hard to redefine yourself after so many years of knowing who you were. Maybe we aren't always who we are. Or can't be. Or shouldn't be."

"Well, God knows I understand that," Cleo said. "I think we used to think we'd have it all figured out as adults. Didn't we used to think that? We were in such a rush to be grown-ups."

MaryAnne nodded, then shook her head.

"We didn't know *shit*," she said, and Cleo couldn't help but laugh. Then she quieted.

"Do you really think I'm a bad person?" Cleo asked. She realized that maybe that was also why she'd come. She thought it was to apologize, but it was also for penance.

"For a long time I did," MaryAnne answered. And it was honest, so Cleo didn't protest. "But I suppose that life is long, and sometimes it is a really stinking slog." She shook the ice in her lemonade. "And maybe it would be nice to believe that people can change. Because if I don't or we can't, then what's the point of any of this anyway?"

Then the two former best friends sat in MaryAnne Newman's kitchen, and they drank their lemonades in silence, but together.

It was better, they each thought privately, than drinking them apart.

It wasn't that everything was smooth for the rest of that late afternoon with MaryAnne. You don't make up for two decades of pain and betrayal over a glass of lemonade and with a simple apology. They made inconsequential small talk and gossiped about Oliver and Gaby, of course. Soon MaryAnne noticed the time, and Cleo stood to go.

At the door, Cleo didn't know if she should hug MaryAnne, so instead she said: "Hey, listen, you know our kids are . . . dating or something?"

"Esme says she prefers not to label it."

"Right, what does that mean?" Cleo said.

MaryAnne rolled her eyes and laughed.

"Well, I was thinking. I'm running for president—"

"You are?" MaryAnne gasped. "I mean, you really are?"

"I'm going to." Cleo nodded. "We'll announce it next week."

MaryAnne held her hands to her cheeks like she couldn't believe it.

"MaryAnne, I thought you were pretty aware that this was in the mix," Cleo said. "Wasn't that the point of the op-ed that started this whole thing?"

"Oh, I was aware, but to think that I might know someone who will be president . . ."

"So, I mean, you can think about what I'm suggesting . . . but back in high school, you were one of the smartest people I knew," Cleo said. And she wasn't being conciliatory, because it was true. It was the two of them, best friends and sidekicks and established intellectuals, and one of them was now running for president, and Cleo thought that what she was about to propose was the least she could do to make up for all the ways she'd stepped on MaryAnne to get a leg up. "What if you and Esme came for a visit? Sat down with my team, figured out how we could put you to work?" She hesitated, realized she was being presumptuous. "Um, if you'd want to support me. I can see now why this sounded extremely arrogant. I offered it only with the best of intentions. But I was thinking—maybe you could work for the Seattle field office or the West Coast division. I don't know. I don't mean to imply that you have to launch your career by working for me. Uh, if you prefer one of my opponents, maybe I can make some calls too."

Cleo stopped talking because she worried she was only making her proposal worse. She hadn't meant to make it sound like a handout. She was only trying to give MaryAnne whatever power back she could.

"I don't have any experience," MaryAnne said.

"You are so smart, MaryAnne, and you work hard, and maybe it could have been you, not me. I don't know. There's no way to know any of that now. And you're ruthless; that's probably the quality you need most."

MaryAnne laughed. "Well, I mean, Cleo, I've been pissed for twenty years."

"Will you think about it?"

MaryAnne nodded. "I will."

"I'd love to have you. I'd be honored. That was the only reason I asked. No motive other than it would be nice to be a team again."

"Madam President," MaryAnne said, shaking her head. "To think I can say I knew you fucking when."

"MaryAnne!" Cleo mock gasped.

"Oh, I watch all those political shows on HBO," she said. "If I come on board, I'm going to need to learn how to swear and not apologize for it."

# TWENTY-EIGHT

In the end, the plan had been a compromise among Georgie, Cleo, and Lucas. Cleo didn't think it was prudent to fly all the way to Seattle and risk Doug Smith being out of town or unreachable, so Friday, just before Arianna bought their plane tickets, she had asked Matty to track down Doug's email, and she wrote four drafts, none of which was her best work, and then sent off the one she found most acceptable and prayed. (And Cleo never prayed. Plenty of her detractors were happy to point this out.)

> Dear Doug-
>
> I don't know if you remember me, but we were acquainted at Northwestern our senior year. I am planning to be in Seattle for the weekend, where I have heard you now live. I was hoping to find some time to sit down. Perhaps I could take you to coffee?
>
> Sincerely,
> Cleo McDougal

Cleo hadn't mentioned the intention of the visit. She knew it was selfish and probably not fair to blindside Doug completely, but she at least wanted to fulfill her promise to Lucas and give him a fighting chance of meeting his father.

Doug wrote her back within the hour.

Dear Cleo-

What a surprise! I, of course, remember you and have watched your career ascend with pride, even though I didn't really know you well. I'm hoping, perhaps, this is about cybersecurity, which you must know is my specialty, since you tracked me down at work. (Damn you, government!) (Ha ha.) (I'm only partially joking. My whole purpose here is devoted to firewalls, so I must admit I'm surprised you got my email . . .) Anyway, yes, I am in town this weekend and happy to meet. I live in Queen Anne. Will you be nearby? Or I can come to you.

All best,
Doug Smith

Cleo didn't know why he signed his first and last name, since she clearly knew who he was by emailing him in the first place, but she didn't want to be nitpicky. She also didn't want to correct his assumption about why she was reaching out. She was intent on being truthful, but she was still a politician and knew that sometimes obscuring the full facts led to the better end result, even if it made you feel a little dirty while you were doing it.

Cleo had proposed the vegan restaurant where she and Gaby and Lucas had eaten just weeks before—it was at least one less surprise, familiar ground, and besides, now that Cleo was dabbling in new things, she thought maybe she'd like a vegan omelet after all. Cleo sat in the back of the Uber with Lucas, who was fidgety and nervous but trying not to act like it by ignoring his mom and otherwise being snappish, and she marveled that it had been only a few weeks since their prior visit. She'd read that it took several weeks of consistently drilling down a habit to ensure real change, and she wondered if this couldn't also be true for her: if by practicing being more open and asking for help and welcoming support when she genuinely needed it (and eating a healthy breakfast), it wouldn't just become second nature by the time her campaign was in full swing this summer. She hoped so. Even with all the recent upheaval, she felt more settled than any time since her parents had died. And twenty years was a long time to be unconsciously spiraling.

Her leg jittered in the back of the car, and her underarms were clammy, and her eyes felt like they were sinking into the back of her head. She hadn't slept well for obvious reasons, and she rehearsed her script in her mind because what she was about to say mattered. She didn't care if Doug Smith hated her forever, but she cared for Lucas, and for that reason, this speech felt more critical than anything she'd ever delivered on the Senate floor or on her reelection trail.

Too soon, they were there.

She'd discussed the plan with Lucas—let her go in first, explain the situation, as if she could possibly explain the situation over a cup of coffee. She wasn't sure if she'd even recognize Doug Smith. That's how vague that night was for her; that's how poorly she knew him. But then she saw him through the vegan restaurant window, and she didn't know if she recognized him from back then or if she recognized him because he was so familiar—he was honestly a snapshot of who her son would be in two decades—but there he was, hunched over his table, scrolling through his phone.

"Hey, Doug."

He peered up and stood, a grin on his face. Cleo went to shake his hand, and he went in for a hug, so she tried to act casual and laughed and accepted his arms folding around her. He was still athletic; Cleo now remembered that—his broad back, the way he could absolutely kill it at beer pong, which was of course not a sport but gave you an indication of hand-eye coordination—and he had Lucas's eyes and jawline and brown-black hair. Now that she was staring at him, it was hard to believe that she'd ever thought Lucas looked like her at all.

"I didn't know what to get you," he said. "The choices for lattes are almond milk, oat milk, cashew milk, or soy milk." He shrugged. "I went with cashew. I don't know why. I think I was intimidated by the choices."

Cleo's gut roiled, and she couldn't imagine drinking a cashew milk latte, so she asked the waitress if they could just bring her a plain drip coffee, which they could not—they did not offer plain drip coffee—so she agreeably opted for cashew milk because her brain was racing too quickly and she just wanted this to be over, one more disaster behind her. *"Only Forward!"* she thought, though she also realized that they were going to have to change this campaign slogan in light of the past few weeks.

"It's great to hear from you!" Doug said. "I can't believe that all these years later, you even remembered me!"

Cleo thought that it was best to probably just rip the Band-Aid off. She didn't know how you showed up and told someone that he had a kid who had been living on this planet for fourteen years and the conversation didn't turn out terribly. MaryAnne was right in many respects—she could see this now. She *was* a bad person. Or had been. Good people didn't unilaterally make the decision to conceal their pregnancy under their graduation gown and then flee like hell to law school. And then indignantly tell the media during her first congressional run that the father was not involved by choice and perpetuate that lie to her son until he discovered otherwise.

Doug wore a wedding ring, and Cleo didn't know if this made it better or worse—that he likely had a family and a wife who had to make this adjustment too. And she and Lucas had discussed it last night—that it was Doug's prerogative not to be as gracious as they hoped. These were the ramifications of making bad decisions, Cleo knew. As a lawmaker, she had established a well-earned reputation of making people bend to her will. In her personal life, she was now seeing that the same wasn't true, nor should it be.

"He has the right to be very upset with me," Cleo said to Lucas as they were getting ready for bed. "All I can do is try."

Despite her script, Cleo fumbled for words, which she'd suspected would happen, which was the point of the script in the first place. The waitress brought her the cashew milk latte, and it left a weird film on her tongue, so she grimaced and tried to just jump in. It occurred to her that perhaps Doug had seen photos of Lucas online—from time to time, he was photographed with her, though she tried her best to keep him out of the fray, and the press was usually respectful. (And surprisingly had taken her at her word early on that she had full custody, and it was the dad's decision.) She didn't think there were many recent public pictures, though, and Lucas had changed so much in the past few years, and besides, what are the chances that you see a child of a woman you once slept with and make the leap that he's yours? Cleo could feel herself spiraling now, and she told herself to say it, just *fucking say it!* she screamed inside her brain.

She met Doug's eyes, and then she watched his gaze drift over her shoulder. Something changed about his demeanor, like when an animal goes into fight-or-flight. His already good posture straightened up even more; the lines on his forehead folded. He returned to Cleo's eyes and then back again, and Cleo knew, even before she swiveled around, that she never should have trusted a teenage kid to follow his mother's instructions.

Lucas was standing by the hostess's table, staring at Doug, looking more vulnerable and terrified than Cleo had ever seen. And she didn't mean to and she didn't fucking know what was happening with her, but she felt the swell of tears rush forward, and there was nothing she could goddamn do to stop them. She knew that Doug knew, because how could he not? Seeing the two of them together was like slipping back in time or, for Doug, like looking in the mirror at his younger self.

"I don't . . . ," he started, and Cleo watched his face go slack and then turn a very deep shade of red, which she prayed wasn't rage.

Cleo stood, wiped her damp cheeks, and walked to Lucas, pulling him tight. She grabbed his hand and squeezed. She had to absorb his terror; it was the very least she could do and also the most she could do. This was what parenting was.

"Come on," she whispered. "We can do this."

Doug rose, then sat again, his face moving from Cleo to Lucas to Cleo to Lucas. Cleo reached for a chair from the abutting table and slid it across the floor and offered Lucas her seat, then sat in between them.

"I didn't email you about cybersecurity," Cleo said. She tried to draw on the confidence she used whenever she made a public speech. It didn't work as well as she hoped, but at least she had stopped crying, though her voice still shook. She blew out her breath, tried to steady herself, and Lucas, the love of her life, now reached for her hand too. "I emailed you about Lucas."

In her script, she had followed this with some line like *He's your son* or *He's our son*, but she knew that she didn't need to. Doug's stunned silence conveyed everything she needed to know.

"I left Northwestern and didn't tell you," Cleo said. "Obviously. And you can hate me, and you may, and I can live with that. But please, I hope you won't hate him. And I composed a whole script to justify what I did, but there really isn't any excuse."

Lucas glanced toward his mom then, their hands intertwined and his eyes wet, and she said, "How you could ever think you were a regret—" Her nose stung, and her chin quivered again. "You're the best accomplishment of my life. And I'm sorry that I have made a mess of this for you." She looked at Doug now. "For both of you. I'm sorry."

❦

Doug really didn't know how to react, which was both reasonable and justified. But he asked Cleo to give him some time alone with Lucas so they could talk, and though her instinct was to stay and protect her son, she realized that maybe her instinct was to stay to protect herself. Lucas was now the age where he could see how deeply flawed she was, and she couldn't shield either of them from the mistakes she made and the ripple effects that she passed on.

"I'll text you when we're done," Lucas said, and Doug looked at him, bewildered, as if he couldn't believe he had a teen who could text his mother and also had the fortitude to sit in a café and drink a cashew latte with the man he just learned was his father. Doug probably couldn't believe it, actually. If he had, Cleo might have been more alarmed.

She tried to calm herself by walking around her old neighborhood, where she and MaryAnne used to roam after school. She peered into shop windows and occasionally wandered in. She turned a corner and found a store devoted exclusively to mirrors, which she thought was a little niche, but she was no longer this area's target market, so what did she know?

She stepped inside and squinted: the light from the sun outside was bouncing off the dozens and dozens of mirrors—the brass-framed ones, the antique warped ones, the bold floor-to-ceiling ones. She was inclined to slip on her sunglasses but reconsidered; she thought she'd be missing the point.

"Let me know if you want something," a disinterested twentysomething with dyed black hair and too much eyeliner said without looking up from her phone.

Cleo peered closer at herself in a giant mirror in the shape of a star. She had lines around her eyes now, and she was going to have to do something about the stray gray hair or two before they launched the campaign. Women couldn't be perceived as old, she knew. Through the mirror in front of her, she saw her reflection all around the store, from every unflattering angle, and from the well-lit good-looking ones too.

She straightened up and checked her phone for a text from Lucas. There wasn't one.

She thanked the cashier and tugged the door open and stepped back onto the sidewalk into the Seattle sun. She resolved right then, in her hometown, on her old stomping grounds, that she wasn't going to dye those gray hairs after all. Through everything, her parents, her pregnancy, Alexander Nobells, Congress, all of it, she'd earned them.

*Fuck that,* she thought without any sense of apology, without any hint of regret at all. *I'm going to show up just as I am.*

# TWENTY-NINE

Doug, though extremely upset with Cleo, took none of this out on Lucas. So Cleo was correct in remembering that he was a nice guy. And in fact, he had a story of his own. After moving to Seattle postcollege for the tech scene, he also discovered the thriving gay scene and further discovered that there was a reason he had to be eight beers in to sleep with Cleo and anyone else of the female persuasion. And thus was now happily married to a man named Bradley, who was a private chef. They had two beagles but no children, though they were considering it. They played for an amateur soccer team on Saturdays, which explained a lot about Lucas's golden foot.

Lucas told Cleo all this once he finally texted her about an hour and a half later.

Doug invited Lucas to dinner that night but did not extend the same invitation to Cleo, and she thought this was quite fair. She insisted on accompanying him to their house, though, and Bradley shook her hand and said, "Well, this is certainly strange, a senator and two gays and a surprise teenage son," and she liked him immediately, even though he closed the door on her shortly thereafter.

She found a wine bar that served tapas in the neighborhood and asked for a table for one.

"Just you?" the host asked.

"Just me," she said. And then she sat at her table and texted Georgie and texted Gaby and also texted Emily Godwin, who had left her a voicemail earlier (which Cleo listened to) when she'd heard about the trip from Benjamin. And she knew it wasn't just her after all.

⁂

They were on a flight out the next morning, but Cleo rose before the sun and made her way down to the Seattle waterfront, just as she had those few weeks ago. She knew she would never be a painter, much less a dancer like her mother, never see the world like she did, likely never take the time to appreciate its vivid colors and landscapes and detail and the beauty of a perfect grand jeté. She leaned over the concrete guardrail in Waterfront Park and stared at the drop below into the dark water. Then she righted herself and stayed there until the sun came up.

It was remarkable, she thought before she turned and headed back to the hotel to retrieve Lucas and go home: how the whole world could look different just by shifting your perspective. How over the course of just a few minutes or even a few weeks, everything could become a little brighter, a little clearer, but only if you opened yourself up and allowed for it.

⁂

Bowen finally returned her email while she was on the plane home. Cleo had to laugh because he was so fucking smooth that he knew to time his reply to when she had finally quelled one fire and before she started another with the campaign kickoff.

He accepted her invitation for a drink, though he insisted it would be his treat.

She wrote him back that they could split it. And she started to explain why—because they were equals and she didn't need him to take care of her and it was the day and age when women should pay for men too!—but Lucas looked over and read the email and said: "Oh my God, Mom, give it a rest. Not everything needs to be spelled out."

So she deleted those sentences and clicked a smiley emoji and a thumbs-up, which also made Lucas groan, but she didn't care and hit Send.

"No regrets," she said to Lucas.

And he rolled his eyes and returned to his own phone, but then he glanced up and smiled and said, "Ha ha."

And Cleo took this as a victory.

～ͽ

Cleo had vowed to burn the list once she returned home. Georgie had offered to stay on FaceTime while she did it, but Cleo waved her off.

She didn't know what was stopping her. It was just sheets of paper, just notations of a past that she now had control over. And yet, after she said good night to Lucas and reminded him four times to brush his teeth, she wandered to her office, where the list was resting on her desk, no longer locked away, and she found that she simply could not.

She understood the symbolism of why she should. Georgie had made a compelling case about turning your regrets into ashes and blowing them into the wind, but when it came time to find a lighter and turn it into flames, she instead folded the list neatly three times, found a padded envelope, and sealed it shut. Her list would end with 233 items, and if she screwed up in the future, which she would, she'd have to figure out how to move forward without relegating it to a sheet of paper and hoping that would absolve her.

Burning it wouldn't have changed anything. Or maybe that was just an excuse. Her mother's painting hung in the hallway outside her office, but this was what she had left of her dad. The list, for all its complications, had made her feel less alone for so long, she realized. It tied her to her father, whom she never had said goodbye to—she'd been at MaryAnne's when they set out for their anniversary trip.

Maybe in the future, she'd burn it.

For now, she dropped it in her top drawer, where it had sat since she moved to Washington as a young congresswoman with her five-year-old son, and she turned off the lights to her office and went to find herself something to eat. Cleo had thought ahead and thawed some of Emily Godwin's casserole from her freezer.

∽

Her Senate office was a beehive on Tuesday. Veronica came for a sit-down, and she smelled as lovely as ever, and Cleo and Gaby were anxious but not nervous because it felt like with the three of them collectively, they were going to be invincible. At the news of her likely candidacy announcement, several of the men who had already declared their own quest for the office started making statements about her likability and her fitness and, of course, her stamina, but Cleo knew that if they wanted to come for her, they were going to have to come with more than that.

"Stamina?" Gaby had shouted self-righteously but also sarcastically. "Please! Three of these guys are nearly eighty! If they want to have a fight about stamina, let's get in the ring."

Cleo sat behind her desk and envisioned jumping into a boxing ring with the former governor of Minnesota, who was indeed seventy-eight and had been credibly accused of pinching his staffers' asses yet still had the gall to run for president, and while she didn't want to be responsible for knocking him unconscious, she also admitted that she wouldn't have minded either. As it was, Senator William Parsons's chief of staff was nervy enough to call Gaby and ask if he couldn't be in the running for the VP nod. Gaby hung up on him.

"We're not going to punch back," Veronica said. "This isn't going to be a campaign of tit for tat."

Cleo placed her elbows on her desk and dropped her chin into her palms. "You don't think we need to counter them?" she asked.

"No," Veronica said with the authority of a woman who knew things. "This isn't going to be about stooping to their level. This is going to be about them chasing you as you rise above."

"I like that," Cleo said.

"It's genius," Gaby echoed.

Cleo's phone buzzed, and there was a text from Bowen. He had an unexpectedly free evening; could she meet for that drink tonight? Cleo had planned to spend the evening catching up on work because Lucas was going to a movie with Marley. But one drink, maybe two? Perhaps it might slide into three? Cleo grinned as she thought of it.

Then she typed in a simple answer: yes.

She dropped her phone into her top drawer.

"Everything OK?" Gaby asked.

"Perfect," Cleo replied.

And then they raised their pens and put their heads down and got busy writing their future, which was much more gratifying than writing a list about their past. And as their staff came and went with ideas and statistics and polling, they stayed that way all day, the three of them, because no one was going to do the work if they didn't do it for themselves. So they did. And they would. And already they knew they were changing the world, step by step, without apology. Exactly as it should be.

Only forward. No regrets.

# ACKNOWLEDGMENTS

I am enormously grateful to my agent, Elisabeth Weed, who had the patience to bear with me as I recalibrated and reworked several other manuscripts until *Cleo McDougal* called out to me, and we both knew that I was finally writing the book I was meant to. Sometimes, like Cleo, I need to take a few side steps to figure out how to point myself forward, and Elisabeth has never once complained about my circuitous route. I'm similarly grateful to Danielle Marshall at Lake Union, who embraced the manuscript without pause or hesitation, proud to put the story of a complicated, powerful woman into the world. Thank you to the entire team at Lake Union for championing *Cleo* and all that she and I dreamed.

Tiffany Yates Martin, as always, took my early drafts and worked alongside me to hone them into something even better than I initially envisioned. Kathleen Carter is a wonderful cheerleader and an even better publicist.

I picked the brains of several DC insiders, who gave me their time and insights, both of which I know are extremely valuable. If any mistakes were made about the heady whirlwind of DC politics, they were my own or intentional—I was aware at all times that Cleo lived in a slightly fictitious bubble, and I tweaked certain elements of her world to reflect this. But I owe a huge debt of gratitude to Philippe Reines, Scott Mulhauser, and Lisa Beaubaire for answering questions both big and small (and possibly annoying—many of my emails or texts did indeed begin with "sorry to be annoying," an attitude Cleo surely would loathe).

Thank you to my Twitter friend, BetsyBoo, who came to my rescue by suggesting the amazing Calamity Jane quote after I couldn't use my initial epigraph by the legendary Leslie Knope.

I should also note that I grew up in Seattle and have nothing but the fondest of memories from my childhood. Nothing about this story or any of the characters is based on my own life or any of my friends there, who, unlike Cleo, I happily stay in touch with. MaryAnne and Esme and Oliver and Matty and Beth and Maureen and Susan. All of them and every situation and relationship sprung from my own imagination, nothing more.

I am so grateful to have wonderful parents—I write a lot about less-than-wonderful parents—but mine are examples of parenting done best: supportive, involved, and loving. My mom read this manuscript, as she has all of mine, with a red pencil and an eagle eye and copyedited the hell out of it. I love me a comma, and she put me in my place.

I have two teens, who deserve a lot of credit for helping me shape Lucas, my favorite character to write. Campbell and Amelia are the delights of my life, and my joy in parenting them is reflected on every page. Thanks to my husband, Adam, for doing so alongside me.

In the end, I wanted to write a book not about politics but about power, about the state of being a woman in this specific moment in history, about learning to take up space without apology. But I'd be remiss not to thank all the women who spoke their difficult truths these past few years; who stepped forward to seize their moments; who ran for office; who took their swing in 2016, in 2018, and beyond. Thank you all. *Cleo McDougal* is the better for it. We are all the better for it.

# ABOUT THE AUTHOR

*Photo © 2015 Kat Tuohy Photography*

A *New York Times* bestselling author, Allison Winn Scotch has published *Between You and Me*, *In Twenty Years* (a *Library Journal* Best Books of 2016 selection), *The Theory of Opposites*, *Time of My Life*, *The Department of Lost and Found*, *The One That I Want*, and *The Song Remains the Same*. Her novels have been translated into twelve different languages. A freelance writer for many years, Allison has contributed to *Brides*, *Family Circle*, *Fitness*, *Glamour*, *InStyle*, *Men's Health*, *Parents*, *Redbook*, *Self*, *Shape*, and *Women's Health*. A cum laude graduate of the University of Pennsylvania, where she studied history and marketing, Winn Scotch now lives in Los Angeles, where she enjoys hiking, reading, running, yoga, and the company of her two dogs . . . when she's not "serving as an Uber service" for her kids. For more about the author, visit www.allisonwinn.com.